D0465647

PROLOGUE

"HOUSTON, THIS IS Acting Commander Catherine Wells of *Sagittarius*. Do you read?" Catherine leaned over the comm panel, watching the swirling colors of nothingness outside the ship.

"Mom, they can't hear you." Aimee sat on the edge of the console, twisting the end of her long braid around her index finger. She was wearing the PROPERTY OF NASA shirt David had bought Catherine the Christmas before she left.

She was right, of course. But any moment now, the blurry colors of the wormhole outside her window should resolve into normal space, meaning that she'd arrived back in her own solar system. Back within radio contact. Finally.

The ship's chronometer told her she had been traveling for at least six years now. It felt much longer. She wasn't sure she trusted the reading, but at this point, her mind was even more untrustworthy than the chronometer.

When she looked at Aimee again, her daughter had gone from being an eight-year-old in an oversize shirt to a five-year-old holding a stuffed stegosaurus. She fidgeted in her chair. "I'm tired of waiting. Are you going to be home soon, Mommy?"

"I hope so, baby girl. I hope so." She reached out to push a lock of Aimee's dark hair behind her ear. Her hand went straight through her daughter, bumping against the heavy glass window separating her from the dark vortex of space outside.

Catherine knew, of course, that the Aimee in front of her was the result of too much time alone—more alone than any human had ever been before.

She'd had a crew once. The other five individual quarters on the ship were empty now, but each bore marks and remnants of its former occupant: a data disk labeled in Claire's neat handwriting, Richie's battered Mets hat, photos of Ava's children on a shelf, Izzy's copy of *Catch-22*, Tom's antique compass. If she closed her eyes, it almost felt as though they were right there, just as Aimee was, present but beyond reach. She couldn't remember the last time she'd seen them. Or why they weren't with her now.

All she knew was that she had to get home. To Aimee. To David. To Earth.

The ship gave a small lurch beneath her and for the first time in years, she saw stars again, the blackness of space stretching out before her, drawing her toward home. Her breath caught.

"Try the radio again, Mommy!" Aimee said, bouncing in her seat.

Catherine smiled at the vision of her daughter. She was still too far away for communication, but she had to try. For Aimee. She leaned over the comm panel again.

"Houston, this is Acting Commander Catherine Wells of *Sagittarius*. Do you read?"

All that met her was silence.

———

Tucked away in a corner of a basement of a satellite NASA office in Houston, largely forgotten, was central command for the Sentinel program. Its sole mission was to monitor the Einstein-Rosen bridge that had opened up past Mars's orbit in 1998, in case something came through it. Calling it "ERB Prime," as if it might be the first of several, seemed ridiculous then and even more so now. In the fourteen years that Kenny Turner had been working the graveyard shift for Sentinel, nothing ever came through. In fact, in the entire lifetime of the Sentinel program, exactly one thing ever had: the *Voyager 5* probe, expected and ahead of schedule. Until now.

At 0341 central standard time, the alarm went off, startling Turner away from his nightly perusal of various subreddits. With hands suddenly clammy, he scrambled to his computer to see if he could identify what had just appeared out past Mars.

He couldn't believe what he was seeing.

The ship's transponder identified the craft as *Sagittarius*, a ship that wasn't supposed to exist anymore. A phantom ship. Kenny's skin crawled. The crew of the Sagittarius I mission had been lost six years ago. After some initial earthshaking reports back from TRAPPIST-1f—evidence of the existence of primitive, mostly microscopic life on the planet—all transmissions had abruptly stopped, and the life-support readings for all six members of the crew failed.

Who the hell should he call? There were protocols in place if something unidentified came through the wormhole, and for when a planned mission made its return . . . but there was nothing on the books for what to do about a ghost ship.

The Sagittarius I mission was over, finished, and the mission's original flight director had died two years ago. Sagittarius II was still in the works . . . maybe he should call that flight director. No, Kenny decided, this was too big for anyone but the top. He placed the call to Sentinel's director, George Golding.

"Golding," came the growling voice over the phone. "This better be good."

"Sir, this is Kenny Turner. We have a situation at Sentinel."

Kenny could hear his boss snap to full attention. "Tell me."

"*Sagittarius*, sir. It came back."

"Is this some sort of prank, Turner? Who put you up to this?"

"No joke, sir. I'm picking up the transponder signal loud and clear. No radio contact yet, but it'll be a bit before we hear."

"Jesus Christ on the cross." Golding took a deep breath. "All right. We gotta wake up the folks at JSC. I'll call the administrator. Oh hell, you should probably call someone with Sagittarius II. Llewellyn's off on some godforsaken wilderness trek right now. Morganson's covering for him. Call him."

Kenny stopped short of groaning. "Sir, don't you think that call would be better coming from you?" Kenny had heard about JSC's wunderkind. He'd never met him, but everyone knew his reputation. If there was a problem to find, Cal Morganson was the guy who was going to find it. And he walked into every situation expecting to find a problem. It was too damn early in the morning to deal with that.

Golding laughed. "You woke *me* up; you get to wake *him* up, too. Call Morganson and I'll handle the big guns." He hung up without another word.

Kenny took a long swallow of coffee gone cold and grimaced before looking up Cal Morganson's contact information.

———

Cal Morganson drove like the devil from his apartment in Midtown, Houston, to Sentinel's tiny office. He'd been awake when Kenny had called, staring at the ceiling, his mind swirling with logistics and timetables and question after question, all unanswerable. The closer they got to the launch of Sagittarius II, the greater the specter of Sagittarius I's unknown fate loomed over the crew and staff.

Sagittarius returning! It was impossible, more than they could have hoped for.

Now, finally, they could get some answers about what had happened out there.

The Gulf Freeway was nearly empty this time of night, and he made it much faster than he'd expected. He jogged through the darkened office building that served as Sentinel's home base, bursting into the control center.

"What's their ETA for Earth?" he asked Kenny immediately. "Does JSC have a plan for getting them back on the ground yet?"

"Current trajectory puts them back in Earth's orbit in about three months. Director Golding is probably on the phone with the folks at Johnson as we speak."

Before Cal could throw out any more questions, the radio crackled to life.

"—of *Sagittarius*. Come in, Houston. This is Catherine Wells calling from *Sagittarius.*"

Cal fought the urge to whoop. "*Sagittarius*, this is Houston; we read you loud and clear. Boy are we glad to hear from you!"

"Oh, thank God." The relief in Wells's voice was palpable, even across the millions of miles. "Any chance I can get a landing trajectory from you guys?" She laughed, the sound faint and staticky. "I'd like to come home now."

Something was wrong, something in the shaky tone of Wells's laugh, in the way she said "I" instead of "we."

"Colonel Wells, this is Cal Morganson. I don't think we've ever met, but I work with Aaron Llewellyn. Who's with you up there? Status on the rest of the crew?"

"It's just me. They're . . . they're not here."

Before keying the mic again, Morganson glanced at Kenny. "Are you recording this?"

"Yes, sir."

Cal turned back to the mic, leaning into it as if he could get closer to her that way, could reach through space and pull the answers out of her. "What happened, Catherine? How long have you been alone?"

There was a long pause before she answered, long enough that Cal wondered if they'd lost contact. "Almost six years. I think."

I think? What the hell were they dealing with here? "We lost your life-support signals about six years ago." He drew a breath and said, "Colonel Wells . . . you and your crew have been presumed dead for those six years. Are you telling me the other five *are* dead?"

"I don't know. I . . . I think so. It's just me. No one else is on board."

"What do you mean you don't know?" This might be Cal's only chance to get unfiltered, raw answers. The more time Wells spent talking to other people, the more her story might shift and change. Right now, her relief to be talking to anyone would be the only thought on her mind.

"I don't remember." Her voice turned plaintive. "When can I talk to Aimee and David? I want to talk to my daughter."

Kenny shut off the mic. "Sir, she's been isolated for six years. We don't know what her mental state is. She sounds unstable."

"I know the effects of long-term isolation, Mr. Turner." He didn't bother to keep the chill out of his voice as he turned to Kenny. "By now, Wells has probably experienced hallucinations and breaks with reality."

"Then why ask her anything?"

"Whatever she tells me right now might not be real, but it won't be untrue. Don't you think it's odd that she doesn't remember *anything*?"

"Are you saying you think she's lying?"

Cal loved the astronauts he worked with like family, but he wasn't blind to their faults—they were family he understood all too well. "I'm saying, Mr. Turner, I want to get as much information as I can, as quickly as I can." He turned the mic back on. "We'll have someone contact your family, Colonel Wells. I'm sure they'll be overjoyed to hear the news. In the meantime, can you tell me what you *do* remember?" To Kenny, he said, "Let me know when command contacts her family."

"Yes, sir."

Cal watched the radar displaying the ship's continued path home. *What happened to you out there? And how do we keep it from happening again?* Catherine—unstable or not—had those answers, he knew she did. He just had to dig until he found them.

———

Aimee Wells jogged down the stairs and headed for the kitchen. Her dad was at the stove and Maggie sat at the kitchen table with a cup of coffee, reading something on her tablet.

"Morning, Aims," her dad said. "How do you want your eggs?"

She wrinkled her nose. "On someone else's plate. I'll just grab some cereal. Morning, Maggie," she said as she went to grab a bowl.

Aimee was glad when Maggie and her dad finally stopped pretending that Maggie wasn't basically living with them. She'd been about to tell them to stop when they finally sat her down and told her what she already knew, that they loved each other and were talking about getting married someday. Maggie was great, and she made Dad happy. They'd been practically a family for years now anyway. Maggie wound up helping Aimee with her homework more than her dad did, especially when Aimee got into advanced math. Her dad had a natural, instinctive understanding of calculus—which meant he had no idea how to help Aimee understand it. Thankfully, Maggie had struggled with it a little more, so she knew how to help.

"Morning," Maggie said, looking up with a distracted smile. "Sorry, getting ready for an early meeting."

"Who is it this time?" Aimee poured some granola into her bowl then mixed in some cornflakes. It was one of the many things she'd picked up from her mom. Memory was weird. Aimee could remember her mom's habit of mixing cereals with crystal clarity, but she couldn't remember the last words her mom said to her, or how her laugh had sounded. It had taken her a long time to stop feeling guilty about that. She smiled at Maggie. "Eccentric billionaire who wants to be buried in space, or rogue start-up that says they can colonize Mars?"

"Neither, thankfully." Maggie and Aimee's dad both worked for NASA just as her mom had, David as an engineer, Maggie as a consultant.

"That's—" Before David could finish his statement, the house phone rang. "—not a cell phone," he finished, and got up to answer it. "Hello? Yes, speaking." He paused. "Director Lindholm, I—"

Aimee and Maggie exchanged glances. Paul Lindholm was the director of NASA. Why would he be calling their house before eight in the morning?

"What's going on?" David asked. He met Aimee's eyes as the voice continued on the other end. "I—" The color drained out of her dad's face. "Are you sure? How is that—?" He leaned heavily against the counter behind him. "Yes. That's . . . that's wonderful." It didn't sound wonderful, whatever it was. "No, I'm just surprised. After all this time . . . yes. Thank you. Thank you so much. We'll come down there this morning."

He hung up the phone and looked at Maggie and Aimee, reaching out for both of them.

"Dad? What's wrong?"

"That was . . . Aims . . . I don't know how to say this . . ." His gaze moved to take in Maggie as well. "*Sagittarius* came through the wormhole last night. Catherine . . . your mom's alive, Aimee. Your mom's *alive.*"

Maggie's face went pale. David hesitated for a second, then broke into a smile and pulled them both in for a hug.

Aimee didn't understand what he was saying at first. Losing her mom had been the worst time of her life, but it was over. It had been years. How could she—The full meaning of her dad's words hit Aimee, and she grabbed him tight. "Mom's coming home?"

"She's coming home."

1

ALMOST HOME.

That was the thought that kept going through Catherine's mind as she showered and dressed for her last day in isolation. The room was small, ten by ten, with a twin bed, a desk, and a pocket-size bathroom. Once she'd made contact with Houston, the ship had felt more confining than ever, and the three months it had taken her to reach Earth interminable. She hadn't thought anything could be more frustrating, but these past three weeks in isolation had almost been worse. She was so close to her real life, to the outside world, yet she was still trapped. Knowing it was just feet beyond her reach made the wait all the more maddening.

But one more briefing, and then she'd be able to see Aimee and David for real, without layers of heavy glass between them. She could finally hold them both.

Now she knew: nine years. Nine years had passed since the launch, and Aimee was nearly eighteen, almost all grown up and looking so much like Catherine's mother, Nora, that Catherine had choked up on seeing her. Nora was still alive, now in hospice care near Catherine's sister in Chicago. A decade after Nora's Alzheimer's diagnosis, that was still better than Catherine had hoped to find.

Not all the surprises were pleasant ones.

She tried to push aside thoughts of Maggie, someone Catherine had known and loved as a friend. Maggie, who'd been in their wedding, who'd been one of the first to show up at the hospital after Aimee was born. Who'd sat at Catherine's dining table for countless dinners.

Maggie, who had always been prettier than Catherine, more poised.

Maggie, who was now stepping aside but who somehow still felt so present.

It was no one's fault in the same way that a hurricane was no one's fault: even without anyone to blame, the damage was immense. So now there was nothing to do but try to rebuild what was broken, put the pieces back together.

There was a knock at her door. Aaron Llewellyn was a tall, tanned cowboy of a man. As flight director of Sagittarius II, he was her new boss by default. He was a good man, but she desperately missed Michael Ozawa, Sagittarius I's flight director. He'd been a friend, and he hadn't deserved to die thinking he was a failure.

Catherine took a deep breath to clear her thoughts. Her flight commander Ava Gidzenko's voice in her head was a steadying presence. *Keep your shit together, Cath. Tell them what you know, one last time, and then you can go home.*

"You ready?" Llewellyn asked. "I know you've got to be sick of telling your story, but thank you for humoring us. Cal and I just want to dig into a few more details that might relate to Sagittarius II."

Cal Morganson. There was another unexpected—unpleasant—surprise. From the gruff voice, the barely there Texas accent, she would have expected someone who looked more like Aaron Llewellyn, NASA's version of the Marlboro Man, not the tall, wiry young guy who'd introduced himself on her first day back. She'd since learned he was a NASA prodigy of sorts, a fixer. In several briefings, she'd caught him watching her with cold, blue, wolfish eyes behind tortoiseshell glasses (*oh* God, *were those trendy again?*), studying her as if she were a problem that needed fixing. If it weren't for those eyes, for that expression, she would've said he was cute.

"I'm not sick of it," Catherine said truthfully. "I keep hoping that if I talk about it enough, I might start to actually *remember* more of it." She was the only person alive who had set foot on a planet outside Earth's solar system, and *she couldn't remember any of it.* What sort of massive cosmic joke was that? Even the parts of the mission she did remember felt like something that had happened to someone else. Dr. Darzi, her psychiatrist, kept saying this was normal.

Normal. She was already sick of the word. It didn't feel normal. Nothing about this felt *normal.* She was forty-three years old, and a huge chunk of her life was just . . . gone. From shortly after *Sagittarius* and her crew entered the wormhole until six months after Catherine left TRAPPIST-1f alone, there was nothing but a blank spot on the recording in her mind. She was forty-three, but she'd never been thirty-seven.

Of course Claire Tomason and Richie Almeida would never see thirty-seven either, but for a different reason. After nearly six years alone in space, Catherine thought she was through the worst of the grief for her crew. Coming home had reawakened everything. It was like losing them all over again.

She hadn't expected that so much about coming home would hurt this much. The pain of understanding the scope of her memory loss. The pain of learning about Maggie. The pain of returning without her crew. And the pain of just being. Even stepping out of her quarters into the hallway hurt.

The lights of the hallway stabbed into her eyes, and she reached for the sunglasses she now carried everywhere. The lights on *Sagittarius* had been designed to acclimatize the crew to the perpetual twilight of TRAPPIST-1f. No doubt there'd been a similar acclimatization program planned for their trip home, but Catherine had never found it. Since her return, she'd been wearing progressively lighter sunglasses. The lights in her quarters had started out dim, slowly brightening, although they were still low. The lights in the hallway were not.

Llewellyn noticed her squinting. "I've had them turn the lights down in the conference room. It shouldn't be so bad there."

"Thanks." The lighting wasn't the only physical difficulty. The gravity on TRAPPIST-1f was weaker than that on Earth, and Catherine hadn't kept up with her exercise program on the way home. She'd been badly deconditioned when she'd landed. Walking across a room had left her winded and tired. Even now, despite extensive physical therapy, her body still didn't feel like her own. She'd felt the same way after giving birth to Aimee—that her body was forever altered in ways she would keep discovering for years.

"Here we are." Llewellyn looked down at her and gave her a reassuring smile as they reached the door of the conference room. "You ready to get this over with?"

"Hell yes," Catherine breathed. After this, she could go *home*, go back to work, and resume her interrupted life.

The conference room was taken up by a long table, a little ridiculous with its single occupant down at one end with water glasses and a pitcher. Cal didn't look up from his tablet as they came in. Only when she and Aaron took their seats near him did he glance at her. "Good morning, Colonel Wells."

"Good morning." Catherine poured herself a glass of water. She took off her sunglasses, then folded her hands on the table, clasping them tightly to suppress the urge to fidget.

Cal fiddled with his tablet and started the recording. "This is Cal Morganson, here with Aaron Llewellyn and Lieutenant Colonel Catherine Wells." He stated the date and time, then pushed the tablet forward, between the three of them.

Aaron started. "You've said in prior briefings that you have no memory at all of the time between roughly Mission Day 865 and Mission Day 1349, a gap of four hundred eighty-four days. There's still absolutely nothing you recall from that period?"

"No," Catherine answered, wishing she could say otherwise. It was as if she'd talked to Ava right after they entered the wormhole, and then a moment later she was alone on the ship, with all the evidence telling her she'd left the TRAPPIST-1 system six months earlier. "All of it is still a complete blank. Dr. Darzi says that some memory loss is to be expected. I understand the last astronaut who went through ERB Prime also had some memory issues."

"Iris Addy didn't forget sixteen months," Morganson commented, looking through his notes.

Everyone around NASA knew about Commander Iris Addy. She'd been the first to go through the wormhole, nearly ten years before the launch of *Sagittarius*. Just a quick trip through and back. Except Catherine heard the rumors that she'd come back wrong. Hearing voices. Claiming to have no memory of parts of the trip. All Catherine knew for certain was that Addy had gotten violent with another astronaut and washed out. No one had seen or heard from her since. No one talked about her officially anymore. It was as if she'd never existed.

Llewellyn stepped in before Catherine could respond. "Commander Addy's trip was much shorter. And we know now there may have been a few . . . additional factors related to her problems after returning home. I think we can agree that Colonel Wells's experience is unique. There's no way to compare it to anyone else's." He turned to Catherine and gave her a reassuring smile. It was a smile that said *I'm on your side. You can trust me.* Which automatically made Catherine suspicious.

"Tell us the last thing you remember before the gap, and the first thing after," Llewellyn said.

You can do this. Would this be the time she remembered something new? "The mission was going as planned. We were on schedule traveling through ERB Prime, and the planned experiments were going well. The last clear memory I have is of a conversation with Commander Ava Gidzenko about adjusting our ETA, since we seemed to be ahead of schedule. That was sometime around Mission Day 865, because Commander Gidzenko commented on it in the ship's log." The logs were the only reason she knew for certain that they'd even reached the TRAPPIST-1 system, but the entries stopped shortly before they landed.

Cal spoke. "Commander Gidzenko's private logs mention some tension among the crew around that time, but she didn't go into specifics."

That was new information. Had Ava been referring to— She hadn't written that down, had she? She'd promised. *Cath, I'm not even calling this a verbal reprimand. Call it being a worried friend. Deal with it before it blows up, and I'll keep pretending I don't know anything.*

A sudden paranoia grabbed Catherine by the throat and shook her. Each of the crew had written private log entries. She had reviewed the public entries, but she couldn't access the private ones. Her own personal log entries had been wiped sometime during her blank period, leaving nothing before Mission Day 865. She had no idea when or why they'd been deleted. It wasn't as if she'd written anything incriminating . . .

But what had the others written? What had they seen? How much did NASA know? *Breathe. If they knew everything, you'd know by now.*

"Colonel Wells?"

"Sorry, sir." She clenched her jaw. It galled her to call him "sir." "That's news to me. Commander Gidzenko didn't talk to me about any problems among the rest of the crew." That was the absolute truth.

"And the first thing after the gap?"

Catherine shook her head. "It was like waking up from a dream. There are snatches of memory, doing some of the planned experiments, making a meal . . . Day 1349 was the first day it really came to me that I was alone, and that I shouldn't be. I thought the ship's mission clock had to be wrong at first, but there was so much evidence on board that we'd landed—the Habitat module wreckage, the depletion of the supplies, the missing rover . . . That's when I first realized things were terribly wrong."

She could still feel that panic clawing in her mind even six years later, and remembered how she'd run blindly from one crew quarters to another, praying she'd find her missing colleagues there.

At times it felt as if she might drown beneath a massive tsunami of delayed grief. Every time she sat down to retell her story in yet another debrief, there were ghosts behind her, pushing at her, needing her to tell their stories as well. But how could she tell their stories when she couldn't even remember her own?

The questions came from both men now, fast and hard.

"And so nothing out of the ordinary was going on before *Sagittarius* left the wormhole, nothing that was kept out of the logs?"

"No sir." Another technical truth.

"You have no memory of Mission Day 1137, or of any of the circumstances around it? Nothing about what happened to the rest of the Sagittarius I crew?"

"No, sir, I wish I did." *God, I wish I did. How can I ever face Ava's kids and tell them I don't know what happened to their mom?*

"What about the Habitat debris on board *Sagittarius*? Do you remember anything about that?"

"No, sir. All I know is what I've been told since coming home. On Mission Day 1137, all contact between Earth and TRAPPIST-1f ended abruptly, and all life-support signals from the crew ceased, including mine." *She survived; what if the others had as well? Had she just abandoned them? No, she wouldn't have. She* couldn't *have.* "I've thought about it, and all I can figure is that if the Habitat was destroyed, I would have tried to bring the debris back with me, for analysis, to figure out what happened."

"Colonel Wells." Morganson spoke up again, and he lifted his head to look at her. She was struck again by how attractive he might have been, with his messy brown hair and boyish features, if there'd been any hint of warmth to him. "What do *you* think happened on Mission Day 1137? Surely in six years, you've formulated a theory."

"I—" Catherine looked at Aaron, but he seemed interested in her answer as well. "I've asked myself that question every single day." It was more than that. The question tormented her. Over the six years that she was alone with nothing to do but think, she'd come up with a thousand possible scenarios, some more improbable than others, most of them—at least to some degree—her fault. Coming home, she'd hoped that maybe, finally, someone at NASA might be able to help her find the answers. She took a breath and gave them her least improbable possibilities. "There might have been a problem with the Habitat, or an accident of some sort. I know now that we did find signs of microorganisms in the water there, so there could have been an illness that hit us, but given how suddenly everything stopped, and that the Habitat debris shows signs of fire, my best guess is that something catastrophic happened to our life-support systems in the Habitat."

"And the others?" Morganson asked.

Catherine couldn't meet his eyes. Instead she focused on her hands. "The logical assumption is that whatever happened on Mission Day 1137, I was the sole survivor." She hated that answer. That for some unexplainable reason, she survived and the others didn't. "I can't think of any other reason why I would have come back alone."

"Oh, I can think of a few," Morganson said.

"Cal," Llewellyn said sharply. "You're out of line."

"I'm sorry, Aaron, but no one else around here seems willing to say it," Morganson said. "It's incredibly convenient that Colonel Wells 'doesn't remember' anything, and that all information from the Habitat, including public logs and telemetry, stops abruptly three days prior to the Event, not to mention that all of the crew's personal logs after Day 865 are gone. All we have are Colonel Wells's personal logs after Day 1349."

The Event. NASA had always been fond of euphemisms for tragedy. The fear and anger and frustration that had been simmering in her for years bubbled over. "Well, it's pretty damned inconvenient for *me*. Especially since you seem to be implying that I'm lying."

"No one thinks you're lying," Aaron said, looking pointedly at Cal. "No one. We're in awe of you. You went through an unimaginable experience out there and the fact that you came back is a miracle, yes, but it's also a testament to your strength and resilience. No one has ever survived alone in space for as long as you did. You're a goddamned hero."

The word rankled her. She'd spent years training for a mission she couldn't even remember. And she couldn't shake the feeling that somehow whatever happened up there was her fault. How else was she the only one to return?

"I think that's all we have for now." Aaron stood up. "Come on. Your family must be waiting for you. Let's get you to them."

"Thank you." Catherine stood as well, reaching for her sunglasses.

Aaron accompanied her from the room and down the seemingly endless corridors that lead from the depths of the building to the waiting area. Escaping the room felt like escaping prison, and now for the first time in nine years, she was going to find out what it was like to be free again. Her heart thudded painfully in her chest, and her mind raced with the thought of seeing Aimee and David for real, without any barriers between them.

As they rounded the corner, Catherine could see them standing on the other side of the glass doors. David was pacing the waiting area, his arms folded across his narrow chest. Aimee was chewing on her thumbnail.

She was the one who spotted Catherine first, looking up with a bright smile and waving enthusiastically. Aaron touched Catherine's shoulder and smiled. "Go on. Get out of here."

Catherine started out walking down the long corridor but wound up running. Her eyes stung and her throat ached long before she got to the door. *Finally. Finally.* Her heart beat that one word over and over as she stepped through. David and Aimee rushed to embrace her, and she wrapped her arms around both of them fiercely, burying her face in Aimee's hair and letting the tears fall.

2

"WHAT THE HELL was that about?" Aaron Llewellyn waited until he and Cal were well away from the conference room, on the way back to Aaron's office.

"Come on, Aaron. It doesn't add up. It's too neat. How are all the personal logs gone? Even if Wells's amnesia were fishy—which it is—she couldn't have wiped those records." Something wasn't right here. It didn't piece together. His instincts were yelling it loud and clear, and his instincts rarely steered him wrong.

Maybe he shouldn't have pushed it so hard in the debrief, though.

"If she couldn't have wiped the records, then why did you go after her so hard? You think . . . what? That the crew survived and Catherine abandoned them?" Aaron shook his head.

"No, but . . ." Cal paused. He'd considered that, but there was no evidence. And as good as Aaron was about listening to some of Cal's more out-there ideas, floating sinister theories about Wells was a bad idea right now. Everyone on the team was protective of her. Cal got that. Whatever the truth was, she'd been through hell, and no doubt was still going through it. "There's just something she's not telling us. I can *feel* it."

Aaron stopped walking and turned to face Cal. His expression was flat and the way he crossed his arms over his chest didn't bode well for Cal. "Listen, kid. I'm *letting* you step up on this mission. You don't have to start shit to try to make yourself look good. Don't make me, or anyone else, regret this."

"I'm not starting shit—"

Aaron gave him a look.

"*This* time. I'm not. I swear."

Cal never meant to start shit. He saw things that other people overlooked. Worse than that, he was terrible about just going with the flow. He couldn't let things slide, especially not for the sake of a feel-good story for the history books. NASA ran on myths and legends as much as it ran on funding and science. And Cal just couldn't buy into it.

"Well, just . . . lay off for a bit, would you?" Aaron started walking again and Cal hurried to keep up. Aaron might as well have asked him to fly, as far as Cal was concerned, but he'd try. "She's a hero around here. After what happened with Sagittarius I, NASA needs all the heroes it can get. And right now, Sagittarius II depends on what she's able to tell us."

But she's not telling us everything. Cal sighed. "Yeah, all right. I'll lay off." It *was* just intuition right now, something about the way Wells told her story. Nothing concrete. The problem was, the more people defended Wells, the more people talked about her like she was a hero, the more Cal wanted to puncture that bubble, find out what she might be hiding. The higher the stakes got, the more important it was that he find the truth.

His promise to lay off didn't even make it to lunchtime. He was just checking on something, that was all. For his own peace of mind. He pulled up the transcripts of Wells's initial debrief right after she landed.

WELLS: *The mission was going as planned. We were on schedule traveling through ERB Prime, and the planned experiments were going well. The last clear memory I have is of a conversation with Commander Ava Gidzenko about adjusting our ETA, since we seemed to be ahead of schedule. That was sometime around Mission Day 865, because Commander Gidzenko commented on it in the ship's log.*

That sounded familiar—too familiar. Her second debrief was with the psychiatrist present and was filmed. Cal watched the video briefly, then fast-forwarded to the same question.

Catherine, who had been interacting normally, paused and looked straight ahead. Cal hit Play.

"—ahead of schedule. That was sometime around Mission Day 865, because Commander Gidzenko commented on it in the ship's log."

Then his recording from earlier today: the exact same story, word for word. Memory didn't work that way. When people talked about a traumatic event, it was rarely the same story twice—they misremembered, they forgot, they revealed things out of order, and they found new memories between one telling and the next. That was one reason NASA did so many of these damned reviews: to coax out as many details as possible, a few at a time. He and Aaron had hoped that in a slightly more relaxed setting with just the three of them, focused specifically on what happened to the others, that maybe a few more details would emerge.

But Wells was telling the exact same story every single time. As though she'd memorized it. As though it had been prerecorded, so to speak. On its own, it wasn't enough to take back to Aaron, not while everyone wanted to keep Wells on her pedestal, but it was enough to raise Cal's hackles. He just had to—

"I knew it. I knew you forgot me, man." Dr. Nate Royer leaned against Cal's office doorframe. "You stood me up. I sat there in the cafeteria all by myself."

"Nate! Oh shit, I'm sorry." Cal closed his laptop guiltily. He got out from behind his desk and greeted Nate with a clap on the shoulder. "I had that Wells debrief this morning and it threw off my whole day."

"It wasn't a total loss. I looked so pitiful, one of those cute new engineers must've felt sorry for me. Came over to say hello."

Cal grinned, motioning Nate into his office and shutting the door behind him. "I bet you milked it for all it was worth, too, didn't you. You dog."

Nate shrugged eloquently, his teeth flashing bright in a quick grin. "We talked about the fickleness of straight boys. Especially the cute ones like you."

Cal rolled his eyes at the long-standing joke. "Did you at least get his phone number?"

"What kind of a man do you think I am, Morganson? Of course I got his phone number."

"See, wouldn't've happened if I hadn't zoned out." Cal sprawled in his chair again while Nate took his usual seat on the other side of the desk.

"So . . . Catherine Wells, huh? How'd that go?"

"If you're asking if we nailed down everything that happened on TRAPPIST-1f, then the answer is no. We're not much closer than we were before." He pawed through the papers on his desk for his tablet and the notes he'd taken during the debriefing. Nate was slated as the crew doctor for Sagittarius II. Even if they hadn't been close friends, Cal would be doing everything he could to make sure Nate and the others got the answers they needed before they risked their lives.

"Damn," Nate said. "She doesn't know *anything*? I mean, if you're going to send me up there, it'd be nice to know my chances of coming back were getting better."

"We're still working on the assumption that something catastrophic happened to the Habitat . . ." Cal trailed off. He really wanted to be able to give Nate the party line. Nothing to see here. Move along.

"Uh-oh. I know that look. There's a 'but' coming."

"No, not really, just—" Cal pushed his tablet aside. "Never mind, man. I shouldn't be talking to you about it."

"You know I'm going to see the full debriefings eventually, right?" Nate beckoned, like *Bring it on.*

Cal glanced at the closed door. "It's nothing concrete. Something's not adding up yet. Just a feeling."

"Oh lord, not one of your feelings." Nate groaned and ran a hand over his face dramatically.

"Listen. How often have I been wrong?"

"It's not *how often*, Cal; it's that when you *are* wrong, it turns into a colossal clusterfuck." Nate would know; he'd helped mop Cal off the floor enough times.

But once again, Cal wasn't going down without a fight. "Oh, come on. It's not that bad. Name one clusterfuck."

Nate raised his eyebrows. "You really wanna play this? All right. Let's go. You spent a month convinced that TRAPPIST-1f was actually a volcanic hell planet."

"The science was there! With the other planets in the system so close, volcanic activity should have been—"

"It was speculation! You were *guessing*, Cal."

"I was a kid. Come on, we were still in college. Besides, it got me the job offer with NASA, didn't it?"

Nate was unimpressed. "You nearly got the whole program scrapped."

"Considering what actually happened, would that have been so terrible?"

"They weren't killed by volcanoes, were they?" Nate stabbed a finger at him. "No moving the goalposts. You were wrong."

"We don't *know* they weren't killed by volcanoes . . ."

"Cal, we've got the crew's surveys from orbit right before they landed. 'Volcano' is probably one of the few causes we *have* ruled out."

"Yeah, yeah. Okay," Cal admitted grudgingly. "Fine. I was wrong once."

"Once." Nate snorted. "What about that time you were working on Sentinel and you thought—"

This game wasn't fun if Nate was going to show off his flawless recall of "every time Cal Morganson was an idiot."

"All right, all right. Maybe more than once." Cal leaned forward, pointing at him. "But how many times have I been *right*?"

Nate leaned back in his chair, grin on his face. "Not enough times for me to stop giving you shit every time you say you have a feeling."

"I'm wounded, Nate. I'm deeply wounded." Cal pressed a hand to his chest.

"You'll survive. Your ego has made it through worse." Nate gave him a shrewd look. "You know, we're not all *really* keeping score on how often you're wrong here. You're the only one counting, man."

"Can't tell if you're winning if nobody's keeping score." He focused on Nate again, growing serious. "I can't shake the feeling that something's off. It could be something big." Cal didn't care if Nate laughed at him; he probably deserved it a *little*, and Nate was allowed even if Cal wouldn't put up with it from anyone else. "I just don't want a repeat of whatever happened. Not with you guys. You're my team."

"I know. I get it. And we appreciate it, Cal, we really do." Nate grew more serious as well. "Six years is a long time. It would be easy to treat Sagittarius I like ancient history. We all had a chance to get over it and move on. Now that Wells is back, it's stirring up a lot of old stuff for us. Everybody's feeling it."

"How's the crew doing?"

Nate shrugged. "Better, actually. Nobody talked about it, but it was kinda rough, being the crew to follow a mission where everyone died."

"I worried about that, how you guys would handle it." Cal had been tracking the crew's psych evals. Every one of them was understandably anxious. Anxiety was normal, but it led to errors, errors Cal didn't want to risk.

"But now that it turns out there was a survivor, in a weird way it makes it better. Maybe if we can find out exactly what happened, we'll avoid making the same mistakes. If there were mistakes."

"That's what we're working on."

"Yeah, I know. I trust you, Cal," Nate said easily. "As long as I keep believing you guys are gonna get us up there and back, I'm fine. I think everyone else feels the same way."

And that, right there, was exactly why Cal needed to get to the truth of Catherine Wells's story. He owed it to his crew, to Nate, to make sure they were as safe as possible. It might make people hate him, it might get him demoted even, but he couldn't risk Nate and the others for the sake of the narrative that made Wells a hero and left his team vulnerable.

3

NONE OF THEM spoke at first. They clung to one another. Catherine was sobbing and so was Aimee, her slender body shaking with the force of it while Catherine held on to her and David held on to both of them. *I'm home, I'm home, I'm home.* She couldn't stop thinking it, unable to believe it was finally happening. *Our families will be so happy to see us; we'll be able to make everything work out.* Ava had been right.

David leaned in to kiss her carefully, their first kiss in nearly a decade. It was sweeter than she remembered. Catherine closed her eyes and they were twenty-three again, leaning toward each other on a boardwalk bench still warm from the setting sun. She'd been laughing, daring him to kiss her, their mouths sticky with cotton candy like children's. He still smelled the same twenty years later, still wearing the same cologne.

David drew back and brushed a hand over her hair. "Come on. We're taking you home."

Walking out into the sunlight—Earth's light, not artificial light, not starlight—was like walking out under a spotlight. Everything was so harsh, overexposed, bright. She was walking into a nuclear blast and half expected to see her shadow burned into the concrete behind her. The shapes were all wrong. While she was in quarantine she'd noticed the obsession of Earth architecture and design with having everything squared off. After the curves and contours of *Sagittarius*, that blocky squareness felt wrong. It felt dangerous. There were too many sharp corners to cut herself on.

What didn't feel wrong were the two people with her. Squinting despite the sunglasses, she kept David on one side of her, Aimee on the other, her arms around their waists as they headed for the car.

A *car*. She laughed at the sight of it sitting there, delightfully ordinary. David wasn't driving the exact car he'd had nine years ago, but it was the same in all the ways that mattered: midsize sedan, comfortable, safe, and a little dull. She used to tease him relentlessly about it: "You drive the slowest, most boring car of any future astronaut I know." The rest of their training cohort were notorious speed junkies, an impressive collection of sports cars and classic muscle cars among them. Then David had washed out of the program, and the jokes stopped.

Catherine settled into the passenger seat and found herself savoring the overheated air from the late spring sun.

"Are you hungry?" David asked. "Do you want to stop and get anything before we get home?"

"I just want to go *home*." Catherine couldn't stop looking at both of them, cataloguing changes. David's auburn hair was a little thinner at the temples, and there were wire-framed glasses covering his gray eyes that hadn't been there before. But really, he looked the way he'd always looked. From the cologne to the car to everything else, David never changed. He was her rock, steady and unmoving and always *there*.

Except he did change, didn't he? Your rock moved on. To Maggie. Ava's voice. Catherine willed the thought away. She just wanted to enjoy this.

Aimee was a wonder. For years, Catherine had carried the image of the nine-year-old tomboy in her head, and she scarcely knew how to credit this ethereally beautiful seventeen-year-old sitting behind her. She'd always had David's friendly features and Catherine's pale skin, but there was no trace of the tomboy in her now. Her dark-brown hair was pulled back in a loose braid, and she was wearing a perfectly tailored gray dress. It was the kind of thing Catherine would never have had the fashion sense to pick.

"Mom. You're staring." Aimee's smile stayed as bright as ever, but she fidgeted with the phone in her hands.

"You just both look so *good*. You have no idea." She shook her head. "I remember I used to have to fight to get you to wear anything other than jeans or overalls. That dress is amazing."

Aimee glowed beneath the praise, sitting up a little straighter. "Isn't it great?" She played with the skirt, straightening it out. "Maggie helped me pick it out for the last science fair we—" She stopped, gaze darting to her father and then down for a heartbeat.

Catherine's smile tightened but stayed in place. "It's all right." She reached back to touch Aimee's arm. "I'm glad she was there for you."

And she was . . . but she still had to suppress a rush of jealousy that sat side by side with her gratitude that Aimee had had some sort of mother figure while Catherine couldn't be there. All the time she spent drifting through space, imagining her homecoming, she'd never imagined she would come back to find that David had moved on and Aimee had been close to calling another woman "Mom." The two of them were hers again, but Maggie's shadow still lingered. Maybe Maggie had been a better mom, a better partner . . . Catherine could never know for sure, and she'd never be able to ask.

"So," she said, trying to find her way out of the mire they'd stumbled into, "science fairs are still your thing, huh?"

"Aimee hasn't lost a science fair since she started high school." David beamed with pride. "This last time one of the judges said he had graduate students that could learn something from her work."

"Daa-ad, that's not what he said. He said they could learn from my work *ethic*."

"That's still fantastic. I want to hear all about school," Catherine said. "Do you think they'd mind if I came to visit? I'd love to see it."

Aimee made a face, but shrugged. "They'd probably *love* it and want you to do a whole assembly or something."

Catherine laughed at the expression on Aimee's face. "Okay, okay, I won't come and embarrass you right away. I just . . . I've missed you." She glanced over at David's profile. "Both of you. I've got a lot of lost time to make up for."

———

As they got closer to the house, Catherine grew quiet, watching the neighborhood outside the windows. So much had changed, but so much was exactly the same. The supermarket she used to go to all the time was still there. Those quiet early Saturday mornings had been an oasis for her; leaving David and Aimee sleeping while she wandered the aisles, finding something meditative in the simplicity of it, looking at labels, checking things off her list. The stores around the supermarket were all new—a pet store had replaced the hair salon where Aimee had gotten her first haircut; a storefront computer-repair place was where the dry cleaners had been. It was like seeing a familiar photograph with some of the faces rubbed out and replaced with those of strangers. Once in their own cul-de-sac, the feeling intensified. Houses changed colors, the cars were all wrong. Somehow she'd sideslipped into another universe where the McIntyres' house was green instead of blue and Aimee was a grown-up fashion plate instead of a freckle-faced tomboy.

The flutter in her stomach worsened as they reached their house. Would Catherine be able to tell that another woman had been living there?

David pulled into the garage and jumped out to open Aimee's and Catherine's doors. He huffed out a breath and then gave Catherine a bright smile that was a little forced. "So, welcome home!"

She stepped inside. Nothing had changed that she could see at first. Aimee followed her into the living room while David hung back in the kitchen, closing the garage door. "I'll be right back. I need to change out of this before I get something on it." That, at least, sounded like the Aimee that Catherine remembered, and she smiled as Aimee took the stairs two at a time.

Looking around the living room, she could see them now, a million little changes. The drapes were different. And the furniture. Unbidden, the mental picture formed of David and Maggie furniture shopping, redecorating the living room in celebration of the new life they were planning . . .

Maybe it hadn't happened that way at all. Maybe David and Aimee had done it to welcome her home. Maybe—

"You doing okay?" David pressed a cold glass into her hand and kissed her on the cheek. "They said we needed to make sure you stayed hydrated. It's just club soda and lemon."

"I'm fine." Catherine forced a smile and gave him a one-armed hug. "Thank you. It's all . . . a lot."

David took her words at face value and smiled back before glancing around. "Where's Aimee?"

"She went upstairs to change."

"She goes through about five outfits a day these days, seems like." He shook his head.

"I was like that at her age, too."

They fell silent. Catherine couldn't tell if it was because neither of them knew what to say, or that they had so much to say that neither of them knew where to start. David leaned in and rested his head against hers, lingering there. What did she look like to him? How much had she changed in his eyes? It was hard to imagine. She'd always been pale, but now she was ghost-white from years without direct sunlight. There were creases around her eyes that hadn't been there when she left, and she was starting to find the occasional gray hair in the straight, nearly black strands. The first year she was alone on *Sagittarius* she'd taken to cutting her hair to keep it from falling into her eyes. As time went on she stopped caring, and ended up pulling it back in a ponytail or a braid. One of the first things she did after she'd landed was get her hair cut into a short, blunt style. She still wasn't sure she liked it; she was afraid it made her look too severe.

Catherine took a sip of her club soda. David still wasn't talking. Should she be talking? She'd craved human contact so much while she was alone, sprawled on her hard bunk on *Sagittarius*, and now that she had it, it didn't feel anything like she'd imagined. Leaning against him this way should have been natural and soothing. She could feel each breath he took, his body moving lightly against hers. A wave of revulsion washed over her. He was too soft. Touching him was like touching some sort of grotesque bag of seawater and viscera, wrong and unnatural and . . .

She looked at him, and for a moment didn't recognize what she saw, seeing something alien in his familiar features. She blinked, and her vision cleared. David was just David again, and leaning against him felt the way it had always felt: comfortable and warm.

Still, her heart thumped uncomfortably, even as she told herself it was just an adjustment issue. She'd been alone for so long. She wasn't used to touching things that were alive.

"Oh." David seemed unaware of any discomfort and took her hand. "Come over here and see what we put together." He led her over to the wall next to the fireplace. It was lined with photographs of Aimee and David, arranged chronologically from the time Catherine left—literally from the day: she recognized the outfit Aimee had on in the first photo as the one she'd worn on launch day. There were photos of birthdays, Christmases, several science fairs . . . all the things Catherine had missed.

Her eyes stung and she blinked rapidly to clear her vision. "This is . . . it's amazing."

He looked pleased. "I tried to get photos of everything. There are a lot more that we didn't manage to put up. And videos. I have hours and hours of videos."

As heartwarming as the photos were, something about them made her uneasy. It took her several moments to see it. None of the photos had Maggie in them. Even photos that Catherine might expect her to be in, like holidays and birthdays. There was no sign of Maggie at all. David had carefully edited all traces of her from his and Aimee's life. Catherine was equal parts touched and disturbed. Was it so easy to erase someone from your life? Had he done that with her while she was gone?

Aimee came trotting downstairs in jeans and a T-shirt. "You found the pictures!" She smiled and bounded over. She hovered there, tension rippling through her, as if on the edge of a decision, then reached out to give Catherine an enthusiastic hug.

"I love them," Catherine said, returning the hug tightly. This was the sort of hug she'd dreamed of while she was away, unrestrained and affectionate.

"Well," David said, clapping his hands together like a master of ceremonies, "now that you're home, what do you want to do first? Do you need to rest a bit?"

"I've been 'resting' for three weeks now." Catherine smiled. "I'm so glad to be here, I don't even know where to start."

"Let's show you the rest of the house." David offered her his hand and she took it, twining their fingers.

"I did live here before, you know," Catherine couldn't help but tease, but

David's offer made it obvious: right now, she was still a guest in her own house.

He recognized his misstep and tried to make a joke of it. "Well, yeah, of course, but . . . I don't know. This is just so much more room than you're used to, I want to make sure you don't wander off and get lost."

"All right, all right. Commence with the grand tour." Catherine played along with him, but couldn't help but wonder, now that she was home, how long it would be before this really *was* home.

4

AFTER UNPACKING WHAT little she'd taken on the mission with her and call
ing her sister, Julie, Catherine went downstairs for dinner. She'd been expecting to cook, but when she walked into the kitchen she was greeted by the
sight of Aimee at the oven and the scent of roasting onion and garlic.

"You're just in time," Aimee said, setting the pizza on a cooling rack before grabbing a salad from the refrigerator.

"Oh, that smells *good*," Catherine said appreciatively.

"Thanks!" Aimee said. "How's Aunt Julie?"

"She's . . . good. She can't wait to get here for your party." Julie was coming for Aimee's graduation party in a few weeks. Once Catherine had gotten
back in radio contact and learned how close it was to Aimee's graduation,
her biggest wish the rest of the way home was to make it back in time. After
so many years away, she was desperate to be there for at least a few of the
milestones in her daughter's life. She had, and even though it was still weeks
away, Catherine could barely wait. Along with wanting to celebrate with
Aimee, she'd missed Julie desperately, missed that connection to one person
who knew her so intimately, and had for so long. Their phone conversation,
though . . . it had been rougher than Catherine expected.

"Have you told her yet?"

Julie sighed. *"The doctors aren't sure yet how best to approach it. There's no
precedent for this, obviously."*

"I miss her."

"Cath, I see her every few days, and I miss her." Julie's voice was soft. *"She's
not really there anymore, most of the time."*

The diagnosis had come about a year before *Sagittarius I*'s launch, a few months after Nora began to get more and more forgetful and erratic: early-onset Alzheimer's. Catherine had wanted to back out of the mission. Nora was the one who spelled it out on Catherine's last visit home. "Cathy, you're leaving for six years. Anything could happen to any of us during that time. Hell, you know the chances of *you* not making it back. Whether you go is your call. Don't change it because of what might happen while you're gone."

And so she'd gone, and nine years later, she'd lost more than she'd anticipated. Her mother was still alive, but so far gone that the confusion of learning that her presumed-dead daughter had returned could be too much for her. Catherine might never get to see her again.

"Mom?" Aimee interrupted her gloomy thoughts, holding out a stack of plates for her to carry.

"Yeah, sorry. Julie's good. She misses you guys." Catherine quickly changed the subject. "How long have you been cooking?"

"Awhile . . . And I remember that pizza used to be your favorite, so . . ."

"It is! And this looks way better than any delivery pizza. This is like magic, I swear." Catherine gave Aimee a quick one-armed hug, pressing a kiss into her hair.

"Cooking is just science, Mom." Aimee was smiling as she said it, her cheeks turning pink. "Um, Maggie taught me a few things, but most of it I learned from you," she quickly added.

Maggie's a better cook than me. Why am I not surprised? But Catherine forced a smile onto her face. Maggie had been part of the family; ignoring that didn't do anyone any favors, not even Catherine. She ruffled Aimee's hair, and Aimee ducked away with a grin. "I'm going to be learning from you now, looks like."

"Anytime you want a lesson . . ." Aimee teased.

They walked into the living room where David was sprawled on the couch. He sat up to make room for them. "Don't let her fool you," David said. "A 'lesson' means she'll make you chop all the vegetables while she does the fun part."

The three of them spent the evening curled up on the couch together the way they'd spent so many weekend nights when Aimee was younger. Aimee and David stumbled over each other to tell Catherine stories of things she'd missed while they ate dinner.

"So most freshmen arrive on campus a week before classes start for orientation," Aimee said.

"You're coming with us," David said to Catherine. It wasn't a question.

Catherine laughed around a mouthful of pepperoni. "Of course! Are you kidding? My genius kid is going to MIT—I want to see where she'll be living."

Sitting here with the two of them, Aimee sandwiched comfortably between her parents, Catherine felt ready to throw herself into the busy life of a mom of a college-bound senior. She was looking forward to meeting Aimee's friends at her graduation party, though the irony wasn't lost on her that every person there would know her daughter better than she did.

"Last slice." David held up the pizza plate. "Who wants it?"

"Ooh, me," Catherine said. She'd forgotten how good a hot, greasy slice of pizza could taste.

Two hours later, it turned out she'd also forgotten how much she could regret that same slice of pizza (or three). Standing in the master bathroom she'd shared with David for years, she was hesitant to open the medicine cabinet. It felt, somehow, as though she were snooping. It wasn't just pepperoni that had her insides in an uproar. In a few minutes, she would go back into the bedroom to share a bed with someone for the first time in years. She hadn't even been this nervous the first night they'd spent together.

David peeked his head in to rescue her. "Antacid is still on the top right of the cabinet."

"Thanks," Catherine said sheepishly.

"I knew you were going to be in trouble when you ate that third slice," he teased. "Nice to see some things haven't changed."

"Hey, do you know how long it's been since I had pizza?" They shared an amused moment, then Catherine made a shooing motion at him. "I'll be right out."

The antacid was exactly where David said it would be. In fact, while she couldn't be entirely certain, everything looked like it was exactly where it used to be. Nothing had changed. Was that weird? Or was it weird that she thought it was weird? It was hard not to read into it, to wonder what it might mean for them if David hadn't changed in nearly ten years, when she had changed so much. Even if the mission had gone as planned, it still would have altered her. As it was, she felt . . . new, somehow. As if she'd come out of *Sagittarius* reborn into someone else's life, and she wasn't quite sure where she'd fit into it yet.

Here. She fit in here. Catherine reminded herself of that sternly. She belonged *here.*

She'd brought her pajamas into the bathroom with her, not quite ready to change clothes in front of anyone else, not even David. She changed into them and brushed her teeth, telling herself that this was what she'd looked forward to, and no matter what happened, she and David would work through it together.

You have to tell him. He has a right to know.

Ava's voice again.

Not yet, Catherine argued. *I don't want to ruin it.*

"Are you going to spend your entire afterlife playing Jiminy Cricket to me?" Catherine muttered ruefully. "I know. I know. Just not . . . not yet."

"Cath? You okay?" David's concerned voice came from the bedroom.

"I'm fine," Catherine called with excessive cheerfulness. "I'll be right out."

David was sitting up in bed, and he put aside the book on his lap when she came in. "You look beautiful."

Catherine ran a self-conscious hand down her pajamas. They were silk but not revealing, feminine without screaming sex. "I'm a mess."

"Yes, but you're my mess." There was that grin she'd always loved.

They'd met during one of the initial interview rounds for the Sagittarius program, and Catherine had been charmed by the way he never postured or bragged. David had been a dry wit in the middle of the often macho bluster that permeated the astronaut training program—even among some of the women, including her. She'd been all over the place then, twenty-three and a bit of a hell-raiser. All she wanted was to fly, the higher and faster the better. NASA was the ultimate in high and fast. She wound up sitting next to him during one of the introductory lectures, and his quiet asides had her fighting to keep from laughing out loud. They went out to dinner that night, and from the moment they both moved to Houston for Sagittarius, they were an item.

Of the two of them, David was the explorer. Where Catherine just wanted to *go*, he wanted to go see what was out there, figure out how the universe worked. Catherine thought he was so grown up, even though he was her age. He had everything together, his life mapped out. Somehow, she wound up fitting on his map. They worked, mostly. David calmed her down and gave her more focus, and she got him to let go and unclench a little. Sometimes she wondered if the things that made him stand out to her were what made him invisible to their trainers, if someone above them had interpreted his quiet self-assurance as a lack of ambition or drive.

They'd been wrong. That much she knew. She climbed into her side of the bed, sitting next to David. "Yeah . . . I am. Every messy bit of me."

David took one of her hands. "I know we're going to have to get to know each other again. I'm not going to rush you into anything."

"I know. I've missed you so much. All I could think about was getting home to you and Aimee."

"Come here." He put his arm around her and pulled her close. Catherine made herself relax, lean her head against his shoulder, no matter how awkward it felt. They were quiet for a moment, and then he said, "I'm so sorry, Cath. I know how close you and your crew were."

No you don't, not completely.

She sighed, guilt and grief trying to rise up and swallow her again. "I keep thinking about how young Claire and Richie were."

"Richie." David snorted softly. "Did he ever take anything seriously?"

"You know, he really did, when it was important. I know you guys didn't always see eye to eye, but he was brilliant." Catherine closed her eyes against the ache. "They all were."

"Ava was one of the best mission commanders I ever saw." Leave it to David to get to the heart of her grief.

"Sh-she was . . ." Catherine trailed off, slipping her arms around David's waist and relaxing into the luxury of giving in to the grief she'd fought for so long. Grief overrode everything, even her awkwardness about touch. How could she have left them? More than that, she couldn't help wonder how she'd left them. Were they buried? One image that haunted her over and over was that of Ava and her crewmates staring sightlessly up into TRAPPIST-1f's sky, maybe forever. The alien bacteria there, combined with the lower oxygen levels in the atmosphere, might prevent decomposition from ever taking hold. They'd be staring up into that crowded sky until the winds managed to cover them with alien dust.

The thought made her cry harder.

"Shh. I know, I know." David stroked her hair and let her cry—something else she'd always appreciated about him. No matter what she was feeling, he gave her room to feel it. He might try to fix it later, but not then. It went on for what felt like forever, but finally she started to run dry, hiccupping in David's arms.

He kissed her forehead. "You know, Aimee and I met up with Jana and the kids every year on the day we lost contact with you."

"I should call her," Catherine sniffled. Ava and Jana had been a lot like Catherine and David, two opposites drawn together into a single whole—Jana was exuberantly social, a bubbly schoolteacher who had a knack for drawing quieter people, including her astronaut wife, into the spotlight.

"She'd love to hear from you, I'm sure."

"I just— I can't help thinking that she blames me somehow, that they all do."

"Hey, hey." David drew away and looked down at her, his forehead furrowed. "Where did that come from? Why would they blame you?"

"I don't know." The words to explain the amorphous guilt sitting in her gut wouldn't come to her. "Blame is the wrong word, maybe. Resent me. I lived and Jana's wife didn't. How can she not hate me a little?"

"Listen to me." He cupped her chin and made her look him in the eye. "The absolute worst part of this whole ordeal was that we knew we might never find out what happened to you. Director Lindholm got the funding for Sag II in part because he pitched it as the only way we had to investigate. With every other tragedy that's hit NASA, sooner or later, some investigation gave families the answer: 'This is why your loved ones died. This is how we'll make sure it doesn't happen again.' The Sagittarius I families knew we were never going to have that. There was never going to be any closure at all. You're our closure. The start of it, anyway."

"And I can't remember a damn thing."

David pulled her back into his arms and rested his chin on top of her head. "There's the ship data, and you'll start to remember, maybe. But you're home, and honestly, that's all I care about." He leaned down and kissed her, and immediately she felt the difference in his kiss. He wasn't going to rush her, but he wasn't going to be shy about his interest either.

The arms that had been comforting a moment ago now seemed too tight. Catherine looked within her for the same surrender that had let her give in to her grief, but it wasn't there. How many hours had she spent dreaming of being with him again? Why was this so hard?

A face drifted in front of her thoughts. Tom. *No, no, no, go away. You're not welcome here.*

David pulled back with the same worried look he'd just given her. "Too soon?"

"No. I mean—I missed you so much, it's just—"

"I understand." He let her go, but kissed her hand. "It's been a long time. The NASA docs told us you'd still be recovering physically, too."

"I'm so sorry." Anxiety sat in the hollow of her throat. She was screwing this up. One of the most important parts of coming home, and she couldn't get it right.

"Do you want me to sleep in the guest room?" David offered gently.

"No! No, I don't want that."

"Are you sure?"

"Yeah, I am."

"Cath—" He halted, and now he was the one fidgeting. "We should talk about Maggie—"

"No . . . we don't have to, not tonight." *Please not tonight.* Catherine wasn't sure she was ready for this.

"I need to." David's gray eyes were pained as they sought hers out, and he took her hands in his. "Cath . . . I'm sorry. Maggie and me, we didn't plan for anything—"

"Stop; you don't have to apologize. You thought I was dead." But again, once the door was open, thoughts rushed out. "I know the two of you have been friends for a long time. Longer than you've known me, even. She was always there for both of us. When you thought I'd died . . . I get it. She's a great person. Aimee clearly thinks the world of her. I know you love her. I—"

"Cath—"

"No, let me finish." Catherine took a deep breath and pushed on. She needed to give David this chance. "You moved on. You should have moved on; that was the right thing to do. I want you to know . . . I get it. You spent years rebuilding your life, and I never wanted to come back and upend it. If— If you want me to step out of the way . . . I mean, you're not obligated—"

"Cath, stop." David reached up and gently put his fingers on her lips. "What Maggie and I had, yeah, I cared about her. She was there for me and Aimee in ways I still can't describe."

"Then why—"

"I *am* obligated. I didn't stand up with her in front of my family and hers and make a bunch of promises. Catherine, I love you. You're my wife. You're alive, and that's a miracle I don't fully understand yet. But I'll take it." David held her gaze with his, then leaned in and carefully kissed her. A quiet warmth grew in her chest—not desire, not yet, but it could easily turn into that. "I never stopped loving you, not for a second. When they told me you were dead, Aimee was all that kept me going. But between the grief and the publicity, I wouldn't have been able to keep it together without Maggie's help. But now I have you back, and . . ." He trailed off and pulled her into a hug. "We can fix this. We *are* fixing it." He pulled back suddenly, searching her face. "If you want to, that is. I'm not the only one who went through a lot; if you—"

"No, I do. I want to be with you." And she did.

Are you going to tell him? Ava asked.

But it would only hurt him, and Catherine didn't want to hurt him just for the sake of unburdening her conscience. "I love you."

"We can fix this," David repeated, his smile turning soft. He reached up and touched her cheek, and now she did feel that initial spark of desire, *finally*, after so long.

That feeling of ease faded as they started undressing, kissing as they peeled away each other's clothing. David must have sensed it. He paused and drew back. "You okay?"

"Yeah." It was a lot of sensory input at once, most of it so unfamiliar it might as well have been the first time. Catherine took a breath, half expecting the strange feelings of wrongness and disgust from earlier to reemerge. Thank God they didn't. She tried to smile, watching the heat in David's eyes and letting it fill her. "I just needed a minute."

"We've got all night."

Catherine had another uncertain moment when David laid her down on the bed, a moment of unreality that overtook her, as if she were just an observer and not a participant. David's hands moving over her skin brought her back, helping her focus in the here and now.

This was where she wanted to be. This was where she belonged. *Home.* The word repeated in her mind and heart as they moved together, David's breathing warm and humid in her ear as he murmured endearments. The word swelled in her with each moment that passed until they were both crying out with the strength of it.

After, she lay in his arms and listened to his heartbeat as he pressed kisses against her hair. "I love you," he said.

"I love you, too." She looked up at him and smiled. There was a flicker of guilt that tried to insinuate itself into her thoughts but she pushed it away.

As exhausted as she was, she lay awake afterward for a long time, acutely aware of every movement David made. He was right; it had been a long time since she'd been intimate with anyone. It just hadn't been as long as he thought.

Sagittarius I Mission

DAY 859
SOMEWHERE IN ERB PRIME

"No, I'm just *saying* that initially NASA was determined to only send committed couples on these long missions together." Tom leaned against the tiny galley counter, unsteady on his feet while Catherine tried to wrestle open another bottle of wine. It was New Year's Eve on Earth, and the crew was celebrating, here in the middle of nowhere.

There wasn't a huge store of alcohol on board, but there was enough for a few decent parties during the mission, at the commander's discretion, of course.

Plus, as Izzy said, monitoring how alcohol affected their behavior, both in the wormhole and planetside, could prove scientifically interesting. And since the whole point of this mission was to maybe find somewhere for humanity to settle, they'd have to spend some time living as normally as possible to gather the information.

"Yeah, but committed couples never would have worked," Catherine countered, scowling at the recalcitrant wine bottle. "They'd never find a couple who could both pass the training, for one thing." And she should know. David had been as likely a candidate as anyone, but there he was, sitting at home while she was out here, over two years of travel away.

"See, then the answer is clear," Tom said, swaying around to point at her. "They gotta encourage matchmaking *during* the training, between the candidates who don't wash out." He grinned. "Come on, how much easier would this trip be if you had a partner with you?"

Catherine snorted, uncorking the bottle. "For me? It wouldn't. It would be easier for *you*, and for Izzy, and Richie . . . but for me and Ava and Claire? Nope."

"Why not?"

"Proven fact, in heterosexual relationships, a man's happiness improves, a woman's happiness stays the same or declines. I'd just have somebody else to look after."

"Cynical."

"Married," she shot back.

"Look, just because your marriage isn't great doesn't mean that all men are like that."

Catherine paused midway through filling her plastic wineglass. "Hang on, I didn't say my marriage wasn't great."

Maybe it wasn't perfect, and admittedly, there was a sense of freedom in being away from David, as much as she loved him. Sometimes she wished he were here—and he might have been, if the washout rate among prospective astronauts weren't so high. They'd met in the training program but after they got married, David washed out. At first, he insisted he was happy for her, happy that at least one of them was going into space. As time went on, though, she got glimpses of his resentment. She started censoring herself, trying to protect his feelings. It was nice, not having to be concerned about anyone's emotional well-being but her own on a day-to-day basis.

"Oh, come on." Tom took the bottle away from her and finished filling their glasses. "You don't agree to take off for six years with limited communication if you're completely happy at home."

"There are lots of married astronauts—"

"There are," Tom agreed. "More married than single, I think . . . and look how many of them aren't on this mission."

"So you're saying that because Ava and I are out here, we were miserable at home?" Catherine folded her arms and leaned against the counter.

"Cath . . . be real. David? Buttoned-down, wears a belt and suspenders David?" Something in Tom's voice caught her attention, and she looked up just in time to find him standing too close. "You jumped at this mission because you were bored out of your mind back home."

"That's not true." Catherine didn't meet his eyes, though. *It wasn't boredom. It wasn't that simple.* How could she explain that sometimes she felt trapped? They'd had Aimee within two years of getting married, wanting to give her a chance to grow up with both parents before one of them had to leave on a long mission. And then David washed out when Aimee was still a baby, and Catherine constantly felt pulled between pursuing her career and trying to make sure David didn't feel bad about it.

Tom slid his hand over her arm. "I'm not asking you to take care of me, Cath," he said. "Let me take care of you. Let someone do that for a change."

Maybe it was the wine, but it was tempting. She liked Tom well enough. They'd been instant friends the moment they'd met in training. And she couldn't deny that there'd always been a flirty little spark between them. She didn't *need* anyone to take care of her, but having someone offer was . . . nice.

When he slipped a hand behind her head and pulled her in for a kiss, she didn't stop him. His mouth was sweet against hers, and after being away from home for over two years, touching someone like this felt so good. Catherine put her wineglass down and returned the kiss for a moment or two.

No, no, no. This is a mistake. It was against regulations, and it was a complication that neither of them needed, and besides, she loved David. She pushed a hand against Tom's chest, separating them.

"Tom. We're drunk, and I'm married. This is a bad idea."

"But—"

"Trust me, tomorrow you'd regret the whole thing."

"I wouldn't." Tom kissed her again, more feverishly this time. "I swear I wouldn't. I've wanted you for ages." He caught her face between his hands. "I know there can't be any emotion here. I get it. It's fine. I just . . ."

It was a mistake to still be standing there, but his eyes were so soft, and for all her cynicism, she missed having someone. Even the wrong someone. This time when he lowered his mouth to hers, her hand against his chest softened, and stopped pushing him away.

"Come on." He took her hand and led her from the galley. "We can't make out in the kitchen like teenagers."

Their individual quarters were tiny, and the idea of sharing a bunk for any length of time was laughable, but by the time they'd spent several minutes kissing up against the closed hatch of Tom's quarters, the bunk wasn't looking so laughable after all.

———

She wasn't laughing when she woke up in that bunk a little while later. She checked the chronometer set in the wall and saw that it was still the middle of the ship's night cycle. She and Tom were crammed together in his narrow bunk, and his arms were still around her.

What the hell did I just do?

Guilt settled on Catherine like a weighted blanket, pinning her in place. It wasn't just that she'd cheated on David—although God, wasn't that enough?—but that it was the first time in her career she'd not just broken but *shattered* a regulation. Maybe it wouldn't jeopardize the mission, but it sure as hell would jeopardize her career, and probably Tom's.

She needed to get up, get back to her quarters, and try to pretend this never happened. Then hope to God that Tom did the same thing.

As she sat up and reached for her clothes, Tom stirred behind her and reached for her. "Where're you going?" he mumbled.

"I can't spend the night here; we'll get busted." Catherine started pulling her clothes on.

"Good point." Tom sounded more awake, and sat up behind her. He leaned in and started kissing her shoulder. "Too bad, though. Sure you don't want to stay a little longer?"

Catherine paused, halfway through pulling her socks on. She sighed and straightened, turning to look at him. "Tom. We can't do this again."

"Sure we can. We'll be careful. Besides, I don't think anybody would care, really." He tried to kiss her again and she leaned back.

"*I* can't do this again. I'm sorry. This was a bad idea." She stood up and finished pulling her clothes on.

"Cath, come on. Didn't you have a good time?"

"That doesn't matter—"

"It matters to *me*!"

"Shh." The last thing they needed was for Tom to wake someone up. "Tom, don't make this a thing. We were drunk and we made a mistake, okay?"

"'Don't make this a thing'? We've been dancing around this since training!" Tom stood as well, and in the small quarters they were in each other's face.

"No, you were the only one dancing, Tom." Catherine ducked out through the hatch, a sense of dread and shame tightening her chest and sitting like a rock in her belly. The feeling only intensified as she crept back to her quarters.

The six of them were stuck together for the next few years. Catherine hoped she hadn't just signed them all up for a nightmare.

5

"BREATHE, WILL YOU?" David reached across the front seat to take her hand as they drove in together the first morning.

Catherine released her two-handed death grip on her travel mug and took David's hand. "I'm breathing, I'm breathing." She glanced over with a smile. "Hey, I haven't had to go to the office in over nine years, so cut me some slack for being nervous."

David brought her hand to his lips, keeping one eye on the traffic as he drove. "That's my girl. Strap her to a rocket and she's cool as a cucumber, tell her she's got to face rush-hour traffic every day and she's worried."

It wasn't that, and David knew as much, but Catherine was grateful to him for making light of it. "Yeah, well. NASA produces better pilots than Houston does drivers." They shared a grin and some of the tension drained from her. "It'll be good to be back, part of things again." She took a deep breath and let it out. "One more step back to normal life, right?"

And, despite the nervousness, she *was* eager to get back. Llewellyn had offered to give her more time off, but with Aimee finishing up her senior year and David working, there didn't seem to be any point in Catherine's staying home. They'd taken Aimee out of school for a week or so, and there'd be ongoing family counseling to resolve any adjustment issues. Besides, with only a month and a half to go before the Sagittarius II launch, she knew Llewellyn could probably use every pair of hands he could get. She was looking forward to meeting the new crew and helping them however she could. It was the least she could do.

"I saw John Duffy is the flight commander for Sag II," she said. "I couldn't believe it. Don't tell me he's grown up and gotten all responsible."

"Listen, I still can't believe he made it through training," David said with a snort, giving her the crooked grin that had first stolen her heart. "He was so busy playing pranks and chasing tail I didn't think he was actually *learning* anything."

"Oh come on, he wasn't that bad."

"You only think so because you were one of the tails he was chasing the hardest, 'Catherine the Great,'" David teased.

Too late, Catherine realized that despite David's grin, she'd stumbled onto a sore spot. Duffy had been in their training cohort, and despite his antics and David's quiet, intense dedication to learning everything he could, Duffy went on to finish the program and David hadn't. The two men were nearly diametric opposites, and given Duffy's tendency to flirt as easily as he breathed, the tension between them was unavoidable.

"Ugh, I forgot he used to call me that." She tried to find a way to recover. "I guess I'll find out today if he's changed or not. I'm meeting with him and the rest of the crew this afternoon for the simulation test."

"Yikes, that's today?" David looked at her closely. "Are you ready for that? What time?"

"May as well jump in with both feet," Catherine said, trying to smile for him. "It's early this afternoon, after that planning meeting."

"Which planning meeting?"

"The one at eleven, with Aaron Llewellyn. It's not on your calendar?"

David's smile was still firmly in place, but even after more than nine years apart, Catherine could see the strain beneath it. "Nope, that's the weekly meeting for department heads and up. You're in that one?"

"Yeah . . . it's probably a one-time thing, to talk about my mission."

When David let go of her hand to put both hands back on the steering wheel, she tried to tell herself it was because freeway traffic was getting heavier, and she wrapped her fingers around the stainless steel of her cup, staring straight ahead.

"Maybe not," David said, a little too casually. "You're a superstar now, kiddo. I'm just a grunt in the trenches."

She was right back in the moment they'd learned that David had washed out of the program. He'd had that same casual, too-faint smile on his face then. If she asked him, he would say he was fine, and that he was excited for her. It was probably true. But it wasn't the whole truth.

"Yeah, well, you're my grunt, and I love you."

"Love you, too, Cath. I'm proud of you." Now when he looked over at her, the smile looked a little more real. "Always have been."

——

JSC was one of those places that never changed, even while in a constant state of flux. The displays were different, the faces were different, but even if she'd been dropped in the middle of a hallway, Catherine would have known where she was. She found her office without difficulty, a small, blank space with a desk, a computer, and a decent-sized window. Tomorrow she'd bring in a few personal things.

The planning meeting was something new, a glimpse behind the scenes she'd never had before. The only crewman there was John Duffy, and he gave Catherine a quick wave as they sat down.

She knew, of course, that immensely detailed logistics went into every NASA mission, but listening to the others go over the minutiae of weight limits, fuel calculations, supply needs, etc., it seemed a miracle they'd ever gone into space to begin with.

When the meeting ended, Duffy made his way over to her before she could leave the conference room. He came forward with an outstretched hand and, when she took it, he pulled her into a hug. "Here's our hero," he said with a grin.

"Oh God, no," Catherine said, grimacing. "Don't start that."

"I damn near did a dance in my living room when I heard you'd come back," he said, finally letting her go. "Bad enough to lose Ava and the others, but not Catherine the Great." Duffy eyed her closely. "How is it? Being home?"

"It's . . . weird, but good."

"Come on. We've got time for a cup of coffee before we have to meet the rest of the crew."

Over coffee he filled her in on some of the agency gossip she'd missed out on: who was jockeying for a promotion, who was probably sleeping with whom, all the things the briefings left out.

"We did learn a few things from Sagittarius I before the Event," Duffy said. "Mike Ozawa figured out pretty quick that we were receiving the data but you weren't getting our return messages, so he got the engineers working on it. They think they've got it resolved. Guess we'll find out in a couple of years."

"Road testing new equipment is always exciting."

"Tell me about it. That's the problem with what we do, Cath. There's only so much they can do to re-create actual conditions on the ground."

"You know, it's nice talking to another astronaut again," Catherine admitted. "Someone who gets it."

"Catherine, I don't know if any of us can really *get* what you went through," Duffy said, playing with the stirrer in his coffee.

"You've been out there, though. You get that. Being alone." Catherine had expected that the feeling of aloneness would stop once she was home, but it lingered like a bad smell. Even though she was home, sometimes it felt as though David and Aimee weren't really seeing *her* when they looked at her. Maybe that was because she still didn't quite know who she was now. Here at NASA, she'd been part of a unit, her crew, for so long. It felt weird to make a decision without running it by Ava, or to get through a day without Richie's saying something to make her laugh. It was like missing limbs.

"Yeah," Duffy said quietly. "I do get that. I'm sorry."

Catherine smiled at him with a tight expression, fighting to keep her eyes dry. "Yeah. I am, too." She changed the subject. "How is it being flight commander? How's your crew?"

Now it was Duffy's turn to grimace. "Oh *God* they're young. They're so young. I hate them." She laughed, then listened as he went on to give her some background on each of them. By the time they walked toward another, smaller conference room together, she felt as if they were already familiar to her.

Her first thought on entering the conference room was *Oh, they* are *young*. Had she ever been that fresh-faced? Llewellyn wasn't there, and she and Duffy alone didn't do much to raise the average age of the room.

Some of the faces she'd seen around JSC. Duffy, she knew, of course, and Cal Morganson, in his role as flight activities director. *That ought to be fun*, Catherine thought dourly.

John squeezed her shoulder and brought her in to face the rest of the room. "Y'all know Catherine, I'm sure. Catherine, this is my crew." He indicated a woman with a close-cropped Afro and a flyboy smirk. "Leah Morrison's our pilot." Catherine recognized a kindred spirit right away. She would bet money that Morrison had been a test pilot once, too.

"I was there the day you took the B-87 prototype for its test run," Morrison said, standing and offering her hand. "I'm glad it was you flying that day and not me. I was barely out of Basic at the time."

Catherine laughed and shook Morrison's hand. "Yeah, they had to go back to the drawing board with that one. I'm just glad *both* engines didn't go out."

Next down the line was a man with wide brown eyes who looked like a teenager. "This is Zach Navarro, our flight engineer. He's the baby of the bunch," Duffy said.

"Hey!" Navarro protested.

"Not my fault you're a child prodigy, kid." Duffy ruffled his hair while Navarro made a face, but smiled at Catherine.

"Kevin Park is our mission specialist," Duffy went on, pointing to a man with pale white skin and a shock of dark hair. "He's an exobiologist. After what you found up there, he's hopeful."

"I'm glad they're sending you," Catherine said. "Claire Tomason was a hell of a scientist, but she was a geologist." Claire had been the baby of *their* crew, and they'd all been mildly protective of her.

"I can't wait to see it all for myself," Park said. "Who knows what we'll be able to find."

But there's nothing else there to *find*, she thought, although there was no way she could know that. She pushed the thought away and turned her attention to the systems operator, a bubbly blonde named Grace Kowalski. "It's an honor to meet you, Colonel Wells," she said. "I was so glad you didn't die—I mean, I was glad you came back safe." She pushed up her glasses, flustered. "You know what I mean."

"I do," Catherine said. "No worries."

"Last but not least is the man who's going to be there to save our asses, Dr. Nate Royer, our physician."

Nate was attractive, with warm brown skin and an easy smile. And Catherine didn't miss that he was sitting next to Cal; the two of them looked close, as much friends as colleagues.

"And of course, you've already met Cal, our resident cat herder."

"Colonel Wells." Cal nodded briefly, and Catherine would've sworn the temperature dropped in the room.

John's phone beeped and he checked it. "Okay, the techs tell me they almost have the simulator ready for us. Hang tight for a bit; soon we'll be able to take a look at what our new home is going to be like."

The TRAPPIST-1f simulation was equal parts virtual reality and real-world environmental changes, like temperature, gravitational pull, winds. At first Catherine hadn't seen the point of her joining in. It wasn't as if she could verify how accurate they were. The science team was working off the little bit of information that had come back from Sagittarius I, not anything useful from her.

They settled in to wait for the techs to give them the go-ahead, and Morrison scooted over to sit next to Catherine. "Hey, I've been dying to ask. Is there anything about flying in ERB Prime that I should know? What's the handling like?"

Catherine was thrilled to have a question she could actually answer. "Well, you're hopefully not going to do that much *flying* in it. At least not in terms of controlling the ship. There's only one way to go, and that's forward." She reached down for her water bottle. "It's . . . like being on a track. All you control is the speed, not the direction."

"What do you think happens if you go off the track?"

"I don't think that's possible."

Morrison grinned. "But you tried it, didn't you." It wasn't a question.

Catherine laughed. "Busted. That *was* part of our mission, to learn as much as we could about the makeup and properties of the wormhole. I did try to steer the ship off course."

"What happened?"

"Not a damn thing. The ship twitched a little, but that was it. A tunnel. That's a more accurate description. It's like flying through a tunnel." She paused. "Except you can't hit the wall."

Morrison looked as if she wished she were taking notes. "How close are the flight simulators to actually flying *Sagittarius*?"

Catherine had mentored new pilots before, when she was in the air force, but this was something different. She was the first to fly the *Sagittarius* model ship, and so far, the only. That added a little pressure to get the information right—there was no one else around who could correct her if she got it wrong. "They're pretty close. As close as sims can get to the real thing, anyway. I think we pulled more Gs on liftoff than the simulators said we would. It was one hell of a push to get us going. Other than that . . . yeah, pretty close."

There was a knock at the door and one of the techs stuck her head in. "We're ready for you in the planetary simulation now."

The six of them—Catherine plus the Sagittarius II crew, except for Commander Duffy, who was observing with Cal—suited up in the same space suits used on the first mission. The only difference was the VR headsets implanted in the helmets.

They started going through the planned "mission" for the session, gathering "samples" from the environment. The room was hot and humid, close to surface conditions on TRAPPIST-1f. The light dimmed and brought relief to Catherine's strained eyes.

"You know, this is going to take away all the wonder from actually getting there," Navarro complained. "It's gonna feel like standing in a room in Houston."

Before Catherine could say anything, a strange feeling came over her. She was hot enough to start sweating—that wasn't so surprising—but it was harder to breathe. They had oxygen on. Even if the atmosphere in the room was a match to the planet's, the oxygen would counter it.

It wasn't a memory, exactly. More a feeling of uneasy familiarity. Her skin was crawling and she couldn't explain why.

"Yeah, except it's hotter in here than in the other sims we've done," Park said. "And the commute's a hell of a lot longer. I dunno, this is pretty exciting to me. We get to see another planet without the long trip."

"Park, are you the kind of guy who spends his vacation touring the world through VR?" asked Morrison. When he didn't answer, she laughed. "Oh my God, you are. Would you seriously rather spend most of the week exploring Venice via a headset rather than actually going there?"

"It's not that, it's just . . . *easier* that way," Park said defensively.

Sweat beaded along Catherine's temple. Through the VR goggles, she could see the projected landscape of TRAPPIST-1f. It might have been a desert anywhere in the Southwest: rocky ground, hot. The sky was a dull red, and was crowded with the other TRAPPIST planets, close enough to be clearly visible. *They've got it wrong. Everything's wrong. Something's missing.* It was a feeling, a deep, unsettling feeling, but it didn't come with any memory of what the landscape had really been like. A shadow fell, and something glimmered in the corner of her eye. She turned sharply to the left. Nothing was there, but the feeling persisted. *I'm being watched.*

"All right, enough with the chatter," Duffy interjected. "Wells, your vitals are going wonky. Heart and blood pressure rates up. Are you all right?"

"Yeah. Yeah, I'm fine." There was a bitter, coppery taste in the back of her throat, adrenaline flooding her body. She laughed shakily. "You guys must have gotten this sim close to the real thing. I'm having déjà vu." *Of course you're being watched. Half of NASA is observing you.*

"Catherine, are you remembering anything?" That was Cal's voice.

"No, it's just . . . weird. This feels familiar." *Familiar but wrong.* It was as if her vision were doubled, one image superimposed on the other, but the image in the background was too blurry for her to see it.

"Catherine, your blood pressure is shooting up, and I'm not liking your heart rate. If your vitals don't stabilize, I'm going to pull you out," Duffy warned.

"It's okay. I'll be fine," Catherine insisted, even as dark spots clouded her vision.

The stones are missing. It was her last thought before she fell to her knees and everything went black.

6

WHEN CATHERINE OPENED her eyes, she was in the simulation control room, a tech holding her helmet and Duffy and Morganson hovering over her.

"Her vitals are getting better, Commander," the tech said.

"What did you see?" Cal asked.

"Come on, give her a second to breathe," Duffy said.

Catherine blinked. The real world felt false to her, the lights too bright again, everything too loud. The strange feeling of standing back on the planet was fading. The last thing she remembered was Duffy threatening to pull her out.

"The simulation, like everybody else," Catherine said finally, gingerly sitting up. "What happened?"

"You passed out," Duffy replied.

"Oh come on. I never pass out." Heat rose in Catherine's cheeks as she realized Duffy wasn't teasing her. She'd never showed weakness like that before. It was why Duffy had started calling her Catherine the Great. To have passed out in a *sim* . . . The team was going to think she'd rushed back too soon, that she wasn't ready.

"Still, it's encouraging," Cal said, speaking to Duffy as much as to her. "Clearly something in Catherine's brain was triggered by the simulation of being on TRAPPIST-1f." He addressed Catherine directly. "We need a team to keep an eye on you next time, in case that happens again, but I think we should put you back in there as soon as we're cleared. Tomorrow, at the earliest." With that he seemed to dismiss her.

Duffy stayed behind and squeezed her shoulder. "You sure you're okay?"

"Yeah, I'm fine, I promise. It was a little strange, is all." She could still taste the adrenaline in her mouth.

"We have to keep you in top form," he said with a smile. "You're our star trainer right now. The crew likes you. They know you *get* it, and you know what you're talking about."

"What I can remember, anyway." Catherine sighed.

Catherine felt uneasy about what had happened, but Duffy's praise stayed with her for the afternoon, along with the easy way that Leah Morrison seemed to look up to her. No matter what had happened, she was still capable of doing good things here. She could hang on to that.

———

Sometime after lunch there was a knock on her office door. "Catherine?" The last person Catherine expected to see: Maggie.

Why is she here? With Maggie working here, too, Catherine knew they would run into each other sooner or later. She didn't expect Maggie to come and find her. Bracing herself, she said, "Come on in."

Maggie poked her head around the door. Although she was roughly Catherine's age, she looked younger, and had long blond hair that was always styled perfectly. Catherine used to admire that about her; now it was just intimidating. "I heard what happened with the simulation and wanted to check on you. Everything okay?"

This would be so much easier if Catherine could hate her. "Thanks, but I'm fine. Oh God, people aren't making a thing out of it, are they?"

"No, don't worry about that." When Catherine gestured, Maggie came in and shut the door behind her, sitting in the chair across from Catherine's desk. "My team had a hand in the sims, so we got the reports afterward." She hesitated, then said, "I know they're using you as a resource for Sagittarius II, but don't let them put too much pressure on you."

"I won't." Catherine smiled faintly. "Besides, what would they have done if I had stayed dead?" *What would* you *have done, Maggie?* That wasn't fair of her. Maggie at least had thought Catherine was dead. Catherine had known full well David was alive when she slept with Tom.

Maggie must have caught the edge in Catherine's question; a furrow appeared in her smooth brow. "I wanted to say . . . I don't have to go to Aimee's graduation party this weekend if it's too awkward for you."

Catherine paused. A piece of her wanted to take Maggie up on her offer, to tell her to stay away. But the rational part of her knew that wasn't fair, to Maggie or Aimee. "No, you should come. You were there for her in high school. It wouldn't be right for you to miss it."

Maggie leaned forward and looked her in the eye. "I'm not going to say this isn't hard, or isn't weird. I care about David and Aimee. I . . . I miss them. I can't say I'm sorry for what happened. We were all doing the best we could."

"I know." The difference was, Catherine's best involved six years alone in a ship designed for a full crew, terrified and not sure she would ever make it home. Maggie's best involved sleeping with Catherine's husband and raising Catherine's child.

Stop it. That's not going to help anything.

Instead, she took a deep breath. "I didn't get to say thank you. I know you did a lot for Aimee. She needed a mom."

"She's a great kid." Maggie gave her a sincere smile. "She's a pleasure to be around. But . . . if you need me to back away a little—"

"No." Catherine shook her head, although this was one of the hardest conversations she'd had since coming home. "Please don't. She still needs you. I'm sure she still feels more comfortable confiding in you than in me." More than anything, she wanted her daughter back, but pushing away someone Aimee had come to rely on wasn't going to help that.

"David and Aimee are lucky. If either of them ever acts like they're forgetting that, tell me, okay? I'll knock some sense into them."

Yeah. This would be easier if she could hate Maggie. Catherine smiled. "I will."

"You sure you're okay? You still look a little pale."

"I really am, I promise. Thanks for coming to check on me."

"You bet." Maggie stood and Catherine walked her to the door. Once Maggie was gone, Catherine decided she needed some coffee to face the rest of the afternoon.

She stepped through the door Maggie had just used, and everything was wrong.

The hallway was wrong. The hallway outside her office—outside the door she'd *just walked through*—had been a main corridor: brightly lit, broad, busy. The hallway she was standing in now was dim, narrow, and empty.

Catherine looked around. What the hell had happened? She turned to go back into her office. Maybe she'd gone out the wrong door.

But your office has only one door.

The door behind her wasn't her office door. It was locked, a heavy-duty security door labeled AUTHORIZED PERSONNEL ONLY.

What—

Where was she? Looking around gave her no clues. Sometimes at home she used to take afternoon naps on the patio. When she slept too long and the weather was too hot, this was how she felt on waking. Groggy, disoriented. Nothing made sense.

Footsteps sounded down the hall and around the corner. She should hide. But where? There was nowhere in the tiny hallway to go. The bitterness in her mouth was overwhelming, and her heart pounded wildly in her chest. There was nothing to do except brazen it out. She started walking toward the footsteps, wishing she had some files with her or something.

Two men came around the corner. One of them was an engineer on Sagittarius II—she couldn't remember his name. The other was Cal Morganson—of course, of *course* it would be him.

"Afternoon, Colonel Wells," the engineer said. Both men were looking at her curiously, and she smiled. "Hey."

Suddenly Catherine felt her awareness *shoved* back, like getting pushed to the back of a bus. In her dimming vision, the two men in front of her turned into pale, grotesque monsters, the same repulsive, too-soft creature she'd seen when she looked at David.

No, not here . . .

An overwhelming mental image came to her, of slamming their heads together over and over until their skulls broke and the seawater inside them ran out red and thick. She almost screamed before she realized it was only in her mind.

"Didn't expect to find you in the archives." Cal's voice brought her back, her heart racing sickeningly. His eyes were focused too tightly on her. As though he knew what she was thinking.

"Don't tell me somebody stuck *you* on research duty," the engineer said with a laugh.

"I'm here by choice, believe it or not." Catherine faked a laugh with him although she was trying not to vomit. The archives? She had no reason to be in the archives. How the hell had she gotten down here? "I— I had to look something up and it . . . wasn't in a digital file yet," she stammered. "It's a nice change, though; it's quiet here."

"Too quiet. Gives me the creeps." The engineer was a round-faced, cheery sort, and she was grateful he was there to act as a buffer to Cal, who hadn't said anything further.

"Yeah, that's for sure." She took a step backward, hoping her legs didn't tremble beneath her. "Well, I'll let you both get to it."

It wasn't until she found the elevator that she thought to check her cell phone. Maggie had left her office around two thirty.

It was nearly four in the afternoon.

That was impossible. Her phone was wrong.

She got off the elevator on the ground floor and checked one of the clocks showing the world's various time zones.

Her phone wasn't wrong.

An hour and a half of her day had vanished in the time it took her to walk through a doorway.

7

SHOULD I EVEN be driving? Catherine gripped the wheel as she drove in alone to JSC the next day, focusing on the things that were *real*: the firm steering wheel against her fingers, the sun coming through the car window, hot against her skin despite the fierce air conditioner.

For the past eighteen hours, Catherine had been clinging to reality like a life preserver. She focused on sensory input as much as possible, trying to ground herself in things that were unmistakably real, like counting the mile markers on the side of the highway as she drove. Watching them reassured her that she wasn't losing track of time. As far as she knew, the loss of time hadn't happened again, but the constant vigilance to try to prevent it was exhausting. Especially since she had no idea *how* to prevent it. She found herself checking her watch every few minutes, making sure the time that had passed felt like the right amount of time.

It had been worse last night. David let Aimee go out with friends after dinner. On a school night. She didn't get home until eleven, and every minute she was gone seemed to stretch, further distorting Catherine's sense of time.

Focus on the steering wheel and the warm sun. Let everything else go. And don't tell a soul.

She wasn't sure what would happen if she did, but she couldn't bear the thought of going back to isolation, of losing the freedom she'd so desperately yearned for while she was in quarantine, and, before that, all those years alone...

She still hadn't decided what to tell Dr. Darzi when she sat down in her office for her therapy appointment. Compared to the rest of JSC, Dr. Darzi's office was warm, homelike. In a hive of squared-off, sharp-edged scientific minds, clinical surroundings, and industrial buildings, hers was the one place that was soft and quiet. The overhead fluorescents stayed off in favor of incandescent lamps, and the cinder-block walls were covered in peaceful artwork and soft fabric hangings. Catherine often wondered if her male counterparts were comfortable in these surroundings.

Still, Catherine had liked Dr. Darzi from the start. She didn't dress or act like most of NASA's administration, favoring long, flowy skirts and dresses, and wearing her tightly coiled black hair short. She didn't take any bullshit from anybody, Catherine included.

"It sounds as if you're settling in well at home." Dr. Darzi sat across from her in a wingback chair while Catherine perched on the edge of a love seat, not quite able to relax.

"It's good to be back with my family," Catherine said. "David and I are . . . we're in this weird place where we're getting reacquainted, but it's going okay."

"And with Aimee?"

"It's amazing," Catherine said. "She's great. I just . . . have to keep reminding myself that she's not a little girl anymore. And David's a little more lenient than I would be."

"Are you feeling out of control?"

"No, it's not that," Catherine insisted. "I just . . . want her to be safe."

"Of course you do, but it's also natural to want to reach out and grab on to what we're certain of, what we know we have control over." Dr. Darzi peered at Catherine over her glasses. "There's an awful lot in your life that you can't control right now."

Did she know? How could she know? Suddenly the draped office felt suffocating. "I don't feel out of control," she lied. Was that it? Did she want to be controlling at home to make up for everything else?

Dr. Darzi didn't answer.

"I don't— I mean, I'm not, necessarily. I mean, no more out of control than anybody else, right? Things are going great here. I'm fine. I'm settling in, like you said." The longer Catherine lied, the more desperate she felt, needing to believe it herself. Maybe more than she needed Dr. Darzi to believe it. She stopped trying and went quiet, staring at her hands.

The silence spun out until Dr. Darzi said, "Sooner or later you're going to have to talk about you, Catherine. Not your family. Not your job. *You*. I know you feel like you abandoned Aimee and David, but you were abandoned, too, in a way."

"Me? By who?"

At first Catherine thought Dr. Darzi wasn't going to answer. Instead, she asked, "How long did you know Commander Gidzenko?"

"Ava? We met in training."

"And the rest of your crew?"

Catherine realized where the doctor was going. "They didn't *abandon* me. They died."

"You lived with them for three years. Trained with them for how long before that?"

"I don't know, several years."

"The six of you experienced something no one else has ever experienced. Ever. You lived together like a family. And now you're the only one left."

"But we weren't like that," Catherine protested. "Ava and I were close, yes, but the others, they were just my coworkers." *Sure, your coworkers, like Tom.* The guilt was like a gut punch.

"Catherine?"

"I'm fine." She tried to smile, and felt it falling flat.

"Are you sure?"

"Yes." Catherine closed her eyes for a moment and took a breath. "Doctor, am I ever going to get my memory back?"

Dr. Darzi sat back in her chair, crossing her legs. "It's hard to say. I know that's not what you want to hear. Retrograde amnesia is tough to treat in the best of cases. You went through an enormous emotional trauma; it was six years, and for all we know you could have experienced some sort of physical trauma as well. Plus, we knew ahead of time that traveling through ERB Prime can have some effects on memory."

"Yeah, but I didn't know it would be like this. Did Iris Addy ever get any of her memory back?"

Dr. Darzi flinched so imperceptibly that Catherine wondered if she'd imagined it. "Iris Addy was a special case."

"The stories say she came back hearing voices," Catherine pressed.

"Are you hearing voices?"

Catherine thought about the moments when she heard Ava's voice in her mind, as clear as if she were standing right next to her. But that felt different somehow, more like grief, like she was trying to keep Ava with her. She shook her head.

Dr. Darzi put aside her notepad and leaned forward. "The astronaut screening program isn't perfect, and sometimes things slip past the tests. Yes, Iris Addy came back with some issues, and yes, some of those issues were similar to yours. However, she refused to let NASA help her with them. Our hands were tied." She smiled. "You, clearly, aren't making the same mistakes she did."

"Well, I'm trying not to." Catherine tried to return the smile, though she couldn't help but hear a faint warning in the doctor's words.

"Memory loss is upsetting and disconcerting, I know. What you're experiencing is normal, Catherine. You just have to give yourself time to recover."

"But how long?"

The doctor laughed, but gently. "It's been little more than a month since you got home. I promise you, you're making great progress. If I see a problem, I will tell you. All right?"

"Yes. Okay." Catherine didn't feel any better. Dr. Darzi wasn't seeing the things she was. Dr. Darzi didn't know everything.

"What are you afraid of, Catherine?"

"What am I *not* afraid of," Catherine said with a laugh. "That list would be a lot shorter."

Dr. Darzi didn't laugh, but kept looking at her with patient brown eyes.

Catherine sighed. She wasn't getting out of this, not unless she wanted to spend the rest of her session in silence. She couldn't make the words come out at first. "What if something went really wrong up there? What if . . . what if the reason I can't remember anything is that I'm the reason it went wrong?"

Admitting that took all the willpower she had, and she held her breath waiting for the response.

"That's a normal feeling." Dr. Darzi folded her hands on her lap. "Something did go wrong up there. Very wrong. As the sole survivor of a tragedy, you're going to feel guilty. You're going to look for reasons why you were the one who survived when no one else did. For some people, this manifests as a drive to find their purpose in life, for others, it's proof they were somehow responsible for the tragedy."

Despite Dr. Darzi's reassuring words, Catherine couldn't help remembering how badly she'd wanted to hurt Cal and the engineer when they'd found her in the archives. Not just hurt them—destroy them. And then there was the missing time . . .

"I . . . there has to be some reason I survived and they didn't. Any sort of destruction of the Habitat . . . I would have been there, too. Or else, someone would have survived with me if we were on an expedition when it happened." Catherine fumbled along, trying to explain the fear that had been hovering in the back of her mind. "If it was some sort of sickness, what are the odds that I was the only one to survive? And I suppose there's a chance that I just took off and left them behind, but . . . I think the five of them would have been able to stop me."

Dr. Darzi put aside her notepad again and looked at Catherine seriously. "When we go through trauma, afterward we try to make sense of it. We look for signs, for some pattern to show us the meaning behind what happened. But Catherine, often there is no meaning. Bad things just *happen*."

"But . . . since I've been home, I've . . . I've had thoughts. Frightening thoughts. About hurting other people. Not my family," Catherine was quick to reassure her. "It's like . . . like it's someone else having those feelings."

"I see. Do you feel threatened by the people you want to hurt?"

"Well, I . . . yes. Yes, they seem dangerous."

"Those are called intrusive thoughts, Catherine. They're not uncommon with PTSD, but they're just thoughts. Most likely, the people who trigger that response in you somehow remind you of whatever happened on TRAPPIST-1f, and your mind instantly wants to defend you from the danger.

Pay close attention to when it happens; try to figure out what those people have in common. It may yield some insight."

"But—"

"If they continue to trouble you, we can look at starting you on some medication to stop them."

Catherine fought back a sense of frustration, of not being heard. Finally she admitted, "I'm . . . still forgetting things sometimes."

"More amnesia?"

"No, not exactly. It doesn't feel the same as what happened on the ship." She'd lost years of her life then, a vast yawning emptiness. Losing an hour here and there couldn't be the same thing—could it?

Dr. Darzi reached for her notepad again. "I see. What sorts of things are you forgetting?"

Catherine laughed lightly, waving a dismissive hand. She should never have brought this up. "Oh, it's just silly. Like forgetting that I put something on the stove, that sort of thing."

"Hmm. What does it feel like when that happens?"

"Nothing, really," Catherine said. Half-truths were her home these days. She was getting very good at telling them. "Just like . . . I disconnected for a little bit, distracted."

"It might be some mild dissociation. That's also not uncommon with PTSD. Are you frightened by it?"

"A little." Catherine didn't tell her about the nearly obsessive way she was watching clocks, or the constant worry that she was living in a moment she'd soon forget.

"Dissociative responses often come in response to a trauma trigger. Can you think of anything that might have happened before you dissociated?"

Had something happened? Before the incident here at Johnson she'd talked to Maggie, and it started with the planetary simulation. "Maybe, yes. But . . ."

"But what?" Dr. Darzi prompted.

"What if it keeps happening?"

Dr. Darzi sighed. "I wish I could promise you that it won't, but chances are very good that it will. The good news is, the further you get from the original trauma, and the more work we do here, the less frequent and less severe your symptoms will be."

"I just . . . I just keep thinking that if I could *remember* what happened on the mission, all of this would get better much faster," Catherine said.

"I know, Catherine. But that may not ever happen, and you need to work on accepting that." Dr. Darzi's voice was soothing. "I think our time might be better spent if we start focusing on the here and now. You may never fully recover your memories, but you can—and should—live in the now."

Dr. Darzi's words made sense, but something didn't ring true. "But what if there's something important that I'm forgetting?"

"Catherine. This is becoming counterproductive for you. It's time to stop focusing on the past and focus on the present and the future. Trying to relive what happened isn't going to fix anything. You're back, you're alive, you're a hero. Don't let your mind trick you into poking holes in that."

Catherine was growing to hate the word *hero*. It wasn't just that she didn't feel like one. It was that NASA pulled that word out whenever they wanted her to stop thinking about what had happened on the mission. It was like a code phrase: "No, everything is fine, nothing went wrong that we can't fix, you're fine, now *be* fine so there are no loose ends."

But at the same time, Dr. Darzi was right. There was no way for her to force the memories to come back. All she could do was fix what was happening now.

"I'm trying, Doc. I really am."

"I know, and you're doing great, Catherine. This is hard, scary work that you're doing. The good news is you're not alone anymore. You have a miraculous second chance here. We're going to help you make the most of it."

Catherine stayed quiet, then conceded. "All right. Yes. You're right. I'll do my best to stay focused on the present from now on."

"Great. You're not going to regret it, I promise you."

Catherine left the office, hoping against hope that Dr. Darzi was right. But another part of her wondered how she was supposed to focus on the present when she was haunted by the gaping black hole that was her past.

She couldn't shake the feeling that she *needed* to remember what had happened to her after Mission Day 865. When had they landed on TRAPPIST-1f? What had happened then? Dr. Darzi wanted to know what she was afraid of. She was afraid that the hole in her memory starting on Day 865 would expand, one blank period of time, until there was nothing left of her.

Sagittarius I Mission

The crew was crowded into the command module, watching as they passed over TRAPPIST-1f's dark side. They didn't get their first clear glimpse of their new home until they reached the terminator line that divided permanent day from night on the planet. Catherine guided them through their orbit, giving Claire Tomason, their mission specialist and resident scientist, time to do a full analysis of the surface conditions.

"Water!" Richie Almeida, their systems operator, spotted it first. "A lake. That's a fucking lake! Are you seeing this?"

A large patch of blue winked at them from a valley, and there were other similar blue spots dotting the landscape.

"Scientists back home are going to lose their minds when they find out," Ava said.

Tom craned his head over the communications panel he was manning, trying to spot something else new. "Doesn't exactly look welcoming," he muttered.

"What is your deal?" Richie nudged him in the shoulder. "It's a *new planet*. You're allowed to be excited!"

Tom pushed his hand away with a scowl.

Ever since New Year's Day, when Catherine had crept out of his bed, Tom had been snappish with the rest of the crew.

At first, it had been awkward as hell. The ship was too small for her to avoid him completely. Two weeks after New Year's, Tom approached her once more, trying to persuade her to come back. When she said no, he stopped talking to her altogether, unless absolutely required. He started spending most of his downtime alone in his cabin, rebuffing anyone who tried to draw him out.

She had hoped that maybe reaching their mission objective would help him come around, but it didn't sound like it was working. Everyone else was happy, but he clearly was not.

They certainly all had reason to be happy. Finding water on the planet's surface was exactly what they'd hoped for. Surface water greatly increased the chances that the planet could be habitable and, even more exciting, that there might already *be* life down there.

"That's not all," Israel Riley—Izzy to his friends—said, pointing out the porthole. "I'm seeing a lot of green out there."

"Good eyes, Doc," Claire said, nodding. "It looks like some sort of moss or lichen. It's everywhere." Claire was a geologist by specialty, but she'd spent time before the mission working with everyone from paleontologists to botanists to epidemiologists—even exobiologists, although that field remained mostly speculative without concrete data to study. As their only scientist, she'd needed a broader grasp of what they might encounter out here.

"Claire, what are those rock columns?" Catherine asked. Gray-blue pillars of what looked like extensions of the rocky ground stood scattered, clustered on both sides of the terminator line. It was hard to tell size from this distance, but Catherine would have guessed they were at least one and a half times as tall as she was, and the width of a large tree trunk.

"I . . . don't know, actually. I've never seen any formations like that outside of a cave . . ." Claire's excitement was palpable. "We'll have to take a closer look!"

Sagittarius continued its orbit around the planet, passing into the dark side, where it was impossible to see what lay below.

"Catherine, ETA on landing?" Ava Gidzenko asked.

"We'll reach the terminator line again in about twenty minutes," Catherine said. "We'll cross the light side one more time, then reach our landing coordinates. I'm plugged in and ready to go. We should be able to land on this pass."

"Excellent." Ava clapped her on the shoulder and smiled. "Okay, team. Prepare for landing. Let's take a look at where we're going to be living for a while." She sat down in the commander's seat and grinned back at the rest of the crew, who were strapping themselves in. "*Then* maybe we can go meet the neighbors."

After nearly three years in space, everyone on board *Sagittarius* breathed a sigh of relief when Catherine touched them down on the surface of TRAPPIST-1f.

"Atmospheric analysis is almost done." Claire looked up from her display. "It's not far off from what we thought. Slightly higher CO_2 concentration, humidity and atmospheric pressure comparable to Earth's. We'll be more comfortable if we use oxygen. Temperature outside right now is a balmy thirty-one degrees Celsius, winds are holding steady at forty kilometers per hour. It's breezy out there, folks."

"All right, everybody," Ava said. "Get ready to go for a walk. We'll maintain pressure discipline and quarantine measures until we're sure nothing here is going to kill us."

They drew straws, and Richie got to be the first to set foot on the unfamiliar world. "Damn," he said, "I should have thought of something clever to say."

"You're not on live TV. When we get back, we'll tell everyone you were brilliant." Catherine tried to contain some of her exuberance, but this was it—this was the thing they'd trained so long for, and now, after over two and a half years, they were here.

When it was her turn, Catherine tried to focus on just how momentous this was as she stepped down onto the planet's surface. It crunched beneath her feet like any rocky surface back home would. The landscape looked like a desert—and the heat only added to that impression—with hills and outcroppings and canyons in the distance. It looked like parts of Arizona except the sky had a reddish cast to it, and in that sky, the shapes of the other TRAPPIST-1 planets loomed, along with the system's sun, TRAPPIST-1 itself. TRAPPIST-1 was smaller and cooler than Earth's sun, but its seven planets were warmer due to their closer proximities and dense atmospheres.

Catherine had never imagined such a crowded sky. From Earth, planets looked like bright stars, visible only at night. The other TRAPPIST-1 planets loomed like boulders hanging overhead, some so massive they seemed like they might fall at any moment. Just looking up into that sky made her feel claustrophobic. The light was much dimmer than she'd expected, and wouldn't change throughout the day. All the TRAPPIST-1 planets were tidally locked like Earth's moon, each with a permanent dark and light side. Their landing area was in the space between, in permanent twilight.

Claire had been right about the winds—they were enough to make walking difficult. But on the other hand, the gravity was just over half the strength of Earth's gravity, which gave them the buoyancy of walking through water. Ahead of her, Richie and Izzy were laughing and jumping into the air, seeing if they could reach the top of one of the rock pillars. It was surreal to see them putting NBA stars to shame, clearing more than a meter each time with ease. Tom and Claire watched, Tom with his arms folded across his chest. Claire smiled and said something to him, but he just turned away and walked back to the ship.

"You know you're going to have to deal with that sooner or later." Ava's voice came from over Catherine's shoulder.

"Deal with what?" Catherine tried to sound perplexed, smiling as if she didn't know what Ava was talking about, but Ava didn't buy it.

"It's a small ship, Catherine. Everybody knows something happened between you and Tom. "

"Shit," Catherine said, stomach sinking. "Ava, it only happened once. We were drunk, and—"

"I don't care when it started or when it ended; all I care about is that Tom has been at less than one hundred percent since. I kept hoping he would move past it, but he hasn't, and now that we're here, we need him at one hundred percent."

"I'm not sure what to do," Catherine said with a sigh. "It's been over a month, and he won't let it go."

"You're the only one who can try, and keep trying."

Catherine was afraid to ask, but she had to. "How much trouble are we in for this?"

"Cath, I'm not even calling this a verbal reprimand. Call it being a worried friend. Deal with it before it blows up, and I'll keep pretending I don't know anything."

"Thanks, Ava."

"Cath . . . be gentle if you can. We don't have a lot of extra space where he can blow off steam."

———

Within a few days of landing, she had her first opportunity to talk to him. They were scheduled together for the first EVA on the planet's surface, just after they finished setting up the Habitat. They reached their assigned area and started to work. Tom didn't say anything at all, and Catherine tried to figure out how to bring it up.

"Well . . . we're finally here," she managed. "It's exciting, isn't it?"

"Yeah." Tom didn't look up at her; he was busily scraping some of the lichen they'd spotted earlier off the rock in front of him into a vial and sealing it up. Every bit of contact with the lichen produced small gray-green puffs of what Catherine assumed were spores.

She checked the list of EVA objectives they needed to fulfill. Acquiring the initial samples was the biggest priority, so Claire could get to work analyzing everything. "I can barely believe we've found actual life. I can't wait to hear how folks are reacting back home." Communication to Earth would take a long time. All they could do for now was send all the data they gathered and wait.

Tom's flat voice filtered through his faceplate, and he didn't look up at her. "Yeah."

Catherine took a deep breath. Standing out in the middle of an uninhabited planet seemed to be about as private as things were going to get for them.

Catherine took Tom's arm. "Tom . . . while we're out here, can we talk for a minute?"

"Now?"

"I'm sorry, but . . . I can't keep avoiding this. What happened on New Year's . . . never should have happened."

"Really." His tone remained uninflected.

"Tom . . ."

"No, I'm serious. It was ages ago, and you're standing here telling me it was all a big mistake. So tell me, if it was such a mistake, why'd you do it?"

"I don't have a good answer for that. I wish I did." Catherine fidgeted with her gloves. They were standing close to each other, even though the suit comms didn't require it. She could see the growing anger on his face and wished she couldn't.

"Well, I do. You were bored and maybe you were, I don't know, pissed at David about something. And I let you. Cath . . . you have to know how I feel about you, how I've felt about you for years."

Oh God, don't say it, please don't say it.

"I love you." He said it. "And I swore to myself I wouldn't tell you, because you're married, but then New Year's happened . . . and now you barely even talk to me."

"I'm sorry that you're upset, Tom—"

"You can't tell me that night didn't mean something! You weren't happy with David before you left. I know you weren't."

"I was!" *I know things were tense before I left, but I wasn't actually unhappy . . . was I?* "This doesn't have anything to do with David. Ava knows. Hell, everybody knows. If you can't get your shit together, sooner or later someone's going to have to report that we broke the regs. You're risking our careers with this."

"Screw my career! We could have something here. I'm not willing to let it go because of some outdated rules."

"Oh, outdated rules, like the fact that I'm *married*?" She needed to hold on to her patience, but honest to God, he was turning this into some sort of thwarted true-love scenario in his head. "Tom, we're done. It was a mistake. I'm sorry. I have to put my family and this mission first."

"Y-you can't, Catherine, you *can't*. Don't do this to me." Anger was fighting its way past the hurt in Tom's eyes.

"I already did." As empty a gesture as it might have been, she reached out to put her hand on his arm. "I didn't want anybody to get hurt—"

"Don't touch me. I don't need your fucking pity." He started off toward the rocky hills that edged deeper into the dark side of the planet.

"Tom, wait!"

"Leave me alone. I'll finish the EVA. Just give me a few goddamned minutes, will you?"

She sighed. "Stay in radio contact."

By the time they brought their samples back to the Habitat, Tom had cooled off some, but his responses to her and everyone else were monosyllabic before he headed off to shower.

Ava caught Catherine's arm. "You talked to him?"

Catherine, pretty done with talking herself, nodded. "I don't think it helped."

"It had to be done." Ava didn't look any happier about it than Catherine, despite her words. "Oy, it's going to be awkward around here for a bit. It's a small enough place without somebody sulking over a breakup."

"I know. I'm sorry." Catherine was saying that a lot today.

Ava put a companionable arm around her shoulder and gave her a shake. "Honest truth? Mission Control expected something like this might happen. Six years away from home, someone was bound to get an itch. We dealt with it, it's over. Come on, let's go see what Claire makes of your samples."

Ava could put a good face on it if she wanted to, but Catherine had seen Tom's expression, and she doubted that it was over.

8

"YOU'D THINK BY this point we'd have managed to do every sort of low-gravity experiment known to man," Zach Navarro complained.

The crew of Sagittarius II was crowded into Cal's office, perched on a couple of borrowed chairs, Cal's desk, the windowsill.

"That's the point," Kevin Park was saying. "Experiments are supposed to be *repeatable*. So, we repeat them."

"Again and again and again," Navarro said.

"Trust me, you'll be glad to have something to do." Cal was in his office chair, his feet up on the desk. "You're going to be stuck in that ship for over two years on the trip out. Plus, you're going to be on TRAPPIST-1f for less time than Sagittarius I was, so we've got to fit in as much prep work as possible on the trip there."

"Did we ever find out why Colonel Wells took so much longer to get home?" Kevin asked.

"Initial analysis of the ship's trajectory suggests she was just . . . wandering for a while before she reentered the wormhole," Cal said. "She may have had navigation problems on her own. We won't know unless she remembers. But you"—he changed his tone to something more upbeat—"won't have to worry about that. Because we hired Duffy for his excellent sense of direction."

The tension broke with a chuckle that went around the room, and they went back to studying Cal's planned itinerary. Cal kept his expression light, but the mention of Catherine sent him into what was now a familiar thought spiral. He kept thinking about finding her in the archives, about the odd look on her face, confusion mixed with fear mixed with a strong sense of guilt. Guilt about what?

"Why does Nate get a pass on some of the experiments?" Kowalski looked up from the initial version of the schedule Cal had put together. She didn't sound put out, just genuinely curious. "I don't see him listed as often as the rest of us."

"Perks of being the FAO's best friend." Nate grinned and nudged Cal with his foot.

"Come on, seriously?" Navarro still wasn't good at recognizing a joke.

Commander Duffy spoke up from his seat on the windowsill. "No, not seriously, Zach. I'm guessing Dr. Royer here is going to be doing all sorts of experiments on *us*."

"Extended artificial gravity followed by a year in a low-gravity setting; the physiological possibilities are a dream," Nate agreed.

"Wait a minute," Leah Morrison said. "Y'all aren't planning to use any of us as some kind of control to see who winds up all weak and messed up when we land, are you?"

"Nah, it'd compromise mission efficiency," Nate said, straight-faced.

He got the response he was looking for. " 'Mission efficiency!' What the hell, man?" Morrison looked appalled.

Nate waved a hand. "Plus, there's that whole ethics issue around human experimentation."

Duffy cracked first and snickered.

"Yeah, yeah, very funny," Morrison muttered, folding her arms.

"But I will be collecting data and doing analyses on how y'all are doing," Nate said, dropping the act. "And if need be, altering the physical conditioning routines you're each going to be following if it turns out we underestimated the performance drop. There's no point in doing all the training now if you're going to lose it on the trip there."

"In a very real sense, maintaining your health and well-being is *the* central purpose of the entire mission," Cal said. "We need to know if TRAPPIST-1f can support human life adequately. And for all our theorizing and testing and probing, the only way to confirm that is to send humans there and see. You've got one sort of bonus—you're not the first. Whatever happened to Sagittarius I, it doesn't seem like it was a direct result of the planet's environment.

"I need you guys to understand something. If I think anything is going to endanger you—aside from normal mission risks—I will do everything in my power to fix it or stop the mission. You know me. I don't back down when I know I'm right."

Nate grinned. "You don't back down when you're wrong either, man."

The rest of them laughed, and even Cal had to grin. "Then you know you're in good hands."

The meeting broke up shortly after that, but Nate hung back.

"You mean it?" Nate asked him once the office held just the two of them. "You really think everything's kosher for us?"

Hating himself a little, Cal lied to his best friend. "I haven't seen anything that proves otherwise. And believe me, I'm looking out for it." He paused. "But . . . I'm glad you stayed behind. I need to pick your brain."

"My brain is yours," Nate said with a smile, and settled back onto the couch in Cal's office, a battered old thing that had seen Cal through far too many late nights.

"I'm chasing something. It might be nothing."

Nate rolled his eyes and folded his arms. "Oh brother, here we go again."

"Nate. Humor me, okay? The doctors are assuming that Catherine Wells's amnesia is the result of psychological trauma. What if it isn't? What if it has a biological component? What sorts of things could cause that?"

Nate frowned. "No one's considered this yet?"

"Not that I've heard."

"Well, there are a lot of possibilities. Brain damage is the most likely," Nate said first thing. "Lack of oxygen, dementia, a brain tumor . . ." He paused. "Doesn't her mother have Alzheimer's? I thought I heard that in the gossip mill."

"Yeah, early-onset, too," Cal said, "but Catherine's not showing any other signs, and memory loss with Alzheimer's doesn't act this way. She's had every scan imaginable, so we can rule out a brain tumor. Any other sorts of diseases?"

"Anything that causes inflammation in the brain. Any sort of encephalitis. We're seeing fungal infections more often these days . . ."

"So it's possible."

"What are the guys analyzing the data saying?"

Cal had the grace to look sheepish. "I haven't really talked to them. Aaron gave me a pretty stern warning to stay away from Wells, at least as far as investigating her goes."

"And yet here you are."

"Nate . . . she's lying about *something*. I can feel it. Her story has holes in some places, but is too ironclad in others. I have to find out what it is." He leaned across his desk, needing to make Nate, of all people, understand. "If it turns out that something she's keeping from us is the very thing that can keep you guys alive . . ."

"I get it." Nate didn't seem like he was about to start making jokes about Cal and his paranoia. "I'll tell you what. *I'm* not under orders to stay away from Wells and her info. I have every reason, as the crew's doctor, to want to see the medical records from the previous mission. If I find anything, I'll let you know."

Cal hesitated, despite the urge to jump on the offer. "Don't get yourself in hot water over something that might be me seeing volcanoes again."

"I'm a big boy. And you know I'll tell you if you're going off the deep end."

"Thanks. I just . . . want you guys to be okay."

Nate stood up. "Yeah, I know. That's your job. And we're counting on your sorry ass." He grinned and headed out the door. "Climbing gym tonight?"

"Yeah. Seven sound good?"

"You bet."

After Nate left, Cal debated with himself for a long time whether he should talk to Aaron. With Catherine's visit to the archives . . . his instincts were screaming. Sure it was possible she had access and Cal didn't know about it, but she was acting much too guilty.

He headed for Aaron's office.

"How'd it go with the crew?" Aaron said by way of greeting.

"We're good, I think. Morale's been high lately. They're getting excited." Cal shut the door behind him and sat down in front of Aaron's desk.

"Of course. With Catherine back safe and sound, everybody is relieved."

"That's . . . what I wanted to talk to you about." Cal figured Aaron opened that door, so he was going to march right through it.

"Cal." That tone didn't bode well. "Please tell me you're not coming in here with more conspiracy theories about Catherine Wells."

"I am absolutely not coming in here with more conspiracy theories about Catherine Wells," Cal answered. "I have nothing but what I've seen and heard myself."

Aaron leaned back in his chair, rubbing his face with his hands.

"Aaron, I'm not trying to start shit. I swear."

"All right. Let's talk this through. Suppose whatever it is you have is something worth worrying about." Aaron sat forward, his elbows landing on his desk. He pointed at Cal. "You come up with something. We postpone or even cancel Sagittarius II. What happens then?"

"Well—"

"Unless you were about to say 'a political and public-relations cluster-fuck, Aaron,' you're wrong. After we lost contact with *Sagittarius I*, we damn near lost the program. You weren't here for that. I was."

This was not going quite the way Cal had planned. "I know the history," he started.

"I *lived* the history, Cal." Aaron stood up, pacing to his window. "Without Paul Lindholm schmoozing his ass off on Capitol Hill, neither of us would have a job right now. The days after we lost that signal were some pretty fucking dark days. There was so much outrage, there was worry that NASA would lose most of its funding for its projects. Paul saved us all."

Paul Lindholm was a rarity: a former astronaut who'd made it into the NASA administrator's chair. He exuded an air of hail-fellow-well-met with bright-blue eyes and graying blond hair, and smiled too much for Cal's liking. On Capitol Hill, though, he inspired confidence and had won funding for NASA even in some of the bleakest situations. Cal trusted him about as much as he trusted any politician: not much.

"But how much worse will it be if we wind up losing a second mission, *and* it comes out later that we had the information to prevent that?"

Aaron sighed and folded his arms. "All right. No promises, but what have you got?"

"Does Wells have access to the archives on B2?"

"She hasn't asked for access, so no. Why would she need it? None of her records are down there, as far as I know."

"I found her down there yesterday. The day she joined us on the TRAP-PIST simulation."

"Well, she might've—" Aaron stopped. There was nothing else down on that level, and certainly nothing Catherine might need. Cal knew—he had checked already. "What did she say?"

"That she'd been in the archives doing research," Cal said. "But she hesitated and her cheeks were flushed, like she was lying."

"Maybe she got lost, and just felt embarrassed about it."

"How could she be lost? She was at NASA for years before she left."

"I know, but with the memory loss she's experienced, it could happen. And that would certainly make for an embarrassing situation."

"She didn't look embarrassed," Cal insisted. "She looked guilty."

"Guilty or not, this isn't the sort of thing that warrants postponing an entire mission. Any longer than two weeks and we'll miss the launch window. The next one might not be for months." NASA's engineers had carefully calculated the Earth's rotation and position around the sun to come up with the optimum launch window. Anything outside that window ran the risk of *Sagittarius* running low on fuel too soon. They were already cutting it close. Finding another window could take months, possibly years.

"I'm not saying postpone. Not yet." Cal debated telling him about the automatic way she told part of her story, and how false that felt to him. Feelings, though, weren't going to get through to Aaron.

Aaron fell silent for a time, going back to his desk and sitting down. He was thinking it through, and that was a hell of a lot further than Cal had expected to get today. "This program is Paul Lindholm's baby. It was his initial idea; he's set all our benchmarks. He's not going to sit by and let us play with timelines and mission schedules because you've got a feeling."

"If it turns out that I'm right, it's not gonna be just a feeling." He took a quick, discreet look at his notes. "Look. Catherine's memory loss is worse than Commander Addy's was. Say it was caused by something out there, something we don't know about. Commander Addy may be our best-case scenario instead of the worst, and I know nobody wants that."

"Cal, if Sagittarius II goes down, it doesn't mean just your career, or my career." He pinned Cal to his seat with a dark-eyed look. "As hard as Lindholm fought to keep our funding after Sagittarius I, and the promises he made to Congress about the program's potential, if we go down, we might drag the rest of NASA down with us."

Paul Lindholm, Cal thought, was either a fool or the single most optimistic man on the planet.

"All the more reason to make sure we're not sending our crew into a bad situation," Cal insisted. "We can't put them at risk."

Aaron laughed harshly. "I'm sorry, did you just say that we shouldn't put the people who *signed up* to let us strap explosives to their asses and launch them trillions of miles from home at *risk*? Risk is what they signed up for, Cal. We minimize what we can, but the Sagittarius program is about more than just individual people; it's about the greater good. The crew of Sagittarius I paid the price for that, but they knew they might."

"I know what the normal operational risks are; you know I'm not talking about that. I'm talking about the risks that the crew *didn't* sign up for. The ones they don't know about."

"Oh, come on," Aaron said. "You know there're plenty of risks they never know about. If they knew everything, they'd never have signed up. We talked about the Longbow Protocol, remember? You didn't argue against it. And you, in fact, argued that we should keep the information from everyone on board *Sagittarius* except for the commander."

"That's different." Longbow was a thing Cal didn't let himself think about too often. "We designed Longbow in case *Sagittarius*'s return put the entire planet at risk. Longbow is about protecting the planet from alien infection or radiation. If—God forbid—we ever trigger it, we'll be sacrificing six people in order to save billions. You won't balk at that, but you're hesitating at stopping and taking a second look?"

"So what are you suggesting we do?"

"I don't know. Stop the mission clock until we've got this figured out. Look, we're talking about sending six people into an unknown situation, one where things have already been *spectacularly* fucked up, on the off chance that it won't happen again, so that *maybe* we'll find a planet to colonize." Common sense was taking a close look at the storm brewing on Aaron's face and telling him to shut up, but Cal and common sense didn't always see eye to eye. He pushed on. "Sending Sagittarius II without more information could mean sacrificing six people so you can cover your ass with Lindholm."

Sometimes the only way Cal could see the line was when he looked behind him to see if he'd crossed it. Judging by the look on Aaron's face, he'd cleared it by several feet.

"Let it go. I'm not postponing an entire mission because you think a traumatized woman is acting weird. If I'd gone through what she has, I'd be acting weird, too."

"But—"

"We're done. Humanity *has* to find another home. Now, before there's an emergency threatening Earth. Sagittarius is moving forward. Let this go."

"Yes sir." Cal managed to keep any trace of sullenness out of his voice as he rose from the chair, dismissed.

He thought of Nate and the rest of the crew, how they'd all looked to him. He had no intention of letting anything go.

9

THE SATURDAY OF Aimee's graduation party, the weather was glorious: warm, but not too warm as the day slowly turned into evening. Catherine checked the ice in the coolers and refilled one of the canapé trays spread across a long table against the far wall. The house was overflowing with a mix of Aimee's friends, David and Catherine's friends and colleagues, and a few family members from both sides, including Julie, who'd arrived last night. They spilled through the kitchen and into the yard, filling every seat on the patio.

In the middle of it all, Aimee moved from group to group with utter ease, a gracious host. As Catherine watched, Aimee charmed Aaron Llewellyn, one of the few members of the Sagittarius II staff to make it—understandable, since launch preparations were getting more intense by the day. Catherine was lucky *she* was able to be here.

"Did you tell her to do that?" David caught Catherine by surprise, appearing at her elbow. "I half expected her to run off to a corner with her friends."

Catherine glanced at him and smiled. "No, it didn't even occur to me, to be honest."

"We may have a natural politician on our hands."

"Good God, where did she get that from? Not from either of us, that's for sure."

"I bet I know." David nodded toward Maggie, who was talking to Paul Lindholm and watching Aimee with the same pride on her face that Catherine felt.

"Remind me to thank her," Catherine said, and meant it.

Aimee moved back to her friends and settled in with them, digging into a plate of food.

Paul Lindholm came over, his usual broad smile in place. "Colonel Wells, David, congratulations."

Catherine smiled, but internally winced at the difference in address between her and David. Thankfully, David didn't seem bothered by it and took Lindholm's offered hand.

"Thank you, sir," David said, "but Aimee gets the congratulations. She did all the hard work here."

Lindholm drank from his half-empty glass, and to judge from the flush on his cheeks, this wasn't his first. "Nonsense. My wife and I raised three boys; I know how much work went into this day."

"David did a great job," Catherine said, for once without a twinge of guilt.

"You get some of the credit, too, young lady." Lindholm extended a finger to point at her. "You may have been on a mission, but it's clear how much influence you've had in her life. Did I hear that she's going to MIT this fall?"

"She is." David puffed up a little bit. "She's still trying to decide what branch of engineering interests her the most."

"Ahh, so she takes after her father." Lindholm gave Catherine's shoulder a friendly pat. "Hope you're not too disappointed," he teased.

"Not at all." She gave him a smile in return. This all felt so easy, like a glimpse of what her life might have been if she'd never gone into space, if she'd stayed home with David and helped raise Aimee. "You'd better watch out for her, though. She's already said she wants to work for NASA after she graduates."

"Well, if she's anything like her parents, we'd be thrilled to have her." Lindholm drained his glass. "I need to head out, but congrats again. Aimee's a great kid."

"Thank you," Catherine said. "And thank you for stopping by."

Once he was gone, Catherine and David exchanged a glance and David shook his head with a rueful smile. "I'm always going to be Mr. Catherine Wells where NASA is concerned, aren't I?" So he hadn't missed that after all.

"Sorry." Catherine wrinkled her nose and slipped her arm through his. "Although, if it makes you feel better, you make a great trophy husband."

"Cath." Julie caught up to them. "Can I get your hand in the kitchen for a minute?"

"Oh, sure." Catherine kissed David on the cheek. "Stay right here and look pretty, trophy husband."

"Sure, I might even smile a few times," David deadpanned before waving them off.

The kitchen was quieter than the rest of the house, and Catherine didn't realize how much she could use those few minutes of quiet.

"How's it going out there?" Julie arranged some chopped vegetables on a tray.

Catherine came to help, the two of them still working together in a habit born of a lifetime of family holiday dinners. "It's good. Aimee is a natural at this."

"And you're doing okay?"

"Yeah. I really am." Catherine couldn't keep a note of surprise from her voice, but it was true. She was connecting with the Sagittarius II team at work, and she, Aimee, and David had settled into a rhythm at home. She couldn't quite describe it all as normal, but they were getting there. And there had been no more lost time.

"You look more like yourself than you did on our last Skype call." Julie reached into a cupboard and pulled down a pair of wineglasses. "Here, I tucked this bottle away because I know it's your favorite." She took a bottle of pinot noir from the sideboard and poured them each a glass. When Catherine picked up hers, Julie clinked it with her own. "To Aimee, who is going to do great things, just like her mom."

Catherine chuckled. "Hopefully greater things." She drank, and the taste of the wine brought back the vivid sense memory of standing in the ship's galley, the taste of the same wine in her mouth along with the unexpected and unfamiliar feel of Tom's mouth against hers.

How long would that memory still ambush her? Thankfully, it hadn't happened when she and David were making love, but she was afraid it was just a matter of time. It was maddening that the clearest memory she had was the one she didn't want.

"Hey. You in there?"

Catherine pulled on a smile. "Yeah, sorry. It's been a crazy week."

"Yeah, I'll bet it's been." Julie leaned against the counter. "So . . . Cath . . . I know this is probably a bad time to bring this up, but with getting ready for the party I didn't get to talk to you last night, really, and I'm leaving tonight, so . . ."

"Is everything okay?"

"Yeah, yeah, it's fine. I've been talking to Mom's doctors, and . . . they think she might be able to handle seeing you."

Catherine had given up on the possibility of seeing her mother alive again a long time ago. Hearing Julie say that, she had a sudden inkling of how David and Aimee must have felt, hearing that she was coming home. "Really? Are you sure? Are *they* sure?"

Julie made a small, amused sound, looking down at her wineglass. "No. But given where she's at right now, we can't be sure about anything. And it's not as if there's a lot of published literature about how to reintroduce an Alzheimer's patient to a presumed-dead family member."

"I don't want to make things worse, though." Oh, but the thought of being able to see her mother again, even just once . . .

Julie looked up at her solemnly. "Cath, I don't know that it's possible to make things much worse. We're probably looking at months now, not years. And—and when that does happen, I don't want either of us to have any regrets. Or, at least, not this particular regret."

Catherine wrapped her arms around Julie tight, and Julie returned the embrace. "I'm so sorry. I'm sorry you've been dealing with this all alone."

"I knew what I was signing on for, and Mom would've kicked my ass if you'd tried to stay home to take care of her." Julie kissed her on the cheek and stepped back. "So when I get back home, we'll start talking dates, all right? Sooner rather than later, I think."

"Yes. I'll talk to David and Aimee . . . The launch is soon, but I should be able to get away for this." Catherine met Julie's eyes and tried to smile. "Thank you. So much. For everything."

"That's what big sisters are for." Julie took her by the shoulders, turning her toward the living room. "All right. Break time's over, kiddo. Time to go play hostess again."

"Ugh. Okay, but you come, too. Don't stay in here fussing with things."

Julie handed her a huge tray of sandwiches. "All right, I'll be out soon. Take this with you."

Catherine carried the tray out and set it down in time to see Aimee stand up and climb onto the fireplace hearth in the living room.

"Excuse me," she said, her clear voice ringing out, "if I can get your attention for a moment."

Catherine moved over to David's side. "What's she doing?"

"No idea." He slipped his arm around her waist.

The party quieted down, a few people filtering in from outside to see what was happening. Aimee, bright-eyed and smiling, had a fluted glass of the sparkling cider set aside for the kids. One of her friends, sitting on the hearth, muttered something and she kicked him lightly, laughing. "Shut up."

Then she looked up at the guests and smiled again. "I just wanted to say thank you all for coming today. You all know it's been kind of an . . . *interesting* year for me, for my family, but I am so happy that my mom is home and able to be here, and I know my dad is, too."

Catherine's eyes stung and she looked up at David, whose eyes were also overbright.

"I wouldn't be where I am right now without both of my parents." Aimee lifted her glass, her cheeks turning pink. "So, here's to my mom and dad. My dad stayed here with me to make sure I kept my feet on the ground, but my mom taught me that it's possible to fly, and it's important to, even when it's scary and you don't know when or how you're going to land."

Glasses rose around the room, and Catherine let the tears fall down her face unabashedly. She met Aimee's eyes and mouthed *I love you*, and Aimee smiled. Still, there was a sense of incompleteness, and honestly, there was an elephant in the room that needed to be addressed.

Catherine cleared her throat and spoke up: "I'd like to mention someone else who has been an important part of Aimee's life, too, and deserves plenty of credit for helping her reach her goals."

Maggie was standing on the edge of the room looking at Aimee with a soft smile. "While I was gone," Catherine said, "Maggie was able to be there for Aimee when I couldn't, and I am so grateful for that." Maggie looked over at her, surprised, and started to shake her head, but smiled when some of the crowd's appreciation turned to her as well.

David kissed Catherine's temple and murmured, "Nicely done."

"I knew Aimee wouldn't mention her for fear of making me feel bad." She leaned against David and gingerly wiped away her tears.

After Aimee's toast, the crowd started to thin out a little, work friends leaving first, with Catherine showing them to the door as it began to get dark.

She followed Leah Morrison out to her car and waved as she drove away. As she turned to go back up the front walk, a twig snapped. There was an audible murmur, and then silence. A peculiar sensation prickled at the back of Catherine's neck. It wasn't terribly dark yet, but there were shadows everywhere, plenty of places to hide. She stood by the garage, frozen in place, straining her ears for the slightest sound. Her breathing was loud in her ears so she held it, still listening. She couldn't shake the undeniable, overwhelming feeling that she was being watched. She glanced around, half expecting to see a man with a knife or a gun standing in the yard looking at her.

Nothing.

Except—

A shadow disappeared around the side of the house, an unmistakably human-shaped shadow.

Catherine sprinted around to the back of the house, trying to catch whoever it was, but she was too late. There was no one there, and no sound of rustling branches or anyone running away. Nothing at all.

She stood with her hands on her hips, trying to still her racing heart. Had she imagined it? The feeling had been so real, she could still feel the gooseflesh broken out on her back. No use standing out here fretting about it. Catherine headed back inside. But she wasn't going to see anyone out farther than the front door for the rest of the night.

———

"I can't get over how grown up Aimee's acting all of a sudden," David called from the master bathroom over the sound of running water. "That toast was about the last thing that I expected."

Catherine had changed from her party clothes into her favorite pair of old sweatpants and an ancient Air Force T-shirt and was sitting up in the bed, feeling a content sort of tired after a long but good day. "I know. She's just one surprise after another."

David appeared in the doorway, shirtless and drying his face off with a towel. "I think it's time for us to face it. We managed to create a whole person with all of her own ideas and plans that don't have anything to do with us."

"Isn't it great?"

"Well, yeah." David hung up the towel and came to bed, crawling in next to her. "But admit it: Don't you miss the days when she was more dependent on us? I think I kinda miss being the center of her universe."

"Well, you're just going to have to settle for being the center of mine," Catherine said, leaning over to kiss him.

"I love you, but it's not the same," David said with a grin. "I mean, we're both still young; there's no reason we couldn't—"

"Stop right there, mister." Catherine raised her fingers to his lips and pressed them closed. "If you're about to say 'there's no reason we couldn't have another baby,' I've got about forty-three of them."

"Forty-three isn't that old," David cajoled, slipping his arms around Catherine's waist. "Just think about it, all those cuddles and silly songs and giggles..."

"And all those diapers and two a.m. feedings and teething ... uh-uh. No way." Catherine gestured at her midsection. "This baby factory is closed for business. Besides, what if I came back with some sort of genetic issue they haven't figured out yet. Do you really want to take that chance?"

"No ... I know. You're probably right," David said, sighing.

Catherine pressed a kiss to his forehead. "If you want something little in the house again, we can talk about getting a dog or a cat or something, but you gotta let go of having a little girl, Dad. She grew up on you."

"That she did." David sounded so proud Catherine couldn't help but smile, the smile interrupted by a yawn.

"Okay, proud papa, this mama needs to get some sleep." She settled down on her side, reaching up to turn out the light. David curled loosely behind her, his hand on her hip. Today had been everything she'd fought to get home for. Catherine closed her eyes, feeling as if her real life had finally begun.

10

CAL DUCKED DOWN in the front seat of his car, trying to catch his breath after his mad dash out of the Wellses' yard. Sweat trickled down his forehead from his hairline as he waited to see if Catherine had spotted him, fully expecting to hear her pounding on his window demanding to know what he was doing in her yard.

What the hell *was* he doing here?

At first, spending the afternoon and evening watching Catherine's house seemed like a good idea. All of his instincts were screaming that something was *wrong*. He'd spent hours poring over her personnel files, the transcripts and recordings of her debriefs, and nothing. Nothing! Nate had tried to pick the brains of the medical team to find out more information about Catherine, but they had nothing useful to offer yet. Cal did manage to get a copy of her medical records and the telemetry from *Sagittarius*, and after going over both, he felt that the answer was right there in front of him. He could almost see it. *Something* wasn't adding up, but he couldn't figure out what.

He kept coming back to the rote way she described her last memory of the mission. And the guilty look on her face when he'd found her down in the archives. The whole thing felt wrong. And yet, all of Dr. Darzi's reports to the administration cleared Catherine of any form of instability and any problems that would keep her from working. If her therapist didn't see anything wrong with her, how could Cal be so sure?

On the face of it, Cal knew he was being ridiculous, but he also had made a career out of following his instinct, sometimes to places others would never have considered, and so far it hadn't let him down. Much, anyway. Besides, he'd tried to leave it alone, but the overwhelming feeling of "wrong" wouldn't leave *him* alone. So he wound up here, spending a Saturday afternoon and evening parked outside Catherine Wells's house, looking for some aberration or sign of what was wrong with her.

When he saw there was a party going on, he almost turned around and went home. Whatever was wrong, he likely wouldn't see it while she was occupied with her guests. But curiosity drove him to stay, watching the guests arrive—some of them well-known to him, which meant ducking down in his car—watching for glimpses of her through the windows of her home as the sky darkened. Laughter came from the house, and every time he saw Catherine, she was smiling and at ease—a far cry from the tightly wound Catherine he knew. Cal felt an uncharacteristic stab of regret. He liked the Catherine he saw in the window. Maybe in another life they might have been friends, arguing about trajectories over beers and swapping stories.

As the evening wore on, it sank in just how far across the line he'd stepped. Spying on Catherine at home? Aaron was pissed enough at him for prying into the records. If he found out about this, he'd rip Cal a new one—and rightfully so.

Still, as the guests started to leave, Cal stayed. The compulsion wouldn't fade, no matter how uncomfortable this intrusion made him feel. The thought of driving away now and the risk that he might miss *something*, however small, some clue to Catherine's secrets, was worse than the shame of turning spy.

When the flow of guests slowed to a drip, Cal took the massive risk of leaving his car and creeping into the Wellses' yard. He could see more clearly now, and hear snatches of laughter and conversation through the windows, opened as the night started to cool off. There was nothing out of the ordinary. The party had been a graduation party for Catherine's daughter. Cute kid. Going to MIT, from what he had overheard, so she must be smart, too.

When Catherine came out with Leah Morrison, the two of them laughing and talking, he ducked behind some shrubbery and watched her. A mad urge to jump out of the literal bushes to talk to her seized him, but he managed to resist. Morrison drove off, and as Cal watched, Catherine paused and looked around. His heart thudded sickly against his chest, as she seemed to look right where he was hiding. He imagined that her eyes met his and that the game was up.

He panicked. The moment she looked away he darted into the backyard.

It was a mistake, because then she saw him for sure and gave chase. He used his head start to loop back to the street and dive into his car, and now here he was, practically ready to piss himself and shocked at his own obsessive behavior.

Five minutes passed. Then ten. Catherine didn't bang on his window. No police showed up. He was safe.

Let it go. You have to let it go.

The voice in his head was Aaron's, but Cal was starting to agree with it. Maybe Nate and Aaron were right. Maybe he was jumping at shadows.

But still, he couldn't make himself start the car and drive away.

Finally, the Wells house quieted, and the lights went out, one by one. It looked as if the family had gone to bed. There'd be nothing else to see tonight.

Except.

Just as Cal was about to leave, Catherine came out a side door wearing dark sweatpants and a T-shirt. She climbed into one of the cars in the driveway and backed out, flipping on her lights and driving down the narrow street.

Before he thought about it, Cal had pulled out a short distance behind her, feeling as if he were in a movie. How close could he follow without her realizing she was being followed? Surveillance techniques were not part of the standard NASA training. Wrong government agency.

This is gonna be embarrassing if I end up following her on a midnight run to the store for ice cream.

But the same instinct that was pushing him along this path to begin with said this was no innocuous search for a midnight snack. But if he was wrong, he vowed to turn right around and go home. If he was wrong, he'd give this whole stupid mess up and fall back into line. He'd risked his career enough for one night. For one lifetime.

He followed Catherine through the Saturday night traffic. When she took the highway exit for Johnson Space Center, he felt a surge of triumph.

Oh shit.

He couldn't follow her directly through security, as he'd be spotted for sure. But if he held back too long, he ran the risk of losing Catherine in the complex. Damn, damn, damn.

He waited for what felt like an hour—although the clock said it was barely two minutes—then followed her through the security gates, showing his ID to the night guard.

"Busy night tonight, Mr. Morganson?" the guard asked. "Don't usually see any traffic at all at this time on a Saturday, and there's two of you Sagittarius folk one right after another."

"Huh. Who else is here?" Cal asked nonchalantly, fighting the impatient awareness that Catherine was getting farther and farther ahead of him.

"Catherine Wells came in a couple of minutes ago," the guard said. "Didn't say what she needed, just handed me her ID and looked straight through me. Was kinda creepy, to tell you the truth."

Cal's neck prickled. He forced a smile up at the guard. "This time of night, who knows. Maybe she was sleepwalking," he joked.

"It's funny you should say that. I got a kid who sleepwalks, and she looked a lot like that—she might've been in her pajamas, come to think of it."

The prickles turned into the hair on the back of his neck standing up. Cal took back his ID and gave the man a wave. The guard punched the button to let him through.

"Have a good night, Mr. Morganson."

He passed Catherine's parked car as he reached the building where the Sagittarius program was based, and his heart thudded sickly in his temples. Rather than waste time parking, he stopped his car in front of the building and ran inside, waving his ID at the night guard as he passed.

Cal didn't wait for the elevator but took the stairs two at a time to the third floor, where their offices were. Catherine's door was closed and locked, and the hallway was dark. All the other offices were dark as well. The wing was deserted. Where could she—

The archives.

That's where she'd been that day last week, the first time she was somewhere she shouldn't have been.

Cal flew down several flights of stairs, skidding to a stop at the bottom in near-total darkness. That wasn't right. There should have been exit lights at least. He held his breath, straining to hear anything: footsteps, rustling, anything.

He took a few cautious steps forward. If his memory was correct, the archives were about fifteen feet ahead on the left. The hallway was so narrow he could almost touch both walls if he stretched out his arms. In the darkness he could swear he felt the already-low ceiling pressing down toward him. His imagination was no help: it provided an image of a blank-eyed Catherine waiting for him by the archive door, ready to pounce.

He kept walking, although his skin was crawling, certain that at any moment a cold and clammy hand would reach for his.

Finally, once he was surely next to the archives, he couldn't stand it anymore and turned on his phone's flashlight. He shined it around him, but the hallway was empty. No Catherine, blank-eyed or otherwise. Plus, he was still a good ten feet from the archive door. He checked it, but knew what he would find. It was locked. If Catherine had been down here, she was gone before he arrived.

11

THE LIGHT THAT filtered into the bedroom told Catherine it was mid-morning, possibly later. Catherine winced after opening her eyes, grimacing at a sudden spike of pain between her eyes. Hungover? No. She wasn't sick to her stomach, and besides, she hadn't had that much to drink last night. She glanced over at the clock on the night table. Nearly eleven. When was the last time she'd slept so late? She sat up and stretched, wincing again. Everything ached, as though she were about to get the flu. The ache in her muscles was deep, and her back muscles were twinging, just on the edge of a spasm.

The other side of the bed was empty—not a surprise. Catherine swung her feet onto the floor and stared. *What the hell?* She'd taken a shower before bed last night, but now her feet were nearly black with dirt, grime beneath her nails and between her toes. She went cold as she studied her feet.

What did I do?

Nothing. It had to be nothing. Sleepwalking, maybe. Yesterday had been stressful. Maybe she *had* had one too many glasses of wine. That's all it was. Or sleepwalking.

You don't really believe that. She wanted to. God, how she wanted to.

Catherine went to the bathroom and got in the shower again, washing off her feet. The dirt rinsed away and vanished down the drain, disappearing forever. If only her fears would disappear so easily.

David wasn't home, but Aimee was in the backyard, sprawled in the sun reading a book.

"I hope you're wearing sunscreen," Catherine said, stepping onto the patio and closing the door behind her. She sounded so normal. Okay, she could do this.

"Yes, Mother. I'm wearing so much I bet the sun isn't even touching my skin." Aimee looked up with a grin and put down her book. "I was wondering if you were ever going to get up. Go get changed; we have plans this afternoon."

Catherine raised her eyebrows. "We have plans? What plans?"

"Well, *someone* has been working her ass off to give someone else an amazing graduation party, so *someone* deserves to get spoiled for an afternoon." Aimee pushed herself up from her blanket and picked it and the book up.

"You don't have to do anything for me," Catherine protested.

Aimee laughed and walked up onto the patio, taking her mother by the arm. "I told you. Made plans to spoil you. Come on. I worked it out with Dad and everything. We're going to lunch, then to the spa for a few hours, and then we're meeting Dad for dinner at Tony's."

"Oh Aims, no. I'm not a spa kind of person . . ."

"Yes you are. Today, anyway. Come on, I'm not taking no for an answer." Aimee pulled her into the house. "Go on, go change!" She put her hands on her hips and watched until Catherine smiled and went upstairs to obey.

The thought of keeping her normal face on all day made her insides twist. But how could she say no to spending time with her daughter? She changed into a sundress that wasn't too outdated and put on a little bit of makeup before going back downstairs.

"Okay, let's go!"

It was still a novelty to see Aimee driving, but Catherine agreed to let her, settling into the passenger seat. They wound up at a trendy vegetarian café for lunch that had an entire wall lined with succulents. They looked like a normal mother-daughter pair, ready to spend a Sunday together.

The food was delicious, and Catherine tried to focus on it rather than on the unending echo in the back of her head, asking what she'd done last night.

"Thank you for this," Catherine said, trying to match the picture of normalcy.

"Oh, this is nothing," Aimee said, grinning. "Wait until you see what's next!"

Aimee wasn't kidding, either. There was a type of Texas womanhood that Catherine could never manage to emulate, the Junior League types, with their impeccable grooming and tasteful clothes . . . and now she was surrounded by them. The spa itself was a feminine wonderland: white and neutral tones everywhere, billowing filmy fabrics, and quiet, elegant women in pale-gray coats leading women in robes around. A small dark-haired woman greeted them, and Catherine felt enormous and gawky, towering over her.

"It *is* you!" the woman said. "I knew it! I tried to tell the other girls that it really was *the* Catherine Wells that had an appointment booked. We're so proud to have you here!"

Catherine fought the urge to wince and deny everything. She glanced over at Aimee, and to her surprise, Aimee was beaming with pride.

"That's her. That's my mom," Aimee said.

"I . . . well, yes, that's me." Catherine smiled uncertainly. "My daughter, Aimee, and I are here together."

"Of course, I can see the resemblance. I'm Teena. We've got y'all lined up for our Teaser package, so if you ladies will come this way, we'll get started!"

Thankfully, it seemed that most of their time would be spent in a quiet room. In spite of the questions that plagued her, the masseuse managed to hammer away some of the physical tension in Catherine's body, making it easier to keep smiling.

As their hostess led them to the next room, Catherine said, "I haven't had a facial in years." She laughed self-consciously. "I guess that goes without saying, huh?"

She and Aimee settled into side-by-side chairs and were given strict orders to close their eyes and keep them closed, before they were each given eye masks. Aimee chatted idly with their aesthetician while Catherine fought to keep from gripping the arms of the chair as the aesthetician spread some sort of cool gel on her face before putting the mask in place.

Relax. Just relax. She couldn't. She kept thinking about her dirt-caked feet. Her aching muscles. How much time had she lost? What had she done?

The eye mask made everything worse, the darkness overwhelming. It made everything feel unreal. Like she was back on *Sagittarius*, drifting slowly home, talking to Aimee to keep herself alive.

You are on Earth. Aimee is right here and seventeen now. You are in a spa, Catherine kept telling herself over and over.

"I'll be right back," the aesthetician murmured and slipped out of the room.

"Mom? You okay? You went quiet."

Catherine peeled up one corner of the mask and looked over. Behind Aimee's mask Catherine could see her brow furrowed with concern.

"Yeah. I think I might have dozed off." She lay back down and put the mask back in place, breathing easier.

"That's a good sign, right?"

"It must be."

She had to let it go. She promised herself she'd let go of the past and be more present. No matter what happened, Dr. Darzi would tell her it was normal, and maybe it was. Who the hell knew what "normal" was in a situation like this, anyway?

"Sorry, Aims," Catherine said. "I'm not doing a very good job with the whole mother-daughter-time thing."

"Hey, the idea was for you to relax. Napping counts."

"I know, but . . ."

Aimee's self-conscious laugh was an echo of Catherine's, and Catherine couldn't help but smile. "At least you're here. When you first came home, I don't know, I was afraid something else would take you away from me. Or that you'd vanish. Or that you would have changed so much that you wouldn't be . . . *you* anymore."

Am I still me? Really me? All the time? "I kept worrying I would vanish, too." Catherine tried to laugh it off as a joke then winced at the drying gel pulling at her skin.

"Mom? What made you decide to do it? To be an astronaut? And go away for so long at a time?"

It was a fair question, and Catherine owed her a true answer. "When

I was younger, before you were born, I wanted to see the stars more than anything. I wanted to be out there among them. After you were born I still wanted to see the stars, just not *more than anything*. Remember that, Aims: you don't stop wanting things just because you have a baby; you just try to get better at making compromises."

"And your compromise was to . . . leave?" Aimee's voice was careful, as if she recognized that Catherine was working through her thoughts, too, that both of them were trying to find their footing.

"I know that sounds terrible." Catherine still remembered the tension between her and David, but every time she asked, every time she tried to talk about it, he insisted it was fine and that she should go. "The Sagittarius missions are so important, Aimee. Now that we can reach planets outside our solar system, there's a better and better chance we can find a planet like Earth. The Earth may be fine during my lifetime and yours, but . . . it might not. I told myself," here Catherine's voice started to thicken, remembering how difficult the conclusion had been, "that I might be away from you for six years, but I was part of making sure you would always have somewhere safe to live." Remembered sadness faded into wry humor. "Oh, the irony; my biggest adventure yet, and I don't remember a damn thing about the actual destination."

"I'm sorry. That has to suck."

All the lost time, during and after the trip, all the worry, losing nearly a decade of her life, and Aimee had managed to distill it down to four words. "Yeah." Catherine allowed a laugh—because it was either laugh or cry—and said, "It definitely sucks."

The aesthetician returned, much calmer than when she'd left. "Ladies, I apologize for taking so long."

"Oh, we're not in any hurry," Catherine said, managing a smile that felt real behind the mask. The question still lingered in her mind. Had she made the right decision? Hindsight made it easy to second-guess herself. Would she still be asking herself this if the mission had been a success? It was an unanswerable question, as unknowable as her missing memories.

———

"Tony's for all three of us?" Catherine kissed David's cheek before he held out chairs for both her and Aimee. "Are you spending my hazard pay?" she teased. She'd been able to shake off her melancholy thanks to Aimee's obvious enjoyment of their outing and brute determination on her part not to spoil it.

"No, Aimee's college fund. She made out so well at her graduation party, I figure we can get away with it."

"Hey!" Aimee protested good-naturedly. "I worked hard for that graduation money!"

David picked up his menu, but then let his eyes linger on Catherine. "You look radiant, both of you."

Catherine and Aimee had finished the afternoon by getting their hair, makeup, and nails done. Catherine had to admit, it was the most glamorous she'd felt in a long while. "Your daughter is clearly better at being a girly-girl than her mother ever was."

"Director Lindholm was telling me at the party that he wants you to start doing TV interviews. You should see if someone there can do your makeup if you do," Aimee suggested.

Catherine groaned. "Is he still pushing that idea? Every time I think I've gotten him to give up, Paul tries a new angle to get me to agree."

"The man is a bulldog. He doesn't give up on *anything*," David said.

The waiter arrived and they gave him their orders, then talk turned to Aimee's plans for her dorm room. Even facing the fact that her daughter was going to go thousands of miles away in a few months was more appealing than thinking about Lindholm and his hunger for media coverage. More important, it felt *normal*.

"You should see the rooms, Mom. They're so tiny! I don't know how they expect future engineers to live together in such a small space. There's hardly any work space at all . . ."

"We'll get it figured out," Catherine said.

After she and Aimee decided what dessert they wanted to split, Catherine realized something else had been weighing on her since yesterday. "Julie mentioned something at the party yesterday . . ." She toyed with the napkin in front of her. "The doctors have decided it's all right to tell Mom about me coming back. Julie wants us to come to Chicago to see her this summer. 'Sooner rather than later,' she said."

"Cath, that's fantastic."

"It is and it isn't." God, Catherine hated to bring this up here. "It . . . might not be much longer now. We might be going to, well, . . . say good-bye."

Aimee took her hand. "Mom, we've known that for a long time now. It's just new to you." Aimee, as always, cutting right to the heart of the matter.

Goddamn it, she wasn't going to sit here and cry in the middle of a restaurant. Catherine held her eyes open to keep the tears from spilling out, holding on to her husband and daughter. "Yeah, I guess it is. I'm sorry, I shouldn't have "

"It's *fine*," David said. "We'll figure out the next weekend you can get away, okay? Talk to Aaron Llewellyn; he'll find you some time."

With the launch of Sagittarius II just weeks away, that was going to be hard. It might have to wait until after the launch, but now that Catherine knew she *could* go, she wanted to desperately. She missed Nora so badly, and couldn't help feeling that seeing someone else who knew her, someone who knew her deep down in her bones, would help her shake this feeling of unreality and disconnection.

"Yeah, okay. Thank you." Catherine was able to swallow the lump in her throat and smile at both of them. "I'm so lucky to have you both." The idea of visiting Nora hung before her like a glimmer of hope, and she was going to reach for it with both hands.

12

"**SOME THINGS DON'T** change around here, do they?" Catherine sat in the cafeteria across from David on Monday, enjoying the sunshine coming through the atrium windows. "The politicking, the jockeying for the right sort of attention . . ." She nodded over to where a small group of systems engineers sat, and she could read enough body language to see a competition between two of them to get control of the conversation—even over lunch. Conversations like that happened all over NASA. Catherine had been in her fair share of them.

"Admit it—you missed it, didn't you?" David teased.

"You know, it's weird. Yes, in a way. People in large groups act so differently from those in smaller groups. I mean, you'd think people are people, right? But it's . . . different." Catherine shook her head. "I guess I just mean it's nice to be back with everyone again."

David smiled, then his gaze moved to a point behind Catherine. Cal Morganson stood there with a chilly smile. "Sorry to interrupt. David, can I steal Catherine for a few minutes?"

David stood up. "Of course. Cath, you want me to wait here?"

"Sure. I shouldn't be long, right?" Catherine smiled curiously at Cal and stood as well.

"No, I won't keep you," Cal said, still radiating ice.

Catherine expected Cal to ask her to follow him to his office, but instead he surprised her by leading her out into the courtyard off the cafeteria.

"Let's walk for a moment," he said.

He led her away—from potential listeners, she realized. Once they were out of earshot, she asked, "What can I do for you?"

Cal didn't answer, uncharacteristically quiet at first. Catherine waited, curious to see what sort of game he was playing.

Finally he said, "I was here late Saturday, finishing paperwork. I looked out my office window and saw you drive up a little after midnight. I just wanted to make sure everything was all right."

"Saturday?"

Sunday morning. Her dirty feet with no explanation. *Oh God.* She'd been so careful, on guard every waking moment to keep from losing time again. And so it happened while she slept. She'd lost time again, and, worse than that, she'd driven herself here. And, of course, Cal Morganson had to be the one to have seen her.

Cal was watching her expectantly, and she managed a bright laugh, her heart beating so hard it was making her feel sick. "Saturday was a frantic day. It was my daughter's graduation party. Some of the folks here gave me cards for her and I'd forgotten them, so I came back to get them."

"That late?"

Catherine just smiled at him. "I can tell you've never thrown a graduation party, Cal. We had dozens and dozens of people in and out of the house all day, but I worried about those damn cards all afternoon. You know how it is when you get something stuck in your head. I felt bad that she hadn't had them to open at the party."

"Funny how that is," Cal said without a smile. "But you never came up to your office. I went by to say hello."

"We must have missed each other. I wasn't here long. Just long enough to pick up the cards and go."

"Catherine, you never went up there. I know you didn't." Cal was looking at her the same way he'd watched her in her last debriefing, as if he not only knew she had a secret but also knew what that secret was, and was just waiting for her to confess.

"Cal, honestly. Why would I lie about something like that?" She tried to keep her voice calm, despite panic rising in her gut. If she hadn't come up to her office, what was she doing here? She had an image of herself wandering mindlessly through the dark halls of JSC on a Saturday night like some sort of zombie and had to suppress a shiver. The early-afternoon sun was warm on her shoulders and she tried to focus on that, to let it ground her.

Cal wasn't going to give her that chance. "People lie for all sorts of reasons." He stopped walking and looked her dead in the eye. "Catherine, I *know* there's something wrong. You're not telling us everything."

"Of course I'm not telling you everything!" Catherine cried, exasperated. They were going to have this argument, right here in the middle of the courtyard. Sure, no one could hear them, but plenty of people could see them, so she tried to control her body language as best she could. "Do you think I want my official record to talk about how many times I *hallucinated* having my daughter in the cockpit with me?" She met his eyes, feeling as if her free-floating anger and anxiety had finally found a valid target. "Do you want a day-by-day record of all the times I was certain I was going to die alone in space and that my corpse would go drifting through the cosmos forever?

"I know something terrible happened out there, Cal. I would give *any-thing* to be able to tell you the whole story of what happened, but I can't, because I don't know what the whole story is."

"Do you want to know what I think, Catherine? I think you remember more than you're saying." Cal folded his arms, but she read uncertainty in his eyes, as if her words had struck home.

"Cal, I swear to you. I don't know how to make you believe me, but I don't remember a single goddamn thing that happened on that planet, and it's going to haunt me for the rest of my life."

"I'm not going to let anything put my crew in danger."

Catherine was struck dumb, the breath knocked from her lungs. "Do you seriously think so poorly of me that you think I'm capable of that? I care about them! Leah is my friend. I would never—"

"Ava Gidzenko was your friend, too." Cal let that sink in while he watched her. "If you're hiding *anything*, tell me. Let me help you."

"There's nothing." Catherine felt a small tremor in her hands.

"Well." Cal walked them back toward the atrium. "If you change your mind . . ."

"If I know of anything that will help, believe me, I'll say something."

"Catherine, this isn't personal."

Catherine, who had started to walk away, stopped and looked back at him. "You're accusing me of harming my crew. That feels pretty fucking personal."

"No, I'm not saying—"

Catherine stopped listening and left Cal behind. She was shaking inside, and trying to keep it from showing. Her thoughts ping-ponged between *how dare he accuse me* and *oh God, he knows everything*. David was still at their table, checking his phone.

"What was *that* all about?" he asked.

"It's nothing. Just Cal being Cal." Talking about this was out of the question.

But David hadn't gotten that message. "It didn't look like it was nothing. What's going on, Cath?"

"It was *nothing*, okay?" Catherine spat.

"Hey, hey." David lifted his hands in surrender. "I'm on your side here, remember?"

"Then stop pushing me, David!" A few heads turned in their direction, and Catherine leaned closer, lowering her voice. "Jesus. I get grilled enough here as it is without you joining in."

"There's a difference between grilling you and just wanting to reconnect with you, Cath."

"I talk to you all the time!"

"Bullshit." David kept his voice low as well despite the vehemence of his words. "You never talk about the mission. Not to me, and not to Aimee. Believe me, she's noticed."

"Don't bring Aimee into this. This is about you. Since when have you wanted to connect with me at all about my work?"

"What the hell . . . Where is this coming from?"

Maybe Catherine wasn't being fair, but why should she be when nothing else seemed fair? "We used to *talk*, really *talk* about what was going on here at NASA, about missions, about the future . . . and all that stopped the second you knew you would never be an astronaut."

"Come on, was I supposed to be excited that you were going to leave me behind?"

"Excited?" Catherine laughed bitterly. "Christ, David, I would have been happy if you'd even acted *interested.*"

"I'm sorry, I was too busy being interested in how I was going to raise our daughter alone."

"What do you want from me?" Catherine asked with deadly calm.

"I want you to tell me what's going on!" David was speaking through clenched teeth now. "Let me help you, for once in your life. God, some things really don't change. Catherine the Great, able to do everything by herself, just like in training."

"I'm alive right now because I *can* do everything myself, so I guess it turned out to be a damn good thing, didn't it?"

They both froze, looking at each other.

"Sorry." David's voice was quiet. "I'm sorry."

Fuck. Catherine sighed and pushed her hair back from her forehead. "I'm sorry, too." Was sorry enough? For now it had to be. "Cal is just— he's been on my case ever since I got back. He's sure I'm lying about the mission somehow."

David had his listening face on. They were going to act like a normal couple again, it seemed. "He doesn't think the amnesia is real?"

"I don't know. Maybe. I think he hates me."

"Cal's just an asshole. Everybody knows that."

Catherine looked down at the table. "I think . . . I think he thinks I did something up there, maybe even something that got everyone killed." Just saying it aloud hurt more than she expected. Frightened her more than she expected.

"He doesn't." David finally reached for her hands, ducking down to look her in the eye. "I know he's brusque, I know he asks all sorts of annoying questions, but that's his job. He's good at that sort of thing, getting to the bottom of problems, solving them."

"Well, he's decided that I'm one of his problems to solve." Catherine felt the warmth from David's hands and tried to draw on it. David was trying to fix everything, the way he always did. That was a good thing. Wasn't it? And he wasn't wrong. Cal *did* look at her as if she were a problem, not a person.

"I wouldn't worry too much about him. Most people around here see him as kind of an oddball. A useful oddball, but an oddball nonetheless."

She thought about the odd way he conducted himself at meetings and briefings, focused on his own information, and thought of the way Aaron Llewellyn seemed to rely on him. "Not everybody. Everyone working on Sag II takes him pretty seriously."

"Cath, trust me when I say nobody outside your department takes him seriously. You've got Lindholm in your corner, and that's all that matters. Plus, your psychiatrist, right?"

Catherine remembered how Dr. Darzi pushed for her to let things go. "Yeah. She says I'm fine," she said, with a trace of irony in her voice.

"Then don't worry about Cal Morganson. He's terrible with people. Just ignore him and everything will be fine."

So many people were telling her that everything was fine. But how could she be fine if she was losing time? How could she be fine if she'd gone to JSC without realizing it?

And how could she be fine not knowing what actually happened to her crewmates?

What if Cal was right? What if she'd gotten everyone killed?

Sagittarius I Mission

DAY 1134, THREE DAYS BEFORE THE EVENT
TRAPPIST-1F, TWILIGHT LANDING AREA HABITAT

Tom was sitting in the command center of the Habitat when Catherine came in. The command center was a small room, made more crowded by all the system monitors and communications equipment. There were intercoms and suit comms, and the long-distance comms, which so far had remained silent. "Oh, hey," she said.

He made a noncommittal grunt. Since their talk, he'd been friendlier with the rest of the crew, but he still barely said two words to her.

"Still no word from NASA?"

"No. We knew it might be months." He looked up at her. "Why are you here?"

"Oh, uh. Richie needed a hand with some air-lock alarms."

Tom stood up. "I'll get out of your way. Wouldn't want anyone to gossip about us being alone together."

"Tom—" But he was already gone. Catherine sighed and sat down, turning her attention to the monitors Richie needed her to watch—and frowned at what she saw. Richie was in one of the air locks, checking the seals after some alarms had gone off.

"Hey, Richie. You got a buddy out there you need to tell me about?" Catherine asked.

"Just me and my shadow. Why?"

"Your shadow's got a fever then. Thermal monitoring is going bonkers in here."

"Nah, everything's fine."

"That's weird." Catherine watched the numbers on the thermal scanner and eyed the outlines on the spectroscopic monitors, the skin on the back of her neck starting to crawl. "I'm getting localized readings of nearly forty-four degrees. Do you not feel that? You should be roasting."

"Nope, I'm cool as a cucumber. Damn it. The seals are fine out here, and now you're getting weird readings. Looks like I've got two fucked-up monitors to try to fix." Richie sounded as though he were just waiting for one more thing to go wrong.

"Everything else is green across the board." Catherine kept her voice neutral. "Are you sure there's not a hot spot out there?"

"Yeah, there's nothing."

Richie was right. He had to be. That much heat couldn't possibly remain in such a single tight area without dissipating. And a random warm spot in the Habitat wouldn't have clean, well-defined edges. The monitors were glitchy. The rest was just her imagination.

Later, she caught up with Ava in the corridor, still trying to put it out of her mind. "Are we getting any information through to NASA?"

"Tom said he thought some of our information might be getting through, but we don't know yet how long the transit time is for sure. The wormhole wreaks havoc on all the calculations. We haven't received any communications at all from Houston."

"So we're on our own out here." They knew it was a possibility from the start, but it was the worst-case scenario.

Ava looked at her more closely. "Everything okay?"

"Yeah. I'm just homesick." Catherine smiled at her faintly. What she saw had spooked her; it would've been nice to know they could contact NASA if something went wrong. Not that NASA could do anything at this distance. "Richie and I found a couple of monitoring glitches, too. He can probably give you more information than I can."

"Ugh, this is what I hate about being the first to use new tech out in the field." Ava rubbed her forehead. "All right. I'll make sure it gets reported. Between this and the issues we've been having with the oxygenator, I'm tempted to send the testing department a very strongly worded letter."

The dry humor in Ava's voice made her laugh. " 'Dear Sirs: Why were you not able to replicate working conditions precisely in a location no human had ever seen before?' "

Ava grinned at her. "Yeah, yeah, okay. Maybe I'm not being fair."

Claire came down the corridor, suited up for going out. "Cath, are you ready?"

"Oh shit, I'm running behind. Give me a few minutes and I will be." She and Claire were going to take the rover out and explore the landscape around the terminator line. They were going to go deeper into the dark side of the planet than they ever had before, and Claire was chomping at the bit to see what changed across the border.

Catherine pushed all her worries aside and went to get suited up.

———

Claire steered the rover slowly between some of the large rock formations that dotted TRAPPIST-1f's landscape. With each EVA, the team was venturing farther and farther from the Habitat to gather data and samples. Full dark and full daylight were both too far from the Habitat to reach by rover, but they were going as far in either direction as they could. Catherine had initially volunteered for this EVA because she needed a break. A few hours away from the occasionally tense atmosphere of the Habitat sounded perfect.

The more data they gathered on their current home, the more like Earth it seemed in many ways. After a lot of discussion with Izzy, Ava gave the okay to reduce pressure-suit protocol on EVAs. As a result, Catherine and Claire both wore oxygen masks instead of full pressure suits; although the planet's atmosphere was breathable, it wasn't optimal, and there was always the question of potentially harmful microbes. They kept their skin covered, but the lighter suits were much more comfortable in TRAPPIST's intense heat.

"Man, we really *do* need to get a botanist up here," Claire said. "I'm not an expert, but the way the plant life changes as we get closer to the dark side . . . I feel like I'm watching evolution happen."

The wonder in Claire's voice made Catherine a little envious. It wasn't that things weren't amazing here. They were. After the constant twilight of the Habitat's surroundings, to drive deeper into the dark was exciting as hell. But no matter how exciting things were, Catherine was constantly aware that she was responsible for the friction that still lingered among the crew.

"Look over there." Claire pointed to one of the flatter rocks they were passing, caught in the rover's ambient light. "See? That lichen is growing in similar patterns to the stuff that's all over the place on the light side, but . . . it's *bigger*."

Catherine could see what she meant. It seemed to be growing taller here in the dark, which given what little Catherine knew about plant life, didn't seem possible. Lichen didn't grow that way, did it? Something else caught her eye as well.

"Hang on. It looks like it's glinting. Do we have samples of that? Pull over and let me grab some."

"It's a crystalline structure!" Claire said, now sounding even more excited. "Of course. It looks like . . . I don't know, like it's merging with the rock." The rover started going faster as they moved down a small slope.

At first, Catherine laughed. "Wrong pedal, kiddo; I said stop."

"I'm trying! Shit. Shit! Cath, the brakes are out!"

"Try the emergency brake." Catherine tried to keep her voice calm, glancing up to see a large cluster of rocks in the rover's headlights, straight ahead. And the rover was picking up speed. She pinged the comms for the Habitat. "Wells to Twilight Base. Having a rover malfunction, do you read?"

"The emergency brake's out, too!" Claire cried.

"Bail out," Catherine ordered, watching the rocks get larger. "Get out, now!" She fumbled with her own door to do the same herself.

"The belt's stuck, hang on—"

Before Catherine could turn back to help her, there was a loud crunch and the rover lurched. Catherine, unsecured in preparation for bailing, was thrown against the windshield with a rattling crack of her head, leaving her stunned.

"We read you." Tom's voice came over the comms. "Sensors went dead on the rover; are you there?"

He sounded worried. Catherine tried to answer, but she couldn't at first. Her head was spinning, and she was faintly aware of the sound of Claire groaning.

"Colonel Wells." Ava's voice, her stern commander voice. "Mission Specialist Tomason. Status report."

"We . . . crashed. Into a rock," Catherine managed to get out. Something warm was running down the side of her head, but at the same time she felt something a little cooler, a breeze against her skin. After a second or two, she realized why. There was a rip in her hood where she'd hit her head. "Suit breached. And I'm bleeding."

Panic tried to take over, but Catherine pushed it down savagely. If TRAPPIST-1f's atmosphere weren't similar to Earth's, she'd be dead already. That didn't mean she was safe. They still didn't know what types of bacteria populated the air.

"I've got an open cut exposed to the air," she repeated, trying to keep her voice calm. She tried to hold her suit together at the tear, but it might have already been too late.

"Hang on," Ava said. "Richie and Dr. Izzy are on their way. We've got your last known about two klicks from the south ridge. Is that right?"

"Yeah. Yeah, that's right." The worst of the confusion was fading. She pulled herself back to a sitting position, ignoring the way her head tried to spin. "Claire. Claire, are you okay?"

"I'm okay." Claire was slumped in the driver's seat, and sat up with a wince. Her eyes widened. "Cath, your head."

"I know. We're gonna find out how friendly the microbes are here." She'd have to go into quarantine for ten days while Dr. Izzy tried to figure out what she'd been exposed to, if anything.

She should have been terrified. Something that could kill her might be invading her bloodstream right now through the cut on her head. She might never see Aimee and David again. The thought hurt, but it was a distant pain. More than fear or pain, she felt weirdly fatalistic. Not making it home had always been a possibility, and all she could do was wait and see.

It didn't take long before they heard the sound of the other rover approaching, and Richie hailed them over the comms. "You two okay?"

"Some bruises," Claire said, "but Cath's suit is breached."

"All right," Izzy's voice came next. "We know the routine here. Sorry, Catherine. It's gonna suck to be you for a little bit."

"Are you kidding?" Catherine forced a laugh, smiling so Claire could see her. "I was supposed to be on KP this week. Couldn't have happened at a better time."

When the other rover stopped next to them, Izzy jumped out. Catherine waved him over to Claire first, but he ignored her. "Okay, it's not deep," he said of the cut. "We'll have to see about the rest. The sooner we can get you on prophylactic antibiotics the better I'll feel."

"Working on it," Richie said, hooking up the crashed rover to the working one so they could drag it back.

Izzy repaired her suit breach then moved on to Claire, giving her a quick exam. Within ten minutes, they were headed back to the base, with Richie pushing their speed the whole way.

Claire went to the infirmary for a more thorough exam while Catherine wound up in the base's quarantine unit. It was stark; an empty bunk stood in one corner, and various monitors and bits of medical equipment sat in the other. The only real form of entertainment was a tablet. This was going to be a long ten days. Through the observation glass, she could see Ava and Richie, and after a short time Claire and Izzy. Where was Tom?

She didn't have time to ask before Izzy came through the decontamination air lock, still in his sealed suit. Catherine had taken hers off and was waiting on the bunk. He patched up the cut on her forehead and took some X-rays and an MRI before giving her a shot. "I'm gonna have you wired six ways to Sunday," he said apologetically. "I'm going to keep track of all your vitals, and if I see so much as a hint of any sort of infection, we've got another collection of antibiotics to try."

"It had to happen to one of us, right?" Catherine wore the same smile she wore for Claire, determined to keep presenting a cheerful face. Her feelings were still a numb sort of mystery, and until they sorted themselves out, she would keep her best "okay" face on. "Besides, I know you were dying to see if the atmosphere was safe for us or not."

"Yeah, I just hope you're not dying to get the answer." Izzy was smiling, too, with a grim sort of humor. He attached one electrode after another, to her scalp, her chest, her back.

"I'm not worried. As far as I'm concerned, I just got a ten-day vacation." She looked up at the module's observation glass and saw the others standing out there looking stricken. Especially Ava. Catherine gave them a wave. The room was miked, so she said, "Will you guys stop looking like you're at a funeral? I'm fine."

"She is," Izzy agreed. "I'm going to run some more tests to be sure, but I don't think she even has a concussion."

"Claire told us what happened." Ava still looked grave. "We're going to check out the rover and see if we can figure out why it failed."

"Well, I can't do much from in here, but I'll help however I can."

Izzy gave Catherine a clean bill of health except for the cut and some bruises—and, of course, whatever organisms might have invaded through that cut. Eventually the others drifted away and Catherine settled in with the tablet. Her comment about being on vacation wasn't accurate. There was still some work she could do in here, and the first job was to write up a report about the rover crash.

She was halfway through the report when Ava's voice interrupted her. "Catherine?" She looked up to see both Ava and Richie standing in the observation window. Richie's eyes were dark with rage, and Ava didn't exactly look happy either.

"What happened?" Catherine put the tablet down and sat up.

"The rover didn't have a mishap. Richie says the controls were tampered with. The brakes in particular."

Catherine couldn't believe it. "Richie, you sure?"

"I'm sure." His voice was unrecognizable, low and dark. "I saw the damage."

"But why would somebody *do* that?"

"I can think of several reasons, all worse than the one before," Ava said, folding her arms. "And it's more than that. I had Richie dig deeper into the problems we've been having with the oxygenator. It looks as if it's being tampered with, too."

"*What?* That— I mean, anyone who's messing with that has to know they're putting themselves in danger, too!" Catherine's head spun. The oxygenator filtered the air and made sure the inside of the Habitat was as close to Earth's atmosphere as possible. Anything that needed oxygen to survive needed the oxygenator. "What are we going to do?"

Ava leaned closer to the mic. "You and I are going to go over the security footage and see what we find."

Catherine had never wanted so badly to be wrong, but only one person kept coming to mind, one person who had been quieter than usual, more withdrawn. *God,* she thought, hoping she was wrong.

What about the shadow in the air lock?

No way. *That* she pushed firmly out of her mind.

Richie went to double-check the rest of their essential equipment while Catherine and Ava divided up the security footage for the twenty-four hours before Catherine and Claire took the rover out. The two of them painstakingly made their way through it, Catherine on her side of the observation glass, Ava on hers. Hours later, Catherine found the smoking gun. Early that morning, long before anyone else was up and about, the cameras showed Tom Wetherbee sneaking into the rover bay and opening a panel on the side. Catherine told Ava the video time stamp, almost too shocked to speak, and they watched as he did something they couldn't quite make out, then closed the panel.

"Go back to Day 1033," Ava said. "Check the footage around the equipment room."

"You didn't do this before?"

"No. I didn't think it was sabotage."

The two women scrolled through the footage and Catherine drew a quiet breath when—again, in the middle of the Habitat's night cycle—Tom showed up. He went straight to the oxygenator.

It had failed for the first time the following day.

"What are we going to do?" Catherine asked.

"We'll have to question him. Confine him to quarters while we try to figure this out. At least to start." Ava's brow creased. "I don't know. I want to get a message to NASA. They may not be able to reply, but they at least should know what we've found." She shook her head.

"I take it they didn't give you any contingencies in the case of a crew member trying to kill everybody?" Catherine meant for it to sound dry and sardonic, but the truth of the statement, once spoken, was unavoidable. *Tom tried to kill us. Or at least hurt us.*

"Not . . . quite like this." Ava rubbed her forehead. Catherine didn't envy the position she was in. "Cath, I'm going to bring him in here to talk to him. Maybe he'll say something in front of you that he wouldn't in front of just me."

"And here I thought I was going to get bored in quarantine," Catherine said.

When Tom came in to the observation area, he rushed to the window. "I heard what happened. Are you all right?" Worry was written all over his face. It looked real to Catherine. "I'm fine for now." She glanced over his shoulder at Ava, who looked equally nonplussed. "We'll see if I come down with anything."

"What's going on?" he asked, and now he looked between her and Ava. "Is there something I can do to help?"

"Tom, sit down." Ava gestured to a seat and took one herself. *She's calmer than I would be in her shoes*, Catherine thought.

"What's wrong?" He looked worried about more than just Catherine now.

"Were you in the garage at all last night?" Ava asked.

"Last night?" Tom shook his head. "No. I haven't been out there since . . . well, whenever my last EVA was."

He was lying. He had to be lying, but damned if Catherine could read any sign of it on his face.

"All right." Ava nodded. "What did you do last night, then?"

"Nothing unusual . . ." Tom looked to Catherine and she thought she saw a trace of fear in his eyes. "What's going on? Why do you think I was in the garage?"

Catherine glanced at Ava through the glass and she gave a faint nod, so Catherine drew a breath. "Tom, there's security footage of you. We both saw it. You went into the garage and did something to the rover. The one Claire and I were in."

"No, there's some sort of mistake!" His hands gripped the edges of the table, his knuckles going white. "I didn't do that. Cath, I know we've had a rough time, but I would never hurt you; you have to know that."

She would have thought so once, but after seeing that video she wasn't sure anymore. Rather than answering, Catherine called the footage up on her tablet and turned it to the glass for Tom to see.

Tom watched and started shaking his head as soon as he saw himself head for the rover. "No. I didn't do that. It's a fake." He looked between them like a trapped animal. "Richie. He's got access to all the security systems, and he's been pissed at me for ages. He could have changed the footage, edited it somehow."

He couldn't expect them to believe that. Catherine sat back and looked at him, folding her arms.

"I swear it wasn't me!"

Ava tensed, and Catherine worried that there was no one else in the room with her for backup if Tom got violent. "Tom," Ava said quietly, "I promise you, I'll look into that possibility, but in the meantime, I have to restrict you to your quarters. You understand that, don't you?"

"I do, but . . ." Tom didn't look violent. He looked lost. If Catherine weren't literally looking at the video footage, she would have believed him.

"All right. We're going to do that now, okay? And if you didn't do it, we'll figure out who did." Ava spoke to him as if she were talking him down off a ledge. "You've got to trust me, Tom. All I want is to make sure we're all safe. You want that, too, right?"

"Yeah. Yeah, of course I do."

Ava took Tom by the arm and he didn't resist. As she led him out, Catherine slumped against her seat. Two crew members out of commission. How the hell were the other four going to keep everything going? And if Tom really was a danger to them, what could they do, so far from home and on their own?

13

"FOR NEARLY SIX years, we mourned the loss of *Sagittarius* and her crew." Paul Lindholm's voice came through Cal's car radio as he drove in. He was giving a report to Congress, which the local news reported in loving detail, but it sounded more like he was giving a sermon. "But then early this year, we received the radio transmission that rewrote NASA history when Colonel Catherine Wells returned to our solar system, alive and well.

"Thanks to her bravery and determination, we have a much clearer understanding of the tragedy that befell the Sagittarius I mission, and knowing what happened on TRAPPIST-1f, we can move forward, wiser and more prepared for the next mission."

Cal snorted. Catherine hadn't given them a clearer understanding of anything. How could she have? All they had was the information on board *Sagittarius*, and so far that had yielded little.

"And we *will* move forward! If NASA excels at anything, it is moving forward, and moving our great nation forward."

Cal snapped off the radio. NASA was doubling down on its mythology-building. Once Cal had thought it was just PR, but it wasn't. It was a belief that was religious in its fervor, with astronauts as NASA's demigods and goddesses. From the very start, the moment Catherine had reappeared, Lindholm had written a specific narrative for the Sagittarius I mission, and he was not going to let anything stray from that narrative.

Anything else was heresy.

Cal might literally be the only person on the entire planet who gave a damn about the truth of what happened out there. No, that wasn't entirely true: Catherine no doubt cared passionately about the truth of what happened. He just hoped it wasn't because she wanted to make sure no one else found out.

As he walked to his office, he couldn't forget the anger on Catherine's face when he'd confronted her. He was used to people getting pissed at him for his work, but this felt different. She'd looked and acted defensive, yes, but there was something else. Something about it reminded him of the Catherine he saw at her daughter's party. She'd looked *real*. As though he were seeing her without her mask, seeing the Catherine he might have been friends with, anger and all.

What if she was telling the truth, and the things she was holding back were only her private fears while she was alone out there? Maybe those secrets were hers to keep, but he had to be sure. She might think his investigation was personal. It wasn't, not really.

John Duffy caught up with him in the hallway. "Hey, Cal. Listen, we're only a week out now, and the kids are getting nervous. There's still no confirmation of what happened to Catherine's crew?" Duffy asked.

Cal dreaded the question every time it was asked. Every time, he wanted to have a better answer, and every time, he didn't. "The data analysis isn't complete yet. It may not be finished before launch day. So far, we've found some anomalies with the oxygenator, and it looks as if one of the rovers was wrecked, but that's all we know for now."

"Okay; that's not the most reassuring answer, you know that, right?" Duffy, as always, spoke for his team. "That still makes it sound like there are some mechanical issues that could happen again." Cal had always tried to resist an "us vs. them" attitude between administration and the astronauts, but conversations like this served as a reminder that—no matter how close he felt to them—he was administration and they were not.

Cal stopped walking and looked Duffy in the eye. "Right now, the engineers are saying that the likelihood of the oxygenator, or any other system in the Habitat, having the same problems at the same time again is practically nonexistent. I believe them, but I also know they're working to make sure that none of the problems that the Sagittarius I Habitat *might* have experienced happen on your watch. We're not going to send you up there with bad equipment, I swear, John."

Duffy sighed. "I know. I know you won't. Sorry, Cal. Like I said, the kids are getting nervous. We all hoped we'd find out so much more when Catherine came back."

"We did, too, but it looks like we're stuck with what we've got. If she'd come back a year sooner, maybe we'd have had time for more analysis, but . . ."

"Yeah. All right, I'll let them know."

Cal thumped him on the bicep. "If I find out anything else, I'll tell you as soon as I can."

As Duffy walked away, Cal felt the weight of half-truths and partial information hanging over him. He wished he could tell the crew that he was doing everything in his power to try to find out what was wrong, that he was sure something *was* wrong, but if they were nervous now, that would only make matters worse.

They had nine years of data to go through from *Sagittarius*, and the analysis was slow going. It would be years before they had a full picture, so Catherine's landing a year earlier might not have made a difference. Then again, who knew what they'd know about this mission a year from now? Cal knew better than to ask Aaron about a postponement again. If Aaron thought missing the launch window could be NASA's death knell, nothing other than absolute proof of an imminent threat would make him take the chance. No, the public—and, more important, the Appropriations Committee—needed to see NASA produce an on-time, glowing success with Sagittarius II.

He tried to shake off the gloom, and by the time he unlocked his office door, he'd almost succeeded. As he'd hoped, some new information was waiting for him in his email. Cal had specifically requested the data from the day of the Event, Mission Day 1137, and two weeks in either direction. Most of the initial analysis had focused, rightfully, on the Habitat, trying to figure out how and why and even *if* it failed. He settled in behind his desk, propping his feet up as he scrolled through the data on his tablet.

He started on Day 1136. *Sagittarius* was in standby mode—unsurprising, since no one expected to use it. He moved ahead slowly, and also as expected, *Sagittarius* reactivated on Day 1137. Where else would Catherine have taken shelter?

All the data looked normal: energy usage, life-support readings, temperature readings. While it still didn't tell Cal what had happened to the Habitat, it did suggest that Catherine was the sole survivor and that she retreated to the ship. It was . . . vaguely disappointing. Cal hadn't *really* expected to find a smoking gun, but he'd thought there would be—

Wait a minute.

There. On Day 1139, two days after the Event. Cal traced the data with his finger and did some quick math in his head. The first two days after the Event, Days 1138 and 1139, oxygen usage held steady at about 575 liters per day, pretty much what he'd expect for one human occupant. Then suddenly, three days after the Event, Day 1140, usage spiked to over 1,200 liters. Carbon dioxide output had a comparative spike. Temperature readings shifted unexpectedly.

Then five days after the Event, on Day 1142, life-support readings all dropped back to their initial levels. What had happened for those two days?

"Two people," Cal said out loud.

It was right there in front of him. For two days after the Event, there had been two people on board *Sagittarius*.

Cal was in Aaron's office before he had time to give it a second thought.

"Hey." Aaron was all smiles. Unlike everyone else, Aaron always seemed exhilarated as a launch got closer. While Cal was juggling a dozen deadlines to keep on top of everything, Aaron always appeared to have the whole thing tied up with a ribbon.

"Aaron, I need to talk to you."

"Oh hell. You're gonna fuck up my good day, aren't you?"

Cal put his tablet on Aaron's desk.

"Aaron, someone besides Catherine survived the Event."

"What? What the hell are you talking about?"

"Look. Right here." He leaned in, pointing at a graph. "For two days after the Event, the life-support readings are all wrong for just one person to have been on board *Sagittarius*. Oxygen consumption, CO_2 output... it's all wrong."

"That doesn't necessarily mean there was a second person."

"Come on, the numbers line up too well. What else could it have been?"

Aaron shook his head. "There could have been a leak, it could have been a glitch..."

"Aaron, if it was a glitch, systems would've found it already."

Aaron looked at the information for a few long, quiet minutes that felt like hours. Cal's heart pounded in his chest with the hope that maybe, *maybe* he was getting through to Aaron.

"Cal, sit down."

That didn't sound good. Cal pulled over a chair and sat down. Aaron looked at the report once more then closed the folder. "What are you saying? That someone survived and Catherine—what, killed them?"

Cal tried not to squirm in his seat. "No, not exactly, but—"

"Suppose someone besides Catherine *did* survive the Event. Is it so inconceivable that after two or three days trapped or exposed to TRAPPIST-1f's elements, probably wounded, that crew member might have died as a result?"

"Well, no..."

"And do you really want the families to wonder if it was their loved one who lingered near death for three days, possibly in terrible pain?"

Cal knew where these questions were leading, and Aaron's words made sense, but... his *gut*. His instinct. It didn't jibe.

"I know you're anxious, Cal. I get it. This is your first big mission, an you want everything to be perfect. You don't want to be the guy who miss something. Even beyond that, I know you're close with your crew. That's c of the things that makes you so good at what you do. But even if you're ri until we have more information, this isn't something that should get Especially when it really *might* have been a glitch."

"But... the data... plus now with Catherine acting just... wrong. needed to make Aaron see. "There's something bigger here, more th know, and I'm *certain* Wells is the key."

"I've been quiet for a while now about this," Aaron said. "But I can see server logs as well as you can, Cal. You've been snooping through Catherine Wells's files. Even after I told you to let it go."

"But—"

"Shut up and listen to me. Aside from that, I know you've been talking to Dr. Royer about this, when I *specifically told you* not to say anything."

Cal opened his mouth to say something then thought better of it, feeling like a kid in the principal's office.

"All that is bad enough, but I heard from security that you came in here after her one night. Were you following her?"

"The real question is, what was she doing here so late on a Saturday night, Aaron!"

"I'm gonna take that as a yes, that you were watching her and following her. Do you have any idea how far over the line that is? Do you know how much trouble this could cause us if she found out?" Aaron shoved the tablet back across the desk toward Cal. "I ignored it for as long as I could, because you're damn good at what you do, and I couldn't afford to replace you so close to the launch date. But I want you to listen to me right now. I don't know what issues you have with Wells, but they stop here."

"Aaron—"

"Listen to me. Say you're right. Say that your worst-case scenario is true, what does that mean?"

Cal hadn't wanted to give voice to a worst-case scenario, but Aaron had put him on the spot. "Well . . . worst case . . . Catherine was behind what happened up there, and she's lying to cover it up."

"Right. Say that's true. What does it change for Sagittarius II? It's not like she's going to be up there with them, so she's not a direct danger to the mission." Aaron had him pinned with that stern, fatherly look that was a little too reminiscent of his real dad. "Your crew is going to be fine. Even if you're right, she's *staying here.*"

What Aaron was saying made sense. Cal knew it did. But everything in him was screaming that logic didn't apply here, that there was something they were all missing.

"Sagittarius II is a go, Cal. I need you to focus all your time and energy on that, not chasing down ghosts. You have to leave Wells alone. If there are any other incidents, if I see you so much as *breathe* in her direction when you shouldn't, you're out, genius or not."

Cal took back the tablet with a quiet nod.

Aaron's tone shifted to something more conciliatory when Cal didn't argue. "I know you're worried. But I promise you, it's going to be all right."

Cautiously, Cal said, "Yes, sir." Aaron was one of the smartest people he knew. He had the same data Cal did and reached different conclusions. But he knew Aaron had a strong bias toward making the mission happen. That was skewing his perspective. It had to be. He was seeing what he wanted to see in the data, and drawing his conclusions from that. Cal was being more objective, more invested in the truth than in a specific outcome.

Really? Are you sure about that? No biases of your own?

Self-doubt, even a whisper of it, was a new thing for him, and he didn't like it.

"Now, if we're done here, I need to get some things together," Aaron said. Cal recognized a dismissal when he heard one and stood up.

Aaron looked up, peering at Cal over the rim of his glasses. "And, Cal, I mean it. No more. There's too much riding on this mission."

"I hear you, Aaron." Anxiety sat like a rock in his belly. Even though Aaron made some good points, Cal couldn't shake his worry. But if he wanted to keep his career, he had to let it go. Or at least do his best to try.

14

CHICAGO WAS OPPRESSIVELY muggy when Julie drove Catherine, Aimee, and David to Nora's hospice facility. "It's not a bad place," Julie was saying. "It's about as homelike as you could expect, and they have a lot of experience with Alzheimer's patients."

From the passenger seat, Catherine gave Julie a careful smile. "I know you made the best decision. Thank you. For everything you've done to take care of her." She left *I'm sorry I wasn't here to help* unspoken. Most of her life since coming home seemed to involve that phrase.

"I'm just glad you could make it. I know you've got a launch coming up soon." Julie smiled faintly. "And I know this is going to be hard for you. Mom made a lot of noise about not wanting anyone to see her this way. Me included. She said I should just find her a home and leave her there."

"I can imagine how well *that* went over," Catherine said with a dry laugh. Stubbornness was a family trait, and all three of them had it in spades.

"Well, I won that one."

David and Aimee stayed silent in the back seat. They'd seen Nora at Christmas, and had a better idea of what awaited them than Catherine did.

As they pulled off the expressway, Catherine asked, "Is she lucid at all?"

"Hard to say. Some days yes, most days no. There's never any way to tell." Julie maneuvered through the surface streets. "We're early enough in the day that the chances are better, but . . . I don't know. Last time I was there, she didn't know me the whole time. So . . . just be ready for that, okay?"

Catherine nodded, swallowing the lump in her throat. *No, she has to know me. I need for her to know me.*

"The staff has tried to keep reminding her that you're coming, and when I told her you were back, she seemed to get it, but I just don't know."

Eventually they reached the suburbs, and Julie pulled up in front of a long white building with neoclassical architecture and a vast expanse of rolling green lawn. Everything about the place emanated an aura of calm. When they climbed out, Catherine could smell nothing but freshly cut grass and warm parking-lot asphalt—no other trace of the city they'd just left behind.

Once inside, though, there was the unmistakable hospital scent of disinfectant and floor cleaner, but it was fainter than Catherine had feared. There were fresh flowers everywhere, and it was quiet. The staff knew Julie and greeted her, and a few of them recognized Catherine as well.

David took Catherine's hand as they got closer to Nora's room and she gave him a grateful smile.

The door stood ajar, and Julie rapped on it. "Mom? It's Julie. I've brought you some visitors, is that all right?"

A querulous voice that Catherine didn't recognize came from the room. "Julie? Come in, come in!"

As much as she'd tried to prepare, Catherine wasn't ready for what greeted her. The room itself was reasonably homey despite the hospital bed that dominated the center of it. There were armchairs and a coffee table arranged in a small sitting area, and plants everywhere. The chairs were from her mother's old house.

The woman in the bed bore a passing resemblance to the mother Catherine remembered. When she'd last seen Nora, Nora had been a vibrant, quick-witted sixty-three-year-old with straight dark hair like Catherine's. The woman in the bed looked as if some cruel magician had shrunk Nora and turned her hair dull gray with a malevolent spell. She was impossibly thin, as if she'd break under the weight of her own body should she stand up.

Worse, the bright, sharp eyes that Catherine remembered were clouded and vague. There was no spark left in her mother's face.

"Mom, look who's here. It's Catherine. Remember we told you she came back from her mission."

Nora pushed herself to an upright position with a shaking motion that made Catherine ache, and peered at her. "Catherine. I had a daughter named Catherine."

"This is her, Mom. This is your Catherine. Look, she brought David and Aimee with her."

"Hi, Grandma." Aimee had no qualms about approaching Nora, leaning over, and kissing her cheek. Nora smiled up at her and patted her arm. David greeted her as well, and it broke Catherine's heart to see how accustomed they seemed to this.

Nora looked closer at Catherine and beckoned her forward. "You look like my Catherine." She reached out and gave Catherine a pat, then leaned back in her bed. "My Catherine died in space, you know. On another planet."

Julie and Catherine exchanged glances. Julie looked apologetic; Catherine gave her a resigned shrug, her hope fading.

"How are you feeling today?" Catherine wasn't sure if she should call her "Mom" or "Nora," so wound up calling her nothing.

Nora plucked at the bedding at her side before answering. "I'm going to get up later today. The nurses wouldn't let me this morning."

Julie sat in the chair nearest the bed, and Catherine and David sat near the window, Aimee between them. Catherine put her arm around Aimee's waist, and Aimee leaned against her shoulder.

"Mom," Julie said, "they just don't want you to get hurt. You fell last week, remember?"

"Eh." Nora dismissed it with a wave of her hand then turned to Catherine. "How do you know my Julie?"

Catherine looked to Julie for help. Should she remind her mother who she was?

"Mom, that's Catherine. *Your* Catherine. See? That's her husband, David, and your granddaughter, Aimee, next to her." Julie's voice was calm, practiced, used to explaining things. Catherine felt a stab of guilt—again—that Julie was the one who'd developed that skill. Everyone seemed to be playing a familiar role here except her.

"It's me, Mom." Catherine stood and walked over to the bed. "I'm here. I came back." She watched Nora's face, hoping for any sign of recognition at all.

There. There was a flicker—wasn't there? Nora reached out a hand to her and Catherine took it. "Cath? But you died." Her eyes cut to Julie, pleading.

"It's really her, Mom."

"Why did they tell me you died?" Nora started crying and Catherine bent to hug her. As fragile as Nora looked, she felt even more so, as if she might crumble to dust in Catherine's arms. She was fever-warm and smelled like baby shampoo. Her body was all sharp edges and angles, but she had a strong grip. "How did you come back? Catherine . . . my baby girl."

Catherine felt the sob rising in her throat. She was afraid of frightening her mother, so she tried to swallow it. "It was all a mistake. I didn't die. I was just lost for a little while." She couldn't stop the tears, so she let them fall unchecked. Nora finally let her go, but held on to her hand, so Catherine sat on the edge of the bed.

Nora fell silent, just looking at Catherine and smiling while tears trickled down her cheeks. Odd that this was the first chance she had to see someone react to the news that she'd survived. She glanced at David, wondering how he had reacted when he'd heard. Had he cried? Had Aimee?

"I remember when Catherine was a little girl she wanted everything with airplanes on it. Books, pillows, clothes, if it had an airplane on it, she wanted it."

Catherine smiled at the memory. "Dad hated it. Said everybody thought I was a little boy."

"He was proud anyway." Nora's eyes went misty and distant. She wasn't talking to Catherine. It was as if Catherine had disappeared. "He loved that girl. She's smart, you know. She's the smartest little girl in her class. Just the other day she brought home her idea for her science project, and she had to explain it to me." Nora smiled. "Still not sure I understand it."

Catherine and Julie exchanged glances again. "How old is she, Mom?" Julie asked.

"She'll be eleven in a few months. Julie, my oldest, she's fourteen now. They're getting so big." She looked up at Catherine. "Do you have any children?"

Julie nodded at her, so Catherine answered. "One, my daughter Aimee, by the window there. She just graduated from high school."

"Ah, that's a good age." She patted Catherine's hand again. "She going to college?"

"Yes. She's going to MIT," Catherine managed.

David came up behind Catherine and put a hand on her shoulder. "We're very proud of her."

"MIT! Another smart one." Nora chuckled. She fell quiet for a few minutes, and no one spoke. Catherine looked around the room. There was artwork she recognized from her mother's house, but the most prominent item was a large whiteboard with the date and names of the nurses on duty.

Nora touched her arm and Catherine turned back to her. "You know, you look just like my daughter Catherine."

Despair clutched at Catherine's chest and she started to answer, but Julie shook her head. "I do?" was all she managed to say.

"Just like her. She was an astronaut, my Catherine was." Nora reached out for Julie, who came over as well. "If it wasn't for Julie, I'd be all alone. My granddaughter and son-in-law live so far away . . . and I miss my baby girl."

Catherine fought to keep a smile on her face as David's hands tightened on her shoulder.

"I'm going to get up later today," Nora went on, oblivious. "The nurses promised."

"Mom?" Julie indicated Catherine. "Who do you think this is?"

Nora peered up at Catherine. "That's your friend that came to visit me. She looks a lot like Catherine, doesn't she?"

"Yeah . . . she does." Julie leaned down and kissed Nora's cheek. "We should go, and let you rest."

"I have to rest up," Nora agreed. "I'm going to get to go home soon."

It was too much. Catherine squeezed her mother's hand and stood up, ready to flee. "It was good to see you," she managed to say.

"It was nice meeting you," her mother said, and Catherine hurried out of the room. David was right behind her, saying something comforting that didn't actually provide any comfort. A moment later, Julie followed. She took one look at Catherine and the two sisters fell into an embrace in the middle of the hallway. Catherine hated crying, hated it worse than anything, but the sobs tore out of her, quiet but intense.

"I know, kiddo, I'm sorry," Julie murmured. "Come on, there's a chapel down the hall; it'll be quieter there."

The four of them made it into the chapel, but by then the worst of the storm had passed. Catherine wiped her eyes. "I'm sorry. Sorry. She's just so different." Seeing her mother was a glimpse into how much worse things might have been for her. For all Catherine's missing memories, she remembered the important things: who she was, who her family was. The three people around her were still *hers*, were still the most important people in her life.

"I don't know if it's worse to have seen it happen gradually or to see it all at once," David said, rubbing her back as they settled into one of the pews in the small room.

"The first time Grandma didn't know who I was, I think I cried for two days." Aimee offered both women a pack of tissues she'd pulled from her purse, after taking one for herself.

Julie took the tissues and gave Catherine one, wiping away a few tears of her own.

"Does she know?" Catherine asked. "Does she ever understand what's happened to her?"

"Not anymore," Julie said. "It was hard when she started getting bad. You'd see moments where she realized what was happening, and she'd get so frustrated and scared. Now . . . she's in her own little world most of the time."

A world where Catherine was dead. And maybe it was better that way for her. She'd grieved and moved on. A world without Catherine was a more settled world. Not just for Nora. Coming back the way she had had turned all her relationships messy and painful and fraught.

"I'm still glad I got to see her." Catherine steadied her breathing and kept it from hitching. "I think I needed to. Do the doctors— what do they say?"

Julie shook her head. "They can't give a firm time frame, but she's withdrawing. She'll keep getting quieter and more still, they say. A few months, maybe less." She sighed. "I didn't want you to miss out on what might be some of the last days that she's talkative."

"Thank you," Catherine said. It was heartfelt, and she hugged Julie tight. "And she knew me for a minute or so at least. Maybe part of her will still remember that."

The sisters held on to each other for a long time, until Catherine had her composure back.

"Come on," Julie said. "Let's get home."

15

CATHERINE RETURNED HOME from Chicago with a new sense of peace and purpose. Nora might not have been able to give her the sense of self she'd hoped for, but she'd been the last piece of the puzzle, the one part of her old life she hadn't come to terms with. Nora's death would be painful, but Catherine could tell herself that Nora knew, somewhere in her mind, that Catherine was still alive. With that as resolved as was possible, Catherine was able to throw herself back into work, the last few days before the launch.

Leah Morrison sat in Catherine's office, leaning forward with the expression of someone relishing the "no shit, there I was" story she was in the middle of telling. "So then, we finally get the poor bastard back down to the ground and he's got the shakes; he's so sick his hands are turning green, but we're supposed to shake his hand and tell him what a great job he did, because you know, he's on the Appropriations Committee, right?"

Catherine laughed and nodded. Dealing with politicians had been the worst. "How bad was it?"

"Girl, he took off that helmet and his lunch went everywhere."

"He threw up right there in front of you?"

"No!" Leah sat back, cackling. "He already had. Sometime while we were flying!"

"You mean he sat there and—"

"Yes!"

Catherine winced but couldn't stop laughing. "How the hell did he manage that without you hearing him?"

"I don't know, but the inside of that helmet was just wrecked, man." Leah grinned at Catherine. "I'll tell you one thing, that was the last time the captain volunteered us to take a civilian on a test run."

"So something good came out of it at least." Catherine saluted Leah with her coffee cup, marveling at how normal it felt.

A knock at her office door put an end to all that.

Cal Morganson stood there with a bland smile. "Sorry to interrupt the pilot bonding time. Leah, can I speak to Catherine?"

Leah stood up. "I've got a briefing I've got to get to. Wells, I'll call you later this week, all right?"

"You bet." Catherine smiled and stood as well.

Once Leah was gone, Catherine expected Cal to ask her to follow him somewhere, but instead he surprised her by closing her door.

"Can I sit?" he asked.

She motioned to the chair Leah had just vacated, and sat back down herself. "What can I do for you?"

"I have some updates to the launch schedule, and I wanted to make sure you saw them." He offered her a piece of paper—a memo she'd already seen earlier that morning.

"I saw it," she said, putting the paper on her desk. "Was there something in particular I needed to pay attention to?"

"No. I just know you were out for a few days." Cal paused awkwardly, and Catherine watched him carefully. Where was the ambush? Which direction would it come from?

"Yeah. Family issue." *Get to the point already.*

"Listen, Catherine, I wanted to apologize. I was . . . out of line before. I hope there are no hard feelings."

"No, of course not. I know you're just doing your job." Cal thought she'd killed five of her closest friends or God knew what else, but sure, there were no hard feelings. Catherine kept the smile on her face. He wasn't going to see a thing from her, not if she could help it.

"I've been, uh, overzealous before. And it seems as if I was here, too. That's really all I wanted to say."

Catherine had no idea how to respond, so she just kept smiling. "Don't worry about it," she finally managed.

"I should go, but . . . thanks."

She watched him leave, and leaned back in her chair. His apology unsettled her almost more than his accusations did. It wasn't that it felt insincere, necessarily. Cal had sounded like a kid who'd been told to apologize to his sister. Not insincere, but also not entirely willing.

Which meant that he'd been talking to some higher-ups about his concern. Aaron, most likely. The thought was a tight hand around her heart. Cal had seen some of her lost time, some of her strangest behavior. How much had he told Aaron?

Aaron must not be interested in pursuing it or he wouldn't have pulled Cal back, but still. How much did NASA know? How long before her house of cards toppled?

Catherine took several deep breaths. Things were fine. She was much better now, moving forward. She hadn't lost any time since the night of Aimee's graduation party. Dr. Darzi had been right—since she'd started focusing more on the present, things *had* improved. She could deal with a bit of NASA gossip.

She picked up the memo Cal had brought her—now certain it was just a ruse to speak to her—and looked it over again. All she could do now was her job, to the best of her ability. She resolved to do just that. She closed her eyes for just a moment, and when she opened them . . .

. . . she was standing in the middle of a room she didn't recognize. She was at a computer, a collection of files open on the screen. The clock on the screen told her it had been nearly two hours since she'd talked to Cal in her office.

Catherine's breath caught and her pulse spiked. *No. No.*

It had happened again.

She was almost afraid to look around, to discover where she'd gone this time. The room was small and dim, and there were rows and rows of file cabinets and shelves lining the walls. Microfiche storage boxes filled the shelves.

The archives. It had to be.

But why? She looked at the documents open on the screen in hopes of finding an answer, but all she saw was page after page of old emergency protocols and procedures, most of them outdated.

Despair crept up her spine, cold fingers on the back of her neck.

There had to be an answer here, but she couldn't see it. She looked around the room, looking for some sign that she'd accessed something else, but no matter where she looked, she could find no clear answer why she'd come in here. None of it made sense. All the Sagittarius-related data was still too new to be in the archives, so it couldn't be anything about that.

Not to mention, how had she even gotten in here? The lock required an access code that she didn't have.

It hit her that security probably kept a log of every time someone accessed the room. There was probably a camera outside the door.

Suddenly the room seemed even smaller, the walls creeping toward her. She had to get out. No one could find out she'd been here. A cold sweat broke out on her forehead, adding to the chill running through her. Not only didn't she have authorized access but some of the information in here was way above her security clearance. If they knew it was her . . . Catherine had a sudden vivid image of security leading her out of the building in handcuffs, handing her over to the feds. Getting caught committing a security violation was the last thing she—or NASA, for that matter—needed. Aaron might be willing to overlook some strangeness on her part, but a security violation? Hell no.

The image of her in handcuffs persisted. She'd lose everything. Aimee. God, she could already see the hurt and disappointment on Aimee's face. She'd lose her job. David could lose his job.

Because who would believe her if she told them she didn't know why she'd come in here?

She hurriedly closed everything on the computer and shut it down.

Her heart hammered painfully in her chest as she peeked out the archive door before exiting. This time the hallway was mercifully empty, and she looked around and up in the corners, but didn't see any sign of a security camera. Still, she didn't start to breathe normally until she was on the elevator. Three people got on at the lobby level. She smiled and said hello. None of them looked at her strangely. By the time she got to her floor, she thought she must have looked fine.

She settled back in at her desk, prepared to tell anyone who asked that she'd just taken a long lunch. Words on her screen seemed to dance in front of her mockingly, and trying to form sentences of her own was completely futile.

It was no use. She couldn't focus on anything, jumping from task to task and expecting at any moment for Cal or even Aaron to storm into her office with security guards demanding to know what she'd been doing in the archives.

Catherine did something she'd done only once before, when Aimee was tiny and had come down with a raging fever. She couldn't face going to Aaron's office to speak to him directly. Instead, she sent an email to the team saying she had to leave, but would keep an eye out for any urgent emails or messages.

She practically slunk out of JSC, praying that no one would talk to her.

16

THE HOUSE WAS quiet when she got home. David was still at work, of course, and Aimee had a summer job at a nearby computer repair shop. The silence was oppressive.

Catherine went to her computer and turned it on, planning to make good on her promise to keep an eye on anything that might need her attention. But even as she sat at her desk in her own home, a sense of impending doom hovered, as if someone were still watching her.

Images flickered through her mind: getting called in front of some sort of committee, or worse, a federal judge. Scandal. Losing Aimee. No matter what she tried to focus on, her thoughts spiraled out of control.

Without thinking about it, she went to the kitchen and poured a glass of wine.

She sat at the breakfast bar with the open wine bottle next to her. Slowly, the worst of the images started to fade. The second glass wiped them away almost entirely. Finally, Catherine was able to sit there in the kitchen and breathe. A third glass was tempting, but now she at least felt able to focus on *something*, so she decided to go with her other favorite method of distraction.

David hadn't gotten rid of any of her belongings while she was gone, and they were all still waiting for her, packed away in the guest room. Now she could go through some of them—all the clothes that were ten years out of date, that didn't fit anymore, that she never liked to begin with.

As she cleaned, she was better able to think through her options. She should tell someone what was happening. She'd kept this in for too long. Even if Dr. Darzi wanted to insist that everything was normal and fine, it wasn't. It couldn't be. Catherine felt as if a random hand were moving her around like a chess piece, and she had no idea if she was a pawn or the queen. Either way, the strategy in play wasn't hers at all.

But Dr. Darzi was employed by NASA. Could Catherine trust her? If not her, then who? The answer was obvious. David. She could tell David. *Let me help you*, he'd said.

Decision made, she threw all her energy into sorting through the closets, drawers, and boxes full of her belongings.

By late afternoon she was sweaty and a little grouchy, but her mind felt clearer, and all the extra stuff that had been stored in the guest room was cleared out and sorted through. And it was worth it: there were several bags of things to donate as well as to toss out.

In the master bedroom, she worked through the dresser drawers, reorganizing, putting things away. Tucked in the back corner of one of those drawers was a black velvet box. Thinking she might have found a piece of old, forgotten jewelry, Catherine pulled it out. The hinges were stiff and it took more effort than she expected to pop it open.

Inside the box was a diamond solitaire in a gleaming platinum setting. It wasn't Catherine's. Her engagement and wedding rings had made the trip to TRAPPIST with her in her Personal Preference Kit—the collection of personal items all astronauts brought on missions—along with photos of her family and a USAF sweatshirt, and were back on her left hand. Besides, she hated platinum. She took the ring out and checked—it was too small for her fingers.

Maggie had small, delicate fingers. And Catherine had seen her wearing platinum jewelry.

She'd known that David had moved on while she was gone. But, knowing it was one thing. Holding the proof in her hand . . . that was something else entirely. All she could do was stand there, staring at the sparkling item in her palm.

"Hey, there you are. Feeling better?"

She jumped out of her skin as David came up behind her, slipped his arms around her waist, and kissed her neck. "I just got home. Aimee's talking about going out again, so it's just going to be us. I was thinking, we could order something in for dinner, settle on the couch—"

She pulled away from him and turned around, unsure what to say.

David's forehead creased as he looked at her, and then at the ring in her hand.

"When were you going to tell me about this?" Catherine asked.

"Catherine, I—"

"Had you already asked her? Were you planning a wedding when I reappeared and messed everything up?" Something bubbled in her chest and she wasn't sure she'd be able to keep it from boiling over this time.

"I hadn't—" David took a breath and stepped back. "We'd talked about it. I hadn't formally proposed yet. We were talking about it after she moved in here, with Aimee and me."

Logically she knew that David and Maggie had slept in the same bed she slept in every night, the same bed David had been about to try to get her into. But that did nothing to calm her irrational anger.

"In here," she said flatly. "In our bed. How could you do that?"

"You were dead!"

"I wasn't dead. I was never dead. I was in hell, David, but I wasn't dead." Nothing she was saying was helping defuse this, but it felt so *satisfying*, like scratching an itch too hard.

"How could I have known that? If you hadn't gone in the first place—"

"You *insisted* that I go! 'You can't miss this opportunity, Cath, it's once in a lifetime.'"

"What else did you expect me to say? You'd already made it abundantly clear that your career came before me and Aimee."

"What the hell does that mean?"

"Come on, Catherine. You weren't content to do space-station missions like everyone else. You had to be more. You applied for the Sagittarius program when Aimee was still a baby. A six-year mission! You didn't have to do that, but before Aimee could even walk, you were planning—*planning*—to leave us."

"David, you met me in the astronaut training program. Did you expect me to stay home all the time and take care of you and the baby? You *knew* before you married me, before we had Aimee, that I'd be gone sometimes. You could have said something then, if you were worried. Why didn't you?"

"I was supposed to go, too!"

Silence fell between them, and then Catherine barked a laugh. "Is that what's been bothering you all this time? What was I supposed to do, David? Fail, just because you did?"

"Oh. Oh, you've been wanting to say that for a long time, haven't you?" David's smile was feral. "Catherine the Great got stuck married to David the Failure."

"That is not fair," Catherine said. "I never felt stuck. I always loved you." Too late, she realized she'd used the past tense.

"Why *would* you feel stuck? You were free to roam the whole fucking cosmos while I stayed home and took care of the baby."

Catherine realized then she was lying. David had been so calm and steady when she'd met him, but after a few years, she realized that "calm and steady" could also mean "stagnant." He never changed, and he'd hoped that she wouldn't either. Catherine put the ring back in its box, closing it with a snap and setting it on the dresser. Then she looked up at her husband. "I thought we were past this, but all this time you've resented me for doing what you couldn't."

"Of course I resented you. You bailed on us."

" 'Bailed' on you? Really, David? Was getting to spend time with our daughter that much of a hardship? Do you know how much time I spent wishing desperately I was with her?"

"No. No, I don't. Because you never fucking *talk to me* about what happened up there."

"And boy, are you really making me want to confide in you right now." Catherine started refolding some of the clothes she'd planned to keep, pulling open a dresser drawer with a sharp jerk.

"When have you ever? Catherine the Great never needed to confide in anyone." Catherine didn't miss the way David picked up the engagement ring box and tucked it in his pocket.

"Stop calling me that."

"You didn't seem to mind when John Duffy called you that."

"And now we're back to the jealousy." Catherine fought the urge to roll her eyes. "David, do you really think what I did is any worse than what hundreds of men who've gone into space long-term have done? If it had been you, do you think anybody would've talked about how you 'bailed' on your family?"

"You're her *mother!*"

Catherine laughed. "Did you really just—" She stopped, unable to believe what she was hearing. "Are you trying to say that it would have been perfectly okay for you to leave us for ten years, but since I'm not a man, I'm the harpy who left her family behind?"

"You can't understand what it was like here then." David rubbed his forehead as if he had a headache. "Cath, I was there in Mission Control the day we lost contact. Initial reports said there might be cooling issues in the Habitat, so we were working on that. I was talking to Michael Ozawa about what we'd discovered, and you all just . . . vanished. Everyone's vitals dropped to zero. Including yours. I thought I'd just watched you die."

"For all I know, I did watch them die, David. Can you understand that? Five of my closest friends. I have no idea what happened to them, or if I even tried to do anything to stop it." The horror of those initial days alone in the ship came rushing back. Realizing that she was almost six months out from the TRAPPIST-1 system with no memory of ever having been there. Sitting in the cockpit again, wondering if she'd abandoned her crew, trying to decide if she could go back to TRAPPIST-1 and still have enough fuel to get home. "You cannot imagine how completely alone I was."

"No, I can't. God, Catherine, the list of things about you I can't understand could stretch from here to Mars." He shook his head. "I don't know if I've ever fully understood you. You're unknowable—you were then, and you are now."

Quietly, a little afraid of the answer, Catherine asked, "Then why did you marry me?"

"Back then I found it intriguing, but now it's just exhausting." David sank to the edge of the bed, sitting down heavily. "We needed you. *I* needed you. And career or no career, you weren't here. Even when you were here, you were never present. Maggie was *here*. She was the one who helped Aimee through her first day of middle school, who sat down with her when she started going through puberty. Maggie did all of that, not you."

Her hands curled into fists. "Maggie was here awfully quick, wasn't she? Middle school? We were barely through the wormhole when Aimee started middle school. What was Maggie doing here *then*?"

David didn't respond at first.

"Which one of you was just waiting for the chance?" She paused, a horrible thought occurring to her. "Was it going on all along? Right under my nose?"

"No! Catherine, I would never do something like that. And if I had—"

Catherine's eyes narrowed dangerously. "If you had, what?"

"Who could blame me? That wasn't what we planned, not at all. We were both supposed to go into space, to take turns—"

"It's not my fault you weren't cut out to be an astronaut."

"I was doing fine! If you had just supported me a little bit more—"

"The way you're supporting me right now?"

"I can't support you if I don't know what happened."

It was like a flood of anger pouring out of her, and out of David. A small part of her felt the quiet, vicious joy of dancing around a funeral pyre. Another part of her felt like this had been inevitable from the moment she'd returned to Earth.

She started to see it in Chicago. In her mother's world, Catherine was dead and gone, and she'd learned to cope with it. The idea of Catherine returning was too much for her, too difficult. Catherine's return had filled a hole in Aimee's life—she'd found her mom again. Julie had gotten her sister back. But David, David was the only one who had lost something when she came home. Like Nora, his world had been turned upside down. Did he really love her anymore, or was it just habit?

"You want to know what happened? You want me to tell you about the hallucinations? How I thought I'd die before I had a chance to see you and Aimee again? That's apparently what Cal wants to hear." She leaned against the dresser and folded her arms. "Or do you want me to tell you about how I slept with Tom Wetherbee?"

He stared at her in shock.

"There. Now you know. The thing I'm hiding that Cal Morganson keeps trying to find. We got drunk one night with the crew, and I screwed him. It happened once, that I know of, and I felt like shit."

"You cheated on me," David said flatly. "With *him*? Jesus, Cath, I didn't think you even *liked* him!"

"I sure as hell wasn't in love with him! Remind me again, had *Sagittarius* cleared the atmosphere before you brought Maggie around, or did you wait a few days?"

They looked at each other. She knew she'd just shattered something between them irreparably—no, to be fair, they'd both shattered it. Catherine waited to see which of them would be the one to say it. When he didn't, she did. "Should I go?"

"Catherine, I didn't want this."

"Neither did I."

She just kept looking at him, waiting for his answer. Finally, David stood up and sighed, resigned. "Yeah. Yeah, I think you should go."

Catherine turned without a word and fetched one of the suitcases from the closet to start packing.

"Where will you go?" David was still standing there, watching her.

"I don't know yet."

"What about Aimee?"

Catherine stopped, holding a half-folded blouse. She sighed. "Can you send her up here? Let me tell her?" *Christ, I'm leaving her again.*

"Fine." David left and Catherine sank down on the bed. She expected that she might cry later, but for now there was nothing, just a slow-growing sense of relief.

"Mom? Dad said you wanted to talk to me?" Aimee caught sight of the suitcase. "What's wrong? Is it Grandma?"

"No, honey. Your grandma's fine." She patted the bed next to her. "Come sit down."

Aimee sat down, but before Catherine could speak, she said, "You're leaving. Why are you leaving?"

"Your father and I just need some time to think about things." There might be a time to share the details with Aimee, but this wasn't it. "It's not anybody's fault."

"It's Maggie, isn't it?"

"Not really, no. I'm not going far," Catherine said. "I'll stay nearby, and you'll be able to come see me and stay with me whenever you want. I love you, and this is not about you at all, you know that, right?"

Aimee threw her arms around her mother's neck. "I don't want you to go. You just got home."

"I know. I know." Catherine stroked her back, closing her eyes against tears. "I have to, though; at least for a little while." Even as she said it, though, Catherine knew her comforting words were delaying the truth; her gut told her she wouldn't be coming back. She'd already lost her crewmates. And now she'd lost her family, too.

Sagittarius I Mission

"You have to stop beating yourself up, Wells." Ava pushed a cup of what passed for tea into the air-lock slot. "None of this is your fault."

"I knew he was acting weird, though." Catherine waited until Ava had sealed the far side before extracting the molded plastic cup, cradling it in her hands, staring into it. The tea was murky and smelled only faintly of tannins, like a memory of real tea from the ancient tea bags they'd brought with them. "I should have been paying attention."

"By that logic, I'm the one at fault," Ava said. "I'm the commander; it's my job to keep track of each of you, and Tom slipped under my radar."

"Do you really think he did all this?"

"We have him on video . . ." Ava paused, considering another possibility. "The only other alternative is that we've got someone else messing around with us, too."

"The oxygenator was months ago . . ." Catherine could barely stand to look at all the pieces laid out in front of them.

"I know." Ava sighed and lowered her forehead to her hands. "I should search his quarters, make sure he hasn't managed to get his hands on anything dangerous."

"Let me come with you and talk to him again."

"Cath, you're in quarantine."

"I know. I'll suit up, go through decontamination again." Regardless of what Ava had to say about it, Catherine couldn't help feeling guilty. "Come on. You know he might talk to me."

"All right. I don't like it, but all right."

That was how Catherine wound up moving through the Habitat in a full decontamination suit as if she were going on an EVA. She knocked on Tom's door. "Tom, it's Catherine. I have Ava and Richie with me. I'm going to open the door, is that all right?"

"Yeah." Tom's reply was faint, sullen. When she opened the door, he looked up at them with dull eyes, giving a small snort at the sight of Catherine. "Whatever this is, it's important enough to drag you out of quarantine, huh?"

"Tom, I'd like to search your quarters," Ava said, without preamble. "I just want to make sure that everyone, including you, is safe."

Richie stood by the door. He was the biggest guy on the crew, so if Tom tried to bolt or, God forbid, fight back . . .

Tom didn't show any signs of fighting back. His shoulders slumped and he stood up, moving away from his bunk. "Sure. Whatever you want."

While Ava searched, Catherine pulled him aside. "I'm sorry about all this," she said. It was hard to radiate sympathy through a pressure suit, but she tried. And Tom looked so utterly lost that the sympathy wasn't a lie.

"Catherine . . . I didn't *do* this," he said quietly. "I swear to you."

"Son of a bitch," Richie said. "You're on video."

Tom grew more agitated. "I don't know why I'm on that tape! I didn't do *any* of this! You have to believe me!"

The look Richie gave him was one of disgust. Ava looked resigned. Catherine . . . she didn't know how she felt. He sounded so sincere it broke her heart.

"There's nothing here that shouldn't be," Ava said. She'd collected a few items with sharp edges, anything that might possibly be used as a weapon. "Come on."

"Catherine, please!"

Catherine followed Ava and Richie out, but the sound of Tom's voice followed her down the hall. "Ava, hang on. Let me talk to him some more."

"I don't think going back in there is a good idea," Richie said.

"I won't go in. I'll talk to him through the door."

Ava sighed. "All right. Come to the mess when you're done. I think we need to get the crew together and have a talk."

Catherine went back to Tom's door. "Tom, it's Catherine. What's going on, really? Can you tell me?"

Tom was silent for such a long time that Catherine didn't think he was going to answer. "I don't know what's going on," he said, so quietly she barely heard him.

"What do you mean?"

"I mean . . . *I don't know*. Cath, something is wrong with me. Really, really wrong." His voice got stronger, as if he moved over to the door but stayed quiet. "I . . . I don't remember doing any of the things that are on the tape. I don't remember messing with any equipment. But I . . . I guess I must have."

Was he lying? Trying to cover his tracks somehow? Catherine didn't think so, but how could she be sure? "I don't understand."

Tom laughed harshly. "Yeah, I don't either." There was a soft thump, as if he'd bumped his head on the other side of the door. "I don't know what I did last night."

"How do you not know?"

"I mean . . . I remember having dinner in the mess with everybody, then going back to my quarters, and then . . . nothing. The next thing I remember is waking up in my bed this morning. It's happened a few times. Like the night before the oxygenator failed."

At first Catherine didn't know what to say. What he was describing was terrifying, both from her perspective and imagining what it must feel like for him. "I-I'm going to have to tell Ava about this, you know that, right?"

"You can tell her, but she's not going to believe me," Tom said dully. "And I don't blame her. I wouldn't believe me either."

"We're going to get to the bottom of this, I swear," she said. "I'll come back when I can, okay?"

When she got to the mess, the others were already gathered.

"I'm just saying we can't keep him in there forever," Claire was saying.

Catherine leaned against the counter, and the other crew members looked at her with varying expressions: Ava looked troubled, Izzy and Richie looked skeptical, poor Claire just looked shaken.

"It's too dangerous," Richie argued. "How many times might he have tried to kill us already? And he nearly succeeded killing one of us this last time. You wanna give him another chance to try again?"

"Did he say anything, Catherine?" Ava asked.

"He's still saying he didn't do anything."

"How the hell does he expect us to believe that?" Izzy asked. "We've all seen the footage."

"I know." Catherine leaned her head back against one of the cabinets and closed her eyes. She sighed. "He says he doesn't remember doing any of it. And that he's . . . well, that he's lost time. Waking up in his bed and not remembering how he got there. That sort of thing."

"So which is it? Is he saying he didn't do anything, or that he doesn't *remember* doing anything?" Claire asked.

"He's saying both," Catherine said.

"Convenient amnesia." Izzy folded his arms. "I've been doing medical workups on all of you regularly, and I haven't found a single thing wrong with any of you."

"Would some sort of trauma-based amnesia show up on an exam, though?" Ava asked. "Are there any tests you can give him?"

"We don't exactly have the facilities for a full diagnostic battery of tests," Izzy said. "I mean, I can test him for a few things, but . . . the thing about amnesia and fugue states—which are what he's describing—is that they're really fucking easy to fake. How am I supposed to say, 'Yes you do *so* remember what happened'?"

"Ava," Claire said quietly, "don't you think it's time we stopped trying to deal with this ourselves and got NASA involved?"

"I tried." Ava ran her fingers through her cropped hair. "The comms are now completely down. I couldn't send a message of any sort."

"The comms are down? What, did Tom sabotage *them*, too?" Richie said.

"Shit." Izzy looked around the table. "What if he's been doing that all along? What if NASA's been sending us messages and he's just . . . not sharing them?"

The five of them fell silent.

"We don't know for sure that he did anything to them," Catherine protested. "What he's done is worrisome, yeah, but . . . maybe we shouldn't start blaming him for everything." *Not yet.*

"Oh, of course. Of course you're going to stick up for him," Izzy said with an eye roll.

"What do you mean?" Catherine had a sinking feeling she knew exactly what he meant.

"*Sagittarius* is a small ship, Catherine. You think we didn't know the two of you were sleeping together on the trip out?"

"Look," Catherine said, then paused, realizing she was about to defend the indefensible. "Yeah, okay. We did. Once! It was New Year's Eve and I was drunk. Then I told him it couldn't happen again. I know it was a mistake, and it never should have happened."

"Wait a minute," Richie interrupted. "That's when he started acting distant and grouchy. And it got worse when we landed. Are you saying that all of this happened because you screwed him?"

"No!" That couldn't be it. Catherine refused to believe that. "The thing is, no matter what he did, and no matter what happened between the two of us, if we're going to get a message to NASA, we're going to have to let him out at some point. We need him."

"Maybe *you* need him," Izzy sneered.

"Doc, come on," Claire tried to interject.

"No, I mean it." He turned to Catherine. "Your boyfriend might be trying to kill us because you felt guilty and now you're feeling guilty about *that*, so you're trying to believe he's innocent. And you expect us to just trust you. To trust him."

"It's not like that!" Catherine's temper was quickly fraying. "If you had talked to him, you would have seen how rattled he is by this. I don't believe he's lying."

"And I'm supposed to just trust my ass with him because he gave you a big sad puppy-dog look?"

"Enough." Ava cut them both off. "Catherine isn't wrong. We don't know for sure that he's deliberately and consciously done anything to hurt us. But more important, he's the only one who can get us back in touch with NASA. As long as the comms are down, we can't tell them anything."

Richie spoke up. "And if he's the one who sabotaged the comms in the first place?"

"Well, if he was," Ava said, "then he'll know better than anybody else how to fix them. It's in his interest, too. He agrees to fix the comms, we let him out—for a little while at least." She looked around at all of them. "Look, we need to get in touch. This is the sort of thing NASA ends missions over. But it's too big for me to make the call alone. I'm not calling an abort until I've heard from Mission Control. Are we clear?"

The four of them nodded, the men grudgingly.

"All right," Ava said. "Richie, Catherine, come with me. We're gonna see if Tom is in the mood to bargain."

"You're gonna fucking get us all killed," Izzy muttered. "Just watch."

17

CATHERINE YAWNED AND rubbed her eyes, squinting at her office computer. Last night, she'd tossed and turned, unable to get comfortable in the hotel bed that was hers for the foreseeable future; there was no time between now and the launch to find an apartment.

Her phone beeped and she saw a text from Aimee: *there's a new apt complex not far from house. U looked there yet?*

Catherine smiled. Aimee seemed to be taking things in stride so far, eager to help Catherine find a place to settle. Aimee was so perceptive that Catherine wouldn't have been surprised at all if she had seen this coming. God knew Catherine should have.

No, I didn't know about it, she replied. *Text me the address?*

Aimee loved to give her shit about how she texted in complete sentences with proper punctuation, but Catherine had never gotten the hang of abbreviating everything.

She took a sip of her lukewarm coffee and turned her attention back to her computer. She was going to be one of the flight controllers on launch day, a first for her. Tradition said the CAPCOM desk—short for Capsule Communicator, although there hadn't been a "capsule" launched in decades—should be staffed by an astronaut, and as the only surviving member of Sagittarius I, Catherine wasn't just the logical choice, she was the only real choice. When John Duffy radioed the call sign "Houston" on launch day, Catherine would be the one who answered him.

The role was an extremely visible one, one that she'd never have been given if anyone at NASA knew about her blank periods. To distract herself from the fear that she might have one of those spells on launch day, she threw herself into memorizing all the protocols.

An hour later, she picked up her mug and walked to the kitchen area down the hall, smiling at Aaron on autopilot as she passed him.

"Catherine!" The voice was far away and not immediately identifiable.

She stuck her head out into the hallway to see if she could tell where it had come from, her brow furrowing.

After a moment or two, it came again, more impatient. "Catherine, come on!"

The mug of coffee fell out of her fingers, which had gone suddenly nerveless, and shattered on the tile floor.

The voice was Tom Wetherbee's.

That's impossible.

"Let me out already! Be reasonable!"

Catherine's heart pounded. It sounded as if the voice was coming from the end of the hall, down past her office. The only things down there were the stairwell and a supply closet. Was someone playing a cruel joke? Catherine walked down the hall, forgetting the broken mug.

The voice didn't sound again right away. The stairwell was empty. No sounds of movement. No voice. Catherine pushed open the door to the supply closet, heart in her throat. She fumbled for the light switch. No one was in there.

"Catherine?"

This time the voice came from behind her, and Catherine jerked in surprise. But the voice wasn't Tom's. She turned around to see John Duffy standing there, a concerned look on his face. "You okay?"

"John. Yeah, you just startled me."

"Is that your mug on the floor?"

Catherine gave him an embarrassed smile. "Clumsy me. I-I was looking for something to clean it up with."

"Don't worry, I called Facilities; they're sending someone up." Before she could thank him, he said, "Are you sure you're all right? I, um, heard about you and David. I'm sorry."

Sometimes the rumor mill around here moved faster than the rockets. "Thanks. I guess nearly a decade apart was just too long."

"Well, listen, if you ever need someone to talk to," he said, smiling wryly, "or need someone to recommend a good divorce lawyer, just let me know." She must have looked surprised, because he added, "Come on, you have to know how high the divorce rate is around here."

"Oh," Catherine said. "Um, thank you."

She escaped back to her office as quickly as she could, the strain of keeping a normal face on wearing on her too much. Tom's voice hadn't come from anywhere but her own mind. Dr. Darzi would dismiss this hallucination as a completely normal response to trauma. Catherine could probably have a screaming, ranting breakdown in Darzi's office and she'd sit there and say the same thing.

Hell, maybe it was.

But what if Tom's voice was coming from a memory? What if it had really happened? *What if* what *really happened? You locked him up somewhere?*

That didn't make sense. It was just her guilt over the affair bubbling to the surface.

The problem was, it didn't stop once she went back to her hotel that night.

As she was waiting in line for her takeout, she heard him again.

"Catherine! This isn't fair!"

It was so loud and sharp she jumped, looking around. No one else reacted at all. Trembling, she paid for her food and raced back to her hotel, the radio turned up to full volume to drown out any noise—real or imagined.

Once in her room, she had a bottle of wine with dinner, and the voice stopped. Blissful silence. And when she slept that night, she actually *slept.*

The voice was back the next day, so she took a couple of the miniature bottles from the minibar to work with her, tucked in her purse. She told herself it was "just in case." And just until after the launch. Then she'd have time to figure everything out.

By the end of the day, both bottles were gone, but so was Tom's voice.

18

THE ASTRONAUTS' LAUNCH-DAY breakfast was a long-standing tradition. Half the crew—Commander Duffy, Kevin Park, and Leah Morrison—had done this multiple times before for shorter missions, while Grace Kowalski, Zach Navarro, and Nate Royer were all relative rookies, with one or two missions apiece.

Cal was the only true rookie of the bunch. This was his first launch-day breakfast, joining the crew with Aaron and a few of the other support staff. It was embarrassing how ... *emotional* he was. They were sitting in the same room where the greats ate breakfast before heading out: Glenn, Armstrong, Ride, and all the rest. Some of them had never come back. Everyone acted as if it were no big deal, as if this momentous thing that they'd been planning for years wasn't about to happen.

In a nod to tradition, all the Sagittarius II astronauts had ordered the favorite steak-and-scrambled-eggs breakfast, except their lone vegetarian, Kowalski, who stuck with the eggs. It was just as well, because she barely ate anything anyway, but kept a resolute "I'm absolutely fine" look on her face nonetheless. They all did. Including Cal.

He'd done everything he could to prepare his crew. He'd done absolutely everything in his power to make certain that no issues from Sagittarius I would harm them. The rest was out of his hands. That wasn't easy for him to acknowledge, but if he'd learned anything working for NASA, it was that there were always some things that had to be left to chance. He watched the minutes count down on the clock, wondering what random things might crop up on this mission.

When it was time for the crew to suit up, Cal had a chance to say goodbye to each of them.

John Duffy was the first, and gave Cal a hearty handshake and a slap to the shoulder that threatened to knock him off his feet.

"Keep 'em in line up there, Commander," Cal said.

Duffy gave him a salute and a grin. "You know it."

Morrison was next, and she already had her game face on. Of course. While the others would mostly be passengers for a bit, Morrison would bear the brunt of the responsibility following the launch. To keep from distracting her, Cal just offered a handshake. She looked at his hand, then cocked an eyebrow at him before hauling him into a hug. "Relax," she said in his ear. "You look like you're about to get your ass kicked or something. We got this, all right?"

"All right," he confirmed.

When Morrison pulled back she was smiling. "Better. See you, man."

He said good-bye to Navarro, Park, and Kowalski in turn, a lump forming in his throat. He kept it hidden from them under his smile.

Nate was last, and Cal couldn't resist needling him. "Saw you were late for breakfast. You oversleep or something?"

"Nah, I had to make sure I was looking just right before I made my appearance." They clasped hands and pulled each other into a hug, one that was tighter than Cal intended. Nate picked up on it and pulled back with a frown. "You okay?"

"Yeah." Cal cleared his throat. "Yeah, I'm fine. Prelaunch jitters. You know how it is." He tried on a grin and it almost fit. "Dude, my best friend is leaving for six years, I'm allowed to have a feeling or two about it."

"Think of all the stories we'll have to swap when I get back." He gave Cal's shoulder a shake. "Just don't screw up the launch, all right? After that, it's all down to us."

"That's what I'm worried about," Cal teased.

"Yeah, well, next time you can haul *your* ass out there if you don't like the way we do things."

That made Cal laugh, and he felt a bit of tension drain away. "Yeeeeah, I think that ship's sailed, my friend. I'm gonna keep my feet right down here."

"Then quit bitching." Nate gave Cal one last swat to the arm and then turned to go. "See ya."

"You bet." Cal kept smiling, and kept the worry off his face. *I hope I will.*

———

Mission Control buzzed with activity as Aaron and Cal entered the last planned hold of the countdown. Once the clock started again, if all went well, in nine minutes the ship would launch, and the Sagittarius II mission would be underway. Cal tried to focus on his job, tried not to think about how his friends were sitting on top of a giant explosive device, and that this was the biggest moment of his career so far. He'd never sat in one of the flight-controller desks in Mission Control before, and here he was, at the Flight Activities Officer desk, a few minutes away from his first launch. He focused on the display in front of him, determined to do this right.

"Two, stand by for go/no go." Catherine's voice came through his head-set. She was seated next to Aaron at the CAPCOM desk.

"Roger, Houston, standing by." Commander Duffy was terse, no doubt focused on the next nine minutes.

Cal hadn't argued against using her as CAPCOM for the launch. But he didn't like it, and from the tension he felt radiating against his back, it seemed she wasn't exactly at ease either.

"Attention Sagittarius II flight controllers." Aaron sounded as calm as ever, but then this wasn't his first launch. "Give me a go/no go for launch . . . FIDO?"

"Go," the flight dynamics officer replied.

"RENDEZVOUS?"

"Go."

Cal listened to the check, his heart in his throat. If they passed this check, the only thing that would stop the launch now would be a major emergency. This was the last real hurdle to clear.

"FAO?" Aaron's voice in his ear.

If Cal said "no go" the countdown would remain stopped. He could stall things. Maybe halt them. But despite his reservations, despite everything he'd been worried about, he had no real proof. Aaron had shown him that much. Cal had no real other option. "Go."

"PAYLOAD?"

"We're a go."

Aaron cycled through the entire Mission Control team, finally reaching Catherine. "CAPCOM?"

"Go."

Did she have some of the same doubts he did? Cal wondered. She didn't seem to be at one hundred percent these days. Her skin was sallow and she had dark circles under her eyes. She sat slumped over her desk, her lips drawn in a tight frown.

"Launch Control, this is Houston," Aaron said. "We are go for launch."

"Roger, Houston!"

Launch Control took over, going through their own checks. Cal kept his focus on the displays in front of him, looking for any sign of trouble. From the intercom overhead, he could hear the public affairs officer, sometimes called the Voice of NASA, continuing the countdown for the benefit of the observers gathered around the complex. Each time a launch position was called, Cal couldn't help the small hope that someone would call a no go, but no one did.

"Start the clock," Aaron said.

"Ladies and gentlemen, we are nine minutes and counting," the PAO said as the clock started.

At T-5 minutes, Launch Control armed the rockets that would carry *Sagittarius* away from Earth and activated the auxiliary power. Cal could barely breathe, certain his heart was loud enough for the flight controller next to him to hear.

At T-2 minutes, the crew closed their visors and sealed up their suits. Cal felt as if he might throw up.

At T-31 seconds, the launch autosequencer started. Everything was out of his hands at this point. Normally that would be maddening, but right now things were so far out of his hands that even he was able to let go. Cal felt a strange, sudden sense of calm.

At T-15 seconds, the PAO started counting down over the intercom. Cal felt as if he were floating, weightless in space himself.

"... Ten, nine, eight, seven, six. Ignition sequence starts. Three, two, one. Ignition."

Then the calm broke and the tension in the room heightened. Eighteen flight controllers and Aaron, not to mention the world watching outside, held their breath as the rockets under *Sagittarius* bloomed orange and the massive launch structure began to separate, allowing *Sagittarius* to leave the ground.

"The clock is running," Commander Duffy confirmed.

"We have liftoff!" the PAO told the crowd outside, and Cal could hear faint cheering over the Launch Control comm loop. No one in Mission Control was celebrating, not yet. They still had work to do, but they did allow themselves the luxury of glancing around and exchanging smiles. Cal grinned at Aaron, and then Catherine smiled at him, wary but friendly.

Cal couldn't bring himself to smile back. He now had six years of anxious waiting to get through before his crew came back safely, and he still didn't trust that Catherine had told him everything he needed to know to bring them home.

19

"I SAW YOU on TV talking about the launch. You looked great, Mom."

Aimee and Catherine were putting away groceries in Catherine's new apartment. It was small and dim compared to the bright, airy house she'd left behind in Clear Lake, but, Catherine told herself, it was all hers. And it was in the complex Aimee had picked out for her, close to David's house. It was odd how easy it was to think of it as David's and not hers already. Aimee had come over for the weekend, ostensibly to help Catherine unpack and get organized, but Catherine got the feeling that her daughter was checking up on her.

That was fair enough. Catherine would have been worried, too.

"Thanks." She smiled faintly as she tried to figure out which tiny cabinet should serve as a pantry. "Paul finally managed to talk me into it, so now I'm NASA's go-to for all things Sagittarius these days."

"That's good, though, right?" Aimee was on her knees on the tile floor, rearranging the refrigerator, what little there was in it. If Aimee noticed the many bottles of wine in the fridge and cupboard, she didn't comment. Catherine had finally figured out the exact amount of alcohol it took throughout the day to maintain the silence in her head. It wasn't as much as she feared, and she was able to keep from actively drinking during working hours. She hadn't heard Tom's voice since the launch.

"Yeah. Yeah, it's a good thing." NASA was pretty much all she had these days. Cal Morganson hadn't confronted her directly again. But there was still that strange moment after the launch, when he just stared at her instead of smiling. He didn't talk to her afterward, either, as the flight controllers offered each other congratulations. She got the feeling that while he wasn't actively antagonistic toward her anymore, he was still keeping a close watch on her. "How are things going for *your* big move?"

"It's okay." She grinned up at Catherine. "You know me, I have lists on top of lists and then a list of all my lists. You're still planning to come help me move in, right?"

"Of course. I wouldn't miss it for anything."

Aimee was quiet for a few minutes and then asked, "Even if Dad comes, too?" She stood and dusted off her knees.

"Of course." Catherine sensed something behind that, some bigger topic of conversation, and she wasn't sure she was ready for that just yet.

"Mom, are you two ever going to talk to each other again?"

She and David hadn't spoken much, beyond what was required for joint parenting and for occasionally working together. "So what classes are you taking this fall?" Catherine deflected.

Aimee sighed but went along with the new subject. "Yeah. Calculus, for sure. It's probably going to kick my ass, but I need it as a prereq for pretty much everything."

"Didn't you take AP Calculus in high school? Why do you have to take it again?"

Aimee gathered up the empty grocery bags. "This is more advanced stuff. I actually got to skip a couple of the intro classes thanks to my AP credits."

"Well . . . there're tutors, right? Don't forget to ask for help if you need it."

"You're one to talk."

There was a chill in those words, and Catherine stopped rummaging through the pile of take-out menus she'd already collected and looked at Aimee more closely. "What do you mean?"

"Dad." Aimee closed the refrigerator door with more force than necessary, and Catherine could see the tension rippling through her as she fought to hold back. "Don't think I didn't notice you dodging my question. Did you ask for any sort of help at all to fix things with him? Do you *ever* ask for help?"

"Aims . . . I don't know if I'm ready to talk about this yet."

"You can't avoid it forever."

"I'm not avoiding it. It's just— none of this has been easy, with the launch, and your grandma, and then moving—"

"Just tell me this." Aimee angrily shoved the paper bags into the recycling bin. "Did you even try? You guys were fine! We were a family! One little fight and you just walk out on us again?"

Ready or not, it looked like they were having this conversation right now. Catherine leaned her hip against the kitchen counter and folded her arms. "Honey, your dad and I . . . we did try. But we were apart for almost ten years, and . . . in that time, we both changed. Your father moved on."

"But you were married for almost twenty years!" Aimee's hurt was written all over her face, and it broke Catherine's heart.

"I know, sweetheart. But we spent half of that time apart." Catherine hated like hell that Aimee was learning that loving someone wasn't always enough to make a relationship work.

"So, you just gave up on us."

"Aimee. Aimee, no, I will never, ever give up on you. No matter what happens between your father and me, you are my daughter and I will always be here for you."

"Sure, the way you've always been here. Except for that one time, for nine years." Aimee walked out of the kitchen and Catherine followed her.

"Aimee—"

"You and Dad are both adults, and if the two of you can't fix a relationship after being apart for so long, how am I supposed to be able to? How am I ever going to be able to trust that you're really my mom again?"

Catherine paused in the kitchen doorway, searching for the answer. "It's . . . it's a different relationship, Aimee. I'm always going to be your mom." It was a weak answer, but it was all she had.

"You know, this is supposed to be the most exciting time of my life. I'm going to college! It's scary and fun and everything's new—and instead of focusing on that, I'm stuck dealing with this shit." Aimee crossed her arms over her chest. "I don't know why I came here. You don't need me."

"I'm not supposed to need you!" Catherine snapped. "That's not how this works!"

"You don't need anybody. You never have, have you?"

Aimee was parroting David's words back to her. Had he been talking to her about Catherine? "Did you hear that from your father?"

"No! Mom, I'm not a child anymore. I can see things for myself."

"That's not fair—"

"Why did you come home if you were just going to leave again? It was easier when you were dead. Why didn't you just die?"

Catherine smacked Aimee across the face. It was like watching it from outside herself, watching her hand fly up and back and not being able to stop it.

Aimee stared at her with wide eyes for a moment, and Catherine stared back, the stinging of her hand and the red mark on Aimee's cheek the only evidence of what had happened.

"Aimee—"

"I'm going home." Aimee snatched up her purse and headed for the door.

"Please, no, wait—" Catherine reached for her and Aimee whirled.

"Don't touch me."

For a frightened moment, Catherine didn't know the girl in front of her, and thought she might strike back. Aimee turned and left without another word, leaving Catherine to stare at the closed apartment door.

Oh God, what have I done?

She sank onto the couch, horrified at herself, at her loss of control. At the way she'd hurt the one person she was trying not to hurt. *David. I have to call him.*

She scrambled for her cell phone and dialed David's number. It went straight to voice mail, and she realized he was probably already talking to Aimee. "David, it's Catherine. Aimee and I had a fight; she's coming over there now. Please take care of her. And . . . and if she'll listen, please tell her how sorry I am." She hung up, too ashamed to tell him what she'd done.

You're just terrible at relationships in general, aren't you?

Catherine froze. *Tom.* "Leave me alone!"

I mean, I thought it was just me, but no. Now I see it wasn't me at all. It was you, Catherine. It's always been you. You're the fuckup.

Without thinking, she found herself in the kitchen, grabbing a glass and the open bottle of chardonnay in the refrigerator. She filled the glass and went back to the battered secondhand couch in the living room, her hand flexing against the fading sting. One glass helped a bit. Two, and she felt a little more in control of herself. By the time she'd finished the bottle and started a second one, Tom was quiet, dinner forgotten, and she'd ignored three phone calls. As she stared blankly at some sitcom on her tiny television, there was nothing in her mind but a soft, blissful hum.

20

AFTER THE FIGHT with Aimee, Catherine stopped sleeping almost entirely. The wine wasn't always enough to keep the nightmares and Tom's voice at bay.

She stayed up and watched bad TV, drinking until she either passed out on the couch or fell asleep from sheer exhaustion. Sleep brought an increasingly unpleasant selection of dreams: slapping Aimee; Aimee telling everyone at her funeral she was glad Catherine was dead; killing the entire crew of *Sagittarius I*, laughing the entire time.

Last night, she'd dreamed about Tom. He was sitting on one of the acceleration couches on board *Sagittarius*. He was dead, his eyes filmed over, his skin pale and faintly green. There were burns down one side of his face.

When he turned to look at her, the burns glinted in the light.

"It's always been your fault," he whispered. "Why did you leave us all to die?"

"I didn't mean to," she whispered, stricken.

"You should have let me out." He stood up and reached for her. "You should have died with us."

Catherine jerked awake before he touched her, and stared blindly up at her ceiling until it was time to go to work.

The hours she spent at JSC were a special form of hell. She'd managed to keep her drinking confined to her off-hours, sometimes sneaking a glass or two of wine with lunch. But as time went on, that stopped working. She started hearing Tom's voice again, yelling for her to let him out, accusing her of leaving him to die.

Maybe it was inevitable that one morning she filled her travel mug with something other than coffee. Wine wasn't concentrated enough to get her through the day in an easily portable form, so she filled it with vodka instead.

She promised herself she'd drink it only if she absolutely needed it.

It was a rough day. Her office was too quiet. With the launch well past, there wasn't anything to help her keep focused. By noon, the mug was half-empty. Catherine idly sorted and cleaned out her email inbox, feeling the pleasant, warm glow of the vodka. She should drink this more often at home. It felt so much more soothing than the wine.

The fuzzy, blank feeling was interrupted by her phone buzzing to remind her of a mission-status meeting for Sag II staff. *Shit, shit, shit.* How could she have forgotten it?

She stood up, and things stayed relatively steady. All right. She could do this. It shouldn't be a long meeting. She could just sit in the back and sneak out when it was over. *And stop drinking for the afternoon, Cath. Seriously.*

The huge conference room was crowded with all the engineers, admin staff—everyone with a hand in Sagittarius II at all. David would be around here somewhere. His department had worked on some of the communications systems. Catherine ducked down in her seat to avoid seeing him.

Aaron Llewellyn entered and went to the portable lectern at the front of the room. Stragglers found seats, and Catherine put her most attentive face on.

"All right, I'll try to keep this brief," Aaron said into the mic. "Everything is A-okay with the crew. They're on schedule to hit their planned arrival at ERB Prime."

A small cheer went around the room. Aaron went on, checking in with various department heads. Catherine fought to stay awake.

She started when she heard her name. "As some of you may not have heard," Aaron was saying, "Catherine has been our expert spokesperson for Sagittarius II, and has already made several media appearances to try to make the mission more relatable to the general public." He smiled at her, and Catherine had a sinking sensation in the pit of her stomach. "I hate to put you on the spot like this, but why don't you give us a quick rundown of how it's going?"

This was like that old nightmare of showing up at school naked. Oh God, she was much too drunk for this. What the hell had she been thinking? She stood and dropped her forgotten notebook, scrambling to pick it up as one of the AV techs handed her a mic. Everyone swiveled to look at her.

"Um. Good. It's going good." Was she slurring? She tried speaking very carefully. "After the— Right after the launch the major networks all wanted news—I mean, they wanted interviews. More information. It's slowed down. Wo-once the ship reaches the bridge, it'll get busy again." Catherine couldn't judge how well she was doing from anyone's face. Couldn't tell if she'd faked her way through it or not. Had she said enough? That was probably enough. She handed the mic back to the tech and sat down, her face on fire.

"Uh, thank you for the update," Aaron said with a frown, and Catherine realized she'd blown it.

She spent the rest of the meeting swallowed up with dread, the anxiety making her more sober by the minute. When the meeting ended, she fled to the refuge of her office. The travel mug sat on her desk, mocking her.

Later that afternoon she got the knock on her door she'd been expecting since the meeting.

Aaron stood in her open door. "Catherine, can I talk to you for a sec?"

"Sure, come on in."

"Let's go to my office."

Catherine's heart sank. It was worse than she thought. She followed him like a condemned woman, feeling as if every eye was on her as they went down the hall.

Once inside his office, he invited her to sit and then just looked at her. Finally he said, "Was that the first time you've been drunk at work?"

Catherine started to argue that she wasn't drunk, but knew it wouldn't do any good. "I'm sorry. I don't know what I was thinking. It won't happen again."

"You've had a lot going on lately. I won't ask how you're doing. I can see how you're doing." He gave her a rueful smile. "I know what a hangover looks like when you're trying to hide it, and you've been having a lot of rough mornings."

"Aaron, I—"

"Catherine, you don't want to go down that road. I've been there. You'd be surprised how many of us have." He was looking at her with sympathy, and she'd almost rather he was angry with her. "I want you to take some time off."

"I can't. I know this is a bad time right now—"

"You said yourself that you're in a lull right now until *Sagittarius* reaches ERB Prime. I don't want to say I'm suspending you, but if anybody's earned a leave of absence, it's you." Aaron gave her a stern look. "Take the time, Catherine. Go to some support meetings if you have to. Get yourself back together. Okay?"

Bitterness flooded Catherine's mouth and she felt something surging forward, like a tidal wave she couldn't stop. There was a letter opener on Aaron's desk.

Pick it up.

The voice wasn't hers. She remembered wanting to hurt Cal and the engineer in the hallway outside the archives, seeing them as monsters. *Oh, not again.*

Instead of a sympathetic, concerned boss, Catherine saw a pale, shapeless mass of flesh and had an overwhelming urge to strike out.

Pick it up.

Her fingers itched to touch the cool metal object, already anticipating violence, while part of her wanted to scream. *Not here, oh God please, not here . . .*

She tore her eyes away from the letter opener with an agonizing wrench and realized Aaron was still waiting for her answer. He was offering it as a choice, but she knew better. "How long?"

"We'll figure that out as we go. For now, let's say three weeks."

God. She'd go mad if she had to sit at home for that long. *You almost stabbed your boss with a letter opener. That ship has sailed.* She nodded. What else could she do? She was damn lucky he wasn't firing her. If she wasn't such a public figure, she had no doubt he would have.

"Okay," Aaron said, standing up. "Go on home. And if there's anything I can do to help you—*anything*—I want you to call me. Day or night."

Catherine stood as well, and accepted the hand he extended to her. "I will."

"I mean it. We will do whatever it takes to take care of you. We look after our own."

He wasn't wrong, but it wasn't altruism, either. Damaged astronauts were bad PR, and that was especially true of her.

21

WHEN CATHERINE ARRIVED back at her apartment, she saw the mess with fresh eyes. There were empty wine bottles everywhere, take-out containers piling up, and something in the trash that needed to go out, *now*. Catherine sighed and put her things down before grabbing a garbage bag from the kitchen and starting on the worst of the mess.

It must not have taken long for the news to spread around NASA. She hadn't been home two hours, spending most of that trying to reclaim her apartment, before she got a call from David. Oh Christ, David had been at the meeting this afternoon. She couldn't bear the thought of talking to him. Or to anybody. She was much too ashamed of herself. He called three times before he stopped, and she wanted to collapse with relief.

The following days were a blur—not because Catherine lost time, but because she spent as much of her time away from work being as drunk as possible. Despite Aaron's warnings, it was just easier that way. She didn't go back to the vodka. She comforted herself with that. It was only wine. That made a difference, didn't it? Either way, the voices stopped. When she slept, she didn't have any dreams, and there was no suggestion that she was wandering at night, either. While she was awake, she felt . . . peaceful. Hazy but peaceful.

Aimee still refused to return her calls. If that bridge wasn't already burned behind her, it was smoldering. It wasn't the only one. David came by and knocked on the door several times, but she told him to go away. She'd sent Julie's calls to voice mail more times than she could count. Catherine felt as if she were carrying a box of matches around with her, ready to throw lit ones at every bridge she saw, with the slightest provocation. For the first time since coming home, she thought about just . . . leaving everything. Ditching

NASA, ditching what was left of her family, and just going. Some days, all that kept her in one place was not having any idea where she wanted to go.

It was a Friday night, and Catherine was sitting on her couch, contemplating what it would be like to live in a trailer in the middle of nowhere. The glass of cheap cabernet sauvignon in her hand was so astringent that she could probably have cleaned her face with it. She'd started going to different stores to buy wine now, hoping to avoid that look from the cashiers, the one that said, "Back already?" It didn't matter, though; she was warm and glowing inside, halfway to the pleasant haze she was looking for.

A knock at her door startled her out of her reverie. Who would possibly come to see her? Hadn't David given up already? With Aimee not speaking to her and the only other friends she had either dead or far away from Earth on a spaceship, nobody should be at her door. Wrong apartment, she thought, a little blearily, and ignored it.

"Cath? Are you in there? I can hear the TV going. Come on, it's Julie. Let me in."

That cut through her haze. Catherine set her glass aside, blinking slowly, and pushed to her feet. "Julie? What are you doing here? Is Mom okay?" She undid the flimsy locks and slipped the chain, then opened the door.

Julie stood there with just her purse, no sign of luggage, and her eyes wide. "Cath, what the hell is going on? I got calls from both David and Aimee. David said you wouldn't answer the door. They're worried sick about you."

"I'm fine." Catherine swung the door open to let Julie in. "We just had a fight."

"You don't look fine." Julie gave her the worried big-sister look. "You've been dodging everybody's calls. I came to check on you."

"From Chicago."

"Yes, from Chicago. Cath, I don't think you know how freaked out everyone is. Why are you avoiding our calls?"

"Does David know you're here?" Catherine bristled, feeling defensive. Were they all going to gang up on her now?

"I called him before I left Chicago. When you wouldn't talk to me either, I didn't know what else to do. What's going on?"

"Haven't felt like talking." Catherine turned to go back to her seat on the couch, stumbling over the coffee table. "Bottle of wine on the counter if you want a glass," she said, picking hers up. "It's kinda shitty, though. I wouldn't."

"You're drunk."

Catherine lifted her glass in salute. "End of the week. Time to celebrate."

Julie came around the table—managing not to trip—and sat next to Catherine, plucking the glass out of her hand. "You look like hell," she said brusquely. "And David said you showed up at work drunk."

"Well . . ." Catherine reached for the glass, but Julie wouldn't hand it over, so she just went to the kitchen for a new one. "Turns out I was a shit astronaut, then I came home and found out I was a shit wife. And guess what? I'm a pretty shitty mom, too." She came back and took a sip from her new glass. "Can't pick wine worth a damn either."

Julie sniffed the glass she was holding and wrinkled her nose before setting it on the coffee table. "So, you're throwing yourself a great big pity party?"

"Just until I figure out what else I wanna do."

"Meanwhile, your kid's not talking to you."

"I don't blame her. I walked out on her for nine years. Then you know what I did? I hit her. Slapped her right across the face." Catherine blinked rapidly, determined not to cry. "I wouldn't wanna talk to me either."

"Did it occur to you to apologize?" Julie asked.

"I tried." The truth was, Catherine had started to dial Aimee's number dozens of times more than she actually managed to call. The times she didn't chicken out and actually made the call, Aimee didn't answer. She was almost grateful. She couldn't bear the thought of Aimee hanging up on her.

"Catherine, you're the grown-up here. If you let this go, you are going to lose her." Julie touched her arm. "Look at me."

Reluctantly, Catherine turned to look at her big sister.

"Have you talked to your therapist about this at all? Any of this?"

Catherine shrugged. "I haven't seen her since Aimee was here."

"And you didn't call her?"

"Didn't see the point. I was wrong. I don't need a professional to tell me that." She could just imagine how Dr. Darzi would tsk at her over the whole mess.

"No, but a professional might give you some ideas on how to fix things. Why don't you call her?"

Uh-oh. Catherine knew that tone in Julie's voice. In about a minute, Julie was going to offer to make the call for Catherine, but either way, neither of them was leaving this room until someone called Catherine's therapist.

"Julie . . ."

"Catherine . . ." Julie said in the same tone. "You know I'm right. Where's your phone?"

"It's Friday night; she won't be available."

Julie didn't relent. "Then we'll leave a message."

"I can't call her. I'm drunk." Catherine had a line of excuses ready to keep throwing out.

"I'm sure she's gotten drunk calls from clients before. Come on." She stood up. "Don't make me call David and get the number from him. Phone, *now*."

God, they *were* ganging up on her. She could hear the smug tone in David's voice already. Catherine sighed. "My purse. Hand it here." She pointed vaguely in the direction she remembered leaving it.

Julie handed it to her and she dug out her phone. There was no way out of it now.

Dr. Darzi insisted on seeing her the next morning, even though it was a Saturday. And then, to make sure she didn't avoid it, Julie drove her to JSC for the appointment. Which was probably just as well. Catherine's hangover wasn't the worst she'd had, but it was bad enough.

"I was wondering when you'd come see me," Dr. Darzi said. "I was concerned when you canceled your last appointment."

"There's been a lot going on."

"That sounds like an understatement. I heard about you and David. I'm so sorry, Catherine."

Catherine wasn't surprised that she knew. "That's not the worst of it. I . . . I had a terrible fight with my daughter."

"Why don't you tell me about it?"

Catherine didn't want to. But this was why she was here, wasn't it? "She was at my new place, helping me unpack groceries, and something just . . .

snapped. She got mad at me." Some of the truth bubbled out of her before she could stop it. "She said I didn't need anybody. That's close to what David said the day we split."

"Do you think he said that to her?" Dr. Darzi's voice had that tone that said she knew Catherine was getting close to something major.

"I . . . I don't know. She said . . . she said it was easier when she thought I was dead." Catherine's throat ached, and her eyes were stinging with tears that she hadn't let fall, that she couldn't. If she started crying now, she'd never stop. "She said she wished I had died."

"That must have been incredibly hurtful."

Catherine stared at her hands. "I slapped her across the face. I've never hit her before, not ever. We didn't spank her as a kid. I don't know what got into me."

"You were upset, and you've been going through a lot."

"I know, but I *hit* my child!" Catherine made a frustrated noise, thumping her fist against the couch cushion. "That damn Lindholm. He's trying to trot me out like I'm some big hero, but all I am is a drunk who hit my kid. I'm so fucking sick of it."

Dr. Darzi let her drop the subject of Aimee. "Director Lindholm is just doing what he thinks is best for NASA."

"I get that. I know that. I just—" She cut herself off. Dr. Darzi waited as the silence became too much for Catherine to cope with. Catherine started again. "Ever since then, he wants me to take on more of a spokesperson role, deal with more media, make more appearances talking about the Sagittarius program."

"You're the logical choice to be the face of it to the public, especially since the launch."

"But I'm not," Catherine argued. "I'm a fucking mess. Look at me. My marriage has fallen apart, my kid isn't talking to me . . ."

"Was that why you came to work drunk?" Although her tone was soft, the words were harsh, painful to hear. "Were you looking to get fired?"

"What? No. No, I just . . ." It was on Catherine's lips to tell her about the violent impulses, the voices. But she knew it was too much, too far.

"You just what?"

At first, Catherine was determined to sit in silence and not answer the question. And she tried. She really tried. But Dr. Darzi was better at this game than she was. It was her job, after all. "I'm having nightmares," Catherine finally said. "About my crew. They're so overwhelming sometimes, they're almost real. Could they be memories?"

"They may be. Or they may be ordinary nightmares." She leaned forward. "But what I'm hearing is a woman who feels desperately out of control. You're still trying to focus on the past and the present at the same time. No human being has ever experienced a trauma exactly like yours, Catherine. Survivor's guilt would probably be one of the best outcomes we could expect in such a situation."

Catherine lowered her head to her hands. "But what do I do?"

"Let it go. That's what we're working on here, you and I. Catherine, I've said it before, but you *need* to focus on your life here and now. Today is what you can control. That's all." When Catherine didn't respond, Dr. Darzi continued. "Listen, I know. It's easier to worry about what happened in the past. You're going to be much happier if you focus on rebuilding your life now, fixing your relationship with Aimee, getting back on an even keel."

It sounded so reasonable, but why did it feel so wrong? "But to fix things with Aimee, I do have to look back. I never should have hit her."

Dr. Darzi waited to see if Catherine would say anything else, then asked, "So when you've made a mistake with someone in the past, what have you done?"

"You're telling me I need to apologize to her. I know I do."

"So why haven't you?"

"She's not answering my calls. If she won't talk to me then what do I do?"

"You keep trying. You give her time and try again." They went on to talk about some possible methods she could use to approach Aimee, how best to apologize.

As they were wrapping up, Catherine couldn't help it. She asked again. "If the memories are coming back, how do I tell what's true and what isn't?"

"You don't." Dr. Darzi stood, and Catherine stood with her. "Catherine, you're in a very dangerous place. There's no benefit to going down that path. If you don't believe me, think about Iris Addy. She couldn't let things go either. Travel through ERB Prime has side effects. We know that. You don't want to end up like Commander Addy. I don't want to see that happen to you."

It was a warning, a stern one. Catherine couldn't tell if Dr. Darzi was telling her that she would lose her place at NASA if she pushed, or if she . . . went mad, or whatever it was that happened to Addy.

Either way, the message was clear. If she let things go, she'd have all the help she needed to move forward. If she didn't let things go, she was on her own.

Sagittarius I Mission

They were on their own.

Tom had been working on the comm system for three days. He said he couldn't fix it, but maybe he just didn't want to fix it. That was the problem, wasn't it? They had no way of knowing if he was actually trying.

The irony wasn't lost on Catherine. Tom was out and about in the ship—albeit under constant supervision—while she was trapped in quarantine, and would be for another week. She spent her time cataloging some of the planet's biological samples that Claire provided, but God was she bored.

The rest of the crew came to visit her regularly, except for Tom. Catherine suspected they had some sort of visiting schedule set up, but the only pattern she'd spotted was that she never had a meal alone.

"I feel like it's my fault you're in there," Claire was saying, leaning against the glass between them. She'd come to visit for lunch. "If I'd been paying closer attention, the wreck might not have been as bad."

"Stop that," Catherine said. "It could have just as easily been you in here. I just got the short straw." She leaned forward and glanced out the window to see if anyone else was around. No one was. "How's it going, really?" she asked. "How bad is it?"

Claire sighed and put down her fork. "It's pretty bad. Izzy and Richie want us to abort and go back, but Ava refuses to do that until either we hear from NASA or things are too untenable to continue here. And Tom is . . ." She shook her head. "Every time we let him out he's like a kicked puppy. Perpetually guilty-looking, trying to be friendly with everybody."

"But he's still not fixing the comms."

"Says he can't. He says there's nothing wrong with them, just that the signal can't reach Earth from here."

"But we were sending data before . . ."

"And we never got a response," Claire said. "We have no way of knowing if anything got through then, and now we can't even try."

Catherine studied her plate. "Do you believe him?"

"I don't know *what* to believe. I mean, we *were* having communication problems before, but maybe that was him, too . . . And why would he want to help us, when all Ava is going to do is rat him out to NASA first thing?"

"I hadn't thought about that." She couldn't shake the feeling that all of this was her fault, that somehow what happened with Tom had . . . unbalanced him.

Claire stiffened suddenly, then lifted her head, sniffing the air. "Is that smoke?"

"I don't smell it." But Catherine wouldn't. The air she was breathing was recirculating through her room without ever touching the air outside the quarantine cell. Still, just the mention of smoke was enough to send a chill through her. Despite all the precautions, despite all the safety lessons learned at the expense of other astronauts' lives, fire in an enclosed area was still one of everyone's greatest fears.

Claire stood up. "I'm going to go try to track it down."

"Be careful."

"I will. Wait here. I'll sound the alarm if you need to get out. Might want to suit up, just in case." Claire hurried off.

It might be nothing. It was probably nothing. But Catherine started the arduous process of climbing into her decontamination suit anyway.

She was grateful that she glanced at the clock before Claire left, because five minutes felt like twenty. And it was starting to look hazy outside her window.

Six minutes. Hazier still.

Catherine thumbed the comm on her suit and set the channel to broadcast over the entire Habitat. "Guys? What's going on?"

Six and a half minutes. Nothing.

"Ava? Claire? Somebody?"

The corridor was actually smoky now. She was heading for the air lock leading out of quarantine when a voice sounded in her ear over the comm.

"It's all right, Catherine. Everything's fine." Tom sounded totally calm. The only way he could speak to her directly through her helmet rather than over the overhead speaker was if he was in the command center still, where he'd been working all morning.

"Tom? What's going on?"

"Just a little mishap. Stay where you are. It's not quite safe out here yet."

"I'm seeing a lot of smoke," Catherine said. "Where is everyone?"

"It's fine; it'll all be fine in a minute or two," Tom said soothingly. Something about his voice prickled the back of Catherine's neck and she shoved her way into the air lock, dialing in the commands that would let her out as fast as she could. Her hands were shaking as she slammed the last button and waited for the pressure to equalize so she could get out.

"Come on, come on, come on."

The door opened into the Habitat hallway. The smoke was so thick Catherine could barely see three feet in front of her. The suit's air tank protected her lungs, but she had to get out. *Please let the others already be outside.*

"Catherine, where are you going? I'm showing that you breached quarantine."

"What are you doing, Tom?"

Tom laughed, as if that were the silliest question he'd ever heard. "I'm in the command center, doing what I'm supposed to be doing, what else?"

The door that led out of the Habitat was right in front of her. If the others weren't outside . . . No, but they would be. Whatever game Tom was playing, the others would have evacuated by now.

It was twilight out on the surface, but then it was always twilight.

There was no sound on TRAPPIST-1f except for the wind blowing between the pillars of rock. There was no sign of the others. The rendezvous point in the event of an evacuation was half a kilometer away, not far from where *Sagittarius* sat waiting for their return trip.

There was still no sign of anyone.

Then she heard a low, tearing rumble. She turned back just as the Habitat expanded outward in a slowly unfurling giant cloud of dust, rubble, and smoke, until the walls shattered from the force of the pressure. A fireball rose from within the smoke like a bright orange sun in the dim landscape.

The others.

"No!" Catherine ran toward the flames, her breath coming in harsh, sobbing pants. The debris field met her before she even got close to the Habitat's remains, flying toward her and falling from the sky. There was no way to get closer. The air was too hot. She stumbled back, choking back her tears. As she flattened herself behind one of the stone pillars, she prayed something didn't land on her from overhead.

When she stopped hearing debris slamming to the ground, she took a chance and looked around the pillar. The remains of the Habitat blazed brightly, the skeleton of the structure showing amid the flames. There was just enough oxygen in the atmosphere to feed the fire.

Catherine tried to get closer, but there was still nothing she could do. The fire extinguishing equipment was inside the Habitat, where it was burning as fiercely as the rest of the module.

All she could do was circle what had been her home, helpless. Hoping that someone might come out of the burning wreckage, but there was no one. Everyone was dead except her.

22

IMMEDIATELY AFTER THE launch, Cal was too busy to do anything other than monitor and keep in touch with the Sagittarius II crew. Aaron had stopped glaring at him every time Cal so much as cleared his throat. He commented to him privately that he was glad to see Cal focusing on the right things.

Most of his time was spent in Mission Control, keeping an eye on his people.

The fourth morning running, Leah Morrison started ribbing him. "Hey, Morganson, don't you have anything better to do than *hover*? No home to go to, nothing?"

"I'd love to go home," he said, "but somebody's gotta keep an eye on you and make sure you fly that thing straight."

Commander Duffy piped up, drawling. "Houston, can somebody take a look under Morganson's chair and see if he's got any eggs in his nest yet?"

Laughter rippled through Mission Control, and Cal took it good-naturedly. "All my chicks have flown far, far from the nest, John," he shot back.

"They do that," Duffy agreed. "You gotta let 'em go, momma hen."

"Hey, if I hadn't, y'all wouldn't be out there." Cal *was* hovering; he knew he was. And now that the crew had called him out on it, he'd have to stop.

It turned out to be harder than he expected.

He made himself stay away from Mission Control outside of his scheduled duty hours and tried to focus on the other work waiting for him. It slowly got easier to stop worrying about his crew. That, and he could keep reminding himself that whatever problems they were going to face, they wouldn't happen on the trip out.

There was still plenty of data coming in from Sagittarius I, and as long as Cal didn't focus too much attention on Catherine, he was well within his job parameters. He began looking again at the telemetry from the first mission, making comparisons between the Sagittarius I benchmarks and where Sagittarius II was.

Periodically, his attention was drawn back to the data he initially uncovered. The *only* way the Sagittarius I data from TRAPPIST-1f made sense was if two people had been alive on the ship. But he had no other information. He was trying to solve a jigsaw puzzle with no idea what the final picture would look like. And Aaron ultimately was right: the families of Sagittarius I didn't deserve the pain of knowing that one of their loved ones had suffered terribly.

But then one of the lab techs called him. "Dr. Royer told us to call you when we had something new. We've got the first full set of data on Catherine Wells's blood work. I can't send it to you yet, but you can come down here. Trust me, you're going to want to see this." From the tone in the tech's voice, he might have found something big.

On his way down to the lab, he saw David Wells in the hallway and stopped him. "Hey, I just wanted to find out how Catherine is doing."

Catherine's meltdown had been all anyone talked about in the days following the launch. Cal had missed the meeting where she'd supposedly been drunk, but he heard about it several times.

David gave him a somewhat surprised look. "And here I thought NASA lived on gossip," he said. "I have no idea how she's doing."

"I'm sorry?"

"We split up. Before her ... um, incident."

Cal thought he saw a flicker of guilt cross David's face. He knew about Maggie Bachman; everyone did. That was a particularly popular topic of gossip in the months after Catherine's reappearance.

"I'm sorry," Cal said again. "I hadn't heard."

"I wish I could tell you more."

"Well, if you talk to her, let her know we're thinking of her, all right?"

David looked grateful to be ending the conversation. "I will. Thanks."

Huh. Cal shouldn't be that surprised. The pressure that came with returning from a mission was enormous. And no astronaut had ever been under as much pressure as Catherine had. That had to be a contributing factor.

And some of that pressure was his fault. He wasn't to blame for Catherine's marriage falling apart, but . . .

When he got to the lab, the tech pulled him aside. "Tell me what you know about antibodies."

"Uh . . . just the Biology 101 version. Part of the immune system. When your body detects bacteria or a virus or anything else that doesn't belong there, the antibodies go after it and neutralize the threat." He paused and looked at the tech as if to say, "Is that enough?"

"Right," the tech said. "Each antibody is keyed to a specific antigen—the bacteria or virus. That's often how we can diagnose a specific disease, or at least rule it out. If you have an antibody for a specific antigen, you've been exposed to it at some point. It's why most people don't get the chicken pox more than once."

"Okay . . . so what did you find?"

"It's buried in the prelim report. Probably no one will care much about it, but . . . Colonel Wells came back from TRAPPIST-1f with an antibody that matches no known antigen on Earth."

Cal shook his head. "Sure, but we expected that. She was living on another planet; she was bound to come in contact with something if there was anything to come in contact with."

"Except I've found one other person who carries that same antibody. Iris Addy."

"You're saying they were both exposed to the same antigen?" A sense of excitement, like he was on the brink of something big, was growing in Cal's gut. "But . . . Addy didn't go to TRAPPIST-1f. She never even left the ship."

The tech shrugged. "I'm just telling you what I found."

Cal's thoughts were whirling. "When can you send me the full report?"

"We should have it written up in the next day or two."

"Thank you, this could be a huge help."

He headed to Aaron's office for their regular meeting.

As soon as he settled in, Aaron said, "I wanted to congratulate you, first off. I'm glad to see you took my words to heart. You're back on track, where I expect you to be, and the mission's success so far reflects that."

Cal pasted on a smile, still thinking about the new data. He had to tell Aaron, and just hope that Aaron wouldn't get angry. "I owe it to my crew to give them my best," he said. That wasn't a lie, at least.

"Nobody could fault you for the job you're doing," Aaron said.

"Listen. I really did stop looking into Catherine, but the medical team gave me some data today that I think could be important. It might be a clue to the amnesia that Catherine and Iris Addy both developed."

Aaron lifted his eyebrows, his gaze telling Cal the ice beneath him was getting thinner. "Cal, Addy's medical workup has been gone over with a fine-toothed comb, and we can't have that much information back on Catherine yet."

"Addy's records have been, yes, and it'll be months before we've gotten final results on all of Wells's tests, but today I got some of the initial results." Cal wished he had the written report, but he had to make do with what he had. "We may have found something."

Aaron gave him a small nod, a cautious one, and Cal felt a surge of relief. He was going to listen.

"The folks in the lab found an unrecognized antibody in Catherine's system," he began.

"Not a surprise; we already knew there was all sorts of life on TRAPPIST-1f."

"Yes, but . . . Commander Addy has that same antibody. And as far as the lab can tell, it doesn't match any known antigen on Earth. She never landed on TRAPPIST-1f." Cal could see the skepticism growing in Aaron's eyes, so he rushed ahead to his conclusion. "They both had to be exposed to the same thing out there. What if the amnesia and the erratic behavior have a biological component?"

"You may be onto something," Aaron was forced to admit. "Whatever it is, it's unlikely that it's infectious, or we'd have had a problem before now."

Cal nearly slumped in relief. Finally, Aaron was listening.

"That being said, you need to think about spending some time away from here." He raised his hand to forestall Cal's protest. "Now's the best time. We can follow up on the antibody angle without you. Things should be quiet for a bit, and we've got a couple of months before the ship gets to the wormhole."

"Shouldn't I wait until they're in before I take time off?" Cal countered. "They'll be unreachable then so there won't be anything we can do with them at all."

"You'll be taking time away then, too," Aaron said. "We've got too many staff overstressed right now, but you and Wells are the ones I'm most worried about."

Cal was fine. What was there to worry about? Catherine, though . . . "I heard about her and her husband. It's a shame."

"I'm not surprised, honestly." Aaron could afford to be philosophical, as he had two failed marriages behind him himself. "It's more than that, though. Have you talked to her at all lately?"

Cal shook his head, allowing himself a wry grin. "You told me to stay away from her."

"Yeah, yeah. I'm worried about her."

"So you're sending us both into time-out?"

Aaron shook his head, chuckling. "You know, most people don't consider a few days off punishment. But yeah. Go to your room, Cal. Come back on Monday."

"Yes, sir," Cal sighed.

"I mean it. Pack up and clear out, starting right now. I don't want to see your goofy-ass face until Monday."

———

Cal didn't do well with an excess of free time. The good thing was, he knew that about himself, and was planning ways to keep from going stir-crazy. It was too last minute for him to go on a trip, and he wouldn't want to be too far away from Johnson anyway, in case something did go wrong. The only option that left him was going home to his folks, and he sure as hell didn't want to do that.

And despite what Aaron said, he had every intention of looking into the first mission from home.

The second morning, though, he needed to get out of the house. And he needed to *move*.

The climbing gym that he and Nate favored was mostly empty on weekday mornings. The only people around were people off work for the day, like him, and folks who worked the night shift. Still, there were a few familiar faces, and it wasn't hard to find a partner to climb with.

Climbing with Nate was better, Cal decided, when he was halfway up the wall. It wasn't just that they knew each other's habits, it was also that he was more fun. *Get it together*, he chided himself. It hadn't even been two weeks since the launch. If he started missing Nate now, he'd never make it. Still, it was one thing to logically know his best friend would be out of touch for several years, but now the reality of it was starting to kick in.

It took until his second attempted climb for Cal to clear his mind. Things were so clean here, so simple: find the next handhold, keep moving. The steady rhythm of his heart and the sweat trickling down his face left his mind clear and empty.

Aaron had told him to take a break, but he couldn't stop thinking about the strange Sagittarius readings. Which crew member had made it back onto the ship with Catherine? What had happened to that person?

Maybe following up on the new medical info might provide a way to unlock Catherine's memories. But if Cal was honest with himself, it wasn't just that. Before her discharge from NASA, Commander Addy wasn't only erratic but had also had more than one violent outburst. It hadn't happened with Catherine yet . . . but what if it did? What if it already happened, out there?

And what if that same antigen—virus, bacterium, whatever it was— infected the *Sagittarius II* crew?

It was a lot to think about. Something else to look into. Maybe it was the missing piece of the puzzle, or maybe it was the one maddening piece that wouldn't seem to fit anywhere until the whole picture was almost complete.

Either way, having a new direction to go in lifted a weight off his shoulders. Cal took a deep breath and swung into action, reaching for the next handhold.

hell had she ended up this time? The diploma on the wall was from Cornell. Realization hit her hard.

She was in Aaron Llewellyn's office.

The light from the computer monitor in front of her registered and she looked at the screen. The first words to greet her eyes were "TOP SECRET."

Catherine shoved herself back from the desk with a gasp. What the hell? She turned off the monitor, not wanting to risk even a glimpse of the page's contents.

Why was she in Aaron's office in the middle of the night, accessing something way above her security clearance?

"I have to get out of here." The sound of her own voice startled her. "Turn off the computer." Had it been off when she came in? Maybe she hadn't done anything. Maybe Aaron had left it on when he'd gone for the day.

Yeah, sure. He'd just walked out for the day with a top-secret document open on his computer. That made sense.

Catherine turned the monitor back on and closed out the document without reading it, shutting the computer down. Her heart was pounding so hard she felt sick. Somehow she made it to her feet and out of the office.

How—There was no way she should have been able to get in here like this. She leaned against the wall and covered her face. Last she knew, she'd been home on her couch, it was Sunday night, but she didn't have to go to work the next day because Aaron had suspended her. Had she been drinking? To judge by the sour taste in her mouth, yes.

Was it still Sunday?

Oh God, she couldn't keep going on like this. She had to talk to somebody, but whom? No one had believed her so far.

Someone might.

There was one other person at NASA who didn't seem eager to buy into the hero narrative. One other person who was trying to poke holes in her story.

One other person she might be able to talk to.

23

WHEN HER PHONE rang Catherine almost let the call go to voice mail, but after Julie's visit, she'd promised to pick up the phone when people called. Besides, she was starting to feel a little lonely.

"Hi, Julie."

"How are things going?"

"I'm doing better." Catherine paced the length of her living room, before spinning in the other direction. She sounded normal. Then again, she was completely sober, for the moment.

Julie paused, and Catherine could hear office sounds in the background, before they muted with a thud. She must have closed her office door. "Cath, are you still drinking?"

"No," Catherine lied.

"Just hang in there," Julie said. "Do something fun during your time off."

They hung up a short time later and Catherine dropped her phone on the table, scrubbing her face. She should find something to eat and spend the evening not drinking.

She got half of it right. She managed to eat dinner before opening a bottle of wine.

———

Catherine drew a sharp breath, so disoriented that she teetered off-balance. She caught herself against the edge of something—wait, it was a desk. She was sitting in front of it. Blinking, she looked around the dark room. Nighttime. She could see sodium lights through the half-closed blinds. Where the

24

CAL STAGGERED DOWNSTAIRS in his condo, fumbling to get his glasses on. Christ, he really needed to talk to his neighbor about making sure his ex-girlfriends knew which door was his and which was Cal's. This was the third time in a month he'd had a drunk, crying girl on his doorstep at two in the morning.

He swung the door open. "Look, Steve lives next—"

There wasn't a drunk, crying twenty-year-old on his doorstep.

Catherine Wells wasn't crying and she wasn't twenty. Cal wouldn't vouch for whether or not she was drunk. He stared at her blankly.

"I'm sorry to bother you so late," she said. "I didn't know where else to go." God, she looked like hell. The circles under her eyes were as dark as bruises, and her clothes were mismatched and dirty.

Not knowing what else to do, he stepped back. "No, of course. Come in. What happened?" He had to ask because he couldn't think of a single solitary thing that would cause Catherine to come to him, of all people.

She stepped into his kitchen, her shoulders hunched like a wounded animal's.

"Here. Sit down," Cal ushered her to one of the kitchen chairs. "Are you hurt? Do you need me to call someone?" He didn't miss the smell of alcohol floating around her, although she seemed coherent enough.

Catherine sank into the offered chair, her dark eyes solemn. "I need to talk to someone. You were the only person I could think of who might believe me."

That got his attention, instantly zapping him awake. "Sure, of course. Uh, do you want some coffee or something?"

"That would be great."

He expected her to start talking while he made a pot of coffee, but she sat there, twisting her fingers together with her hands resting on the table. When he pushed the steaming mug in front of her, she ignored the cream and sugar on the table and took a long swallow, wrapping her hands around the ceramic as if it were a lifeline.

Cal couldn't take the silence anymore. "What's going on, Catherine?"

She didn't answer right away.

"Look, if I'm going to help you—and I'm guessing you came here for help—you have to tell me everything."

Her eyes darted left and right like she was looking for an escape. "I . . . haven't told anybody this. Not even Dr. Darzi. Nobody wants to know. Nobody wants to figure out what really happened."

Suddenly it became clear why she'd come to him. He nodded. "Except for me."

"Shut up and be a hero, Catherine," she said bitterly.

"NASA loves its happy endings," he agreed. "So . . . what is it you haven't told anyone?"

When she spoke, she spoke to her hands rather than look him in the face. "I . . . I keep losing time. Like, I'll be somewhere one minute, and the next I'm somewhere else and hours might have passed."

"Like a blackout drunk?"

She winced. "It began before I started drinking."

Cal had a sudden image of the surprise on her face when he'd asked her about visiting NASA the night of her daughter's graduation party. And earlier, finding her down by the archives. "So that night I met you at NASA . . ."

"There weren't any graduation cards in my office. I don't know why I was there." Her voice cracked. "I woke up the next morning and my feet were dirty and I was tired. I had no idea why."

"Okay, okay." Without thinking, Cal reached out a hand and covered hers in a calming gesture. She grabbed his hand with the same force that she'd grabbed the mug, clinging to it for dear life. "What happened tonight, Catherine? What brought you here?"

She took a deep breath. "Cal, I was in Aaron's office. On his computer."

"How'd you get past the locked door, and his password?"

"I don't know. But I did."

"What were you looking at?"

"I don't know that either. It was top secret, so I closed it."

"Damn. That might've been a clue." He was startled at how easily he believed her, but then again, everything she'd said so far fit with what he knew.

"Cal, what if I hurt someone? What if this happened to me planetside and I hurt my crew?"

Her words had a chilling effect on him. "Have you hurt anyone here?"

"I don't think so. But Cal . . ." Catherine turned pale. "I've *wanted* to."

He didn't say anything, just watched her and listened.

"A couple of times since coming home I've had these . . . urges."

"What sorts of urges?"

"To hurt people. It's like this haze, like something's taken over me, and all I want to do is strike out against whoever's in front of me. It . . . It happened with you once. When you found me downstairs by the archives."

Cal tried not to let his surprise show. She'd been so busy looking guilty, he hadn't seen so much as a hint of anything else. "Some anger is understandable—"

"No. It's not like that. When that happens . . . people stop looking *human* to me. They—you—look like monsters. I'm not angry, I'm repulsed." Catherine ran her hands the length of her face. "I really could hurt someone like this."

"You're not going to." A course of action was slowly taking shape in his mind. "Because we're going to keep an eye on you."

" '*We*'—you believe me?"

Time for a few confessions of his own. "I've been looking into what might have happened—strictly off the books. There are . . . a few anomalies."

"How do you mean?"

"Hang on. Come into the living room." He led her there and sat next to her on the couch so they could both see the screen. He pulled up the telemetry reports he'd received. "Look, right here. Here are the readings from the ship shortly after the explosion."

Catherine leaned in to the screen. "That can't be right. That's too high."

"Look at the CO_2 and oxygen. It's about right for two people."

"I wish I could confirm it for you." She shook her head and sat back, looking at him. "You really *do* believe me. Why?"

He gestured at his laptop. "Your story fits the data I have so far. It explains some of the strangeness I've seen in you. It makes more sense than the story you told us initially." He should tell her about the antibody, but he didn't want to frighten her. She'd had a bad enough night as it was. Instead he groped for something to explain the gut feeling he had. "Plus, there's no real reason for you to lie to me about this. The bosses at NASA are happy with your story. And—frankly—they're not listening to me."

"You've talked to them?"

"To Aaron. If it makes you feel any better, he threatened to fire my nosy ass over it." He gave her a small smile. "I was the only holdout, and I can't do anything to you. There's nothing to be gained by giving me a new story. It'd just be more ammunition—if I were still looking for ammunition."

"I get that Aaron wants this story to go away, but why the hell would he threaten your job?"

Cal ducked his head. "I . . . might've stretched a few rules while I was investigating." He looked up to see suspicion in her eyes, and found that it stung more than he thought it would.

"Cal, what were you doing at NASA in the middle of the night?" Catherine asked suddenly. "The night you saw me there."

Paperwork. He'd lied and told her paperwork, that he'd been working. He stood at a crossroads. She'd just told him the truth, as much of it as she knew. Didn't he owe her the same? "That's one of the ways I overstepped." There was no way to make this sound okay. "I, um— I followed you there."

"Followed me?"

God, he didn't want to have this conversation. "From your house."

"What were you doing at my house?" She didn't sound angry, yet. Just puzzled.

"Um. Watching you."

Catherine shook her head. "Why the hell would you be watching my daughter's graduation party?"

"I didn't know there was going to be a party."

"So you . . . what, sat outside my house? What were you expecting me to do?" Now there was a flash of irritation. "I had a houseful of people, I wasn't exactly going to go on a rampage." She paused, her eyes widening. "Were you in my yard?"

He knew exactly what she was talking about and did his best to look apologetic. "I was there when you were saying good-bye to Leah Morrison."

"Jesus Christ. I've already spent months thinking I was going insane. Thinking I was being watched didn't help."

"At least you weren't imagining things." It sounded lame as he said it, but she gave a startled laugh.

"You're an asshole, you know that?" She was grinning as she said it. There was the Catherine he saw at the party. The one he wished he'd met sooner.

He grinned back. "Yeah, I've heard that before."

Some of the tension dissolved. Catherine looked worlds better than she had when she first came in. Her shoulders sat lower, her face was less tight.

"Hey," he said, "if I hadn't followed you, we might not know you ever went to NASA."

She sobered. "I wonder how many times I've gone there without anyone knowing."

"We can find out," he said. "We both want the truth, right?"

"I do. I don't care how bad it is. I have to know. Not knowing is driving me mad."

"All right. We'll work together, okay?" Maybe it was too soon for him to be optimistic, but with Catherine giving him information instead of hiding it, surely they'd find some answers.

Catherine stifled a yawn against the back of her hand. "Thank you. I think— I think I've been sitting on this for too long."

"Wait, I have some questions for you. I've got some printouts in my office that you need to see. Maybe you can help me make sense of them." He jumped up, not waiting for her to nod, and left the room. He flipped on the lights in his home office and rummaged for the transcripts he had of her original debriefings, especially the sections he'd highlighted.

"Okay," he said, coming back in. "When you were interviewed the first time, you said—" Cal stopped. Catherine lay on her side on his couch, eyes closed. "Catherine?" he said softly.

No answer except her quiet breathing.

Cal gathered up their coffee mugs and took them back to the kitchen. When he returned, she was still sound asleep. It was close to 3:00 a.m., and he didn't have the heart to wake her. He fetched a blanket from the hall closet and draped it over her, turning off all the downstairs lights except one dim one in the hallway. He may as well go back to bed, too. They would have plenty to talk about later.

25

CATHERINE OPENED HER eyes and realized two things at once: the head-ache she'd been waking up with every day for weeks was gone, and she had no idea where she was. She sat up on the unfamiliar couch, pushing off the blanket, and then it came to her. Oh God, she'd fallen asleep on Cal Morgan-son's couch. This was going to be the weirdest walk of shame in the history of Houston.

She swung her legs over the side of the couch and rubbed her eyes before running her hands over her hair. She was a wreck, no doubt. Wreck or not, that was the best sleep she'd had in weeks. Her head felt clearer than it had in . . . well, in a long time. Cal believed her. Someone else knew the truth now. That on its own was enough to make her feel less crazy, less alone.

As she tried to finish waking up, she realized just what a mess her life had become. The drinking, the way she was avoiding everyone, her relationship with Aimee. For the first time in ages she felt like it was a mess she might be able to clean up. She needed to get home and start making some phone calls.

Cal came out of his kitchen, freshly showered and dressed for work. She hated him a little for looking neat while she was sitting there with dirty hair and morning breath and clothes she'd been wearing for days.

"Hey," he said. "Look who's up."

"I'm so sorry. I didn't mean to crash here."

"Don't worry about it. You looked like you could use the sleep. Probably safer than you trying to get home, as late as it was." He smiled and she hated him more—it figured he was a morning person.

"Thank you."

"Can I get you some coffee? I promise it's not leftovers from last night."

"No, thank you. I should— I should get home." She stood up, and the room didn't spin. She really was feeling better this morning.

"Are you sure? It's no trouble."

"No, really. I have some things I need to fix."

He nodded as if he understood, and maybe he did. Even if he was still investigating her, he believed her, and it was amazing what a difference that made. "Call me later, and we'll start working this thing through, okay?"

"Yeah."

Cal walked her to the door and there was a weird, awkward moment— considering the intimacy of the conversation they'd had the night before, she was tempted to hug him. They settled on a clumsy handshake, and she fled. She had thought he was cold, but there'd been nothing cold in his eyes this morning, and he'd covered her on his couch and let her sleep.

She stopped to pick up coffee and some breakfast on her way back to her apartment, and ate while checking her emails. There was a message from Aaron asking how she was doing. She replied, telling him how much better she felt, hoping she hadn't ruined things for herself at NASA.

Lingering over her coffee was a luxury she hadn't allowed herself in a long time. She looked out through her sliding glass doors at the morning sunlight while she figured out her next moves.

She needed to call Aimee. Her stomach churned at the thought, but she needed to be the grown-up here. Julie was right. The longer she let that go, the less chance they'd have to patch things up. Catherine swallowed the last of her coffee and picked up her phone. Feeling ridiculous, she took a deep breath and sat up straighter, perched on the edge of the couch as she dialed her daughter's cell phone.

Eventually Aimee's voice mail picked up. "Hey, Aimee. I just wanted to tell you how sorry I am, and how much I love you. We need to talk. Call me, please?"

She hung up and spoke aloud to her empty apartment, hearing the quaver in her voice. "Well, that was anticlimactic."

She needed to call David. There was no getting back together with him. No matter how much better she was doing, their time was done. Catherine felt sure of that. But his offer of friendship was still there, and she was going to need all the friends she could get. She picked up her phone again.

David answered right away. "Catherine. Is everything okay?"

"Yeah. It's fine. I'm sorry. I've been putting everyone through hell." She tried to organize her thoughts. "I wanted to say thank you for everything. I've been pretty pissed at you—at everybody. Julie was just what I needed."

"I'm glad. I knew I wasn't the best choice to talk to you, but you needed someone."

"Is Aimee okay? I called to apologize, but I think she's screening her calls."

"Listen, Catherine, Aimee told me what she said to you. She's ashamed of herself right now and not ready to face it. If you give her time, she'll come around."

"How do you know?" Catherine stood and started pacing. What if David was wrong? What if Catherine had lost her forever?

"I'll talk to her. Don't worry. She needs you; she just doesn't know it right now." David sounded reassuring and Catherine tried to hold on to that, but . . .

"I was out of line. When you talk to her, make sure she knows that I know that."

"I will, I promise." David hesitated then said, "Tell me the truth. *Are* you okay? With everything, and the fight with Aimee . . . please tell me." When she didn't answer, he went on. "Look, whatever's happened between us, I still care. I know . . . I know the last time we talked I said a lot of things I shouldn't have. I'm sorry."

"We both did," she said automatically. "I'm sorry, too." She wasn't actually sure she was, not yet, but she knew an olive branch when she saw one.

"So talk to me. What's going on?"

Standing there, in her dim living room, Catherine was tempted to tell him everything. Instead she just laughed. "It's been kind of a weird year, David."

After a moment he laughed with her, and things felt as though they might be okay between them. Not "married" okay but "still friends" okay. "Point taken. Just remember you're not alone, all right?"

"Yeah. I know." Then because she didn't know what else to say, "Thanks."

"I know you've always wanted to be the best mom possible," David said. "And whatever happens between you and me, I hope we can keep working together as Aimee's parents."

"Of course. Of course, we can."

It was so much easier to talk to David now that she wasn't worried about trying to stay married to him. And now they could both focus more of their energy on Aimee. They chatted a few more minutes, and then Catherine started cleaning her apartment. She moved automatically to the kitchen. Rather than pour a drink, she threw herself into washing the dirty dishes that were days old. Maybe she couldn't fix everything, but she'd fix what she could.

She was almost finished with the dishes when her phone rang. Aimee's name flashed on her screen. Heart pounding, she wiped her hands on a dish towel and picked up her phone, trying to sound calm.

"Hello?"

"Hi, Mom." Aimee's voice was subdued; not quite at full sullen-teenager levels, but close.

"I'm so glad you called," Catherine said. She sat down in her tiny dining area, leaning against the table.

"Yeah, well, I've been talking to Dad and Julie. They both thought I should."

"Aimee, I'm sorry. I never should have hit you. I . . . wasn't in a very good place then, I got hurt, and I reacted badly." Catherine's throat tightened and she swallowed several times.

"I shouldn't have . . . said what I did. I'm sorry."

"You had—you have—every right to be angry with me." The guilt was threatening to swallow her whole, making her want to throw herself at Aimee's proverbial feet. But something Dr. Darzi once said stuck with her: *You can't build a relationship on guilt.* Yes, Catherine had made mistakes, but that didn't make her responsible for everything. She took a deep breath and said, "I have the right to be angry, too. Neither of us handled it well. But I'm the grown-up, and I should have done better."

"I don't want to be angry at you all the time." Aimee's voice quavered. "I just want things to be normal."

Catherine pressed her lips together, her eyes stinging. "I don't know what normal is going to look like for us. But we can get there. I don't want to do this on the phone. Can we meet? I understand if you don't want to come here yet." They needed neutral territory; Catherine could sense it.

Aimee was silent at first then said, "Sure. Yeah, we can do that."

"Great. Today? Coffee shop down the street from you? About two?" More than anything, Catherine needed to see Aimee, to hold her, to make everything feel real.

"Okay."

When they hung up, Catherine went through the apartment cleaning up after the weeks of misery. Everything felt so much lighter today, as though she'd cut all her hair off or shed a heavy coat. There were still questions that needed to be answered, but now she wasn't going to try to answer them alone.

Dr. Darzi had been wrong: the only way she was going to put everything behind her was by remembering everything and getting the full story about what happened. And now with Cal to help her, she was sure she could do it. Sooner or later she was going to remember.

———

The coffee shop was crowded, but Catherine ordered two coffees and found a table while she waited for Aimee to get there. When she arrived, the two of them looked at each other awkwardly, then Catherine stood and carefully reached out to her. They fell into an embrace, and all the tears that Catherine had been holding back started to fall.

"Mom, I'm so sorry."

"I'm sorry, too. I love you so much, Aimee."

"I love you, too."

Conscious that they were drawing attention, Catherine tried to get her crying under control and sat down again. Aimee sat across from her, wiping away her own tears, sniffling.

"It's so good to see you," Catherine said, then had to stop, choking up again.

"I've missed you," Aimee admitted. "Dad is great, always has been, but . . . he's not you."

At the mention of David, Catherine fought the urge to ask if Maggie was coming around again already. This wasn't about David or Maggie. Aimee was the only one that really mattered right now. "You guys did okay without me for a while there," Catherine teased faintly.

"We do better with you. Or I do, at least." Aimee stirred her coffee aimlessly, looking into the cup. "Dad was really worried about you. So was I."

How much should she tell Aimee? She wanted to be truthful, but didn't want to scare her. Catherine focused on her own cup while she gathered her thoughts, then looked up to meet Aimee's eyes. "I was struggling—I'm still struggling. Coming home was so much harder than I thought it would be. I wasn't ready for that." She paused again. "I . . . tried to cope with it by drinking too much." One corner of her mouth twitched into a faint smile. "You see how well that went."

"But you've stopped now?"

"Yeah. I'm trying. If I can't stop on my own, I'll get help, I promise." Catherine laughed wryly. "See, I'm learning to ask for help."

"Maybe there's hope for you yet," Aimee shot back with a grin.

"Yeah. Yeah, I think there might be."

If only she could remember what happened—all of it, no matter how painful the truth.

26

CATHERINE FELT LIKE she had everyone fooled. Just yesterday, Dr. Darzi had commented on how much progress Catherine was making now that she was looking forward and not back. Considering what she and Cal were working on, the irony of that wasn't lost on her.

Her first couple of days back at work were awful. It felt as though everyone was staring at her, waiting for her to have another meltdown. At times the tension in her ramped up so high that she wanted to scream, but she forced herself to toe the line.

Now she sat in Paul Lindholm's office with Aaron, making plans for *Sagittarius II*'s voyage through the wormhole, anticipating the inevitable surge in requests for information and background pieces.

"I think that's all we need to worry about from a media perspective," Aaron was saying. "And once the initial rush of requests dies down, it'll be quiet around here for a good long time."

"I have another idea," Lindholm said, leaning forward with a gleam in his eye. "If you're interested, Catherine."

Cautiously, she smiled. "What are you thinking?"

"Now that you're back on your feet, so to speak, how would you feel about making some more appearances talking about your experiences? I'm still getting requests from the big networks, plus CNN, MSNBC . . . everybody wants to know how you're doing."

Catherine just barely managed to keep from making a face, but Lindholm was right. There was no excuse she could give at this point to keep her face out of the news. "Sure, I can think about that."

"It would give us a real boost," Lindholm said with a smile. "Especially if we could make it a family affair. You, David, your daughter . . ."

"Paul . . ." Catherine hesitated. "You do know that David and I are separated, don't you?"

Lindholm waved his hand dismissively. "You haven't gone public with that yet; no need to muddy the waters right now. How about it?"

Catherine thought about the conversation she and David had had just the night before, and the one they were going to have with Aimee later that day. *No, but it's going to be a matter of public record pretty soon . . .* "Well, I'll need to check with David and Aimee, and make sure they're both on board."

"You do that."

Later, over lunch with Cal in his office, she commented how strange it was that everyone got over her lapse so quickly.

Cal just shrugged. "They were rooting for you, for one thing. You're one of us, and they know you've been through hell. Besides, everyone's eager to move on."

"Dr. Darzi said everything has been a natural response to trauma."

"You could have swollen up and turned green and she would've said that."

Catherine laughed to hear some of her own thoughts reflected back at her. "Well, to be fair to her, it does sound like trauma can do some pretty wonky things to people. So, someone, somewhere, probably *has* swollen up and turned green."

Cal grinned, and she marveled at how quickly their relationship had turned around. There was a decent guy under the prickly exterior. She was struck again by how much warmer he seemed, and how that warmth transformed him from someone forbidding to someone she could get close to. Then his grin softened. "Are you still having dinner with Aimee and David tonight?"

"Yeah." She wished he hadn't mentioned it. At the thought of it, her belly tied itself in knots. "I'm just glad Aimee and I patched things up." They still had a long, long way to go, and Catherine wasn't sure tonight's conversation was going to help matters any.

"She loves you. You'll work everything out."

"I hope so."

That hope stayed with her for the rest of the day, right up until the moment she knocked on the door of her old home. The fact that she was knocking instead of just going in said volumes about how much things had changed.

Aimee opened the door with a tentative smile. "Dad's in the kitchen cooking." Aimee gave Catherine a hug so cautious that Catherine wanted to cry, but at least it was a hug. A couple of weeks ago she'd wondered if she'd ever get that much from Aimee again.

"And you let him?" Catherine teased, trying to get a smile out of her.

"Hey, I've been busy." Aimee gave her a twitch of a smile. It was enough.

They went into the kitchen together and Catherine rubbed her palms against her jeans to dry them.

"Dinner's almost ready," David said.

"Good, I'm starving." Aimee started setting the table in the dining room. Catherine stayed out of the way and watched as the two of them moved as a single unit, getting drinks and napkins and dinner on the table, years of practice showing in their movements. They'd perfected a dance, and Catherine saw clearly how she had come home and thrown everyone's rhythm off.

"Okay." Aimee sat in the dining room chair she'd sat in since she was old enough to eat at the table, between her parents. "How about you two tell me whatever it is you're planning to tell me."

"We can't just have dinner as a family?" Catherine asked.

"Yeah, we can," Aimee said, and now there was a bigger smile. "But that's not what this is. Dad's been acting weird all day. So what's up?"

"Well . . ." David looked at Catherine and she nodded. "There are a couple of things, actually. First, I want you to know how much better your mom is doing."

Catherine was uncomfortable with the praise but smiled at him. "I had a lot of help." Then she sighed. "So . . . the downside of me doing better is that NASA wants me to be more visible. Instead of just playing a spokesperson role, they want me to get more personal, to talk with the media about what happened to me out there."

"That's no surprise," Aimee said. "You said all along that Director Lind-holm wanted that."

"Yes, but . . ." Catherine took a breath. "Now it's going to happen. NBC wants to interview all of us. They want to talk to you and your dad about your experiences, too."

Aimee looked to David with raised eyebrows. He shrugged. "I signed up for this, too, when I initially began the training program. You didn't, though. Your mom is going to talk to them, and I am, too. Whether you do or not is entirely up to you. Your mom and I are happy either way."

"Can I think about it?" Aimee asked.

"Of course; that's why we brought it up," Catherine said. "And if you want to talk it over with either of us, or with Maggie, that's okay, too. Just . . . keep it between all of us for now."

Aimee grinned. "Right, no bragging on Twitter, got it."

That was the easy part. Now came the hard part, the real reason they'd come together for this talk with Aimee. "So . . . the next thing isn't fun," Catherine said.

"You're getting divorced," Aimee said.

Catherine should have known Aimee would figure it out.

"Your mom and I have talked about it, and we think it's best if we go ahead and file. We're not planning to fight over anything. I'm going to keep the house, and we'll divide the rest. You're almost eighteen, so obviously we're not going to fight over custody of you."

Catherine stepped in. "We figured you'd probably want to live here when you're not at school, but you're welcome to stay with me as much as you want."

Then she and David stopped talking, waiting for Aimee's reaction. Catherine braced herself.

Aimee sat with her head lowered in thought. "You know, when Mom moved out, I couldn't figure out what was wrong with you two. I thought you loved each other, and that was all that mattered."

Catherine nodded, not wanting to interrupt.

"But . . . when you came back, I guess things were a mess for all of us for a while there."

"All of us had trouble adjusting," David said. "Your mom and I gave it our best try to fix things, but ten years is a long time." It seemed they weren't going to mention Maggie, or Tom, and Catherine was relieved. Despite everything that had happened, this really was just between her and David.

"I still care about your dad, and we both love you, Aimee. We're still a family. It's just going to look a little bit different now."

Aimee smiled ruefully. "Guess that's nothing new. We've never been a completely normal family anyway."

"Not so much, no," David said with a smile of his own.

"Hey, do me a favor," Catherine said, "don't tell that to NBC if you talk to them, okay? Lindholm would kill me."

"I don't know . . ." David grinned. "Can you imagine the look on his face?"

"I can, hence the caution."

"Okay." Aimee leaned forward and looked at both her parents. "Tell me more about this interview. It might be fun . . ."

Catherine and David exchanged smiles, and Catherine felt some of the knots inside her unravel. It would take time, but for the first time, she had faith that her family would be okay.

27

"ALL RIGHT, THAT'S about it for right now." Cal tuned out the chatter around him in Mission Control so he could focus on the crew, which was now somewhere past Mars and close to ERB Prime. "Anybody have anything else I need to know about?"

On the screen overhead, the crew glanced at one another, and Navarro nudged Nate. "Go on, Doc. Ask him."

Nate sighed. "So these guys—"

"And *you*, too," interjected Navarro.

"Fine; *we* just wanna know why NASA is stealing our thunder." Whatever Nate was talking about, Cal could tell it wasn't his idea to bring it up, whether he agreed or not.

"What do you mean?"

"One of the techs told us about the interview with the Wells family. We watched it."

Cal chuckled. "You and a few million other people, Nate." It had been a ratings bonanza, no doubt fulfilling Paul Lindholm's wildest dreams. Americans had tuned in to hear about the sole survivor of Sagittarius I, and how her family felt after getting her back from the dead. Lindholm probably *hadn't* been thrilled that David and Catherine admitted they'd filed for divorce. But the real surprise of the night hadn't been the announcement, but rather their daughter, Aimee. She'd turned out to be well-spoken and incredibly bright—and already gunning for a job at NASA.

"So who's going to listen to what we have to say about TRAPPIST-1f when we come back?" Nate asked.

"I thought you said you *watched* the interview. Come on, guys. Nobody was paying attention to a few vague artistic renderings from years ago. She came back, yeah, but her memories didn't." Cal was suddenly aware that most of the staff in Mission Control had stopped to listen to what was supposed to have been an ordinary status meeting. "The story there was all about how she survived a tragedy. God willing, that's not the story you guys will be telling—and you'll have some hard information about another planet. Trust me, gang, there's plenty of story to go around."

He swallowed his misgivings. Depending on what he and Catherine learned, the story *Sagittarius II* brought back might be different from anything they could have imagined . . .

But instead, he just grinned at his computer screen. "You bunch of walking egos have anything else, or are we good?"

"That hurts, man. That really hurts." Nate was grinning back, though, and the rest of the crew looked a little more relaxed.

"Yeah, well, they hired me for my brutal honesty."

"We're good," Commander Duffy said. "Thanks, as always, Cal."

"No problem. I'll talk to you all tomorrow." He signed off and closed the connection, pushing back from his station.

Cal headed for his office, thinking about the interview. He'd watched it, too, of course. The divorce announcement caught him off guard, his stomach twisting in a mix of nerves, worry, and anticipation. It was a combination of feelings he really didn't need right now, not while he was still trying to figure out what Catherine was doing during her blank spells.

He got to his office and settled behind his desk. The problem was, he couldn't kid himself that he was objective anymore. But then, he never had been, had he? At first, he was digging into Catherine's records because he wanted to find some evidence of wrongdoing. Now he was looking because he wanted to confirm that she'd done nothing wrong. Whatever she was doing, he was convinced she didn't remember it.

A knock at his door interrupted him. "Cal, hey." Aaron stuck his head in the open doorway. "Just wanted to say good job defusing the interview issue with the crew earlier."

"That was easy. We should've seen it coming."

Aaron chuckled. "Yeah, everybody's gonna wanna write a book when they get back. If they wanted the lion's share of the glory they should've been first, right?"

Cal didn't point out that the other five people who'd been "first" hadn't come home—but that was part of being first. You took the bigger risk. "Right," he said instead.

"And good job with the Wells thing. Don't think I haven't noticed that the ice has thawed between you two. Finally figured out she was telling the truth, huh?"

"Yessir. I believe her story." That wasn't a lie—he didn't say *which* story he believed. "I was just being cautious. That's one reason you hired me, right?"

"You bet. And I'm glad we did." He tapped the doorframe. "Get out of here, would you? It's nearly eight. We'll be busy when the crew gets to ERB Prime soon. Save some juice for then."

"Yeah, thanks. Just have a few more things I need to do then I'm out."

He stared at the door Aaron had just exited through. What had Catherine been doing in Aaron's office that night? Cal had to admire her for not wanting to read top-secret information once she'd come to, but it sure would help if they knew what she'd been after in her altered state.

Maybe . . . he shouldn't even try to do that, but he could . . .

Cal got up and shut his door, although the floor was empty by now. Even Aaron's office light had gone off, thank God.

No one would ever mistake him for a hacker, but he knew how to access and read server logs. Of course, if the files Catherine accessed were out of Cal's security clearance, it still might not help him, but it was worth a shot.

Catherine had showed up at his house at two that morning, so all he needed to do was see what files were accessed from Aaron's computer shortly before then—assuming she'd come right over after being in Aaron's office. He looked through the logs until he found the right time frame. The files she'd been looking at should be . . . there.

Cal stared. That couldn't be right.

He double-checked the date, the time, the workstation.

They were all correct.

Fuck.

Cal didn't need to open the files to know what they were. He knew exactly what they contained. He'd written most of them. And only half a dozen people at NASA even knew they existed. Half a dozen people, and now maybe Catherine Wells.

Before he could think, he grabbed his cell phone and called Catherine. Shit, how was it ten o'clock already? Voice mail.

"Hey, it's Cal. Call me when you get this. It's urgent. I figured a few things out. We have to talk."

While he waited, waffling on his next step, he pulled up one of the docs she'd accessed that night. He knew the text by heart, but looked at the memo anyway.

> *... Longbow Protocol is a last-ditch contingency. When the three-step process is triggered, a signal is sent to the Sagittarius mission craft, at which point the computer will begin to shut down all life-support systems. The crew will receive no warning. An hour after life-support shutdown, the interior modules will be flooded with gamma rays to ensure that no foreign antigen or life-form survives and reaches Earth. This radiation will also neutralize any crew that might have survived the first line of defense.*

Catherine—or more accurately, whatever was controlling Catherine—now knew all about Longbow. Including ... wait. He paused to double-check the server logs again ... Shit. Yes. Including the codes and locations needed to trigger the first sequence.

Fidgeting, he dialed Catherine's number again. Voice mail.

His heart raced in his chest as he pictured her, blank-eyed and determined, coming into NASA that very night to set the protocol in motion.

She's known about it for weeks; there's nothing that says tonight would be the night.

But the skin on the back of his neck crawled with panic. It was fine.

It would be fine, he told himself. He'd just go to her place. Wait, no. She'd moved.

Even if he found her, what would he do, exactly? Tell her what he'd found? *Kill* her? No, of course not; that was a ridiculous thought. But they could talk it through. Aaron was the only one with the fail-safe codes to disconnect Longbow; they might have to tell him everything.

Then a worse thought occurred to him: *What if she's not there? What if she's on her way here right now? Or already here?*

He grabbed his coat and ran.

28

TURN SIGNAL. SMILE at the guard.

They were all automatic responses from deep within. They repressed the disgust they felt on coming in contact with the sickening, soft flesh of these creatures. The dull human wearing a weapon and a uniform waved them through the gate, seeing only Catherine Wells.

Time was running short. They knew what they had to do, but they could feel the wall slowly wearing away in Catherine's mind. She was becoming aware of the forces in her mind that were compelling her. They found that troubling, that one single mind could resist so strongly against their larger, unified whole, many minds working as one.

The time to act was now, before the opportunity was lost. The initial plan, to keep the ship from launching, had failed. Since they could not stop the ship's departure, they'd have to destroy it. The imperative planted deep within Catherine's mind was simple: no ship could make it through the wormhole.

They moved through the building, uncomfortable in their borrowed nervous system. Everything they took in through Catherine's senses displeased them. The building's angles were too sharp, too squared-off. Too mechanical. There was nothing organic, nothing beautiful. No natural stone or soft colors. Perhaps humanity surrounded itself with hardness to give them the armor their soft, flimsy bodies lacked.

It was simple to enter the locked offices in this compound. Child's play. The first office they'd entered before, the one belonging to the man Aaron. They accessed his workstation with a few keystrokes, not bothering to sit down. What they had to do wouldn't take long.

(Stop)

The dim whisper of a voice in their mind, an annoyance brushed away as easily as a buzzing fly.

The codes they had retrieved from this very office were clear and sharp in their memory, and they typed in the first of the three.

SEQUENCE INITIATED, the screen said.

(stop)

Ten minutes now to enter the remaining two codes, and their mission would be complete.

The second station was down the hall. It gave them a special sense of satisfaction to break into this office, the office of the man who couldn't stop meddling.

They quickly entered the second of the three codes.

(please stop, don't do this, don't make me do this)

Now for the hardest part. It would take most of their remaining allotted time to get to Mission Control. That was, they supposed, built into the process deliberately, to reduce the chances that any one person could do what they were doing right now. But no matter. It was well within their capabilities, and when that was done, it would be the end of any further human missions through the wormhole.

They started shutting down Cal's workstation.

"Catherine?"

(CAL STOP HER, STOP ME)

They stumbled back a step. That voice wasn't so much a buzzing fly anymore. They had observed Catherine's behavior for so long that they knew how to respond, turning her smile to him. "Hey, there you are."

"What are you doing in my office?"

"Mission Control said you might still be up here." Acting like Catherine wasn't a problem. It was as easy as driving a car, as chatting up the security guards.

Cal was looking at her strangely, though. "But how did you get in here?"

"It was unlocked. I was just about to leave you a note." The seconds were ticking by. They didn't have much time. "But now I don't have to!"

"Cath, we need to talk."

"We really do." They stepped over to him and put her hands on his shoulders. "And we will, but I have to go. I have to get home. Aimee's in trouble."

Confusion flitted across his face. These people were as soft-brained as they were soft-bodied. "Aimee—what happened?"

(Cal I'm in here that's not me)

"I don't have all the details yet. I'll call you when I know more." Taking a risk, they leaned in and kissed him on the cheek. They had observed Catherine's thoughts and feelings, but the look of surprise on Cal's face said they had misjudged. "We'll talk when I get back." They breezed past him and walked out of his office. There was still time to get to Mission Control.

"Wait!" Cal's voice came from behind them. "Why a note? Why not just call me?"

They kept going, walking a little faster.

"Catherine, stop." It sounded like an order.

They broke into a sprint for the stairs.

Behind them, Cal cursed and they heard running feet on the tile floor. They hit the stairwell door with both hands and jogged down the first set of stairs.

(stopstopstopstop)

They tripped as Catherine swept forward, trying to take control of her body again, but they shoved her down. *Behave, or you'll get yourself killed.*

It was enough of a stumble that Cal caught up with them, grabbed them by the arm. "Cath, what are you doing?"

Catherine's smile vanished as he whirled them to face him, and they responded with the instinct of two different species. They hissed at him, a dry, sibilant warning, but Catherine's body had its own set of defenses when it came under attack and it responded to him as well. They broke free of his hold and drove a hand up into his chin with a solid *thunk*.

(no!)

Yes. They pushed her advantage, knowing they could be more ruthless with him than he would be with her.

He blocked the next two punches, but a third got through, smashing into his soft cheek and through to the bone with a satisfying crunch. He staggered back into the landing wall.

(Cal run, get away from me if you can't stop me)

That voice. It was getting louder. Their time was running out. They had to act fast. They grabbed Cal by the shirt, pulling him away from the wall and turning him toward the stairs.

"Cath. Catherine." He grabbed them by the arms and spoke urgently, looking them in the eyes. "I know this isn't you. I know you're in there. Can you hear me? Come on. You can stop this; you have to fight it."

He was heavier than she was, and stitches in his shirt ripped as they tried to spin him toward the stairs.

"Catherine, come on. Come back. What you're doing is going to kill six innocent people. You have to stop. Please."

(I can't, I can't stop this)

His feet dragged. Just a few more steps. He stopped trying to hold on to her and started trying to pull free, realizing what they had planned. They could see it, envision it, his body tumbling down the stairs, hitting his head. Would it break?

(YOU CAN'T! DON'T HURT HIM)

But they could, and they were going to. They had to. The mission was waiting. How long did they have now? How many minutes remained?

They hauled Cal up, ready to let go.

(stop this let him go let him go let him—)

"—go, let him go, let *go!*" Catherine's eyes widened as everything snapped into focus and she surged forward, taking control of her body again.

29

THE STAIRWELL WAS the first thing that came into focus, and Catherine staggered backward, staring down at the step below her feet as if she'd never seen a step before. Her hands were clenched in Cal's shirt. There was blood on his face. "Oh my God." She let him go and took several steps back.

"Catherine?" Cal stepped toward her, his hands out. "Can you hear me?"

"What did I do?" she asked. Everything was vague and fuzzy. She was at Johnson, she could see that much. The clearest thing was the sense of urgency that she had to—she had to—but whatever it was, it was gone. Cal was looking at her with faint horror, and from the way her knuckles ached, she was sure she was the cause of the blood on his cheek. "*What did I do?*"

"Nothing. You—you tried. But I stopped you." He reached for her as he got closer, and it took an act of will for her not to step away.

"I hurt you."

He touched his cheek absently and winced. "You've got a good right hook on you. I think you might've cracked a molar."

"I'm so sorry—"

"Shh. No. It's okay. You didn't know what you were doing." He slipped an arm around her and they started back up the stairs.

"You knew what I was doing, though." She stopped at the top of the stairs and looked at him. "How bad is it?"

He didn't look at her; instead, he opened the fire door for them to go through.

"Cal. You're gonna have to tell me sooner or later." The longer he was silent, the worse things got in her head. What had she done?

"I know; hang on." He went to his office, expecting her to follow. She did, though she felt unsteady on her feet.

Once in his office, he closed the door behind them. "I'm about to break the law, but really, I can argue that you already broke it, and on some level you already know what I'm about to tell you anyway."

Catherine resisted the urge to grab him and shake him. The tension was growing unbearable. "What are you talking about? Tell me!"

"I'm talking about the documents you accessed when you broke into Aaron's office. They contained instructions on how to destroy a Sagittarius mission ship remotely."

She opened her mouth to interrupt.

"Hang on," he said, raising a hand. "It was a fail-safe, in case the ship picked up anything that was a threat to Earth. Top secret for a reason, obviously."

"And you didn't tell any of us? Cal, I was on that ship, and someone could have—"

"Ava knew," Cal said quietly. "John Duffy knows. No one else needed to. Chances are so remote that we'll ever need to use it, we decided there was no need to worry the entire crew."

"But Jesus, are you saying that I . . ." The full import of it hit her. Her knees wobbled, and Cal pushed a chair behind her, easing her down into it. "I almost killed them?" She couldn't say it above a whisper.

"You didn't, though. You didn't enter the third code." He knelt beside the chair and took her hands. "You didn't. I stopped you. *You* stopped you."

"But how did you know I was going to do it?" Her eyes stung.

Cal looked down before he answered. He was debating a lie, so it must be bad. His shoulders dropped and he looked her in the eyes. "It was pure luck. I realized what you'd been looking at that night, and you didn't answer your phone when I called. I got paranoid. I knew you'd have to start in Aaron's office and then mine, then Mission Control—so I started looking."

Catherine started to shudder. She'd— she'd almost— oh *God*. Cal rose up on his knees and put his arms around her.

"Shh," he said, and lowered her head to his shoulder. She stared blankly at his office wall, unable to accept his comfort. He held on to her for several minutes, until her shaking stopped, then he helped her to her feet and out the door. He made sure to lock his office door behind him. "Let's get you home, okay? We'll figure this out, I promise. You're not in this alone anymore."

Sagittarius | Mission

Alone.

No human had ever been as alone as Catherine was. She had an entire planet to herself.

Since the explosion, she'd been trying to figure out what happened. Had Tom set a fire? Stayed behind in it to die with the others? The command center was in the middle of the Habitat. The chances that he could have set a fire and gotten out in time . . . No, she had to assume everyone was dead.

She was no closer to any answers than she'd been a day ago.

She sat in the command module of *Sagittarius*, eating a cold MRE out of the pouch as she stared blankly out the windshield. Through it, she saw the vast rock formations of TRAPPIST-1f, glinting in the reflected light of her sister planets. The soil was the color of old, dried blood in this light.

Survival was the best thing she could manage right now. She wanted to make a plan to get home, but was there even any point? How was she going to fly back all by herself?

The comm screen beeped loudly and Catherine gave a small scream, jumping out of her chair. She was just about to write it off as her imagination, but then it beeped again, and she thumbed the receiver.

The screen flashed just two words: *SURRENDER, CATHERINE.*

Her makeshift dinner threatened to come back up her throat, stopped only by the fear that constricted it. She leaned in to the mic. "Who the hell is this? Tom? Is that you?" Her heart pounded so hard that it only in-

creased the sick feeling in her belly, and she swallowed the rush of saliva in her mouth.

The screen flashed again. *GIVE UP. GIVE IN. SURRENDER.*

Fuck that. "Fuck you." She enunciated clearly into the mic. "Whoever you are, if you want me, you'll have to come and get me."

She rubbed her mouth with the back of her hand, staring at the comms, waiting to see if there was an answer. It was Tom. It had to be Tom. But how could he have gotten out of the Habitat?

Maybe he'd lied when he'd said he was messaging her from inside. If nothing else, it was clear that he'd wanted her to stay inside so she'd die with the others. But if he was outside in a suit, why didn't she see him when she came out?

The others were dead; she was sure of it. Once the fire had burned itself out, she'd explored the ruined Habitat. She'd found at least three bodies, but otherwise there hadn't been much to identify; the fire had burned hot and fast in the Habitat's oxygen-rich atmosphere. When no one else turned up, she made the logical assumption that she was the sole survivor.

I have to go home. I have to tell the others what happened, if nothing else.

Except . . . what could she tell them?

She stared at the comm screen while she thought. At one point she checked the message log and confirmed that yes, those messages had actually come in.

Okay. If she was going to go home, leaving was going to take some preparation. The ship itself wasn't stocked with enough supplies for the long trip back. There was a supply shed on the far side of the landing area, on the other side of the Habitat—far enough to have been untouched by the blast. She'd have to raid and transport things one rover-load at a time. Thank God the second rover hadn't been close enough to the Habitat to be destroyed, too.

After the first round of messages, the comms had pinged throughout the night, destroying any chance Catherine had of restful sleep. No matter how hard she tried to convince herself that she'd imagined the whole

thing, the string of messages telling her to surrender was real. She'd deleted them in a fit of fear and bad judgment. It wasn't supposed to be possible to delete any of the comm records, but Tom had shown her how to bypass those protocols, showing off for her with a cheeky grin.

Tom. He was still out there, and he expected her to surrender.

There was a tiny cache of weapons on *Sagittarius*, intended for protection against any unfriendly fauna on TRAPPIST-1f. When there had been no fauna to be found, those weapons—modified roughly from standard handguns to fire in different atmospheres—had been locked up shipboard. Ava had confessed to Catherine one night that NASA had also meant for those weapons to serve as a last-ditch solution for the crew, should the worst happen. One usage NASA probably hadn't anticipated for those guns was for the crew to protect themselves against one of their own. But the guns were locked up, and she had no real way to get to them. Ava had been the only one with the passcodes.

"Okay. Okay. No guns, then. Fine." Ah, well, the ability to improvise solutions in a crisis was one reason NASA had chosen them all, wasn't it?

No weapons at all, and she still needed to start getting things together. She grabbed the tool kit from the ship's storage area and slid a heavy wrench into a pocket of her jumpsuit. It might be useless as a weapon, but the weight of it made her feel better.

She drove the rover across the landing zone to the storage shed and started gathering some of the supplies. The entire time she worked, hauling crates onto the rover's storage rack, the back of her neck prickled. Was Tom out there, watching her?

While she was in the shed, she heard a thunderous crash outside, and ran out to see all her carefully stacked crates spilled to the ground.

It was Tom.

He was coming at her from around the rover. His expression was utterly blank, slack-jawed. One side of his face had livid burn marks on the cheek. There was no light in his eyes at all, almost as if he weren't even looking at her.

"Tom. Come on, it's me. It's Catherine."

He stopped, and his eyes focused, fixing on her, still dead and cold.

"We have to work together to get home."

"Surrender." His voice was flat, unemotional.

He started toward her again, at a steady, relentless walk. She pulled the wrench from her pocket. "Stop. I don't want to hurt you."

Tom didn't stop. But Catherine couldn't make herself swing the wrench at his head. At the last second she spun and tried to flee, but he caught her by the shoulder, reaching for her throat. His fingers burned hot through the material of her suit as they closed around her neck.

Catherine fell back on her training. She fought hard and dirty, slamming a foot into Tom's, clawing at his hands. Finally she hit backward with the wrench, connecting with his skull through his hood. Tom grunted and his hands loosened from her neck. She fled, leaving the rover behind for now. She looked back to see Tom still on his feet, blood on his head and his hand. He began to chase her.

Once she was in the shadow of the rocks, she ducked and wove through them, hiding behind one to listen for his footsteps.

He was easy to hear, trampling over the ground without any attempt at stealth.

She waited for what felt like hours, until the footsteps receded and all she heard was silence. She had no way of knowing where he was, if he was searching for her in the distance or lying in wait. All she knew was that she couldn't stay here. Slowly, quietly, she pushed herself upright, the wrench clamped tight in her fist.

Silence.

She didn't see Tom. Couldn't hear him. This was her chance.

She sprinted back for the rover, her heart thudding in her chest. Everything was just as she'd left it. The metal crates were still intact. She shoved them up onto the rover, less careful about stacking than before, no longer interested in loading as much as she could in one trip. The entire time, her skin crawled, waiting, listening for the sound of Tom. Despite everything, she didn't know if she could kill him.

She climbed into the rover and started it up, pushing the little motor as fast as it would go back to the ship. Even if he pursued her, the ship was far enough away, and she had enough of a head start, to give her time to unload the rover before he could reach her.

By the time she finished loading the crates on board *Sagittarius*, Catherine was exhausted and sweaty. Not to mention starving. She sealed up the ship, finally able to relax a bit knowing that Tom couldn't reach her in here. Whatever had happened to him, he seemed too far gone for her to get him back.

The question was, did that mean she was going to leave him behind when she left?

———

After she cleaned up, luxuriating in the feel of clean clothes, she started pulling together dinner. She was so hungry that waiting for everything to heat up felt like an eternity. She was just about to sit down in the galley when the comms started pinging again.

Catherine froze, halfway between sitting and standing, her appetite vanishing. With her stomach twisting in knots, she went to the cockpit, expecting to see the demand to surrender flash on the screen again. Instead, she got Tom's voice.

"*Sagittarius*, this is Tom Wetherbee; if you're there, come in. If anyone's alive, please come in. Someone must be out there. The ship is locked; I couldn't get in."

A chill shot down Catherine's spine.

"*Sagittarius*, I'm wounded. My suit's torn; I've got some burns. I think something scratched me. Please help me."

Part of her mind insisted this was a trick, told her not to answer him. He sounded so desperate, though. So terrified.

She settled in front of the console. "Tom, it's Catherine."

"Oh thank God!" he cried. "What happened? The Habitat—it's gone."

"Where are you?"

"I'm in the storage shed," Tom said. "The ship was locked, so I thought someone must be inside . . . Tell me what happened!"

"You don't remember the explosion?"

"Jesus. No. Where is everyone?"

I don't know what I did last night . . .

Catherine's mouth was dry when she tried to swallow. "They're dead, Tom. I thought you were dead, too."

There was silence over the comms, and when he came back on, it sounded as if he were barely holding on to himself. "All of them? No. Oh God. How much time have I lost, Catherine?"

"It's been a day since the explosion. How did you get out?"

"I don't know. Last thing I remember I was under the console in the command center, elbow-deep in some wiring, trying to figure out how things had gotten so fucked up. Then I'm sitting in the middle of nowhere burned and bleeding." He paused. "I think something attacked me."

Did he really not remember? Or was this all a ploy to draw her out? "You tried to kill me today. You've been sending me threatening comm messages."

"That's ridiculous. I would never— I could never hurt you." The betrayal in his voice sounded so real that she wanted to believe it.

"I've got the bruises to prove it."

"I don't remember that!" The quaver in his voice also sounded real. "Cath, I think I'm getting a fever."

"I can't let you back on the ship. You've got to be quarantined, Tom." *Even if I trusted you, which I don't.*

Tom's voice grew hard. "You're going to leave me behind. You're going to just let me die."

"No." *Yes. Maybe.* "Look, there's plenty of food and supplies still in the storage shed. I'll leave the antibiotics and painkillers you're missing outside the ship. I-I'll wait through your quarantine with you."

"You're a shit liar, Wells."

"Hang on." Catherine ran to the infirmary and grabbed the promised medication. If he was lying and was right outside instead of in the storage shed, she was taking an enormous risk, but she had to. Even if she wasn't sure she could trust him, she needed to be trustworthy herself.

She opened the ship's main hatch. Tom was nowhere to be seen. She put the containers just outside the hatch before ducking back in and resealing everything. When she got back to the comms, she said, "The meds are waiting for you now."

"I don't know if I can walk that far."

"You tried to choke me. I'm not coming to you."

"Fine. God, you always were a heartless bitch." That was real, even if the tears had been fake. "If I die, my blood is on your hands."

Yeah, well, she knew that much.

"If the meds work, we'll talk." Then she shut off the mic and walked away.

There were no other messages that night.

Exhausted as she was, Catherine barely managed to sleep. When the sun came up, she crept to the main hatch.

What she saw shocked her, and, if she was honest, touched her a little. The meds she'd left were gone, and parked in front of the ship was the rover, loaded with supplies. Judging from the other crates stacked around it, there were plenty of supplies for a return trip home. Tom must have spent all night making trips back and forth.

Was it a trick? Then she saw the message scratched in the dirt:

PEACE OFFERING. QUARANTINE 48 HOURS. WAIT FOR ME? WILL MESSAGE.

He was willing to wait outside the ship for two days to see if he came down with something or, like Catherine, stayed well. Even if she didn't trust him, she couldn't turn down what he was offering. The supplies he left weren't tampered with. The seals on all the crates were still intact. He couldn't have gotten to the contents.

Faced with the prospect of trying to get a different batch of supplies and possibly having to fight off Tom again, Catherine decided to take the chance. She started loading the crates. It took the better part of a day, hauling things between the rover and the open hatch. By the time she was finished, she'd reached a decision: She'd wait forty-eight hours. If Tom was still alive, she'd worry about making a final decision then. In the meantime, she'd stay locked in the ship where it was safe. With the long trip back home, a couple more days wouldn't make a difference one way or another.

30

CATHERINE WOKE IN her own bed, confused at first, thinking that she'd had a strange nightmare.

The sound of someone moving around in her living room brought it all back. It had been real. Cal had driven her home in her car, made her tea, put her to bed, and—from the sounds of it—slept on her couch.

Details were fuzzy, but she remembered what she'd gone to NASA to do. *I almost killed them. I almost killed everyone on* Sagittarius. The thought stuck in her head, echoing and rebounding. She crawled out of bed and pulled on her robe.

Cal was in the kitchen making coffee. "Hey," he said. "I heard you get up. How are you doing?"

Catherine's voice came out in a rusty croak, as if she had a cold, or had been shouting. "I tried to kill six of my friends last night—seven, counting you—but otherwise, I'm doing okay. You?" There were bruises on his face, but the cut on his cheek didn't look as bad this morning. Her aches weren't physical, but her soul felt bruised. How could she live with what she'd done? And what if she tried to do it again?

"Yeah, okay, so maybe that was a dumb question." He changed the subject, holding up the coffee can from her cabinet. "Seriously? You seriously drink this? You know dirt would be cheaper, right? And probably taste better."

Despite her misery, she smiled. "It gets the job done. Some of us don't care about hand-roasted, carefully ground artisanal beans from some obscure corner of the world. It's caffeine."

"My God. I see I have a lot of educating to do here." He shook his head.

Still, he started the coffee machine and came to sit next to her on the couch. "Were you able to sleep?"

"Surprisingly, yes." She lowered her face to her hands and rubbed with her palms. "Who knew attempted murder was so exhausting."

"You weren't in control—"

"That doesn't actually make it any better." She looked up at him, needing to voice her fears aloud to another person. "What if I try again? What if I already did kill someone, and just don't know it?"

"Now we know what the plan is," Cal countered. "That makes it easier to stop. And maybe it will give us a clue about what's going on here."

"But whose plan? Cal, there is someone in my head. Maybe more than one. I *felt* them!" Catherine sighed, slumping against the back of the sofa. "God. This is such a nightmare."

"I have a theory about that." Cal turned, sitting sideways to face her. "The Longbow Protocol was supposed to prevent any sort of alien life form from coming to Earth without our knowledge, right? The thing is, it already failed. *We* failed. There was one outcome we didn't predict: that someone would bring something back with them, something we wouldn't be able to detect until it was too late."

"What do you mean?" Catherine pulled her knees to her chest.

"You're carrying an antibody that has never been seen on Earth before. It means you were exposed to something during the mission—bacteria, a virus, a fungus—something that got into your body and caused a reaction in your immune system. And only one other human on record has ever had that particular antigen," Cal said. "Iris Addy. The one other person who's experienced similar memory loss and violent impulses after going through the wormhole."

"You're saying we all were exposed to something out there?" A nightmare scenario grew in Catherine's mind, all six of them falling into those fits. Oh God, had they all destroyed one another? Was that what happened?

"It's possible. I don't know." Cal watched her carefully as if he saw the tension spike in her. "Cath, don't start jumping to conclusions. Stick to what we know. You and Commander Addy. That's all we know."

Catherine took a deep breath to steady herself, then let it out. "Okay. Say you're right. How could an infection make us do things and not remember them? How could it . . . control us?"

"Have you ever heard of zombie ants? In Brazil?"

"Zombie ants . . ." As bad as things were, that was just ridiculous enough to make her smile. "No. Please tell me you aren't saying I'm a zombie."

"No! No, not at all. Okay. So there's a fungus called *Ophiocordyceps unilateralis*. It infects certain species of ants and takes control of their bodies. It's not sentient; it just makes the ants go to a specific place that's most favorable for the fungus to spread."

"Something tells me that doesn't end well for the ants."

"Well, no; they die and sprout fungi," Cal said quickly, "but that's not what I'm thinking about here. What if the original antigen represents some sort of similar method of control?"

"But . . ." Catherine paused.

"There's no sign that it's fatal," Cal reassured her. "Iris Addy has been living with it for years."

"You said the fungus isn't sentient," Catherine said. She could remember the distinct feeling of another entity, an intelligent mind, directing her movements. "But there was a . . . a *personality* there. A mind."

"Yeah, it's not a direct parallel. I'm just saying I think the antibodies are related—" Cal stopped. "Catherine. Do you realize what this means? An alien life-form *made contact with you* out there."

"Don't jump to conclusions—"

"It's a small jump—a hop. First contact. Catherine, that's *huge*."

"We could have it all wrong." Catherine wanted to backpedal. He believed her almost too completely. She hadn't counted on that. "What if I'm just crazy?"

"I don't think you're crazy—at least, not delusional." Cal got up to get their coffee, black for both of them. He brought it back to the living room and Catherine wrapped her hands around the mug, hunched over it.

"Even if I'm not, and I have met aliens—or they've communicated with me somehow—they're not exactly saying 'we come in peace,' Cal. They may have already had a hand in killing some of us, and . . . and if . . ." She couldn't make herself say it.

Cal leaned forward and touched her hand carefully, and she didn't pull away. "Come on. Spit it out."

"If they see us the way that I saw people . . ." Catherine shivered. "They want us dead. All of us." A worse thought occurred. "What if they made me kill them all? My crew? If we were all infected, what if we killed one another?"

"Let's verify that they exist first, before we start worrying about that." Cal squeezed her hand and let it go. The warmth lingered on Catherine's skin, more soothing than she wanted to admit.

" 'We,' " Catherine said suddenly.

"Huh?"

"You keep saying 'we.' 'Before we start worrying.' "

"Well . . . yeah." Cal gave her a puzzled look. If he tilted his head, he'd look like a baffled golden retriever, and Catherine had to fight a smile. "We're the only ones who know about this. The first thing we need is more information," Cal said.

"Where do we start?"

Cal rubbed his eyes before answering. "Some of it might come from you, if you start remembering things. There might be some reports hidden away that describe anomalies from your mission, or Iris Addy's. I haven't seen them, but I can look."

"They didn't tell me about any, if there are."

"Yeah . . . that doesn't mean much. Something like that would be classi-fied 'need to know' immediately. And of course," he added, "mere astronauts don't need to know that."

"You know people would say we're both crazy."

"Feh," he said cheerfully. "Wouldn't be the first time someone's said that to me. Besides, they told Galileo he was crazy, right? And probably Einstein. Sometimes you gotta be crazy to make any progress."

"NASA doesn't like crazy these days." Catherine felt a wry smile tugging at her mouth. "Crazy isn't politically expedient."

"Again, I say feh." He really was on her side. He'd been against her only when he thought she was trying to hide the truth. Which . . . she supposed, she had been. She'd been afraid of the truth. She still was, but now she wasn't afraid alone. And that made more of a difference than she could have imagined.

"The way I see it—God, that's awful," he said, grimacing after taking a sip of coffee, "once we have proof of their existence, the two biggest questions we have to answer are how and why. How are they controlling you? And why do they want to destroy Sagittarius II?"

"I don't know." She shrugged. "I've felt—I'm not sure how to describe it. When I've had those violent, repulsive thoughts, it's like I got pushed out of the driver's seat. And . . . last night, when we were fighting, I pushed my way back."

"Lucky for me," he said.

"I'm so sorry."

"Not another word. You didn't do it." Cal leaned back, thinking.

"I don't understand," Catherine said. "We sent probes to TRAPPIST years before Sagittarius I. And you saw the data we managed to send back. Nothing showed any signs of intelligent life."

Cal lowered his mug. "'What if this species, whatever it is, has evolved into a form that we can't track or recognize?"

"Like what?"

"Any number of things," Cal said. He looked for all the world like a graduate student having a theoretical discussion with some classmates. "They might be microscopic. Hell, they might not be made up of anything we recognize as living, organic material."

"How the hell do we find something like that?"

Cal grinned. "I have no idea. But we'll figure it out with some more data."

"Oh God," Catherine said suddenly. "We've got to let the crew know what they're heading into."

"I have a better idea," Cal said, his expression turning more thoughtful. "How about we bring them back?"

"How are we going to do that? If no one wants to know the truth because of bad publicity, they're sure not going to let us do that."

"I don't know yet." Cal leaned back into her sofa. "We've got just over three weeks to find evidence that letting Sagittarius II land on TRAPPIST-1f would be worse optics than calling them back and scrapping the mission." He glanced over. "You up for the challenge?"

"I am if you are."

"It's got to be good. We've got to find something they can't argue with. Some sort of proof, hard proof, that these life-forms exist," Cal grumbled, thumping his head against the cushion. "I guess if we fail we can make some good money on the basic cable circuit, right?"

"They'd probably give you your own show." She joked, but he was right. They had to convince people who stubbornly didn't want to believe.

Cal let out a frustrated breath. "If only we had someone who could substantiate your story. Someone else who came back from the mission."

"One more reason being a sole survivor sucks."

Cal laughed, startled. "I bet that's a long list."

She hadn't meant it as a joke, but she laughed with him. "Yeah. Yeah, it really is."

"Right, so no one to back up your story. Too bad."

"Yeah, no one's exactly been in my shoes before—" Wait. Catherine stopped herself. *You don't want to end up like Commander Addy. I don't want to see that happen to you*, Dr. Darzi warned her. What had Addy seen on her own trip through ERB Prime? What had she heard? "Cal . . . what about Commander Addy?"

"Addy . . . she didn't go to TRAPPIST, though—" His eyes lit up. "But she *did* go through the wormhole."

"And every time I started pushing for the truth, my therapist used her as a cautionary tale."

"Yeah, but that's because when she came back, she returned with some pretty wild stories, apparently." Cal broke into a smile and planted a loud, sudden kiss on Catherine's cheek. "And the same strange antibodies you have! Colonel Wells, you are a certified mad genius. If we could track her down, you two could compare stories."

"How are we going to do that?"

"I have some ideas. Worst case, we find her and go see her. You up for a possible road trip?" Cal was the one who looked like a mad genius now, a wild grin on his face.

"Let's find our missing commander," she said.

31

CATHERINE HADN'T THOUGHT Cal was serious about a road trip, but when attempts to reach Commander Addy via email and phone both failed, they started making plans. Cal was able to dig up an address for her, deep in the Arizona desert in a place so tiny it wasn't even an actual town—just a general store and a stoplight.

They planned to take off for a weekend to track her down, flying to Phoenix and driving the rest of the way. Maybe nothing would come of it, but Catherine felt like they were *doing* something. Slowly, the feeling of being helpless, of being frozen, was falling away.

The night before they were due to leave she called Julie, so someone would know where she was going. She didn't want to tell David. The fewer people at NASA who knew where she and Cal were going, the better.

"Wait," Julie said after being quiet. "Who is this guy again?"

"Cal's one of the guys working on Sagittarius II. We've got a lead on some information that might affect the current mission."

"Are you sure you're all right? I mean, this seems sudden after— well, you've been having a bad time lately."

"I'm doing a lot better," Catherine reassured her. "No more drinking. This trip—it's a good thing, okay? It's me taking positive steps."

"But doesn't it seem a little, I dunno—a little risky to you?" Julie was typing as she spoke. "Cal Morganson, you said?"

"Yeah. What do you mean, risky?"

"I mean, this guy you've literally never mentioned before suddenly wants you to go away with him to some remote place . . . and you're being awfully closemouthed about why."

Catherine laughed. "Are you saying you think he's going to *hurt* me?"

"No, I just—oh." Julie stopped typing and her tone changed. "Is there something I need to know about this guy?"

"Like what?"

"I don't know. Are you sure this is just about business? What kind of 'positive steps' are you talking about?"

Catherine was too startled to answer at first. "What? Of course it's business. Why wouldn't it be?"

" 'Cause I'm sitting here looking at a picture of Cal Morganson at NASA, and honey, you didn't tell me he was pretty."

"Cal?" Catherine laughed. "You think that me and Cal—no." Pretty? She'd noticed that he was attractive, and he *was* a lot nicer than she'd originally thought, but . . . that was ridiculous. "He's like, half my age or something."

"Catherine Marie Wells, I am not looking at the face of a twenty-one-year-old right now. Sure he's younger than you, but boy, wouldn't that piss David off?"

"Julie." Catherine paused, patiently. "I am not trying to piss David off. And Cal is just a guy I work with." She laughed again, because *honestly*. "I can't believe you looked him up."

"Kiddo, I've been vetting your dates since you were sixteen. You think I'm gonna stop now?"

"Oh my God, stop. This is for work. Can we drop this?" The humor was rapidly diminishing, and Catherine couldn't put a finger on why her discomfort was growing.

"Fine, fine. I'm just sayin'. You could do worse. But— I'm done. Subject changed. When are you coming back?"

"I don't know for sure. It depends on what we find. Shouldn't be more than a couple of days. I'll have my cell phone, but we're gonna be in the middle of nowhere, so I don't know how good service will be." Catherine paused. "Jules, don't mention this to David, okay? I don't want him to worry."

"You realize that's not making me feel any better about this."

"I know, but just . . . trust me. Please?"

There was a long silence on the line, and then Julie said, "All right. I trust you. Take care of yourself. Call me as soon as you can."

By the time she met Cal at the airport, Catherine was starting to have doubts of her own. It was ungodly early; the sun was barely up. What *were* they doing? What did they think they were going to find, talking to someone so thoroughly discredited at NASA that hardly anyone mentioned her name anymore?

Cal met her at the gate, and she almost didn't recognize him, hiding behind a pair of sunglasses. Like her, he'd dressed casually in jeans. They looked like tourists, and Catherine had to repress the urge to laugh wildly. Somehow they'd both made the decision to look as unofficial and nongovernmental as possible.

"You made it," he said. "I wondered if you'd change your mind."

"I'm sorry, that's not the correct code phrase. If you're my contact, you should be saying something about the rain in Germany at this time of year." Catherine sat next to him at the gate.

". . . What?" The sunglasses came off and Cal looked at her closely.

Catherine gave in to the desire to laugh, which didn't make Cal look less worried. "The sunglasses. You look like you're trying to go incognito."

Cal finally smiled, catching on. "Okay, it's a little cloak-and-dagger. Aaron would kick my ass if he could see me right now."

"He'd probably kick both our asses." She paused. "And then fire us."

"And maybe have us committed," Cal added. They were serious until their eyes met, then they both burst out laughing.

———

The drive from Phoenix to Rough Rock was supposed to take five hours. Catherine drove the first leg. They listened to the radio for a while, with a little bit of conversation here and there, but by the time they switched driving duties, they'd left most of the radio signals far behind.

The rental car didn't do a great job of keeping the road noise out after Catherine snapped off the radio. A dull rushing noise filled the silence as the desert went past Catherine's window. It was bright and hot, the sky white-blue. Despite the rental's air-conditioning, she could feel the heat baking through the glass.

After a period of awkward silence, Cal said, "All right, Wells. Truth or . . . truth. What's the craziest thing you've ever seen or done?"

"Do I need to remind you that I've been to an actual other *planet*?"

"Yeah, but you don't remember it. Still, fair enough. On Earth. What's the craziest thing you've seen or done on Earth?"

Catherine thought for a moment. "You've gone through the astronaut training program, right?" she asked.

"A slightly abbreviated version; I was never a candidate, but I wanted to get a sense of what you guys go through."

"Did you do the simulation?" The simulation was a monthlong exercise where a "crew" lived in a replica of a ship like *Sagittarius*.

Cal looked away from the road as a semi barreled past going the other way on the two-lane highway. "I skipped out on that particular experience."

"Uh-huh. I should have guessed." Catherine grinned. "Well, some of us didn't have that luxury. After the first couple of days, it got dull. We were mostly waiting for Mission Control to throw a crisis at us so we'd have something to do. Except some of us found ways to amuse ourselves."

"Uh-oh."

"I don't know how well you knew Richie Almeida, but that was one man you did *not* want to let get bored. When Richie got bored, he got creative."

"You never want your systems operator to get bored," Cal agreed. "What'd he do?"

"I still don't know how he did it, but he reprogrammed the onboard computer to respond to commands with a verbal response." She shook her head, laughing. "Made the mission 'commander' absolutely batshit. Every time one of us typed in a command we'd hear something like 'Aye, aye, Captain!' or 'I'm afraid I canna do that, Captain.' "

"The onboard computers don't have a voice response system," Cal said.

"By the time Richie was done with it, that one did. He was just using recordings." She laughed, remembering. "It was like being around someone who had the ringtone collection from hell. Any alert we got was prefaced with 'Houston, we have a problem.' "

"I mean, that's funny, but that's the craziest thing? Really?"

"That was just the start. I told you that the simulation commander was losing his mind over this, right? Tried everything to get Richie to change it back. NASA wouldn't interfere since, you know, it was designed to test our responses to the unpredictable. Hell, I'm not convinced that they didn't help him set it up." She chuckled. "The commander in question was David."

"David Wells? Your— I'm sorry, what do I call him right now?"

Catherine wrinkled her nose. "Soon-to-be ex is probably accurate enough. Anyway, yes. And he was not happy. But the kicker came when he did a test 'space walk.' I swear, Richie was saving this for a special occasion. When David tried to come back in, the air lock wouldn't open. He yelled for us to let him in, and the computer said . . ."

"No." Cal started to laugh.

Catherine laughed with him. "Yes. The computer said, 'I'm sorry, Dave. I'm afraid I can't do that. . . . This mission is too important for me to allow you to jeopardize it.' I thought David was gonna have a stroke. Mission Control was in tears laughing. I think everybody saw it coming except him. The rest of the simulation, any time David did anything with the main computer, he got HAL 9000 answering him."

"I'm surprised Almeida didn't wash out after that."

"That's why I think he had the brass behind him, to be honest." Catherine shook her head, realizing something. "That . . . might have been one of the reasons David washed out. He never really talked to me about it."

Cal made a noncommittal noise and they were both suddenly quiet.

"Anyway," Catherine said, shaking it off, "what about you? What's the craziest thing you've seen or done?"

"Well . . . I was an undergrad at Caltech."

"Oh God."

"Aha, I see our reputation precedes us." Cal flashed her a smile. "Can you hand me a water?"

"I've known a few Caltech engineers." Catherine reached into the back seat to the small Styrofoam cooler packed with ice and bottles of water and grabbed two. She handed one to him before cracking hers open. "What'd you do?"

"Well. The head of the physics department was notorious for telling students that if they failed out of school, they'd have to get a job working at a car wash." Cal managed to open the water while keeping his hands marginally on the steering wheel. "He'd say it before every exam. It was annoying as hell."

"That doesn't make sense," Catherine said with a laugh.

"I know. Like, why a car wash, right? Still, by my senior year, we could recite it along with him." Cal paused, took a drink of water. "He also, we discovered, had a classic 1980 BMW that he was *crazy* proud of. It was a collector's edition or something, and the damn thing was his baby."

"Oh, no."

"Oh, yes. He gave us a target. Never," he proclaimed, "give an engineering student a grudge and a target."

"What did you do?"

"We washed his car." He gave her a smug look. "In the men's locker room showers."

"How the hell did you manage to get it in there?" Catherine laughed again.

"Hello, Caltech engineering students. We figured it out."

"What did he do?"

"I think he managed to reverse engineer how we got it in there, but last I heard, he'd stopped using his car-wash speech."

"Air Force pranks were never as good as the stories I hear from you geeks." Catherine leaned back against the seat, smiling.

"Come on. Didn't you, like, steal a general's plane or anything?"

"Not me. I was a strictly-by-the-book sort of girl."

"Besides, you say 'geek' like you're not one. I have bad news for you, Cath. You're an astronaut. You're pretty much Peak Geek."

A sign up ahead said they were getting close to Rough Rock. "Do we know exactly where she lives out here?"

"Well . . . her address is general delivery, and GPS wasn't any help. I think this is going to be a case of finding someone who knows her and hoping they can tell us which landmarks to follow." Cal pointed at the GPS on the dash. "We're gonna go to the main crossroads and start from there."

"Oh yeah, because starting anything at a crossroads isn't ominous at all," Catherine said.

"I'm not planning to make any deals. Not yet."

At the crossroads was a gas station, with a store that called itself a trading post. Cal pulled into the gas station. "Well, this is it: the booming metropolis of Rough Rock, Arizona."

"I expect to see tumbleweeds any second." Catherine climbed out of the car, her legs complaining at the long ride.

"I'm going to fill up the car, if you want to go in and ask if anyone knows Addy."

"Sure." It felt good to walk, like rust falling off her joints in great flakes. The gas station wasn't much more than a shack that held a shelf of rudimentary auto supplies, a collection of snack foods of dubious age and provenance, and a cooler of sodas in the back. After saying hello to the woman behind the counter, Catherine grabbed a couple of sodas and took them up.

"This," she said, "and the gas."

"All right." The woman was short and squat, with black hair streaked with iron gray in a long braid down her back and wrinkles around her eyes from squinting into the sun.

While they waited for Cal to finish gassing up, Catherine said, "Do you know a woman named Iris Addy? She's supposed to live around here."

The woman looked her over with dark olive-brown eyes. "You from the government?"

"What?"

"You and your friend. White people in a rental car, asking after Iris. You ain't dressed like government, but just the same."

"No—not really. I mean, that's not why we're here. We just want to talk to her."

The woman humphed, then started ringing up the total after Cal finished. "That'll be forty-five fifty-one, with the sodas."

Catherine handed her cash and tried again. "I . . . I think I went through something similar to her. We just want to talk."

"Yeah, I know who you are now. I saw you on TV." She handed Catherine her change. "That road out there is Route 59. Follow it up about five miles, you'll see a bunch of power towers. Turn right there. Iris's place is about six more miles."

"Thank you."

"Don't thank me. She ain't gonna be happy to see you."

"Still. Thanks." Catherine took the sodas and left "We're all set," she told Cal. "And I got directions."

"There's only a few hours of daylight left," Cal said. "Should we find a place to stay and try in the morning?"

"Let's not." She handed him one of the sodas. "I have a feeling the clerk is going to give Iris a heads-up that we're coming. Be nice if she didn't have time to run off."

"All right."

When they were back on the road, there was no more easy chatter. Catherine's stomach was tied in knots and she couldn't stop fidgeting with the soda bottle.

"Hey." Cal reached over and squeezed her forearm, giving it a shake. "It's going to be okay. Worst case, she can't tell us anything, and we got to have a nice drive through God's country."

"Yeah," Catherine said, unconvinced. "Sure."

The towers the clerk mentioned were easy to spot, and Catherine wiped her damp palms against her jeans as the remaining miles ticked by. A homestead came into view, a gray, weathered cabin and a few outbuildings equally as weathered. A handful of sheep and goats stood around in a pen, and as they pulled up, a dog started barking.

Cal and Catherine got out of the car and had barely taken ten steps to the house when a woman burst through the front door. She wore denim overalls and a plaid shirt, and had wild hair that spilled over her shoulders. She had a shotgun in her hands, and as they watched, she racked it and aimed.

"Now you just get back in that car and turn right around the way you came," she said.

32

BEFORE CATHERINE COULD react, Cal shoved her behind him and raised both hands. *Well, he gets points for gallantry, I suppose . . .*

"We're not here to harass you," he said.

"I know who sent you," Addy replied. "I'm not telling you anything. I've done all the talking I'm gonna do. Now just go." She gestured with the shotgun, and Catherine had a moment of relief when she saw her finger wasn't on the trigger—yet.

"Commander Addy," Catherine spoke up from behind Cal, and in fact, stepped around him with her hands up as well. "We're from NASA, but they don't know we're here. My name's Catherine Wells."

Addy's brow creased, and she took a closer look at Catherine. "What do you mean, NASA doesn't know you're here? You're their media darling right now, I bet you can't piss without someone keeping track of it."

"Well . . . let's just say they're not real fond of me at the moment, Commander. I think you and I have some things in common. Can we talk about them?"

"Who's he?" Addy pointed at Cal.

"Cal Morganson," he answered. "I work on the Sagittarius program with Catherine."

"You're no astronaut," she said dubiously.

"No ma'am. I'm the flight activities officer for Sagittarius II."

Addy sniffed. "Why aren't you at Johnson? Your people are up there right now, aren't they?"

Cal put on a charming smile. Catherine bet it worked wonders on grandmothers and maiden aunts. "Well, Commander, that's part of the reason we're here."

Commander Addy was older than Catherine by maybe twenty years—it was hard to judge from her face. Her salt-and-pepper hair was ragged and looked as if she cut it herself, and her eyes were the same faded and harsh blue as the desert sky overhead. She was nobody's grandmother or maiden aunt, and she wasn't charmed. But she did lower the shotgun. "Catherine Wells, huh? They say it took you six years to get home, that right?"

"Yes, ma'am."

"It's a hard thing, being out there alone for so long. People like this one," Addy indicated Cal, "don't get that. You do, though. I can see it in your eyes." She kicked the shell out of the shotgun's chamber. "Ah, hell. Come on in. But no snooping."

"Wouldn't dream of it," Cal muttered, and Catherine elbowed him as he passed.

The cabin was clearly meant for only one person. There was just one armchair in front of an overstuffed bookcase. On the table next to the chair was a portable radio. Everything was haphazard and looked slightly off-kilter—a lot like Commander Addy. There was nothing decorative, nothing that didn't look absolutely necessary. The wall by the door contained a rack of guns. The main room's two windows were heavily shaded, making it gloomy even in the bright late afternoon. A ham radio set was on a desk in one corner, but there was no sign of a computer.

Something about the entire place made Catherine feel uneasy. It reminded her of the Unabomber's bunker; all that was missing was a manifesto. And Catherine wouldn't be surprised if there was one of those around somewhere, half-written. Something was wrong here. A deep sense of discomfort was growing inside her, something she couldn't put her finger on, an itch she couldn't reach.

"Don't have many visitors," Addy said, pulling two chairs out of the kitchen. "Sorry." She didn't offer them anything, and they didn't ask, but sat in the hard kitchen chairs.

"No, this is fine," Catherine said. "Thank you so much for talking to us."

Addy humphed, then settled into the armchair with a groan. "Keep your voices down. I did a sweep yesterday, but I can't guarantee no one's listening."

Cal exchanged a look with Catherine. "Thanks for the warning," he said.

"You don't believe me. That's fine. She does." Addy nodded toward Catherine. "You know what it's like to be under surveillance, don't you, Wells?"

Catherine didn't answer directly, especially since Cal had been the one surveilling her. "What happened to you, Commander? Can you tell me?"

"What do they say about me?" Addy asked. "Had a breakdown, unfit for duty?"

"That's . . . yes," Cal said. "No one talks about the details. No one talks about it at all, officially."

"No, they wouldn't." She looked at Catherine. "Is that what they told you, too? Breakdown brought on by wormhole-induced amnesia?"

"Something like that," Catherine responded. Her head was starting to buzz, like the power towers they'd passed.

"Did you get it, too?" Addy leaned forward. "The amnesia?"

"I don't remember anything about our time in the TRAPPIST system," Catherine admitted. "But my doctor thinks it's trauma-based. We still don't know what happened to my crew—"

"I have a few ideas," Addy said. "How's Dr. Darzi doing, anyway? She still trying to tell people to move on and stop worrying about the past?"

Catherine flinched as if struck. "Did she tell you that, too?"

"Don't focus your efforts on trying to remember the past," Addy said in a singsong voice. "You have to live in the now and get back to your life."

"That sounds about right." Catherine smiled in spite of herself.

"And it's bullshit. They don't want us to remember." Addy leaned back in her armchair, trailing her fingers over the worn and faded upholstery on the arm. "It's easier for them if we don't. But I do, now. I remember everything."

Catherine cleared her throat. "Tell me what you remember. Please."

"I didn't have a big fancy ship like *Sagittarius*. It was just me. NASA went old-school for the Persephone missions. One astronaut and a small ship. I had room to move around, a bed, some rudimentary living space." Commander Addy snorted. "They called me a pilot, but I wasn't a pilot any more than Ham or Laika were, back in the days before they put people in space. I was just the trained chimp. Almost all of it was automated. I was along for the ride to see if a human could survive the trip."

"All the logs said everything went according to plan," Cal said.

The buzzing was getting worse, the rattle of an incandescent light bulb right before it blew out. But there were no electric lights anywhere. Not in the ceiling, not on the tables. In fact, as she looked around, the only thing Catherine saw that used electricity was the ham radio.

Addy was looking at her closely. "I know," she said, sounding irritable. She wasn't talking to Catherine or Cal. "I can see it plain as you can." Then she addressed Catherine. "They aren't happy, are they? Your friends. The ones you came back with."

Catherine forced herself not to look at Cal. Friends? "Do you mean . . ." She couldn't believe she was going to say this out loud. ". . . the aliens?"

"Of course I mean them. Do you have any other friends in your head besides them?" She tapped her temple. "My friends helped me remember everything." She looked at Catherine shrewdly. "See, I *made* them my friends, instead of my enemies, and now they're on *my* side."

"You don't . . . they don't . . . control you?"

"Not anymore." Addy sounded smug.

Catherine's mouth went dry. Speculation with Cal was one thing, but hearing it from Addy . . .

Cal spoke up, resting a calming hand on Catherine's back. "How did they make contact with you?"

Addy eyed Catherine a moment longer, then said, "Got to ERB Prime, confirmed that it was, in fact, an Einstein-Rosen bridge, and went through. We had probe data that suggested how long the trip would take, and what space looked like on the far end, but nothing concrete."

"That's a long time to be alone," Catherine said quietly.

"Four years, give or take. You were alone for longer."

"True, but no one planned for me to be alone that long."

Addy smiled thinly. "I don't think they expected me to be alone that long. Absolute truth—I don't think they expected me to come back at all. No one said anything, but I saw their faces when I boarded. They were expecting a one-way trip." She shrugged. "Besides, I didn't mind being alone. I never have." She gestured around her.

"What . . ." Catherine swallowed and fought the urge to reach for Cal's other hand. "What happened next?"

"I'm not going to lie, coming out of that wormhole was probably the most exciting moment of my life. I was seeing a part of space no one had ever seen before, not with the naked eye." Addy smiled at the memory. "I only had a few days. I sent out probes, collected data; that was the busiest time of the trip, really. I had something to do besides be a passenger.

"On the second day, after I'd brought the third probe back in, the messages started."

Catherine sat forward. "What messages?"

"At first they demanded to know what I was doing." Commander Addy's eyes went distant, as if she were reliving the moment. "Who I was, where I had come from . . . believe it or not, there actually was a protocol for what I should say. I sent them the information that was on the Voyager Golden Record and waited."

"I hope NASA updated it a little since 1977," Cal said. "It'd be embarrassing to send aliens an out-of-date mixtape."

Catherine gave him a little shake of her head.

"That's when the demands to surrender started," Addy went on as if Cal hadn't spoken, and Catherine drew a quiet breath. That sparked something in her, a distant memory, a chill running down her spine. The buzzing in her head got louder.

"Your friends don't like me very much," Addy said. "They don't want you to remember."

"Surrender, Catherine Wells, you are ours," Catherine muttered. Oh God, she could see it. It was in all capital letters in her head, on a screen. On *the* screen, the comm screen in *Sagittarius.*

"That's pretty much what they said, all right." She sat forward, watching Catherine with new tension in her shoulders. "Told me they'd come in on one of the probes I sent out, and that they were part of me now."

(kill her kill her now)

The urge was strong and unmistakable, and Catherine reached for Cal's arm, hand tightening hard enough that he winced. "Catherine?"

Addy stood up. "They're telling you to kill me, aren't they? My friends can hear them. They're mad we won't do their dirty work anymore."

"Catherine . . . what's going on?"

"I-I don't know." She could feel that familiar feeling of being shoved back—but it wasn't working. A part of her mind was roiling with fury.

"Listen to me, girl." Addy stepped forward, her eyes gleaming with a divine sort of madness. "It's a hive mind. Only the ones in my head managed to break free of the hive. The ones with you haven't."

"How do you know that?" Cal asked, shifting closer to Catherine, ready to get between her and Iris again.

"Telepathy," she said, as if it were the most natural thing in the world. "That's how they communicate."

Catherine stood up. She couldn't sit still anymore. "Shut up!"

(KILL HER NOW)

The guns on the wall seemed to glow in front of her. They were right there. No one could stop her if she took one down.

Catherine clutched at her head. "Make it stop!"

Cal came over and put his hands on her shoulders.

"Hold her still," Addy said. Before Catherine or Cal could answer, she closed the distance again, and put her hands on Catherine's temples.

It *hurt*. The buzzing in her head turned to a scream, two sets of voices seeming to rise and fall in a language she almost understood. There was a sense of invasion, as if a foreign army had come marching into her mind, planning to wreak havoc. When the searing pain started, she staggered and cried out, but Cal and Addy kept her on her feet.

"What are you doing to her?" Cal demanded.

"My friends are setting her free. Now hush."

Everything went silent. It was a silence like Catherine hadn't known since *Sagittarius*. She wanted to ask what Addy had done, but she couldn't find the words. They were buried beneath images and sounds flooding through her mind, nearly four years' worth of missing memories, somehow unlocked.

Everything. Everything was there in her mind. The entire mission. TRAPPIST-1f. *Tom*.

Oh God, Tom.

Sagittarius I Mission

Catherine moved around the command module of *Sagittarius*, getting it ready for takeoff. She'd tried to salvage as much as she could from the wreckage of the Habitat, thinking it might help the team back home figure out exactly what had happened. She knew that Tom was behind it, but she didn't know how. Or why. She hadn't seen him since the day he'd left her all the supplies. His quarantine was over, but he hadn't contacted her again. She'd tried once or twice to find him, halfheartedly, but had no luck.

She suspected he was dead. And deep down, part of her was relieved at that. The idea of leaving without knowing for sure ate at her, but there was nothing she could do. She could search for weeks and not find any trace of him, alive or dead. Longer, if he was alive and hiding from her. All she could do was go home and hope that whoever came back after her learned more than she had.

She looked around the command module. Everything was locked down and ready. She could leave at any time. One last walk-through of the ship. Just to settle her nerves. Theoretically, she knew how to take off on her own, but in practice . . . Even her experience as a test pilot hadn't fully prepared her for this.

Everything was in place. She was doing one last check of the main cabin, the biggest open space on the ship that served as an all-purpose living, working, and—right now—storage area, looking for any loose items that needed to be stowed when she heard the ominous *click-clack* of a handgun slide being racked behind her.

Tom stood between her and the ship's cockpit. He looked like hell. The burns on his face were . . . Catherine swallowed uneasily. Something was growing on them. Glittering and green, like the lichen outside. He was pale and sweaty, and the hand holding the gun had a faint tremor.

"Don't move until I tell you." Tom's voice was so hoarse as to be almost unrecognizable.

How did he get into the guns? How did he get on the ship?

"Tom? Didn't you take the meds I left you?" Her mouth went dry. Her eyes kept going back to the burns, forcing her to think about the cut on her forehead.

"Shut up. Of course I did. Didn't help, did they?"

"H-how did you get on board?" She had to keep him talking. As long as he was talking, he wasn't shooting her. As long as he was talking, she had time to think. She needed a weapon. Trying to look calm, but with her heart threatening to pound out of her chest, she glanced around for anything she could use as a weapon. Something. There had to be something.

He leaned heavily against the bulkhead, but kept the weapon pointed at her. "You think I brought all those supplies over here out of the goodness of my heart?"

She had, foolishly. But that was—that was days ago. "You've been on board this whole time?"

"Didn't know this ship had so many places to hide, huh?"

A prickle ran down her spine. She thought she'd been safe, and all this time . . .

Tom smiled, and it was more like a grimace, the livid red-and-green burns on his cheek wrinkling and sparkling. "You were going to leave me behind."

"I didn't think I had a choice. I didn't know where you were." Catherine put her hands up, still scanning the room. Her heart was beating so hard she was queasy; she swallowed hard against the nausea crawling up her throat. *Stay focused.* There was the Habitat wreckage. Sticking right out of the top was a big piece of rebar. If she could get her hands on that . . .

"Yeah, I saw how hard you looked for me."

"You attacked me!" That was too sharp. She needed to keep her calm, to just breathe. To get them both through this alive.

"So you said. I don't believe you. Who was abandoning who, here? You tried to *kill* me!"

She took a breath to steady her voice. "You're the one holding a gun."

Tom gestured with it. "Move to your left."

As she did, he stepped right. They kept circling the cabin facing each other, and she realized he was herding her back to the cockpit. As he did, though, she was getting closer and closer to the rebar. She did her best not to look at it as it came close to being in reach. "I don't understand," she said. "If you were safely hidden, why come out now? Why not wait until after we launched?"

Tom gave her a sickly smile. "I said there were places to hide. I didn't say they were good places. Especially not to withstand the g-forces of a takeoff."

"And the gun? How did you get it?"

"Let's just say I was motivated. And now I'm going to make sure you don't get cute and leave me behind." He pulled several sets of plastic restraints from his pocket. "If you'll go back to your seat, we can make sure you get us off this hellhole."

"What are you going to do, tie me to the pilot's seat?"

"Yep," he said. "Go on. Go sit down."

"I won't leave you behind, but Tom, at least let me quarantine you in the med bay." Catherine tried to keep her voice reasonable, calm. A quick side glance showed her she was almost within reach of the rebar. "Whatever's infecting you—if it's not responding to the initial antibiotic dosage, we can't risk taking that back with us to Earth."

"You've already been exposed. It's a two-and-a-half-year trip home, and they can scrub the ship before they let us off." He scowled. "You're stalling."

"Be reasonable. You can't . . . you can't strap me in. You're sick. If something happens to you, we could both die."

"Then you better take off fast. Once we're in space, I'll let you go."

The rebar was in reach. *He won't shoot you. He needs a pilot.* She wanted to believe that, but she couldn't be certain he was thinking about his own best interest right now.

It was as though he'd read her mind. "I will shoot you if I have to." He smiled thinly. "I don't have to shoot to kill."

The infection. If she hadn't already been exposed, an open wound would do the trick. "I'll fly us out of here," she bargained. "You don't have to tie me up."

"Catherine, you hit me, and you planned to leave me behind. I'm not inclined to trust you." He stopped, coughing hard enough to double over. Catherine seized her opportunity, grabbing the rebar. She swung forcefully, aiming for the gun in Tom's hand. At the last second, he shifted, and the rebar cracked into his shoulder instead.

"I knew you wanted me dead." Tom's eyes were empty, despite the angry expression on his face. He raised the gun and pointed it straight at her.

"I don't, but Tom . . . I don't want to die either!" Catherine held the rebar like a baseball bat. They kept circling each other, and she kept looking for an opening to aim for the gun. "Neither of us has to die. You're here, I'm here. Let's just go home."

"Drop the bar first." Tom's hand wasn't shaking anymore, and it wasn't wavering away from her head. She could see his finger tensing on the trigger.

Fear took over and she swung. Her aim was true; the gun went flying from his hand, landing at the hatch to the cockpit. Before she could react, Tom was on her. He knocked her to the ground, trying to wrest the rebar from her. Catherine jammed her knees into his belly, desperate to create distance between them.

Tom tried to grab her arms, but she got a foot against his hip and shoved him away, wriggling from beneath him. She scrabbled for the gun. Tom grabbed her ankle, pulling her back. She kicked frantically, swinging the rebar, but Tom's grip was strong, steady. He had her.

"You're not leaving without me," Tom growled. He hauled her across the floor on her belly, got a knee in her back, and wrapped his hands around her throat.

With his weight on her back, she had no leverage. Dark spots started popping at the edge of her vision as he cut off her air. Tightening her fingers on the rebar, she swung back wildly. She connected, heard the dull thunk of metal on bone. Tom's grip weakened and she escaped again, gasping wildly for breath. Tom's eyes were wide, blood streaming from his temple. He looked at her in surprise and betrayal, and then crumpled, dropping to the deck with a hard thud.

For a moment Catherine just lay there, taking greedy gulps of air. Then she pushed herself up to kneel beside Tom. His eyes were vacant. "Shit. *Shit.*"

Tom wasn't breathing.

"No no no no," Catherine muttered, fumbling to see if he had a pulse. "Please God, no."

But Tom wasn't breathing and he had no pulse.

He was dead.

She sat back on her heels, stunned. Suddenly she had to scramble for the toilet, where she became violently ill. She knelt there, shakily wiping her mouth with the back of her hand.

Catherine had killed before, flying planes in service to her country, but this was different. This was personal and bloody and not at all what she'd intended.

And she had to get him *(his body)* off the ship.

Somewhere down the road, if anyone were to ask her what the worst part of this entire catastrophic mission was, she'd say that it was burying Tom Wetherbee. Assuming she got home to talk about it. By the time she was finished, she was utterly exhausted—mentally, emotionally, and physically.

It had taken six hours to dig Tom's grave. Half-hysterically, she thought, *Claire was our geologist. She should have seen it. She would have been fascinated. All those layers of soil, all those newly exposed rocks . . .*

Now Catherine sat outside the infirmary, the metal of the deck cold beneath her. The cooling systems were working a little too well. She'd need to recalibrate them. Instead of moving to do that, she stared at the red dirt on her hands before wiping them on her pants. Her pants were already filthy anyway, and the dirt on her face had turned to mud thanks to the sweat.

Catherine lowered her head to her upraised knees and took several deep breaths. It was time to go home. She had no way to calculate a launch window, so she'd just have to take her chances. She'd done everything she could do here. The ship was stocked. She was alone.

Once she had washed all the grave dirt off her and put on fresh clothes, she settled into the pilot's seat and started going through the launch checklist.

The comm panel dinged.

She jumped out of her skin. That was impossible. Tom was dead. She'd just buried him. With a hand that was just starting to shake, she turned on the monitor.

The screen flashed. *SURRENDER, CATHERINE WELLS. YOU DESTROYED OUR AGENT. YOU ARE OURS.*

Ice went through Catherine's veins, a fear so profound she felt detached from her body, unable to feel or do anything at first. Instinct told her to run. To take off right now. But logic said if they were calling her their prisoner, taking off might not be an option.

Besides, you're the first person to talk to an extraterrestrial life-form. She thought about Tom. *Maybe second.* Her mouth dry as a desert, she flipped on the mic and leaned into it. "Wh-Who are you? Why should I surrender to you?"

SURRENDER OR YOU WILL DIE. YOUR DAUGHTER WILL HAVE NO MOTHER.

Catherine sat back in her chair. Nothing in their training for potential first contact prepared her for anything like this.

"You didn't answer me," she said, aiming for calm and reasonable, and not sure she was coming anywhere near it. "Who are you? How are you sending this?"

WE ARE. THERE IS NO WHO.

"Ohh-kay." That wasn't helpful at all. "Then *where* are you?"

EVERYWHERE.

"I'm not surrendering to anyone unless I can see you."

LOOK BEHIND YOU.

For a single terrified moment, Catherine's heart stopped. The skin on her neck and back was crawling as she stood and turned around, pulse pounding in her temples, not sure what she was about to see.

There was nothing there. "What . . ."

The air in front of her shimmered and resolved into a vaguely humanoid shape, humanoid the way a child would sculpt the shape of a body out of Play-Doh: two limb-like extensions reaching the ground, two more coming out on either side, a roundish shape at the top. There was nothing Catherine could call a face. Only blank emptiness where a face should be. Its "head" brushed against the ceiling of the cabin, making it at least eight feet tall, towering over her.

The body didn't look like flesh, exactly. There was something intensely familiar about the shimmering gray-blue-green of its body, shining like an oil slick without looking wet. With one "arm," it gestured toward the comms display. She looked and saw another message.

LOWER THE LIGHTS. THEY ARE PAINFUL.

The cabin lights were already fairly low to match the twilight outside, but Catherine dimmed them a little more, and her visitor became more . . . *there*. More visible. "How are you using our comms? For that matter, how do you know English?"

WE OBSERVE. WE KNEW YOU MIGHT COME, SO WE OBSERVED YOU. OUR THOUGHTS ARE OUR MESSAGES.

It took Catherine a moment to parse that. Some sort of telepathy? Learning her language through observation? She had too many other pressing questions to linger on this. "Why couldn't I see you at first?"

OUR MATURE FORMS REQUIRE PROTECTION FROM THE BRIGHT LIGHT OF THE DAY SIDE. WE SHIELD OURSELVES.

"And you . . . took the shield off, just now?"

TO YOUR LIMITED UNDERSTANDING, YES.

"Why do you plan to hold me prisoner?"

NOT PRISONER. YOU AND YOUR KIND HAVE HARMED OUR PEOPLE. YOU WILL ACT ON OUR BEHALF.

It didn't move as it "spoke," but stood as still as a statue. Catherine remembered the strange heat signature she'd seen in the Habitat with Richie not long before the explosion. *It was one of them.*

"We came to this planet in peace." Catherine fell back on some of her training. "We meant no—"

PEACE? YOU STOLE OUR CHILDREN FROM THEIR CRADLE COLONIES. CHILDREN WHO WANTED ONLY TO GROW IN THE LIGHT. WE FELT THEIR PAIN AS YOUR KIND DESTROYED THEM.

"We didn't . . . we didn't realize there were advanced life-forms here, I swear we didn't. We will try to make restitution. Our governments can work together, reach some sort of agreement—"

The comms buzzed loudly as if in negation. *NO AGREEMENT. NO GOVERNMENTS.*

"But I'm not empowered to make any sort of restitution on my own, I'm sorry."

YOU KILLED OUR AGENT. YOU ARE OUR AGENT NOW.

Catherine closed her eyes and held on to the pilot's chair. What she was about to say might cost her her life, and Aimee might well wind up with no mother, but she had no other choice. "I will not. If the choice is to be your agent or die, then I'm afraid you will have to kill me." She opened her eyes and looked at the alien.

It made a sound, a grinding, rattling sound. Was it . . . was it laughing at her?

YOU HAVE MISUNDERSTOOD. THE DECISION IS NOT FOR YOUR MIND TO MAKE, BUT YOUR BODY.

"What does that mean?" She stood a little taller, anger starting to filter in in place of the fear.

YOU ALREADY CARRY US INSIDE YOU. YOUR PHYSICAL SYSTEM WILL SURRENDER TO US OR IT WILL DIE.

Catherine stumbled back, landing on the console as her legs started to shake. "What do you mean I carry you inside me?"

WE ARE EVERYWHERE. WE TRAVEL IN THE ATMOSPHERE, IN THE VAC-
UUM, IN THE AIR. WE HAVE ENTERED YOUR SYSTEM AND LIVE THERE.

She shook her head. "I don't understand . . ." But then she looked at
the creature again. The stone pillars. The ones clustered around the terminator line. It was the same mottled gray-blue pattern. That rock was
all over, and in the brighter areas was covered with the lichen they'd been
collecting, the lichen that grew thinner the darker the land became. *All*
those pillars. Oh my God . . .

YOU WILL GO HOME. YOU WILL ACT AS OUR AGENT. YOU WILL NEVER
RETURN.

Catherine leaned heavily against the console. Tom saying he didn't remember long periods of time. Tom sabotaging the oxygenator, the rover.
Tom trying to kill her more than once. It was because of the creature
standing in front of her.

"Please, I don't understand. What's going to happen to me?"

WE ARE ONE MIND. ONE WILL. WHEN WE ARE ASCENDANT WITHIN YOU,
YOU WILL SHARE OUR MIND. DO OUR WILL.

"Mind control?" Panic was rising in Catherine's breast. "Is that it? You
can't. We're a harmless people, please."

WE ARE ALREADY WITHIN YOU. IT HAS STARTED.

"No, please!" It was too much; all of it was just too much. But the
figure was already leaving the cockpit, shimmering out of sight. The only
sign she had that it was gone was the sound of the air lock to the outside
opening and closing.

Catherine's vision grayed out around the edges, and no matter how
hard she tried to cling to consciousness, she felt herself sink to her knees
and fall to the cold floor beneath her, everything fading away.

Sagittarius I Mission

DAY UNKNOWN

ON BOARD *SAGITTARIUS*, LOCATION UNKNOWN

Catherine was flying the ship. She knew that much. That part seemed all right. But why was she alone in the cockpit? Normally Ava kept her company. Had she said anything to Catherine over breakfast that morning about having something else to do?

Breakfast that morning. Catherine had no memory of it. She didn't remember sitting down in the pilot's chair, for that matter. "Where the hell are we?"

She called up the navigation and the charts. They were flying away from TRAPPIST-1f. Had they landed on it? Had something gone wrong? Why couldn't she remember anything? Catherine swallowed her panic and activated the ship's autopilot, then got up to go find the rest of the crew.

The main dayroom of the ship was empty. There was no sound of anyone talking. Or laughing. Or moving around. The ship wasn't *that* big. She should be hearing someone doing something.

The laboratory was empty. The galley was empty. *This is wrong. This is very, very wrong.* She checked all the quarters. Cubbyholes. Closets.

"Where is everyone?" she cried.

She checked the mission logs, the comm transmissions. There was nothing prior to Mission Day 865, before they landed. For some reason, she'd abandoned TRAPPIST-1f, leaving her crew—or their bodies— behind.

She was alone, and she had no idea why.

33

"THERE," COMMANDER ADDY said, stepping back. "That should hold for a bit."

"*What* should hold?" Cal sounded more and more agitated.

"The hive mind inside Catherine had a wall up between her and her memories," Addy said. "*My* hive mind tore it down. We put the wall around *them* instead." She sounded rather pleased with herself.

Catherine stood between them, stunned by all the images racing through her mind, not even sure where to begin.

"Catherine?" Cal gave her a little shake.

"I remember everything," she said, barely recognizing the sound of her own voice.

"What?"

"All of it. All the lost time, the whole mission."

"But how did you—" Cal started, looking at Addy.

Addy just looked back at him.

"You need to go now," Addy said. "As long as she's around me, her 'friends' will fight harder to get past that wall. They're pissed." Her voice was as calm as a Sunday afternoon on the front porch. To Catherine she said, "They shouldn't control you anymore." Her eyes narrowed. "And you shouldn't let those bastards at NASA control you anymore, either."

"I don't understand," Catherine began.

"Go."

"Wait!" Catherine said. "Commander Addy. Iris. Come with us. We don't understand what's happening, and you do. We need your help. We're trying to get NASA to bring back the crew of *Sagittarius II*, so this doesn't happen to them, too."

Addy sighed, slumping. "Catherine, NASA doesn't want me. And I'm pretty sure I don't want them. I don't think there's anything I can do to help."

"But with both of us telling our stories, they might believe us . . ."

The older woman patted her cheek. "You're still so trusting." She looked at Cal again. "Take her and go."

"Okay, okay, we're going." Cal started shepherding Catherine toward the door. "I've got you, come on." He got her out to the car, having to stop and support her once or twice, strapping her in with her seat belt and pulling back onto the road.

Catherine sat limply in the passenger seat, looking out the window. She felt as if she'd run a marathon. The anger in her mind, the anger that hadn't been coming from her, retreated, leaving her with her new memories, the faint burn of their resentment toward Catherine and Iris buried deep. Catherine knew too much now, and that was not in their plan.

What plan?

Oh, but she knew the answer to that now, too.

Neither of them said anything until they were back on the road.

"You doing okay?" Cal asked.

"I'm not sure. Maybe."

"You really remember everything?" Catherine could tell he was dying to know, but she couldn't muster the strength to tell the whole story just yet. "Cal . . . I'll tell you, I promise. I just . . . I can't right now." She looked at him. "But I *saw* them."

Cal shot her a startled look.

"They're not just . . . voices in my head. I saw them. On *Sagittarius*. And Iris Addy isn't crazy," Catherine continued, feeling suddenly defensive. She looked straight ahead and was quiet for a long while.

Cal didn't push her. All he did was reach for her hand.

He had to drive around for an hour before they found a roadside motel. The sun was starting to set, and Catherine was tired enough by that point that she didn't care. Everyone at NASA thought they wanted the truth, but it turned out they'd had part of the truth all along and had ignored it, dismissed it, and pushed Iris Addy out for telling it. They'd worked so hard to discredit Iris—would they do the same to Catherine now?

She waited in the car while Cal checked them in. He came back with two room keys and handed her one. "Looks like we're the only ones here, so we pretty much had our pick. Not that there's much to choose from," he added dubiously.

Her room was decorated in timeworn colors that might have once been charitably described as "desert sunset," but had more likely been eye-bleeding shades of pink, orange, and brown when the paint was fresh. Still, it looked mostly clean. But if she closed her eyes, she could feel the gritty dirt of TRAPPIST-1f on her hands, grimed in her knuckles.

Cal put the key card on the dresser. He handed her a bottle of water and sat down across from her.

She focused on the water bottle, not able to look at him. "I remember everything."

"Can you tell me?" he asked gently.

"I killed Tom Wetherbee," she blurted. "I didn't mean to kill him. I swear I didn't. He was infected with something and out of his mind, and all I could think was that I couldn't bring him back like that. I had to at least quarantine him . . ." The words broke open long-forgotten pain, and she swayed with the force of it.

"Okay." Cal sounded calm, as though she hadn't just confirmed his worst suspicions of her. "Go back and start from the beginning."

She told him the rest, about the sabotage, the comms, and finally the Event—everything that happened, everything but sleeping with Tom. That still felt too shameful. Too much like everything that followed really was her fault.

"I didn't want to kill him," she said, after describing digging Tom's grave.

"Catherine. Look at me."

Catherine met his gaze.

"I believe you."

Those three words, those three simple words, untied a knot that had been growing inside her. "You do?"

"If he was anything like what I saw from you that night in Johnson, he probably would have killed you before you could get home. You did what you had to do." Cal reached out and squeezed her hand tight, and she clutched it like a lifeline.

"The stone," she said, then shuddered. "All that time, there were aliens *all around* the Habitat. They were there the whole time and we didn't know it. Pillars of stone, moving so slowly we couldn't see it. I still don't know how they infected us, though."

"They called the lichen their children, right? What if that's the literal truth? Lichen on Earth spreads by spores, and if you were exposed, and Addy was exposed, and *Tom* was exposed . . . You know, I bet he carried the same antibody, too."

For a moment, Catherine felt a flare of hope. If this "possession" was just some form of infection, maybe they could treat it. But . . . "But how did Iris get infected? She never landed."

"No, but she did send probes out and bring them back in. What was it that it said? 'We are everywhere,' and it mentioned traveling through a vacuum?"

"But that's impossible. Nothing can live in a vacuum," Catherine protested.

"We know of at least one living creature on Earth that can—the tardigrade. And just like a lichen spore, it's microscopic," Cal said. "It all makes sense. Science has thought for years that our first contact with an alien lifeform was going to be with a microscopic organism of some kind. We just happened to find one that's sentient."

"But I don't understand *why* they would want to infect us," Catherine said. "They hate us. I can feel their revulsion. We're soft; they see us the way we see slugs. Wrong, somehow."

"And yet, they don't want to destroy us completely."

"What do you mean?"

"Catherine, they could have had you do something much more destructive than just destroying a spaceship." Cal ticked things off on his fingers. "They haven't had you sabotage the military. They haven't had you cause massive death and destruction. They're not softening us up for an invasion. So if they don't want that, what are they doing?"

Catherine's eyes widened, the implication suddenly becoming clear. "They destroyed our settlement, and they're doing everything they can to stop Sagittarius II. They could have killed Iris, Tom, and me, but they let two of us come back. . . . Cal, they're not planning to invade us. *We* invaded *them*. They're defending their planet from invading aliens. Us."

"Of course!" He let go of her hand and started gesticulating as he spoke. "We show up and build a place for our people to live; of course it looks like we're about to colonize! I mean, that's why we went, right?" Cal laughed. "God, we're stupid. Do you know we didn't even *talk* about any contingencies in case the planet was already inhabited?"

"To be fair, all our probes showed it was empty."

"I know, but the thing is, we're just assuming we can go out there and find any place we want and claim it as ours." He shook his head, incredulous. "It's like we haven't learned a damn thing from our own history."

Cal was already three steps ahead of her, and that shouldn't have been a surprise. He was brilliant, already considering the political ramifications while she was still grappling with the idea that she had come in contact with aliens.

"What do we do?" she asked.

He smiled at her, a slow-dawning expression that caught her off guard. "Listen to you. You've been through a hell I can't even imagine, and nobody would blame you if you washed your hands of the whole business and tried to get back to a normal life, but not you, no. You're ready to jump right back into the fight."

Catherine focused on her hands, unable to meet his eyes. "Well, considering that I'm partly responsible for us being in this mess . . ."

He covered one of her hands with his. "But you're not." He gave her hand a shake. "What's going on is not your fault. If anything, it's NASA's. We might have sent you to an occupied planet. Any conflicts from that are our fault. You are one of the strongest, smartest women I know. And despite everything you've gone through, here you are."

Their eyes met and held. Catherine felt a rush of warmth in her chest at his words, and at the way he was looking at her right now, his eyes soft and admiring. The moment lingered, then he cleared his throat. "Anything else you remember that I should know about?"

"That's most of it." Catherine smiled faintly. "You know, death, destruction, alien contact."

"When we get back, we'll go see Lindholm. He'll have to listen to us now. We'll have time to call back *Sagittarius* before they walk into the same situation you did, blind."

"You really do believe me."

"I do."

Catherine wanted to relax, to tell herself that everything would be all right now. Cal believed her. The question was, would anyone else?

34

ONCE HE WAS sure she was okay, Cal left Catherine in her room while he got settled in his. She showered, washing away desert dust along with the feeling of being helpless and trapped. Someone believed her, she wasn't losing her mind, and now, knowing the past, she was ready to move forward.

They wound up in a roadside diner for dinner. While they were waiting for their food, Catherine said, "Why does everything out here look like it was decorated about fifty or sixty years ago?"

"The Atomic Age," Cal said. "It's a side effect no one talks about—all the tests out here; the radiation froze everyone's aesthetic in time."

"Ahhh," Catherine said, nodding with equal seriousness. "That makes sense. Given our motel rooms, I can see why the government wanted to hush that bit up."

"Shh. Someone might be listening." Cal cut his eyes left and right dramatically.

That was a little too much like Iris, and Catherine felt her grin faltering. "Yeah, you never know." She toyed with the water glass.

"Shit. Too soon, huh?"

"Little bit." Then she managed a smile. "Maybe give it another hour or two before we start joking about paranoia and eavesdropping."

"Deal."

They were rescued by dinner—or, in Catherine's case, breakfast in the form of a western omelet. By silent agreement, they didn't talk about their afternoon, but instead exchanged childhood stories.

As they were paying the check, Cal said, "Where to? You wanna turn in?"

"Don't imagine there's much nightlife out here."

"It's a desert. It's *full* of nightlife." He held the door for her as they left the diner. "Let's go pick one of these side roads and see where it goes."

"Cal, we've been in the car all day; are you really saying you want to go for a drive?" She couldn't help but smile.

"No, I wanna find somewhere to drive *to.*"

A short time later, Cal turned onto a side road that wasn't more than a flat spot of dirt. They'd left every trace of civilization behind, aside from a few power lines they'd passed.

"If you get us lost in the desert in the middle of the night . . ." Catherine started.

"Nah, I was a Boy Scout. I can navigate by the stars." Cal pulled the car off the dirt road. "And speaking of the stars, c'mon." He climbed out of the driver's seat, went to the trunk, and pulled out the bedspread stolen from his motel room.

Catherine laughed as she got out. "You planned this?"

"Hell, yes," Cal said. "If you didn't wanna come, I was going to drop you off and come back out here. You think I want to miss this view? Look up."

She tipped her head to the sky while he laid the bedspread out about twenty feet from the car. A sense of panic threatened to wash over her as she stared up into the vastness above, full of stars brighter than any she'd see in the city, nebulas and the Milky Way visible to the naked eye. Her heart hammered in her chest and she reached out to rest a hand against the warm metal of the car hood to anchor herself. There was dirt beneath her feet, atmosphere around her. Home. She was home.

"Catherine? You okay?"

Catherine drew a deep breath and let it out. "Yeah. Yeah, I'm okay. It just"—she gestured above—"looks a hell of a lot like the view I used to get from *Sagittarius.*"

"Aw shit. I wasn't thinking straight. I thought that would be part of the appeal." He came over and ushered her to the impromptu seating area.

"It is—now that I'm ready for it."

She sat down, leaning back on her hands. In the distance she could see the shapes of mountains outlined by starlight. Even with no moon, the ambient light was enough to see shapes and washed-out colors.

Cal sprawled on his back and looked up at the stars. "Always wanted to do this. Last time I camped out anywhere dark enough for this was when I was in college."

"NASA keeps you too busy?"

"NASA keeps *everybody* too busy," he said wryly. "I can't imagine doing anything else, though."

"Yeah." She laughed then added, "I'm not camping out here, by the way. Not when I have a perfectly good bed waiting for me."

"Don't worry, I outgrew wanting to sleep on the ground a long time ago," he replied. They were quiet a moment, then he said, "I can't imagine what it's like being driven out. From NASA, I mean."

"That's exactly what they did to Iris." Catherine turned to look at him. "Do you believe her, then?"

"As much as I can. You're both telling the same story. That's hard to ignore." Then he voiced Catherine's own thoughts. "I wonder, though, if NASA could still ignore it, knowing what we know now."

There was that "we" again, like a balm to her soul. "Maybe they could. I might wind up being a crazy hermit in the desert somewhere, too." She made a dry sound that wasn't quite a laugh. "I wonder if there's any land available near Iris's place."

"Catherine." Cal looked over at her. "That's not going to happen."

"No? Do you know how many people have told me I don't want to end up like her? It's starting to sound less like a warning and more like a threat."

"You're not doing this alone, though." He rolled from his back to his side and propped himself up on one elbow, reaching for her with the other hand. "I believe you. And I won't be the only one."

That made her feel warm, but something still troubled her. She still hadn't told him everything.

"Cal . . . there's something else I should tell you."

He sat up. "That sounds serious."

Just get it over with, Wells. Rip off the damn bandage.

Catherine sighed. "There's one thing I've remembered all along, since before I came home. Tom and I slept together on the trip out. It was one night, and I shouldn't have done it. I still don't know what I was thinking."

"Oh, my God," Cal said, and at first Catherine thought he was shocked or disgusted with her, but she looked at him and he looked . . . happy. "I knew it! I knew you were hiding something! I was right!"

"Cal."

He stopped, and looked properly chagrined. "I'm sorry. I was going nuts trying to figure out what it was. For what it's worth, you could have told us. NASA pretty much expected something like that to happen."

Catherine leaned back on her elbows, her shoulders slumping. "Yeah, well, I guess I was . . . ashamed."

"I'm glad you told me. I don't think any less of you. You're just human."

Catherine snorted. "I'm not allowed to be human; I'm a NASA astronaut." She stopped and shook her head. "I can't help but wonder now if that didn't contribute to what happened."

"Maybe that's what pushed him over the edge," Cal suggested, "but I imagine alien possession by itself is a lot of stress to carry."

"Hell, yes it is," Catherine muttered.

Something about that made Cal laugh. At first Catherine shot him a look, but a moment later she burst into laughter, too.

"I'm sorry I've been ineffective at work," Cal gasped between laughs, "but the aliens are distracting me."

"Well, if that excuse would fly anywhere, you'd think it would be at NASA."

"No." Cal grinned up at her. "SETI, maybe."

"Oh shit," Catherine said, as the giggles hit her harder. "We scooped the guys looking for aliens."

Every time their eyes met, they'd start laughing again, and eventually it wasn't even that anything was *funny*. As Catherine was trying to catch her breath, there was something about the way Cal was looking at her, something in his eyes, just visible in the starlight.

To hell with it, said a voice in her head.

She reached for his hand and tugged at it, leaning down toward him. He met her halfway, as if he'd had the same thought. Aside from Tom, Catherine hadn't kissed anyone new in twenty years.

She'd forgotten what it was like, that heart-racing, sweaty-palmed exhilaration of the unknown, the new. This kiss—it was like a key that had been sitting in the lock, just waiting to be turned. Cal let go of her hand to slide both of his palms against her cheeks, into her hair, keeping her close to him.

Abruptly, he pulled away. "Shit. Shit. Catherine, I shouldn't have—I'm sorry."

"I'm not." Whatever came of this, she wanted it. She half expected to see light shooting from her fingertips, feeling alive and bright in a way she hadn't for—well, a good ten years. "I'm not sorry at all."

"But, David—"

Catherine shook her head. "We're finished. The paperwork's already filed." She brushed her fingertips down his cheek then surprised herself by curling her fingers in his shirt, pulling him back toward her. "Don't be sorry."

This time, Cal didn't pull away, and the kiss deepened as he slid his arms around her waist. The world shifted around her, and before she knew it, she was lying on her back, half looking at the stars, half looking at Cal. He was warm and real beneath her hands, against her body.

She closed her eyes to the stars overhead and focused on the ones Cal was making her see behind her eyelids. By the time they'd both peeled away their clothing, neither of them was concerned about the nighttime chill, the stars above, or what might await them back home.

35

CATHERINE WAS DRIVING home from work the following Wednesday afternoon, looking at all the back-to-school signs in the store windows. It didn't make her smile the way it had in years past. While she'd always loved fall, even if Texas didn't have much of one, this year was harder. It wasn't the impending divorce. She and David were on better terms than they'd been since she'd come home. David and Maggie were seeing each other again, and she honestly wished them nothing but the best.

There had been no more lost time or voices since she and Cal had come back from Arizona. As long as Iris's "wall" held, Catherine didn't think there would be again.

Cal. Their relationship was in a strange sort of limbo. They were in constant contact, and he often spent the night at her place, but they hadn't talked about what they were to each other. There just didn't seem to be any *time*, life was moving so quickly.

For the first time since she and David had announced their divorce, Aimee was coming over to spend part of the weekend with her, one last visit before she went off to college.

So really, it should have been a happy time for Catherine. But there was one major problem.

She and Cal were running out of time to put together a solid case to persuade NASA to abort Sagittarius II, and she was no longer sure they could do it. It seemed obvious; she had her memories, Cal had his data . . . but NASA had ignored Iris Addy. They could ignore her, too.

They hadn't talked about what the two of them would do if their plan failed. She knew from Cal's earlier comments that pushing this theory of theirs would end up with his losing his job, maybe his career, if their colleagues didn't believe them. Her future was a little hazier. She was a much more public face for NASA, but then again, they hadn't hesitated to push out Iris.

They had to move ahead with what they had. If they waited too long, hoping for some new concrete evidence to turn up in the data Cal was scouring, *Sagittarius* would be through the wormhole and it would be too late to bring them back.

She parked her car and unloaded her groceries. This was her last few days with Aimee before she went to school. When Aimee got to her apartment, she looked outraged. "Do you know what the temperature in Cambridge was last night?"

Catherine laughed, opening the door and pulling her into a hug. "Is it already winter back east?" she teased.

"No, but do you know how much snow they got last year?"

Catherine couldn't help but grin. "I thought you wanted to go someplace where it snowed."

"Not that much!"

"So what I'm hearing is that we should go shopping for some warmer clothes before you leave."

"Sweaters. Lots of them."

They cooked dinner together, just a simple meal, but it felt good to do something normal. Aimee didn't comment on the lack of wine bottles in the apartment, but Catherine was sure she noticed.

While they were eating, Catherine decided it was as good a time as any to dive in and talk to Aimee. Toying with her fork, she said, "I wanted to tell you a little more about what was going on the past few months, if you're up for hearing it."

"Mom, you don't have to worry about it. I'm not mad at you anymore. I know you were going through a lot."

"I know, but I'd like you to know. I know more now than I did then." She held her breath and waited.

Aimee's eyes widened. "Your memories are coming back?"

"A lot of them have, yes." She'd talked to Cal about how much to tell Aimee, and ultimately decided to tell her only the bare bones of the story, for now.

"Do you know what caused the explosion, then?" It was fascinating—and disconcerting—to see in her daughter the combination of worried family member and budding engineer/scientist. Catherine half expected her to start taking notes for future projects.

"It was sabotage."

Aimee blanched. "What? Who? Mom, oh my God!"

Catherine raised her hand to quiet Aimee. "I know. Tom Wetherbee had some sort of breakdown." She paused, debating saying more, then pushed ahead. "It was just luck that I was outside at the time."

A number of emotions flickered across Aimee's face: fear, worry, relief. "How long have you known that?"

Catherine seesawed her hand. "Not very long; a few weeks."

"And the drinking . . ."

"Trying to keep it from coming back, I think," she admitted. "Aimee, I'm so sorry you got caught up in the mess of me trying to get through all this. You deserved better from your mom."

Aimee pursed her lips, thoughtful before replying. "I did deserve better, but I also know you were doing your best. So how can I fault you?"

It was such a calm, adult, forgiving statement that Catherine's eyes stung with tears. She leaned around the table and pulled Aimee into a hug. "Thank you. I am so proud of you, of the woman you've become."

"Mom." Aimee squirmed away from the compliment.

"I'm your mom, I'm allowed to be sentimental," Catherine teased.

They spent the rest of the evening watching movies and making plans to go shopping before Aimee left for school. The next afternoon, Aimee headed back home to David's house. Once the apartment was quiet again, Catherine settled on her couch with a long, contented sigh. She had a bit of peace before a lot of craziness to come. She and Cal were going to tell NASA soon. She had no idea what to expect from them, if anything. If they believed her, and aborted the mission, the PR would be terrible, and they'd have to do a lot of damage control. But if they didn't . . . her career was probably over, and she'd have the possible deaths of six other people weighing on her conscience.

36

PAUL LINDHOLM'S OFFICE wasn't designed to be intimidating to anyone who entered it. Lindholm was subtler than that. It was calming, relaxing. Cluttered enough to look lived in. It was the sort of place you'd feel comfortable letting down your guard. Talking man to man, really. Cal wondered how many people had fallen for that during Lindholm's tenure as administrator.

He wondered if he and Catherine were about to.

He'd contacted Lindholm before Labor Day, expecting at best to be put off until Tuesday, but here they were on the Saturday of a holiday weekend. Lindholm was behind his desk, while Aaron Llewellyn sat to the side of it. Cal and Catherine stood in front of them. So far, both men were riveted by the information Cal and Catherine were presenting. Cal talked them through the scientific evidence that indicated Catherine hadn't been alone on *Sagittarius* after the Event, and described the foreign antibody that Catherine and Commander Addy both carried.

"Medical can confirm about the antibody?" Lindholm asked.

"That's who gave me the information, sir." Cal referred to his notes. "I included a copy of their full report in the packet I gave you."

Lindholm nodded. "Good, good."

When neither man could poke sufficient holes in Cal's data, it was Catherine's turn.

Using Cal's evidence as a starting point, she told her story. About *why* the data looked the way it did. She told them about the lost time here on Earth. That the memories she'd lost on the mission had returned. (But not how—they'd agreed to leave Iris Addy's role in this out for now.) Finally, she told them about her final confrontation with Tom Wetherbee. And, most important, about her conversation with the alien intelligence.

When she finished, Cal gave her a reassuring smile, then turned to Lindholm and Llewellyn. "We have to abort Sagittarius II," he said. "We don't know what we're sending them into, save that it's a hostile intelligence with the ability to control some of us."

Paul Lindholm leaned forward on his desk, eyes bright. "You're saying that it's . . . I don't know, some sort of parasite, or—or . . . *possession?*"

"They're just trying to protect their home from a perceived threat," Catherine said. She started to go on, but Cal gave a little shake of his head. He'd spent more time pondering Lindholm's question than he would've cared to confess to Catherine.

"We can't know for certain," Cal admitted. "But consider this: whatever has been compelling Catherine to do the things she's done, whatever's resulted in the periods of lost time, there have been no new attempts since we stopped their original plan to trigger Longbow. As it is, it's like we've thwarted Catherine's programming and things have stalled out. Perhaps similar to what Commander Addy experienced."

"Hmm." Aaron furrowed his brow.

"They've made it clear they don't want us on their planet." Cal leaned on one of the bookcases lining the walls. "Until we have a clearer way to communicate with them, and . . . and a plan, we need to steer clear."

"You're talking about us losing years of work," Aaron said. "And a mission abort is going to cost millions, which we'll then have to explain to the American people."

"But . . . first contact," Catherine broke in. "I think that's going to be bigger news than scrapping a mission." She addressed Lindholm. "This is exactly one of the things we hoped to do with the Sagittarius missions. This is 'Mission Accomplished' in one hell of a big way, Director."

Lindholm looked thoughtful, and Cal could see the headlines he was writing for himself in his mind. "Still," he said, "it wasn't exactly a positive experience."

"A cultural misunderstanding," Cal said. "That's been an issue with humanity ever since we first started bumping into one another. That's why it's so vital that we get it right this time."

He had them, he could feel it. Llewellyn especially. Aaron believed him, *finally*. He met Cal's eyes and actually looked a little ashamed. Cal wanted to rush ahead, to say something else, but elected to stay quiet and let them continue to convince themselves.

"We need to talk about this," Lindholm said. He glanced at Llewellyn, who nodded in agreement. "If you two can wait outside my office, give us a few minutes?"

"Sure," Cal said.

The lobby was empty and the two of them sat side by side in the guest chairs. "It went well." Cal wanted to take her hand, as much for his sake as for hers, but refrained. They'd agreed to keep their personal connection to themselves for now.

"I feel like I'm sitting outside the principal's office," Catherine muttered.

"As long as we don't get expelled, I'm happy."

The minutes ticked by, enough of them that Cal started getting restless. He fought the urge to pace, not wanting to show any sign of his growing anxiety, not to Catherine, and not to Lindholm when he called them back in.

As the office door opened, Cal stood calmly and Catherine did the same. Lindholm didn't invite them to sit after he closed the door behind them. Hopefully that meant this would be short. Hopefully that was a good sign.

"Catherine, I've said all along that the ordeal you went through was unimaginable, and now, with all the details . . ." Lindholm shook his head. "It's a testament to your strength that you're standing here." The intercom on his desk buzzed. Lindholm hit the button and said, "Come on in." To Catherine he said, "I'm very sorry."

Before either of them could ask what for, the office door opened, and three security guards came in. Two of them took Catherine by the arms.

"Paul, what's going on?" Catherine struggled, panic rising as she met Cal's eyes.

"Look at this from our perspective. You've told us that you killed

Tom Wetherbee. You've confessed to attempting to sabotage an ongoing mission—and we even have an eyewitness." Lindholm nodded to Cal. "That alone would warrant taking you into custody. And if your theory is correct, if you *are* under the control of a hostile alien entity . . . I'm sorry, Catherine. This is for your safety as well as ours."

Oh God. Cal should have seen this possibility. He'd been *so sure* his evidence was overwhelming . . . How did he not foresee this? "Don't do this," he said.

Catherine's movements grew more and more frantic as she struggled with the guards. "You can't do this. My family will want to know where I am. Where are you taking me?" The words came out in quick succession, as if she could prevent this just by saying the right thing.

"We're going to put you under quarantine for now, until we're certain you're no longer a potential danger." Lindholm nodded at security, who started to take Catherine out.

"Cal! Tell them I'm okay."

The look in her eyes, the fear, cut him deep. He turned to the other two men. "This can't be legal." Aaron Llewellyn wouldn't meet his eyes. Lindholm looked determined.

"It is," Lindholm said. "We're authorized to quarantine any astronaut who might have brought back any sort of threat from a mission."

"But what about my crew—"

"Cal," Aaron interrupted gently, "go home. We'll figure out the best way to deal with this on our own."

To the third security officer, Lindholm said, "Please escort Mr. Morganson to the front door."

Cal looked back at Catherine, who was quickly going from desperate to resigned. She saw the truth as clearly as he did. They were almost out of time to stop the mission, and now they were out of chances, too.

37

AS CELLS WENT, Catherine supposed this one was comfortable. The bed wasn't bad, the toilet wasn't exposed, and she suspected some staff member or other was making the home-cooked meals that showed up three times a day.

None of that changed the fact she was a prisoner somewhere in the depths of Johnson Space Center, or that everyone who came to see her was forced to go through a ridiculous routine of hazmat suits and decontamination, as if she hadn't been walking around freely for months.

The first time they'd brought her food in, she'd laughed. "Seriously?" She recognized the staffer in the suit. "I sat next to you in meetings every week. Don't you think you would have caught something by now?"

If the excuse for holding her was that she needed to be quarantined, then NASA needed to follow quarantine protocol to the letter. It was almost darkly humorous to watch the charade.

At least they let her have some visitors. The second day she was there David showed up at her door right after breakfast.

He gave her an awkward hug through the hazmat suit. "Catherine, what the hell is going on?"

"Is Cal okay?" It was the one question that had been eating her alive. She didn't know if he'd been fired—or worse. Was he sitting in a cell, too?

"Morganson? I haven't seen him. Tell me what happened!"

Each time she told her entire story, it got a little easier. She'd been so concerned about being believed—about what other people would think—she'd never stopped to consider how telling the whole story would make her feel free.

"I'll see what it will take to get you out of here," David said. "Do you want me to hire a lawyer?" He didn't say a single word about aliens, or first contact. Whether he believed her or not, he was still the man with the practical solutions.

"Please. I need to get out of here."

"Catherine, I meant a criminal defense lawyer. They could charge you with killing Tom. With all of them, even."

It wasn't that Catherine was unaware of the danger she was in. They could charge her with whatever they'd like, as long as she and Cal managed to bring back *Sagittarius*. Six people might well die, or worse, because they had failed.

"I know," she said. "But I don't think they will. I heard someone saying they're debating bringing me up on espionage charges, but they're not quite sure how the laws work when the other entity is from another planet. I bet they don't even do that. Not when they can hold me here indefinitely." She smiled thinly. "Better PR if I just quietly disappear. So, make some noise and get me out of here." The only problem was, David wasn't the type of guy to make noise.

"They can't just keep you here; quarantine ends at some point, right?"

"I'm a whole new ball game," Catherine said dryly.

"Then I'm definitely getting you a lawyer," David said. "You're not going to sit here and let them figure out how to keep you locked up forever."

"How's Aimee doing?"

"She's shaken, but okay. She's coming to see you later today."

"I wish she wouldn't," Catherine sighed. "She should be at school, not focusing on me."

"I know, but it's her choice."

"How is she taking this?" She didn't want to ask but had to know. She and Aimee had made such progress. Would Aimee be angry that Catherine had—yet again—not told her the whole truth?

"She's worried sick about you. We all are." There. There was the slightly pitying look. David didn't believe her, not about all of it.

Their time ended with David promising again to find a lawyer for her.

The whole visit was more unsettling than comforting. If David hadn't seen Cal, then Cal must be gone from NASA—unless he was locked up down here somewhere, too; but even if Cal was free, a visit from him was probably too much to hope for. She doubted they'd let her see him, for fear of some sort of conspiracy.

Aimee arrived during the long, dull hours between lunch and dinner, ushered in with the same routine of hazmat suit and air-lock doors.

"Mom!" Another awkward half hug. "How can they do this? Don't they know what you've already gone through?"

They settled in side by side on Catherine's bed, and Catherine filled her in on all the things she couldn't tell Aimee before. Unlike with David, this time Catherine was nervous.

"So . . . actual aliens?" Aimee's eyes lit up. "I mean, that must have been awful, but Mom, oh my God, aliens?"

Catherine couldn't hold back a smile despite everything. "Yeah, I know. It sounds crazy. Which is why I'm here."

"I can't believe NASA would do this to one of their own astronauts." Aimee's face fell into mutinous lines. "If anyone should understand the possibilities here, it should be them."

She didn't know about Iris Addy, and now wasn't the time for Catherine to tell her. "So you're not mad that I didn't tell you sooner?"

"Mom, you work for a government agency. I know there's stuff you can't tell me." Aimee lifted her shoulders in a sheepish shrug. "I might not like it, but I know it's not your fault."

"I promise I will always tell you whatever I can."

"I know you will." Aimee looked around the featureless cell and shivered. "I never knew that NASA had anything like this." She turned back to Catherine. "What can I do to help? There's got to be something."

Catherine was torn. Aimee should stay far away from this, all of it. She should focus on college, move on with her life. But right now, there seemed to be two people who believed what had happened to her: Aimee and Cal. And Cal was missing. Catherine had to find out what happened to him.

Sensing her hesitation, Aimee said, "Mom, come on. Tell me."

"There was a man I was working with. Cal Morganson. He helped gather some of the evidence we found." Again, Catherine found herself on the edge of how much to tell Aimee and backed away from it. Besides, what was she going to call him? He wasn't her boyfriend, not really. She pushed on. "I don't know what's happened to him. I don't know if NASA has him 'quarantined' somewhere or what. Can you find out? Ask your dad; maybe he can help."

"Do you want me to go talk to him, if he's okay?"

"No, honey, you don't need to do that. They're not going to let me see him, so it doesn't matter. I just . . . want to be sure he's okay." *I want to make sure he's still out there, that he's still on my side.*

"I will. I'll let you know what I find out."

When Aimee's time was up, Catherine held her as tight as the suit would allow. If she let go, would she ever see Aimee again?

38

EVERY TIME CAL closed his eyes he saw the despair on Catherine's face as security took her away. He wasn't sleeping much.

Not that it mattered; with only seven days—at most—to go before *Sagittarius II* lost radio contact, he had no time to sleep. And it wasn't like he had anywhere else he had to be. Aaron hadn't fired him outright, not yet, but he was on an indefinite leave of absence. That might have been a bonus, except that meant he had no way to contact the crew directly. And there was no one at NASA he trusted enough to go around the chain of command and send them a message. So he had far too much time to think. To plan. To look for any pieces he and Catherine might have missed, something so irrefutable that NASA would have to listen.

At least three times a day, Cal picked up his phone. One of the science writers at the *New York Times* always came to Cal when she needed information on anything aerospace related. She'd be delighted if Cal handed her the scoop of the century, proof not only of alien life but also that NASA was hiding it.

God, he was tempted. With all the information he and Catherine had collected, there was enough to warrant an investigation, enough to put pressure on NASA and get Catherine released.

Would he be viewed as a whistle-blower or disgruntled employee? If this story broke, how badly could it hurt NASA? Paul Lindholm liked to think of this as NASA's first real golden age since the Mercury and Apollo days, but how fast would the funding dry up if the truth came out? Would NASA ever recover? More to the point, Cal couldn't help wondering if it deserved to.

He wasn't ready to give up on NASA just yet. They could still fix this. He just needed more proof of first contact, and he needed it yesterday.

So he kept his coffeepot filled and spent his waking hours in his home office, going over every bit of information he'd gathered on every single aspect of the Sagittarius I mission. There was something here. He just wasn't seeing it.

A knock sounded at his door. That was the last thing he needed interrupting his thought process.

He ignored it, but after the third flurry of knocks, he muttered and went to answer.

At first, he didn't recognize the girl standing on his doorstep. She was vaguely familiar; he'd seen her somewhere before, but without any context . . .

"You're Cal Morganson, right?" She tilted her head, and Cal realized where he'd seen her. "I'm Aimee Wells. You work with my mom."

"Yeah, I did—I do." Cal could only blink at first, and then he broke through his fog. "Is your mom okay?"

"She's fine—well, as fine as you'd imagine." She glanced around as if making sure there were no observers. "She sent me."

Stranger and stranger. Cal swung the door open farther. "Come in."

She followed him inside and he tried to make sense of it all. Once again, he found himself sitting in his living room with a Wells, and he was baffled. "So you've seen her? How is she? I can't get anybody at NASA to tell me anything. I tried your dad, but he won't return my calls."

Aimee grimaced. "I think that's one reason Mom asked me to come. Dad was ordered not to talk to you."

That was ominous, but it explained why no one else was returning his calls either. If he was persona non grata with the NASA staff, then his career was over. "But your mom is okay? Is anyone helping her?"

"Dad is. Well, sort of. I don't think he believes her story, but he's getting a lawyer for her. She's doing okay, though, really," Aimee said. "They're keeping her in quarantine." A roll of her eyes showed what she thought of that. Cal was inclined to agree with her assessment. "She was worried about you, though."

"About me?" He gestured around himself. "Aside from being currently unwelcome at NASA, I'm okay. Tell her that I'm still working on what we were talking about. Tell her I'm doing everything I can to get her out of there."

Aimee perked up. "What are you working on? Can I help?"

It was sweet of her, sweet enough to make him smile. "I don't think so. I'm trying to find more proof about what happened to your mom. It's pretty dull stuff, and it involves rather advanced science—"

"I'm going to be an aerospace engineering major at MIT," Aimee interrupted, looking unimpressed. "For my senior science project I did an analysis of how the life-support systems on *Sagittarius* might have functioned differently with only one person on board and how that affected my mother's trip home."

Cal blinked. "I stand corrected." He should have known better than to underestimate any daughter of Catherine's. "If you're already familiar with the life-support systems, then I think I have something for you to do."

Aimee's initial assessment, after three hours going over some of Cal's printouts, was filled with outrage. "How the hell is NASA ignoring this? Like, okay sure, they want to use the evidence that Tom Wetherbee survived the explosion to keep Mom locked up, but look at this. Right here, before the explosion. Look at those heat readings in the air lock. It's just like Mom said. Doesn't that seem high enough to suggest two living things were in there?" Cal could sympathize with her frustration.

"I know. It seems like a strong indicator, but it's too easy for them to dismiss as a malfunction." Cal sighed. "I've got to find something completely incontrovertible. Something a layperson could look at and instantly understand."

"You need a picture of a little green man," Aimee grumbled.

"Pretty much, yes."

"So let's find one."

"I wish it were that simple." Cal pushed back from his computer. "I've been over the video footage we have—and there's not much of it. The video feed from when your mom *did* actually see them is long gone. There's nothing else there." He looked up to see Aimee texting. Inevitable, as she was still a teenager, he supposed. Smart or not, she couldn't be expected to stay focused forever.

Or so he thought.

"Sorry," she said, "I had to cancel some plans. I'm going to get my computer and bring it back. We'll save time if we're both going through the electronic records." Then she paused. "If that's okay?"

"Uh. Sure, why not?" A new set of eyes couldn't hurt. And maybe, just maybe, Aimee's inexperience would be an asset here—fewer preconceived notions.

Two heads, it turned out, weren't necessarily better than one. Three days later, they were comfortable enough with each other to be frustrated and irritable. At least Aimee had been able to keep Catherine updated on their progress and was able to reassure her that Cal was fine.

"Are you sure we can't get our hands on more data? Anything?" Aimee asked for what Cal thought might have been the hundredth time today.

"I had to go digging to get what we've got now." Cal was deliberately not thinking about the penalties for revealing classified information to a teenage girl. If this all went south, he'd be revealing it to a much larger audience. The *Times* reporter was still an option.

"Why is so much of it missing?"

"Ask your mother," Cal snapped, then immediately regretted it. They didn't know for certain that Catherine had deleted any of the data. It could have just as easily been Tom.

"I would, but I don't know when your bosses will let me see her again." Aimee didn't seem angry so much as tired. They both were. They'd been beating their heads against this for days and weren't getting anywhere.

"I'm sorry. That was uncalled for." He hadn't been able to contact Catherine in over a week, and he was startled at how much he missed her. He kept seeing the fear in her eyes as NASA security led her away. And always, always, the clock was running in the back of his head, counting down the minutes until his crew was out of his reach and beyond his help.

Aimee interrupted his thoughts. "Okay. So, if we can't get more data, then we just have to find new ways to look at what we do have."

Cal raked his hand through his hair. "I dunno, Aimee. Maybe there's just nothing here. We don't know what these things are, or what we're looking for. Maybe we don't have the technology to even prove they exist."

"We do. We have to." Aimee hummed to herself thoughtfully, tapping at her keyboard. "Maybe we literally need a new way of looking at what we have. What was it Mom said they told her? The adults needed protection from daylight, and they took it off so she could see them? She said it was like a shield. I'm guessing technological, some sort of cloaking device, or . . . I don't know what. But it blocks the visible light spectrum—so cameras are no good. But . . . they were still giving off heat. We've got those measurements." She looked away from the monitor. "There was a spectroscopic camera in the Habitat, right?"

"Yes, but . . ." Cal paused. "I didn't think to—" He grasped what she was getting at. "You're saying to check other spectrums visually."

Aimee nodded, already typing furiously. "What were the time stamps for the increased heat signatures in the Habitat air lock when Mom and Richie were working on it?"

Cal checked his notes and gave her the numbers while she called up the imaging program. "Okay," she said. "Here we go . . ." Cal came around to stand over her shoulder, looking at the monitor.

Aimee sighed. "No, there's nothing—" As she spoke, there was movement in the frame. "What is that? That's not Richie, is it?"

Whatever it was, it radiated heat, but more to the point, as they looked through the infrared spectrum, it was *visible*. The shape was humanoid in the loosest sense—there was what appeared to be four limbs, and something that might be a head.

"That's not Richie," Aimee repeated, more certain.

"It's not anybody from the crew. Wetherbee was the tallest crew member at five foot eleven; your mom's five eight. That thing . . . it's at least seven, maybe eight feet." Cal couldn't stop staring, his heart thumping painfully in his chest. "Got you," he murmured. "Got you, you bastard."

"That's—that's an alien. That's a real alien."

Cal put his hand on Aimee's shoulder. She sounded about as stunned as he felt. "And you found it, Aimee."

"Mom found it."

"Either way, I have to get to Johnson."

Aimee turned and looked up at him, the fright in her eyes reminding him of her mother. "What will you do if they don't believe you? What if they lock you up, too?"

"Listen." Cal crouched to Aimee's eye level. "If I haven't called you in . . . say, two hours, call this number." He texted her the contact information. "That's a direct line for a science writer at the *New York Times*. Give her my name. Tell her what we've found."

"I'm a kid; she won't believe me," Aimee protested.

"You show her that video. She'll believe you." He stood. "Hopefully it won't come to that."

His fate rested in the hands of the bureaucracy at NASA and an eighteen-year-old girl. Right now, he trusted Aimee more.

39

THE FIRST THING Cal worried about was that Aaron wouldn't see him. No, before that, driving over, he had visions of security turning him away at the gate. But he had to try.

Security let him in. As he expected, though, when he tried to swipe his ID card to get past the lobby, it didn't work. He waited while the guard at the desk tried to contact Aaron, fighting the urge to pace.

It was too quiet. This close to the end of a mission stage, there should have been people hurrying about, even out here. He'd been following the news reports, and had seen nothing about Sagittarius II, but something was wrong. He could practically taste it.

It wasn't Aaron who showed up to escort Cal back, but a security guard. Hopefully the same guard wouldn't be escorting him out just as quickly.

Aaron stood and came around his desk. "Cal, I'm surprised to see you." His tone said, *You should have called first.*

"I bet." Cal shut the office door and sat his laptop down on the edge of Aaron's desk before pulling up the video. "I found something I think you'll be interested in seeing."

"Cal, if this is about Catherine—"

"Shut up and look at this, will you?" He looked up at his boss and mentor, wondering if he was about to cross the line between "on leave indefinitely" and "fired," then pushed ahead. "I ran some of the spectroscopic footage against the heat signatures we found." He was going to keep Aimee's name out of this, for now. Someone had to stay out of trouble. "Look."

He pressed Play, and let Aaron draw his own conclusions.

"Is this for real?" Aaron asked after a long silence. He hit Replay and watched the segment again.

"Pull up the same footage from NASA's servers if you don't believe me," Cal said. Aaron did believe him, though; he could see it. "You have to call the ship back, Aaron. You're sending them into hostile territory and they don't even know it."

"I can't."

"Come on! Drop the bureaucratic bullshit! You guys said you needed more proof; how much more proof do you need?"

Aaron was ashen. "Cal, I mean I can't. *Sagittarius* reached the Einstein-Rosen bridge thirty-six hours ago."

Cal leaned heavily against the desk. "How— How the hell did they get ahead of schedule?" There were still a couple of days left. There had to be a few days left.

"You know our schedules are rough at the best of times, especially at these distances." To his credit, Aaron at least looked abashed.

"We have to get them back here." Cal said it, but he knew the odds were slim.

"We're not going to have radio contact again for two years, Cal. There's nothing we can do. Even if we send a message, they'll be on the other side of the wormhole before it reaches them."

"And they'd have to refuel on TRAPPIST-1f before they could come back anyway." A sick feeling sat in the pit of his stomach. He'd failed his crew. Again. The best he could hope for was that they would be able to refuel and come home without encountering any spores.

"I'm sorry, Cal. We'll do the best we can—"

"The best you can?" Cal laughed at him. "Have you, yet?" He stood up and closed his laptop.

"That's not fair."

"You believed her." Cal spoke quietly, feeling like if he didn't, he'd start shouting, and that really would get him thrown out. "I saw your face, Aaron. When Catherine and I were telling our story in Lindholm's office.

You *knew* she was telling the truth. You believed us, and you still let them lock her up."

"She's not locked up; it's a precautionary measure against—"

"Spare me the quarantine speech. NASA has her locked up in a basement somewhere because of what she knows." He took a step forward, gratified to see Aaron lean back. "How could you do that? Not just to her, but our crew? They're counting on us to look out for them!"

"There wasn't enough proof. It didn't matter what I believed—"

"*Locked up*, Aaron. You could have said something!"

"Look, you weren't there. Lindholm had made up his mind before you guys left the room." Aaron spread his hands in a supplicating gesture. "There wasn't anything I could do to change his mind."

"Did you *try*? Or did you just go along with his PR plan?"

Aaron's expression told him everything he needed to know.

"We have to fix this," Cal said. "We owe it to Nate and the rest of the crew."

"There's nothing we can do."

"Fuck that. There has to be." Cal grabbed his laptop. "Let me see Catherine. Let me talk to her. We've figured the rest of this out, and we'll solve this, too."

"You know I can't do that—" Aaron started, but Cal cut him off.

"Let me see Catherine or I go public with this. What kind of a PR nightmare do you think it will be if the public finds out NASA's been concealing the existence of hostile aliens?" He put on a shark's grin. "And before you think maybe you should throw me down there with Catherine, I have a fail-safe. If I don't contact them, they'll be passing the information to the media."

He had him.

"Let me see Catherine."

Aaron sighed and picked up his phone as Cal reached for his. He knew of someone else who'd want to see Catherine, too.

40

WITH EACH DAY that passed Catherine's hope grew dimmer. Her days were all the same now. Aimee hadn't come back since she told Catherine she was working with Cal.

What if NASA overheard them and was keeping Aimee from her? Or worse? God, she never should have asked Aimee to get involved. What the hell had she been thinking?

And there went that cycle of thoughts again. She was driving herself mad, but she couldn't stop.

She was about to get up and pace the cell again, unable to sit still, when the door opened.

"Mom!" Aimee burst in and Catherine caught her in her arms, hugging her tight. For a split second she questioned if this was real, or if she'd snapped and was hallucinating her daughter again, as she had back on *Sagittarius*.

Her sense of reality wasn't helped by the sight of Cal coming through the door after Aimee, smiling. Then it hit her. It seemed unreal because neither of them was wearing a hazmat suit. She tightened her arms around Aimee. This had to be real. Even in the worst times on her trip home, when she'd missed Aimee so much it made her ache, she'd never been able to touch the image of the little girl that had appeared to her. Never been able to smell her shampoo.

"I— What are you both doing here?"

"We found it," Cal said.

"Found what? Who's 'we'?"

"Mom, we found proof. We made them believe you."

"Well, Aimee found it," Cal said, and explained what her brilliant daughter had done. Catherine hugged her again, stunned.

"They're going to let you out," Aimee said.

Catherine looked to Cal for confirmation and he nodded. "They're processing all the paperwork right now. As soon as they're done, you can go." But there was a hesitance on his face as well.

"What is it?" she asked.

"We were too late to stop the mission."

Catherine's heart sank. "They're out of range?"

Cal nodded.

She sat down heavily on the edge of her bunk. "So, it was for nothing."

"The engineers are almost positive they've fixed the comm issues *Sagittarius I* experienced, so we're going to try to leave a message for the ship to pick up when it goes through the far end of the wormhole. They'll get it, and can come back quickly. They'll be fine." Cal was trying to reassure her, but she could see how worried he was. Even if the message did get through, Addy had been infected almost as soon as she'd gone through the wormhole. Who knew how fast they'd taken control? She and Cal still hadn't confirmed that their infection theory of control was correct.

"You don't know that," she said.

"It's the best we can do. It's not like chasing someone down to tell them their tire's flat," Cal said.

Chasing someone down.

"Cal . . ." Catherine began hesitantly. "The first *Sagittarius* was reconditioned and prepped as a backup, right?"

"You can't be serious." Cal might have been looking at her as though she were nuts, but there was the same dawning realization in his eyes that she felt herself. "You're serious."

"You said it. We chase them down." Catherine wasn't an engineer, but she could see the possibilities. "They've got a head start, but with a smaller crew we could push harder, take more fuel on board with us. And we'd still probably get there before the message would." She was talking faster and faster as the idea took shape in her mind. "And even if not, if they run into trouble, they could use some backup. Someone who knows what to look for."

"You're saying 'we,'" Aimee spoke up. "You want to go back?"

Catherine's enthusiasm plummeted. What was she saying? That would be another six years of her life, at a minimum, gone. And that was if everything went well. And who was to say she might not be more susceptible to control a second time around? She looked at Cal, then at Aimee. "No, I don't want to. I'm just saying that whoever goes . . ."

"We don't have a crew prepped," Cal said. Catherine could already see the wheels turning in his head. "I'm probably the only other person most prepared." When Catherine shot him a look, he shrugged sheepishly. "I told you. I went through most of the same training as the crew. I wanted to know exactly what they'd be experiencing."

"You can't go by yourself, though." Catherine reached out and took his hand. "Trust me. You don't want to try."

So there it was. Either Cal went alone or Catherine went with him. She laughed. "It's probably all moot. There's no way Lindholm will approve this."

"I don't know. We've got him over an awfully big barrel." Cal leaned over to kiss her forehead. "I'll let you two talk, and I'll go see just how feasible this is. And see if I can get them to speed up that paperwork to get you out of here."

Once he was gone, Aimee sat next to Catherine on the bunk.

"Were you really the one to figure it out?" Catherine asked.

Despite the worry in her eyes, Aimee grinned. "Yeah. When I went over to check on Cal, I wound up helping him out."

Catherine shook her head. "You're an amazing, brilliant woman. MIT is lucky to have you. And so am I."

Lightly, Aimee said, "By the time you get back, maybe NASA will be lucky to have me."

"Aimee . . ."

"Mom, Cal's right. You're the only one who can do this. It sucks. I just got you back. But this is . . ." Aimee gestured weakly. "This is bigger than me, or you, or our family. It's bigger than just Cal's crew. This is . . . this is world-changing stuff." She tilted a grin up at Catherine. "I can't think of anyone I'd rather have out there representing, like, all of humanity than my mom."

Catherine laughed in spite of herself. "Oh, well, no pressure there." She pulled Aimee into a hug. "We'll see. Lindholm is gonna be a tough sell."

"Cal will make him come around," Aimee said confidently.

"You like him?"

"Not as much as you do, but he's nice. Smart. You could do worse," Aimee answered.

Catherine tightened her arms around Aimee.

The cell door opened and Cal poked his head in, and both women laughed. "Oh, that's never a good sign," he said. "Come on, I'm busting you out of here."

41

CATHERINE SAT OUTSIDE Paul Lindholm's office for the second time, although this time she was alone. It was hard to believe it had been two weeks since she was here last. With her release from "quarantine," she and Cal were both reinstated, but the atmosphere was strained, especially between Cal and Aaron. Cal wouldn't tell her what had happened there, but whatever it was, it had been big.

He was in the office with Aaron and Paul now, making his case for a third—impromptu—Sagittarius mission. Catherine had come along for moral support. Lindholm barely acknowledged her presence anymore. She had officially become a problem he wished would go away.

That was fine. She was pretty much starting to feel that way about him as well.

Suddenly the office door flew open and Cal came out with a hint of a smile. She stood up, her palms suddenly sweating. "Well?"

Cal's smile broadened. "Wanna go for a ride?"

"Really?"

"Really. We're cleared."

———

Sagittarius III (Cal insisted on calling it Sagittarius 2.5) would go down in NASA history as the fastest mission ever to go from planning to implementation. With the ship prepped even before the mission got approval, it was only a few months before Catherine and Cal were strapped into the acceleration couches, waiting for the countdown to end.

Saying good-bye hadn't been any easier the second time around. In some ways, it had been harder. She and Aimee had gone to Chicago together to visit Nora and Julie, and Catherine knew this time it really would be the last time she saw her mother alive. That certainty had made leaving harder. And while she'd spent as much time with Aimee as she possibly could, she still wasn't sure it was enough.

As if he sensed her thoughts, Cal reached across the space between them and took her hand, even though both of them were wearing heavy gloves and pressure suits. "You know, my mom always used to say the surest test of a new relationship was to take a road trip together. Six years might be pushing it."

Catherine laughed. Their words were being transmitted to Mission Control, but they'd quickly given up on trying to keep things a secret. They'd both had enough of secrets for a lifetime. "We might do better than most. Nobody can storm out during a fight."

"I dunno; we've got a couple of EVA suits on board."

"Uh, Three, this is Houston. We recommend against using EVA suits as tools in relationship management." CAPCOM sounded equal parts amused and horrified. "That's a major off-spec use."

"Roger, Houston," Catherine said, trying to keep a straight face. She glanced over at Cal and could see him grinning through his faceplate.

There was no certainty ahead of them—whether they would reach the other ship in time to stop a disaster, whether they would find a way to repair relations with an alien race, even whether they would make it back home.

But at least they were on their way.

ACKNOWLEDGMENTS

ALTHOUGH I'VE ALWAYS been a space geek, writing *Vessel* took a great deal of research. NASA's collection of websites is a treasure trove of information not just on missions but also on procedures, history, and general astronomy. Specific mission logs, in particular, gave me a real feel for how astronauts interact with one another. Also immensely helpful (and highly recommended) is Mary Roach's book *Packing for Mars: The Curious Science of Life in the Void.*

Unexpectedly, a NASA press conference changed everything about this book after the first draft was complete. On February 22, 2017, NASA announced that the Spitzer Space Telescope had discovered a record-breaking seven planets within the habitable zone of a single star. All seven planets could possibly contain liquid water and be habitable. In my first draft, the destination planet was Kepler-452b, which is much farther away. I couldn't resist updating the story with the new discovery.

The biggest issue there, however, is that in the two years since, more things have been learned about the TRAPPIST-1 planets. This book represents the things that were known and conjectured in 2017, and may no longer be accurate. That said, as much as I've striven for overall accuracy, story comes first, and some details may have been changed to accommodate the story.

In other words, any errors, intentional or otherwise, are entirely on me.

Aside from research, I owe a great deal to the following people: Jack Z. Ray and Sarah Feldpausch brainstormed with me to come up with TRAPPIST-1f's unique fauna and flora, and how they intertwine within their life cycles. JoAnn Lucas, LMSW, gave me valuable insights into the symptoms of PTSD and how sufferers are affected. And to Dawn and Jason Honhera, for a lifeline just when I needed it.

Finally, endless thanks to Emily Bestler and Lara Jones with Emily Bestler Books, Lanie Davis and the rest of the staff at Alloy Entertainment, and, of course, Jennifer Udden, the best literary agent I could have hoped for.